Imperfect

ARRANGEMENTS

Frances Mensah Williams

ISBN 978-0-9569175-4-6
eISBN 978-0-9569175-5-3

Typeset by Aimee Dewar
Printed and bound in Great Britain by Lightning Source
Cover illustration by Kate Forrester

'The beautiful, tropical backdrop is the ideal setting for this tale that is crammed with realistic, complex characters. It is an easy-to-read exploration of modern love and relationships. I very much enjoyed this brilliantly written novel.'
Dorothy Koomson, bestselling author of *The Ice Cream Girls* and *Tell Me Your Secret*

'In *Imperfect Arrangements*, Frances Mensah Williams slices through the lives of three couples and presents a witty, true, and, sometimes, heartbreaking portrayal of married life in Accra, Ghana.'
Ayesha Harruna Attah, author of *Harmattan Rain* and *The Hundred Wells of Salaga*

'This novel is a celebration of sisterhood. You'll cheer on Theresa, Lyla and Maku as they navigate life in modern Accra, dealing with difficult bosses, feckless husbands and dubious mother-in-laws. You won't want to put the story down till it ends.'
Chibundu Onuzo, author of *The Spider King's Daughter* and *Welcome to Lagos*

READERS' PRAISE FOR FRANCES MENSAH WILLIAMS

'She has an amazing talent to make you feel you are there with the characters. Perfect, relaxing read that makes you want to go to bed early.'

'Portrays her likeable characters with great skill.'

'An emotional rollercoaster with many laugh out loud moments and a few tears ... someone has got to turn these books into a film and when they do, I will be first in the queue to watch them.'

'The descriptions of Ghana are amazing.'

'Takes you on a journey of self-exploration that looks at not just feelings, but cultures as well.'

'I loved the narrative, the story telling, the history and culture. I laughed out loud and cried at one point.'

'Obviously, I read it in one sitting!'

Also by Frances Mensah Williams

From Pasta to Pigfoot
From Pasta to Pigfoot: Second Helpings
Sweet Mercy (Novella)

Non-Fiction

Everyday Heroes: Learning from the Careers of Successful Black Professionals

I Want to Work in Africa: How to Move Your Career to the World's Most Exciting Continent

Enterprise Africa: A Guide to Planning Your Business in Africa

To find out more about Frances Mensah Williams:
Visit her website at www.francesmensahwilliams.com

Follow @FrancesMensahW

Connect on www.facebook.com/francesmensahwilliams

Connect on Instagram: francesmensahw

For my sister-friends, with love

MARRIAGE IS THE PERFECT
ARRANGEMENT FOR AN ORDERED SOCIETY

FEBRUARY

Theresa

Theresa stared anxiously at the grey-haired physician who seemed in no hurry to break the silence. Instead, he returned her stare calmly, while the pages detailing her test results wilted between his damp fingers.

The doctor's office was stuffy, and the ceiling fan that turned listlessly above his head generated only the promise of coolness. A bead of sweat broke out at the top of his nose but he appeared oblivious to any discomfort and leaned back in his chair with a grin.

Theresa's confused thoughts bumped up haphazardly against each other. *His teeth are amazingly white – I wonder which brand of toothpaste he uses.* His grin widened and she shifted uneasily in the consulting chair, gripping the thin strip of worn leather that cushioned its wooden arms. *Are doctors supposed to smile at you when they're about to break the news you have a terminal condition?*

Apparently deciding he had tortured her for long enough, Dr Owusu finally spoke. 'Congratulations, Mrs Brew.'

Theresa frowned in bemusement. *Even the most insensitive doctor wouldn't congratulate me before telling me I'm dying, surely? Unless this is some bizarre Ghanaian tradition no one's told me about.*

Shaking his head impatiently, the doctor straightened up and pushed the report towards her. 'Here, look!'

Reluctantly, she reached out a hand, her eyes still fixed

on him as she grasped the dry end of the sheets. Without giving them so much as a glance, she dropped both hands, still clutching the report, into her lap and waited.

The doctor's grin faded, and his forehead folded into deep furrows of concern as he watched her fingers nervously crease the papers.

'Mrs Brew? There's nothing to worry about, my dear. You're pregnant, that's all.'

Theresa blinked rapidly as the words washed over her, and then slumped down into her chair as the initial rush of relief was quickly replaced with incredulity. *Pregnant!* Not cancer, not leukaemia, not ME or MS or any of the other alphabet diseases she had imagined while waiting in the airless, stiflingly hot reception area for her test results. Diligent to the point of obsession about taking the pill, this was the only condition she hadn't considered over the past three weeks as constant fatigue wracked her body and almost everything she ate heaved around unpleasantly within moments of swallowing.

'Dr Owusu, are you *sure*? I'm on the pill!' She could hear her voice, normally low, sound almost shrill with disbelief.

'Very sure, Mrs Brew.' Dr Owusu looked pointedly at the report she was now crushing in her agitation. 'The results of your tests are right there. Your iron levels are a bit low, but your blood pressure is good. By the look of things, you will have a strong, healthy baby.'

Biting hard on her tongue to hold back the wail of protest threatening to escape, Theresa watched in dismay as the doctor uncapped a scratched plastic biro and scribbled energetically on his prescription pad. Dr Owusu had come highly recommended, but he must surely have made a mistake. She couldn't *possibly* be pregnant. *No! This cannot be happening to me!*

'Now, you must start taking these vitamins immediately. Baby will need them to help his bones grow big and strong,' Dr Owusu continued, scrawling his signature with a flourish.

Theresa was still grappling with the idea of herself and pregnancy appearing together in one sentence, and she gaped as he turned her shock into a bouncing baby boy. Once again, she reached out dumbly to take the paper he was thrusting in her direction.

'Thank you,' she said dutifully. Her mother's training hadn't been in vain. *The sign of a true lady is her ability to remember her manners, no matter what the situation.* She'd lost count of the number of times Clementyne had parroted that particular one. The doctor's raised eyebrows made it clear the conversation was over, and Theresa stood up. *Well, Mama, I remembered my manners, but I seem to have forgotten where the door is.*

Dr Owusu solved her dilemma by coming around to her side of the desk to show her out.

'I'm sure this is all a shock, my dear, but it's wonderful news. Take my word for it, you will soon be jumping for joy.'

The touch of his hand pressed against the small of Theresa's back galvanised her paralysed legs into action and he followed as she walked shakily out to the waiting room, clutching the report and prescription like certificates she'd just been awarded.

Dr Owusu's modest surgery in the busy commercial district of Accra, Ghana's capital city, was a six-hour flight and a million light years away from the elegant Georgian building that housed her Chelsea GP's practice. Out in the waiting room packed with chairs arranged in tight rows, the muggy heat felt even more oppressive. Theresa struggled to suppress the nausea that was never far away. The rusty electric fans suspended from the ceiling had long since given up any pretence of working, and the patients waiting to see the doctor flapped magazines and newspapers in a desperate attempt to generate cool air.

The receptionist was perched on the corner of her desk and the seductive smile she had been directing at Theresa's driver, Joseph, disappeared the instant she spotted her boss. She reached for a stack of files in a bid to look busy while Joseph took one look at his employer's face and hurried across to her.

'Madam! How you dey? You be sick?'

He glared accusingly at the doctor who hastily removed his hand from his befuddled patient and stepped back, clearly unnerved at a woman reacting so strangely to good news. He plucked the crumpled report from Theresa's slack grip.

'I'll need that for your file, my dear,' he muttered irritably, smoothing out the crushed sheets of paper. He glanced at her, and his face softened, his brilliant white smile returning as he leaned in to quietly add, 'Make an appointment with Rose for two weeks' time, Mrs Brew. I would like to take a scan to make sure Baby's sitting in the right place. In the meantime, make sure you get plenty of rest and eat well, eh? You are growing a new life now.'

Theresa walked unsteadily out of the clinic into the brilliant sunshine and came to an abrupt stop on the uneven pavement, vaguely aware of Joseph behind her. Unable to recall where he had parked the car, she rummaged in her bag for her sunglasses and slipped them on with shaky hands while her driver strode ahead, visibly befuddled by what the doctor might have told his madam.

Parked on the dusty verge of the roughly tarred road, the car's shiny newness seemed completely out of place against the backdrop of uniformly drab wooden kiosks, scarred with peeling paint and displaying identical stacks of tinned fish, toilet rolls, washing powder and mobile phone cards.

Joseph started the car engine and then raced around to open the back door for Theresa.

'Madam, you want buy some medicine before we go house?' His face was clouded with anxiety, but Theresa couldn't summon the energy to comfort him. *Let's not forget our manners.* She forced herself to smile.

'No, Joseph, I'm fine. I'd like to go home now.' *I need to go home now. I'm pregnant.*

Sitting upright to avoid contact with the sun-scorched leather seat, Theresa stared out of the window and waited for the blasts from the air conditioner to cool the interior. Still in a daze, it wasn't until she went to wipe away the moisture from her upper lip that she realised she was still clutching the prescription that needed to be filled. She frowned at the crumpled sheet while trying to decipher the heavy slanted scrawl.

Doctors must take courses in writing illegibly, she mused. Surely no one writes quite so badly without instruction. Struck anew by the reason for the prescription, she took a deep breath to calm the panic that coursed through her.

Pull yourself together, girl, it's not the end of the world. Count your blessings! You can still start the business; you have a beautiful home and a supportive husband... Oh my God... Tyler!

The car swerved sharply to avoid a goat that had broken free from a flock being driven alongside the main road. Joseph pressed furiously on the car horn and lowered his window to swear forcefully at the shepherd, a harassed-looking boy in dirty cut-off trousers carrying a stick. Startled by the loud honk, the errant goat skittered back to join his flock, receiving a fierce whack from the boy.

'Sorry, Madam,' Joseph muttered as he sped away. 'Some of these boys are more stupid than the goats they look after. I blame the government – I mean, why should people be allowed to drive goats in town like that. It's nonsense!'

Theresa sighed. Joseph was excitable at the best of times and it was only his excellent driving skills and the fact that he turned up on time every day – qualities neither of his two predecessors had displayed – that kept Tyler from sacking him.

Her thoughts returned to her dilemma. How on earth would Tyler react to this news? Falling pregnant so soon after moving to Ghana hadn't been part of anyone's plan, but that was unlikely to diminish her husband's relentless ability to focus on the positive. Even if it *had* turned out to be something awful like cancer, Tyler would doubtless have responded with an upbeat and encouraging 'Don't worry, Tee, at least we know what we're dealing with and we can strategise clearly and beat this thing.'

Well, I'm pregnant, so strategise that one, Ty. The Tyler in her head took up the challenge. 'Wow, that's *great*, Tee!

I know we hadn't planned to start a family until we'd been in Ghana for a couple of years and your business was up and running, but a baby is wonderful news, isn't it?'

I don't know, Tyler, is it? I mean, my God, a baby! Theresa groaned silently. What the hell was she supposed to do with a baby? The plan was to start a public relations business, not antenatal classes. *Her* strategy called for arranging meetings with journalists and CEOs, not making appointments with Rose to see if Baby was sitting in the right place.

Then, quite suddenly and for no reason she could fathom, Theresa felt a rush of intense elation. *Oh my God. I'm actually pregnant... Me!* She burst into uncontrollable giggles and Joseph spun around, his eyes wide with undisguised panic.

'Madam, please, if you are not well, let us go to the hospital.'

'Joseph, look out!' she said sharply as the car narrowly avoided colliding with a taxi pulling out into the road. Taking a deep breath, she ran her hands through her hair and tried to speak calmly.

'I'm sorry I startled you. It's just – I've had a bit of a shock, but I'm fine. Really. So please, just drive carefully and let's try to get home in one piece, okay?'

Not another word was spoken and soon the car turned into a short gravel driveway leading to a white colonial-style mansion. Wide shallow steps led from the pink-tiled pathway to a front porch lined with brightly coloured potted plants set in huge ceramic planters.

Leaving the car, Theresa climbed the steps to push open the ornate mahogany double doors and walked into the coolness of the house, thankful to escape the oppressive afternoon humidity. Her high-heeled mules – totally impractical for the dusty streets of Accra, but a girl must have *some* style, she'd decided – click-clacked against the polished terrazzo floor as she crossed the wide hallway into the living room. Desperate to be rid of Joseph's prying gaze, she had thrust the prescription and a bundle of worn notes into his hand with instructions to go to the pharmacy and pick up the vitamins, before returning to duty at Tyler's office.

Kicking off her shoes, she burrowed into the corner of the huge sofa, trying to cocoon herself within its cool depths. I should call Tyler, she thought wearily. I *will* call Tyler – in just a moment when I have enough strength to cope with the inevitable barrage of positivity. Besides, this isn't something he should find out on the phone. *Always let a man have a good meal before you break important news, as Mama would say.*

The thought of her mother's reaction to the news brought forth another burst of giggles. It would almost be worth flying back to London just to see Clementyne I-certainly-don't-look-old-enough-to-have-a-thirty-year-old-daughter Curtis's face when she learned that she was going to be a grandma.

'Madam, please. Are you alright?'

A solidly built middle-aged woman appeared in the doorway of the living room. Theresa's giggles came to an abrupt halt and she bit her lip to hide her irritation. Instead of following instructions, Joseph had clearly wasted no time blabbing to Auntie Sisi, who must have dashed from the kitchen, as she was still wiping her hands on a tea towel, her fleshy upper arms jiggling in time with the brisk movements.

'I'm fine, Auntie Sisi.'

Why do I have to call her that when she's not even a relative? Theresa wondered mutinously. *Yet another African tradition, remember? You must call an older woman 'Auntie' out of respect.*

Ignoring the scepticism on the older woman's face, Theresa added brusquely, 'Actually, I'm feeling rather thirsty. Could you please bring me a glass of—' *No, not wine, Theresa, you're pregnant remember!* 'Cold water?' *And then leave me alone.*

Auntie Sisi was quite unlike any other house help Theresa had encountered. Her wardrobe consisted of an eye-poppingly colourful selection of leggings which she teamed with roomy T-shirts. Theresa's tentative suggestion that she wear a dress had been brushed aside by Auntie Sisi on the grounds that her makeshift uniform was far more practical for cooking and cleaning – particularly when reaching into the dusty corners of the house's high ceilings. Today's choice of leggings was a violent hot pink that did Auntie Sisi's generous contours no favours.

A few moments later, Auntie Sisi was back, carrying a glass tumbler and a water pitcher on a small tray. Setting it down on a side table, she filled the glass and handed it over, watching with hands on hips as Theresa gulped down the contents.

'Joseph said he took you to the doctor,' the older woman remarked, appearing in no hurry to leave, and clearly unmoved by Theresa's raised eyebrow.

9

Theresa met the older woman's unflinching stare with one of her own. She had no intention of sharing her news with her housekeeper before her own husband. Wondering if Maku was right and that she gave her staff too much latitude, she thrust the glass back at the older woman.

'Thank you, Auntie Sisi.' Her curt tone said the rest and the other woman left the room without further comment, her rubber flip-flops smacking softly against the flooring.

The open louvre windows allowed through a tiny breeze that gently lifted the white muslin curtains. Thanks to Auntie Sisi, there was no hint on the huge plasma TV screen of the ubiquitous dust stirred by the dry Harmattan winds, nor on the chrome and glass shelves, decorative vases and colourful abstract paintings on the wall. Theresa scanned the spotless living room and pursed her lips at the handiwork of the high-end interior designers that Tyler had insisted should redecorate their newly rented property. Overriding her caution to hoard their hard-earned savings, he'd preferred to heed the advice of his old school friends that in Ghana appearances were all-important and lavish spending was an absolute prerequisite to making money. Her gaze lingered on the ridiculously expensive cream sofas with their matching armchairs and she wondered how long their pristine newness would last against the onslaught of a baby.

Suddenly desperate to discuss her situation with someone, she reached for her phone to call Lyla before remembering her best friend was out of town at yet another of her church retreats. Maku would be at work and in no mood to help her analyse her feelings about the unexpected grenade Dr Owusu had tossed into her carefully ordered life. She briefly considered phoning her beloved Auntie Pat – Lyla's mother – but then didn't feel quite ready to handle the inevitable enthusiasm her news would provoke. She would just have to wait for Tyler to come home. Remembering her promise to join him for dinner with Jeff, his potential business partner, Theresa sighed, already regretting saying yes. She'd avoided socialising for weeks due to the persistent fatigue and queasiness that had finally driven her to see the doctor and the thought of a restaurant meal made her stomach churn. Even worse was the prospect of being pleasant to Jeff Parnell, but she'd given her word, and Tyler had looked so pleased that she couldn't back out now.

Jeff Parnell was the British CEO of an investment fund – or, at least, that was how he had introduced himself to Theresa at their first and only meeting. After making a fortune in banking, he'd set up shop in Ghana to invest venture capital into what he termed 'sound, scalable, locally managed enterprises.' After three years investing in several fledgling start-ups, Jeff was buoyant about his future in Africa, and Tyler had been pitching for weeks for the cash that would help fund his new property business. *But what if Tyler doesn't get the money?* Theresa stopped her train of thought in its tracks. The idea that her ambitious and dynamic husband could be anything but successful was not one she was prepared to entertain.

A wave of exhaustion washed over her and she glanced at her watch. Four-thirty. The baby was already doing a great job of draining her energy. Maybe if she took a quick nap she might feel more like playing the gracious consort this evening, a necessary evil, since however much she detested the man, Tyler was in desperate need of Jeff's investment.

Pushing herself to her feet, she walked woodenly towards the stairs, feeling as weighed down as if she were nine months pregnant, instead of two. She held onto the banisters and half-walked, half-dragged herself up the stairs and into the large master bedroom across the landing where, with a sigh of relief, she stretched out on her side of the bed, her cotton skirt crumpling against the cool sheets.

Struck by a thought, she reached into the drawer of her bedside table and took out a thin carton. 'Traitor', she muttered aloud, scanning the print on the back. 91% EFFECTIVE AGAINST PREGNANCY. *Great. Nothing here about what to do if you end up as one of the 9%.* She tossed the box of pills away and watched in satisfaction as it landed squarely in the centre of the waste bin.

Her gaze fell on her laptop, still open at the document detailing the business plan she had been finalising, just as it dawned on her that she'd forgotten the afternoon meeting she had scheduled with the editor of *The Business Herald*. She cursed silently; her first opportunity to establish a relationship with a senior figure in the Ghanaian newspaper industry and she had blown it. She hadn't missed the man's amusement at her earnest attempts to flatten her English accent at their first introduction and now he would see her as a complete flake – one of those 'unserious' girls, as Maku scornfully termed them, who wafted in from places like London and New York reeking of entitlement and expecting everyone to bend over backwards to accommodate their unrealistic demands. She sighed, deciding to leave it until morning and then ring and plead an emergency with her car. Overcome with fatigue, she closed her eyes and drifted into sleep.

* * *

The decisive thud of the bedroom door jerked her back into consciousness and, struggling upright, she rubbed her eyes and tried to focus on the tall figure with his back against the closed door.

'Tee, what's wrong? I've been calling you for hours! What did the doctor say?'

Tyler's clean-shaven features were creased into a worried frown as he moved towards her, tugging at his tie. His dark eyes, deep-set under eyebrows that crooked into two convergent straight lines, took in her rumpled skirt and messy hair, and he sat on the edge of the bed and tentatively touched her leg, as if needing to reassure himself that she was there.

Forgetting her mother's instructions on how to impart news, Theresa simply blurted it out, 'I'm pregnant.'

Warily, she watched his eyebrows climb and descend and then a grin of pure happiness spread across his face.

'*Seriously*?'

She nodded, fascinated at the speed with which he was welcoming news she still couldn't fully absorb. Maybe because he's not the one who's going to be perpetually nauseous and expanding like a balloon for the next seven months, she thought uncharitably, before finding a tiny smile of her own to echo his.

With a loud whoop, he seized her in a suffocating embrace, kissing the top of her silky curls before abruptly letting go with a look of alarm.

'Sorry, *sorry*, did I hurt you?'

She laughed, genuine laughter this time, and reached for him. 'Don't be silly, I'm not going to break. But, honestly, Ty, we hadn't planned for this to happen so soon and I just can't get my head around it.'

She shifted a little to let him move up onto the bed and he propped himself against the headboard and cradled her in his arms. He was still in his suit jacket and she felt the roughness of the fabric against her cheek as his deep voice vibrated in his chest.

'I know it's earlier than we had in mind, but it's *great* news, Tee. Look on the bright side,' – she rolled her eyes in silent exasperation – 'at least we know you can get pregnant. So many women have a hard time with their fertility – just look at Lyla.' He raised her chin to look straight into her eyes. 'You know better than anyone what she's been going through.'

Theresa nodded. Lyla's struggles with infertility had wrought a shocking transformation in the childhood friend who had once effortlessly dazzled people with her laughing, carefree beauty.

Tyler's voice bubbled with joy as he continued to list the benefits of an unplanned pregnancy mere months after moving to a new country, into a new home and starting a new business. Once, a few weeks after they'd started dating, and curious about why nothing seemed to dent Tyler's spirits, Theresa had asked him, 'Why do you always do that? You know, always put a positive spin on everything? You act as if nothing ever bothers you, when surely some things must.'

'Of course, I get bothered by things,' he'd protested. 'I just don't see the point in dwelling on the negative when there's always a positive side if you look for it.'

Theresa tuned him out and let the burble continue in the background while she tried to decide what to wear that evening. After a few minutes, weary of the blanket of positivity being draped over her, she pushed him away and climbed off the bed. She peered at her face in the mirror above her dressing table and sighed. Despite the nap, deep shadows sat stubbornly beneath her thickly lashed dark brown eyes, and she made a mental note to check where Joseph had left the vitamins she'd sent him out to buy. She dabbed a little face powder on her nose to take the shine off the smooth coffee-brown skin and tried to brush some life back into her flattened locks.

'What time are we meeting Jeff for dinner?'

Tyler glanced at his watch and the jubilant father-to-be expression was instantly replaced by that of the harassed businessman. 'I said we'd be at the restaurant at eight – I'll take a shower and then we should probably get going. The traffic was brutal when I left the office.' He hesitated and then added, 'Are you sure you're up to coming with me?'

The look of relief on his face when she nodded made Theresa feel even guiltier about her lack of enthusiasm as, given the choice, she would have liked nothing better than to crawl under the sheets and sleep until morning.

Tyler tossed his clothes in the general direction of the laundry hamper and disappeared into the adjoining bathroom while Theresa stared listlessly into the mirror, willing herself to feel some of his relentless energy. Recalling her husband's comment about Lyla, she was thankful she hadn't been able to reach her friend. It would have been wrong to share her ambivalent feelings about her newly discovered pregnancy when Lyla so desperately wanted a baby.

She pulled a black, loose-fitting shift dress out of her wardrobe and laid it across the bed. The baby might be no bigger than a walnut, but she still felt an irrational desire to wear something that wouldn't constrict her waist. Her eyes fell on Tyler's discarded clothes and she stooped to collect them, feeling a flash of irritation at the rapid transformation of the once scrupulously tidy Londoner into an entitled African male. Auntie Sisi might not mind rescuing errant garments from the floor, but Theresa had no intention of getting used to it.

A little later, Theresa was back in the car and, with Joseph now off duty, Tyler was at the wheel. She glanced across at her husband's familiar profile, which was saved from being too perfect by a hooked nose, the legacy of a rugby injury from his English public school days. Sighing inwardly, Theresa listened to him paint happy scenarios of life with their new child, responding with an occasional non-committal murmur as she gazed out of the window at the stream of workers trudging home beside the main road. With the heat less oppressive, Tyler had dispensed with the air conditioner that guzzled up the increasingly expensive petrol. The beams from the sparse street lights gently pierced the falling veil of darkness and she marvelled anew at the contrast between the uniform red bricks of houses in London and the large whitewashed buildings behind metal gates that lined the avenues of their new neighbourhood.

Tyler turned into the car park of a brightly lit building and Theresa glanced at her watch and bit back a smile. Eight o'clock – bang on time. His casual attitude to laundry notwithstanding, Tyler had maintained his very British attitude to timekeeping. Not that punctuality did him any favours in Ghana where being late for appointments was almost a given, she thought ruefully.

Timekeeping was the least of the challenges they'd faced in moving to a country that Tyler had left as a boy and which, since the age of six, she had known primarily as a holiday destination. And yet, cocooned in their two-bedroom Chelsea flat, Theresa and Tyler's plans for a new life in Ghana where they would both run successful businesses had made perfect sense. Ignoring Clementyne's opposition to what she considered a ridiculous idea, and enthused by Tyler's unflagging optimism, they had moved forward speedily with their plans to return to Africa and make a difference. Within weeks of their arrival, the tint of their rose-coloured glasses had completely faded as the financial implications of their decision grew starker. Despite the windfall from selling their London flat, the lifestyle in Ghana was proving far costlier than either of them had imagined. The first shock came with having to pay a hefty two years' rent in advance, although Tyler had recovered sufficiently to proceed with hiring an expensive interior designer for the property. Finding – and then paying for – staff had proved the next hurdle, and Joseph and Auntie Sisi didn't come cheap.

Her thoughts on the money draining out of their bank

account, Theresa retrieved her handbag and stepped out of the car, priming herself to meet the man Tyler was counting on to be his saviour.

'Has Jeff actually agreed to invest then?' she probed, desperately seeking reassurance that tonight's meeting was for a good reason.

Tyler's eyes didn't quite meet hers and Theresa felt a spasm of nausea that had nothing to do with her pregnancy. Their entire life savings were riding on Tyler and her making a success of this move.

Tyler shrugged. 'He's pretty much on board but we still need to iron out a few details and sign the paperwork. Look, I've been pushing him as hard as I can, and – well, let's just say he knows his funding is crucial for this project.'

He grinned and the lines of tension she'd seen earlier disappeared as he wrapped an arm around her and squeezed her shoulders. 'Which is another reason why I'm glad you came tonight. Jeff took quite a shine to you when you met at the club.'

'*Ty!*' Theresa laughed and punched him lightly on the shoulder in outrage. 'You'd better not be trying to pimp me out for business!'

They crossed the car park and walked inside, and she blinked as her eyes adjusted to the brightness and noise. The tables in the restaurant were set close together and laden with bowls of food and piles of flat bread so hot, she could see the steam rising. The aroma of grilled meats, fish and spicy pickles overpowered the air conditioning and the sound of clinking cutlery and animated conversation competed with muted background music. It was clearly a popular spot, and the clientele appeared mostly European, along with a smattering of Africans and Asians.

Jeff stood up as they approached his table, shaking hands with Tyler and swiftly planting three effusive kisses on Theresa's cheeks before pulling out the chair next to him with a flourish. Dressed in stone-coloured chinos with a white shirt open at the neck to expose tufts of dark hair, he carried himself with all the confidence of a wealthy financier. His mahogany brown hair was thick and glossy and brushed back from a narrow forehead and his nose was thin, with nostrils slightly flared, as if preparing to go into battle. His eyes were an unusual shade of grey and in the bright overhead lighting appeared almost transparent.

'I absolutely *love* this place,' he enthused, retrieving the menu he had been studying earlier. 'The food is superb – rather like tapas fused with Lebanese cuisine.'

He scoured the room and raised a finger and a waiter appeared almost immediately with a respectful smile and a small notebook clasped against his chest. 'Good evening, sir. Please, are you ready to order?'

'We certainly are!'

Theresa tried not to show her irritation at the speed with which the man had taken over. She glanced at Tyler but, with a signed deal still in the offing, her husband was clearly not planning to ruffle any feathers. She stared blindly at her menu and wondered why she had taken such an instant and visceral dislike to Jeff because, so far, their second meeting wasn't leading to a change of heart. *Everything* about Jeff annoyed her, she thought moodily. She hated his face and his thin lips, especially the top one that looked like a pale pink slash across his face. She hated the way he spoke, emphasising every word as if each one was hugely significant. She hated his smug, self-satisfied smile and the condescending tone he took with people. But Tyler needed him, so she gritted her teeth and forced a smile.

'Tell you what, let's order a bottle of champagne?' Jeff suggested. 'After all, we *are* here to celebrate, aren't we?'

'Sounds like a great idea.' Tyler nodded enthusiastically and then frowned as Theresa scrunched her nose at the thought of alcohol. She stared back at him in dismay – hadn't he just been the one making plans for their new baby?

Jeff, preoccupied with the drinks menu, had missed the silent exchange and brusquely ordered a bottle, adding, 'And bring us three champagne flutes.'

'Um... just two glasses, actually – and some water,' Theresa interjected. The waiter looked unsure as to who to believe, and Jeff shrugged and nodded.

'Tee's not been feeling great lately, have you?' Tyler broke the awkward silence that descended once the waiter had left, and Theresa gave a reluctant smile.

'Probably just a bug,' she said brightly. 'But I'd better stick with water for the moment.'

Giving her a curious glance, Jeff turned his attention to the menu and the waiter returned shortly afterwards with a bucket containing a bottle of champagne smothered in ice. He twisted open the bottle and carefully filled two glasses and, as soon as he had poured out Theresa's water and moved away, the men raised their drinks in a toast.

'Here's to a profitable and long-lasting collaboration!' Jeff tossed back half of the contents of the thin flute in one gulp and watched Tyler drink his champagne rather more sedately. Theresa sipped her water and tried to dredge up some enthusiasm.

'I know you've been in Ghana for a few years, but what made you decide to leave London and come here?' Her curiosity was genuine even if the warm smile she gave him took a bit more effort.

Jeff refilled his glass and took a gulp before answering. 'Ghana's a great country, that's why. It's not the easiest, mind you.'

He broke off to take another gulp. 'But, for now at least, I think it's the best place in Africa to base my business. The people are decent enough, although you do sometimes want to give a few of them a kick up the bum!'

Theresa winced as she watched Jeff's thin lips part to emit a roar of laughter and even Tyler's smile slipped for a moment. The waiter returned, and Jeff took control once again, ordering several dishes with only a token show of interest in whether they approved.

The next hour crawled by. Although the food was tasty enough to restore Theresa's erratic appetite, Jeff was hardly her ideal companion to share it with and she listened with half an ear as the conversation moved swiftly on to business territory. She suppressed a sigh and glanced at her watch, wishing she was at home and reunited with her laptop to continue the business plan she'd been working on before leaving for the doctor's. Remembering the baby brought a fresh wave of frustration followed by intense guilt for feeling unhappy at the prospect of motherhood.

There was no question of not going through with the pregnancy, but... *dammit!* Coming to Ghana wasn't just about changing countries; it was her opportunity to achieve her dream of her own public relations firm and prove that she was more than just a corporate lackey. The seven years she'd spent at Cromwell McIntosh, the top-flight London PR consultancy she had blagged her way into as a mouthy young intern, had taught her everything she needed to know about giving her clients the best and most effective publicity. Even when she'd been not so subtly sidelined from higher profile accounts, Theresa had still achieved an enviable track record with the clients she had been allowed to manage – usually those with small budgets and sketchy ideas of what to expect from their PR. *Play the hand you've been dealt*, another of Mama's sayings, was the one Theresa had taken to heart when it came to her career. Over time, her creativity and instinctive ability to build rapport and quickly determine her clients' needs had resulted in some of the most innovative and well-known campaigns Cromwell McIntosh had fielded. But recognising that any further progression at the firm was unlikely, she had been longing for years for the chance to go it alone and recreate for herself the success she'd delivered to Ian Cromwell and his temperamental partner Jess McIntosh.

When Tyler had hesitantly broached the suggestion that they relocate to Ghana, Theresa had immediately seen it as the pathway to realising her ambition. Surely in a country where everyone looked like her, she reasoned, the constant slights and thinly veiled suggestions from her bosses to stick with clients who would 'feel more empathy with you', would be a thing of the past? No more working harder and putting in longer hours than her blonde, blue-eyed colleagues to prove she was just as good. No further need to steel herself when greeting new clients who expected an executive with skin colour that matched the name Theresa Brew, and who then spent the first ten minutes wondering how to get the agency to assign someone else before it dawned on them she knew her stuff. No more having to deliver twice as much on half the budget available to her colleagues and swallow heavy-handed dollops of patronising praise and barely disguised astonishment that it was the black girl who had done all this. In Ghana, with her two best friends, Lyla, and Lyla's cousin, Maku, to help her settle in, she could start afresh: build a network in business and across the media, create her own concepts, choose her own clients, and be accepted. *That* was the plan. *Until 'baby' decided to show up.*

'Are you sure you don't want a glass of something stronger?' Jeff looked dubiously at the glass of water Theresa had been nursing. She forced herself into the present and shook her head with a tight smile.

'Thanks, but this is fine. I'm sure I'll feel a lot better soon. So, Jeff.' She could feel rather than hear Tyler's sharp intake of breath at the saccharine sweetness of her tone. 'Is it all official? I mean, you *are* investing in Tyler's business, aren't you?' She sensed Tyler's tension, but she kept up her smile.

Jeff frowned. 'Well, yes, I would say so. We're here celebrating, aren't we – unless there's something I should know?' He followed this with a loud guffaw and tossed back the dregs of wine in his glass. 'You're not getting cold feet, are you, Tyler? You wouldn't be the first person to cut and run back to the UK, you know.'

'No, of course not,' Tyler muttered. He glared at Theresa, not bothering to disguise his irritation. 'We're in it for the long haul, Jeff, I've told you that. Besides, property development isn't an overnight game. Once we get this first project up and running, there's no turning back even if I wanted to. Which I don't,' he added pointedly, his tone making it clear that if Theresa hadn't yet got the message, Jeff certainly should.

Jeff gestured for the waiter to bring the bill, and Theresa noted with annoyance how he hadn't even bothered to ask if they wanted anything else.

'That's what I want to hear, old man,' Jeff exclaimed, 'Things don't happen overnight here – you've got to be prepared to stick it out if you want to succeed.'

* * *

Jeff's words were still ringing in Theresa's ears a few days later as she scrolled through the pages of the business plan she had finally completed. She was determined not to spend any more money than she needed to until her company took off, but instead run the agency from home by making use of the second large living room on the sprawling ground floor. Once she had a few clients under her belt, the plan allowed for renting office space and bringing in an assistant and, in due course, other experienced PR professionals.

An apologetic phone call to *The Business Herald* had persuaded the editor to reschedule their meeting to later that afternoon, and this time Theresa had no intention of missing it. She wondered yet again whether to tell Lyla about her pregnancy. Keeping secrets had never been

Theresa's strong suit – hiding her relationship with Tyler from her mother for two months had been the toughest challenge of her life.

No closer to a decision, she reached for the huge mug, emblazoned with a red London bus, which she'd bought on a whim before leaving the UK, and took a few sips of peppermint tea to stem the incipient nausea. Baby would just have to take a back seat for a few hours while she prepared for the meeting which she hoped would give her a vital ally within the national press.

Tyler

Tyler sat at his desk and willed the phone to ring. Almost six o'clock. It was late, but there was no way he was leaving until this was resolved. He was determined not to call Jeff's office again – well, at least not immediately. It had been clear the last time he'd phoned that Ayesha, Jeff's PA, was struggling to conceal her irritation even as she'd reassured him that the documents he needed to sign had been dispatched.

'Jeff says it's a done deal, so just relax, man,' he murmured. But saying it wasn't the same as believing it, and after a moment Tyler jumped to his feet to pace up and down his office, the largest in the suite of rooms he had confidently rented only a few weeks earlier. Its glass walls gave him a perfect view of the heavy mahogany door leading into the board room, reminding him that he had no board – or even staff, other than Patience. But it was still early days, he reasoned, and besides who in their right minds would sign up to be a director for a start-up property development company with no business?

He frowned at the silent phone on his desk and briefly considered calling his wife just to hear another voice. Thinking of Theresa prompted thoughts of the baby and his frown deepened. While he was ecstatic at the idea of a son – and he had already decided their first child would be a boy – Tyler couldn't deny that it was an additional pressure he hadn't anticipated.

The pregnancy had already brought some unwelcome changes, not least Theresa's frequent absences just when he most needed her. Tyler had always relied on his wife's insights, and her instinctive ability to charm all the right people while steering him away from the wrong ones. But ever since the nausea from her pregnancy had made her reluctant to join him at social events where he could drum up business, he was starting to feel alone and vulnerable and, much as he hated to admit it, ever so slightly resentful. However selfish and unreasonable, particularly now with their changed circumstances, he still wanted this move to be *their* adventure and not one he was expected to experience without her.

It wasn't just Theresa's intuition and charm Tyler needed, he reluctantly conceded. He'd also been counting on her income to support the expensive lifestyle they'd adopted since moving here. With a baby on the way, it was hard to see how she could establish the PR business which had been the main reason she'd agreed to relocate. He knew Theresa badly wanted to prove herself with this new venture and, if anyone could do it, it would be his wife. But there was also no denying that an infant was a challenge neither of them had ever encountered.

The picture of a baby boy in tiny overalls suddenly popped into Tyler's mind and, despite the anxiety gnawing at him, he couldn't help the grin that appeared. *I'm going to be a dad! How awesome is that!* He allowed his native optimism to flood back and raise his spirits. Maybe he was worrying unnecessarily about their finances – once this deal was signed and the apartments in the new development were sold, they would have shedloads of money, he assured himself. And if it meant Tee postponing her business dreams for a while, however disappointing it would be, she could always pick things up again when the baby was a bit older. In the meantime, they still had to get through this first year, and maybe it wouldn't hurt to take Theresa's advice and cut back on their spending. She was already stressed about the strain on their funds and once her mother knew about the baby, he had no doubt that Clementyne would redouble her efforts to pressure Theresa to reconsider their plans.

Tyler's smile faded at the thought of his mother-in-law and he slowed his pacing and perched on the edge of his desk. Clementyne had never warmed to him and had grown even frostier once she'd discovered he'd been seeing Theresa for weeks before anyone had informed her about their blossoming romance. Clementyne was not used to being sidelined by her daughter or having her opinion disregarded and even now, five years after their marriage, Clementyne still hadn't forgiven Theresa's secrecy. Tyler's initial attempts to charm his mother-in-law, a successful lawyer from Trinidad who had moved to London and built a thriving practice, had fallen on consistently stony ground and he had long since given up trying. Clementyne, for her part, rarely let an opportunity pass to disparage him and point out the similarity of his background to that of her late and unlamented ex-husband: *'You African men are all the same. I put my career on hold to live there for three years, so I know what I'm talking about. Full of dreams and no substance – you all do exactly as you wish whenever it suits you and then have the nerve to say it's your tradition!'*

Tyler had spent a total of four years of his life in Ghana

– all of them at boarding school – and to his mind he was much more of a Londoner than an African. Nevertheless, he had resisted responding to Clementyne's stinging taunts because he knew how badly the frequent rows between Theresa's warring parents had scarred her. As an only child, she had found herself torn between a loving but ineffectual father and a fiercely suffocating mother, both of whom were too busy scoring points to notice that the bitter words they hurled at one another hurt no one more than their daughter. As much as she'd adored her father, Theresa had been secretly relieved when he'd finally packed his bags for his native land a week after her twelfth birthday; a relief that turned into anguished guilt when he died suddenly a few years later.

Tyler returned his gaze to the silent phone on his desk and tried to shrug off the sense of foreboding that was creeping back to derail his positive mindset. This deal would happen. After all, Sycamore House was the perfect property for his first redevelopment project and had received a clean bill of health from the structural engineers. He sighed inwardly. He *needed* it to happen. This wasn't just about proving Clementyne and her dire predictions about moving to Ghana wrong; it was about proving his own choices right. He hadn't left a great job with a successful property firm in London – and turned down their last-ditch offer of a promotion – only to lose everything now.

Everyone he had spoken to had said the same thing, '*Africa is where it's happening now*'. Many of the Ghanaian school friends he had stayed in touch with had moved to Britain to study and find jobs and had since found their way back home, where they were doing incredibly well, if their large houses and luxury cars were anything to go by. But, unlike Tyler, most of them had benefited from the cushion of a family home or business and hadn't been forced to gamble their personal savings and a promising career. *Things will work out; they* have *to work out.* He repeated the phrase silently to reassure himself. *Come on, Tyler. Just think positive.*

Moving away from the phone and the temptation to call Ayesha, Tyler crossed the deep pile carpet in search of company. Hearing him approach, his PA broke off from the notes she had been typing and looked up enquiringly. In her late forties, Patience was both highly organised and happily married, key criteria for Theresa who had vetted all the candidates for the job and summarily rejected anyone who might wish to set their sights on Tyler rather than on a computer. Unsurprisingly, Patience had proved a brilliant choice and appeared completely unfazed by the absence of clients at her new firm. While waiting for business to roll in, she had set up files and systems in readiness and researched a formidable mailing list of potential customers, building suppliers, and likely contractors for future projects.

Patience by name, patient by nature, Tyler reflected, intensely grateful she showed no signs yet of abandoning ship and feeling rather guilty for keeping her so late.

'Did Ayesha call back?' He knew the answer but couldn't resist asking.

Her sympathetic smile held no reproach at this second interruption in less than twenty minutes. 'No, sir, not yet. I think—'

Patience broke off abruptly as a sharp knock drew their attention to the main door to their office suite. Patience pressed the button and released the lock with an audible click, and she and Tyler watched in silence as a young man in a white shirt and khaki chinos pushed open the glass door and sauntered in. He mumbled a greeting and glanced hesitantly at Tyler who was rooted to the spot, and then turned towards Patience, unslinging a canvas bag draped across his chest as he approached her desk.

The shrill sound of the office phone broke the silence and Patience picked it up and gestured to the messenger to wait. She listened for a moment and then with a quiet, 'Yes, he's here. Thanks, Ayesha,' she dropped the handset onto the cradle and nodded at Tyler with a wide, relieved smile.

Tyler's head was pounding as Patience stood to take the thick manila envelope the messenger had pulled from his bag. With a murmur of thanks, she scribbled her signature on the well-thumbed receipt book he silently produced and waited for him to leave before turning to offer the package to her boss.

Tyler grabbed it, ripping the envelope in his impatience to open it. Pulling out a bound sheaf of papers, he held his breath in trepidation as he scanned through the first page, and a grin of pure delight lit up his face.

'Patience – we're in business!' he bellowed triumphantly. He dropped the papers on the desk and with an unrestrained whoop that echoed around the silent office, swept a startled Patience into a ferocious bear hug that swung her completely off her feet.

Releasing her, he seized the papers and hugged them

tightly to his chest, laughing aloud with relief. The confidence which had been seeping away returned with full force and he was suddenly fizzing with energy. The swagger was back in his step as he clutched the documents and strode jubilantly towards his office.

'Patience, bring your notebook and let's get started – we've got work to do!'

Maku

The car wound its way through the industrial area and past dark utilitarian buildings fronted by tall placards and signboards, before turning into a dusty untarred road only a little wider than an alley. Driving slowly, Joseph manoeuvred the car along deeply etched tyre tracks that ran alongside uniform L-shaped bungalows.

Coming to a stop in front of a set of blue gates, he tooted the car horn impatiently and from behind the gates an elderly man in flowing robes appeared. He held the gates open and Joseph drove up a sharp incline into a small compound. The guard offered a mumbled greeting when Theresa stepped out of the car, and then waited for Joseph to drive off before returning to the frayed mat he had spread out over the concrete ground.

The front porch of Maku's modest verandah was illuminated by a single light bulb and Theresa carefully picked her way through discarded plastic toys and rubber sandals to knock loudly on the solid wooden door. The sudden noise set off mournful howls from a guard dog chained to a post behind the house and startled a tiny lizard which slithered away through a gap in the verandah wall.

Moments later, the door opened a crack and Maku's eldest child peered out. At eight years old, Samuel was a mini version of Nortey with the same full cheeks, round eyes and skinny legs. He also had his father's habit of pursing his lips when he was deep in thought.

Theresa's gaze wandered over the boy's scruffy shorts and food-stained blue T-shirt and the stand-off continued until Theresa smiled and broke the silence, her voice gentle and slightly cajoling.

'Hello, Samuel. May I come in?'

'*Samuel!* Who's at the door?'

With one hand clasping the squirming child balanced on her broad hip while the other shook the feeding bottle to cool the overheated milk, Maku felt as impatient as she sounded. She sucked her teeth loudly and nudged the boy out of the way.

'Theresa! Come in, come in... sorry for the mess.'

She elbowed the door wide open and glared at her son. 'Samuel! Why did you keep Auntie waiting at the door like that?'

Without waiting for an answer, she ushered Theresa inside and led her down a short narrow corridor, her hips swinging freely beneath a loose cotton dress splashed with purple flowers that rose and fell over her ample curves. Maku marched into the living room and, ignoring the indignant wail of the hungry baby, deposited the milk bottle on a side table and unceremoniously swept a pile of freshly laundered clothes off a brown leather sofa that had seen better days.

'Sorry, Theresa. Here – take a seat. I was just about to fold the laundry away when Abra woke up and started yelling. Don't worry, she'll shut up once she's had her milk.'

Maku plopped down into a chair, the leather on its arms faded from years of wear inflicted by restless elbows.

Reaching for the bottle, she thrust it into the wailing child's open mouth while Theresa obediently took the proffered seat on the sofa.

Still sniffling, Abra sucked greedily on the teat, keeping a tight grip on the bottle with a chubby hand in case her mother dared to remove it again, and Maku shook her head with an apologetic sigh.

'I thought she'd be asleep for at least another hour – one of boys must have disturbed her. *Samuel!*' She glared at her son who was standing in the doorway, his skinny legs protruding from a pair of creased shorts. 'Was it you? Did you wake your sister up?'

He shook his head and glanced over his shoulder before replying, his voice almost a whisper. 'It wasn't me; it was Elijah. He wanted to play with her... I *told* him not to!'

Maku's eyes flashed with irritation. Without warning, she raised her head and roared, '*Elijah!* Come here, *right now!*'

Samuel slipped away and a minute later a smaller version of him appeared in the doorway. Elijah's shorts were even more rumpled than his brother's, and he had dispensed with a top altogether, exposing a round, brown tummy with a small protruding belly button. His face clouded with apprehension as Maku glared at him, and then gestured towards the little girl on her lap.

'Why did you wake up your sister? Didn't I tell you and Samuel to watch TV quietly and let her sleep, hmm? You are not a baby any more – you are six years old and big enough to obey instructions.'

Elijah flinched at the harshness of her tone but was spared a further tongue-lashing by the toot of a car horn followed by the dull thud of metal hitting concrete as the opened gates came to rest against the wall. Diverted by the sound of a new arrival, Maku shrieked again, this time in the general direction of the front door.

'*Sam-u-el!* Go and open the front door – it's Auntie Lyla!'

Maku caught Theresa's involuntary wince and she ran a frustrated hand through her thick mane of braided twists, the roots of which harboured strands of silver.

'I'm so sorry, Theresa, you must think you've walked into a madhouse. It's just these kids – I swear they drive me crazy sometimes. I wanted to put some snacks together and tidy the house before you girls got here, and now look...'

She gestured around the room at the jumble of toys and empty plastic cups strewn across the carpet, now accompanied by the pile of clothes recently consigned to the floor. 'I know this place looks like a pigsty compared to your lovely house!'

Theresa nudged an obviously used and poorly rolled-up disposable nappy out of the way with her foot, and grinned. 'Relax, Maku, it's fine. At least your home looks, um, you know, lived in. Our house looks like something out of a showroom or a magazine. It might be lovely to look at, but it's pretty sterile to live in.'

'What's sterile? You'd better not mean *me*!' Tall and slender, Lyla marched into the room carrying Samuel who was struggling furiously to wriggle out of her hold.

'*Auntie Lyla!* Put me down – I'm too big for you to carry,' he grumbled, and she dropped him carefully, kissing the top of his head before he could protest.

'Hi Cuz.' Maku sat Abra down with a somewhat grubby

soft toy and stood up to hug her older cousin. With Lyla, an embrace was never just the perfunctory squeeze that most people gave. It was always deliberate, firm and loving.

'Hi to you, too,' Lyla smiled, holding on tight for a long moment before releasing her. 'You look tired, Cuz,' she pronounced critically as her dark eyes scoured Maku's face. 'I take it Nortey's not coming home any time soon and that we're definitely staying in tonight?'

Without waiting for a reply, her gaze swivelled across to Theresa who stood up and moved in for one of Lyla's hugs.

'You look *good*! I love that shade of blue on you,' Lyla exclaimed when Theresa stepped out of her hold.

Maku smiled as she watched her cousin admire Theresa's dress. Having been brought up by a mother who owned boutiques, Lyla always noticed clothes – even if she'd stopped dressing like someone who did. Stooping, Lyla rubbed a gentle hand over Abra's soft curls, and the child looked up at her and gurgled happily, releasing a thin trail of milk that drooled down her chin. Maku's smile faded when Lyla rolled her eyes and scooped up the pile of clothes from the floor with an impatient tut.

'Cuz, where should I put these?'

Maku shrugged, only mildly discomfited by the unspoken rebuke. She knew Lyla thought she was a slob – God knows she said so often enough. But when you'd had the epithet '*Bush girl!*' hurled at you for so long, and by so many people, it was like water off a duck's back. Village habits die hard, Maku admitted, but it wasn't that she didn't know better. The truth was she was mostly too exhausted to care.

Grabbing the clothes from her cousin, Maku crossed the room to deposit them carelessly on the dining table which already hosted an assortment of old newspapers, empty plastic water bottles, and several soiled bibs.

'Never mind my laundry – I'll sort it out later.' She avoided looking too closely at the windows where a thick layer of dust blown in by the Harmattan winds had settled on the louvre blades and turned to face her guests with a determined smile.

'You guys are here now, and it feels like ages since we had a chance to catch up. I've fed the kids, so give me a minute to put some nibbles together and we can relax.'

Lyla pursed her lips but sat down without comment and was soon engrossed in conversation with Theresa. Stopping only to wipe Abra's chin with her damp bib, Maku went into the kitchen and pulled open the cupboard where she had secreted the snacks she'd bought the day before from Swanson's, the upmarket grocery store in town. She rummaged behind a stack of canned tomato paste, praying that Nortey hadn't spied the titbits and made inroads into them before he left.

Hearing Theresa's laughter from the living room, Maku hoped she wasn't the cause of the merriment, and then immediately scolded herself for the thought. Tee might be a bit irritating at times with her *obroni* behaviour and precise English mannerisms, but she was a good friend – although she did sometimes wonder if the girl was really an African, what with all her romantic ideas. What was the word that character on the TV reality show had called the black girl with a cockney accent? *Coconut* – that was it! Dark on the outside, but inside as white as any of the *obroni* people who came to tan their white skins in Ghana's sunshine – and exploit the country a little bit while they were at it. No, Theresa was all right, even if all the holidays she'd spent in Ghana with her and Lyla still hadn't taught her much about how things were done here.

A rueful smile played on Maku's lips as she rummaged in the drawer for a bottle opener. Those childhood vacations had been long, but they hadn't all been blissful, not least because in the early years Maku had quite simply hated Theresa. The summer breaks had been unwelcome periods during which Maku had fought an uneven battle to come first with Lyla. Even when Maku had pulled the poor-pitiful-country-cousin-who-had-been-brought-to-live-with-her-posh-relatives-in-the-big-city-to-keep-Lyla-company card, she was invariably trumped by Theresa, who made no attempt to manipulate Lyla's affections and yet still received the lion's share of her attention.

Fed up of Lyla and Theresa whispering and giggling in corners during Theresa's annual pilgrimages to Ghana and feeling pushed into the background, Maku's resentment had grown with each passing year. Why did Theresa get to have Lyla describe her to everyone as her best friend? Wasn't it enough that the girl was slim and pretty with a huge collection of immaculate frocks with straps that tied into neat bows at the back *and* shiny, silky hair? Maku, whose short, kinky locks had never even sniffed a chemical, could stare for hours at Theresa's straightened hair, fascinated by the long, smooth ponytail that fell halfway down her back – just like the pictures of the white girls on the covers of the battered romance novels that lined Lyla's bookshelves. Theresa already had everything, and in later years when the frocks had morphed into hipster jeans and cropped tops that flattered Theresa's flat stomach but would never have been tolerated by Maku's broad hips and heavy thighs, it became even easier to hate her. And hate her Maku did – until the day she exploded in frustration at Lyla, demanding to know why Theresa had a father in Ghana and yet always ended up living with them.

Furious at her younger cousin's outburst, Lyla had immediately silenced her.

'You don't know what you're talking about, so stop being so nasty! She's not *allowed* to live with her father and her mother *only* lets her come to Ghana if she stays with us. Auntie Clementyne doesn't trust Tee's father and thinks he'll stop her from going back to England if she lives with him. She only gets to come and see him because Ma swore that she would look after Tee and put her back on the plane to London at the end of the holidays.'

While it made no sense to Maku that any woman would have the power to tell a man what he could or couldn't do with his own daughter, Lyla's response had made it clear there was to be no shift in the pecking order. When, later in the holidays, she'd stumbled across Theresa weeping softly in the bedroom where she thought no one could hear, Maku had reached the conclusion that maybe exquisite clothes and perfect hair didn't bring any more happiness than that experienced by village girls like her who had been ejected from their homes by parents too poor and too tired to add another mouth to their troubles. When Theresa's father died suddenly, Maku had surrendered the remnants of her jealousy, thanking her lucky stars that, indifferent though they might be to her, she still had two parents – including a father on whom her mother could place no unreasonable demands or, if truth be told, any demands at all.

With her animosity to Theresa out of the way, Maku had graciously conceded the top spot in the ranks of Lyla's affections. No longer at the mercy of Maku's sharp-tongued hostility, Theresa, in turn, dropped her guard and the two had grown close over the years. Theresa's recent move to Ghana had further tightened their bonds of friendship and the three women met as frequently as their busy lives allowed.

Two sophisticated, professional women and one country-bumpkin cousin. The thought flashed through Maku's mind and she sucked her teeth in irritation, forcefully ripping open one of the tightly wrapped cellophane packets. *Why do I still think of myself that way?* Moving to Accra, after growing up in a village so sparsely populated that even the neighbouring town of Adidome had seemed huge, had been a shock to the system. But while it was understandable to feel intimidated when you were an eight-year-old girl torn from a carefree village life to live with family members you barely knew, and had little in common with, it was ridiculous to still feel inferior nineteen years later. She had a job, three children and a husband... well, a sort-of husband. *Stop doing that!* Nortey *is* your husband and you *are* married, she chided herself, but she knew it would make no difference.

Maku opened the fridge and took out the bottles of Coca-Cola she had bought from the kiosk down the road. She was lucky that, despite his grumbling, old Oscar had let her have the sodas. She still had to find the money to pay him for the empty bottles she kept promising to return

41

even though Elijah and Samuel had long since smashed them after using them as goalposts to play football on the concrete patch of ground behind the house.

Thankfully the new bottles felt cold to the touch. This time the power cut had lasted only a couple of hours and the electricity had been restored long enough to chill the drinks. She used the kitchen cloth to wipe three glasses, rubbing away the dried water marks as best she could.

Maku sighed. It would have been nice to offer her guests some wine, but the prices at Swanson's had been ridiculous. With no time to try another shop, it had been a choice between nappies for Abra or alcohol, not both. A picture of Theresa's enormous steel-grey American fridge with its internal wine rack stacked with bottles displaying expensive-looking labels flashed through her mind. It doesn't matter, Maku told herself, determined not to go back down the envy road. Coke will be fine. Thanks to that church of hers, Lyla doesn't drink alcohol, and if Theresa really wants wine, she can have some when she gets home.

Lyla's rich laugh wafted across from the living room into the small kitchen and Maku quickly assembled the crumbly cheese straws onto side plates. She carefully shared out a packet of honey-coated nuts into three of the cut-glass bowls Lyla and Kwesi had given them for Christmas and tossed a few into her mouth before remembering, too late, the diet she had sworn to start that day. Already curvaceous, her figure had clung on to the weight she had gained from carrying Abra, as if convinced that she would fall pregnant once again if she shed it. *What the hell! Maybe I should just forget about dieting. If Nortey*

*doesn't like me this size, then at least I'll get some peace at
night. I can't deal with having any more kids!*

A tug on her dress made her jump and she looked down
to see Elijah staring up at her with an unblinking gaze,
his eyes so like his father's it was unnerving. For a wild
moment she wondered if he had read her thoughts and
quashing a stab of guilt, she gave her son a perfunctory
hug and handed him a bowl.

'Here, carry this carefully and take it to Auntie Lyla. Go
on, I'm right behind you.'

The source of Lyla's humour was obvious as soon as
Maku walked into the living room. Abra was standing on
her aunt's lap, blowing damp bubbly kisses against Lyla's
razor-sharp cheekbones. The baby's distended tummy
stuck out from beneath her pink cotton vest and her
chubby little thighs jiggled as she bounced bare feet on
Lyla's linen skirt.

Maku dumped the tray of drinks and snacks on a wobbly
side table and exclaimed in dismay, 'Lyla, *don't!* Her feet
are filthy and you're wearing a white skirt!'

'What's a tiny bit of dirt when she's such a gorgeous
little thing,' Lyla cooed, covering Abra's cheeks with noisy
kisses in turn.

Theresa got up from the couch and walked over to help
Maku pour the drinks. She picked up a bottle and turned
to watch Lyla at play with Abra, staring so intently that she
didn't notice Maku trying to hand her a glass. Maku looked
at Theresa sharply; there was something different about
her today, something she couldn't quite put her finger on.

'Are you alright? You look like you're a hundred miles
away,' she said when Theresa finally took the glass.

'Sorry.' Theresa smiled in apology. 'It's been a bit of a strange week and I'm still trying to get my head around everything that's going on. Tyler's finally got the financing for the business agreed and he's been at the office until all hours putting plans in place for the new development. I'm sure things will be fine, but well... it's all a bit tense.'

Lyla deposited Abra gently on the patch of carpet in the centre of the room and took the full glass of Coke Maku held out. 'But if it's all agreed, that's *great* news, Tee! You must be so relieved. Now, it's your turn to get your act together – did you get to reschedule your meeting with *The Business Herald* editor?'

Theresa returned to the sofa, pulling her legs up under her and balancing her drink on her knee. 'Yes, and he was really helpful. He's offered to set up meetings to introduce me to a few business journalists. He even suggested I write a regular column for his paper giving PR tips for businesses to raise my profile. To be honest with you, I was shocked he's prepared to go to so much trouble.'

'It's worth it, if he can get you into bed,' Maku said bluntly.

Theresa flushed, and Lyla glared daggers at Maku, who stared back unabashed. '*What*? It's the truth.'

'Not everyone has a hidden agenda, Maku!'

'*Puh-leese!*' Maku said, scorn drawing out the syllable. 'Miss JJC here I can understand, but you, Lyla, you should know better. How many of our men would be that helpful if they weren't hoping to get a little something out of it? Look at Theresa; she's *beautiful* – you think after seeing that face and those big eyes of hers, the man is just doing it from the goodness of his heart?'

'What's JJC?' Theresa was more puzzled than annoyed.

Lyla muttered, 'Johnny just come. It means you've—'

'Only just arrived in the country and don't know anything. I get it,' Theresa finished off. She took a long sip of her drink and smiled ruefully. 'Maku, you sound just like Tyler when I told him about the meeting. I only hope the man means what he promised because I need to have some respectable journalists onside. No good PR can manage without press contacts, and when I start running campaigns for my clients, I'm going to need all the friends I can get.'

Maku wasn't finished. 'Then you can cross Tyler off that list if he's sorted out his money supply. You'd better be ready to handle your business yourself because I can tell you for free that you won't see him for dust.'

'Tyler's not like that,' Theresa protested. 'We *always* support each other, no matter what.'

Maku laughed derisively. 'That's how they all start out. Ask Lyla.'

She ignored her cousin's exasperated eye-roll. 'No, really, how many couples do we know who've come back from abroad and then broken up? Nortey was telling me only yesterday that Mame Oduro and her husband have split up. Ten years of marriage in London with hardly one argument – well, at least that's what *she* claims. Anyway, they've been back here for what, a year? All they do is fight. Why? Because Derek's always out with his friends and then crawls home late every night. Mame's convinced he's got a girlfriend hidden away – which wouldn't surprise me, knowing what *he's* like. Nortey says Derek's always moaning to him about Mame's nagging and how she won't accept things are different here than in London. And now it looks like she's finally had enough of his behaviour because, guess what? *Splitsville!*' She clasped her hands together and then swept them apart to illustrate her point.

Lyla burst into giggles. 'Maku, I swear you watch way too many soap operas – you are *so* melodramatic! Theresa, just ignore her. Lots of couples who return to Ghana make it work. I'm not saying it's easy to make the adjustment, but let's not go overboard here. Not *everybody* breaks up.'

Theresa looked thoughtful as she sipped her Coke. 'I know marriage isn't easy – God knows we've had our fair share of disagreements since we got together. But I also know Tyler, and he's not suddenly going to turn into some traditionalist throwback.'

'Ah, Theresa, this is *Africa!*' Maku said impatiently. 'The men here don't hold your hand and push the shopping trolley around Swanson's, so forget all that romantic, lovey-dovey stuff you guys do in the UK. So maybe I haven't been to England, but don't forget I watch a lot of TV and I've seen how the men over there go into the kitchen and do the washing up and the laundry – and even change nappies! If I decided to wait for Nortey to change Abra, the child would be covered in rashes. My sister, let's be *real.* In this country, it's nights out with the boys "doing business", she raised her fingers in sarcastic air quotes, 'and – if you're lucky – then it's back home to you. If not, it's a quick visit to their girlfriend before the wife ever gets to see them.'

Theresa choked on her drink. 'My God, Maku! You can't just generalise about an entire gender. There are plenty of good guys. Lyla, tell her – you're the one that hangs out with the church-y ones.'

Maku snorted in disbelief. '*Wha-at?* Don't even get me started on *those* guys.'

Lyla raised an eyebrow. 'Cuz, don't exaggerate. We have some very devout and sincere brothers at my church.'

'Really? Then why does Kwesi get annoyed with you for spending so much time at church? He's always going on about the pastors who get exposed in the newspapers for preying on women in their congregation.'

'Kwesi's hardly in any position to criticise men who prey on women,' Theresa said tartly, and then bit her lip, looking mortified. 'Sorry, Lyla, that was mean.'

'So where *is* Nortey this evening, then?' Lyla said mildly, as if Theresa hadn't spoken. Maku almost smiled at the obvious attempt to change the subject. My cousin, the peacemaker. She had long ago decided that being an only child was the reason why Lyla was so uncomfortable with any kind of conflict. *Which is probably why Kwesi gets away with so much.* Having spent her early years fighting for a place among her seven older siblings, Maku had never been afraid of a brawl.

'Who knows?' she replied. 'All I could make out before he disappeared was that there's some crisis or other with his sister. Knowing Nortey, whatever it is, he'll still end up at Jake's Joint for a few drinks with the boys before coming home.'

'Which one of his sisters?' Lyla asked curiously.

'Adoley – you know, the lawyer? The one who works at Regency Bank and thinks she's a real hotshot.'

'She must be doing well. I've heard they pay their staff

really high salaries and only hire the best people.'

Lyla sounded impressed but Maku shrugged, already tired of talking about her sister-in-law. It was hard enough trying to break out of her own dead-end job without having to think about Nortey's condescending sister zipping along her fast-track career.

'Well, she's going abroad for some executive course or other soon, so we won't see her for almost a year.' *Thank God*, she added silently.

Their conversation continued while the children wandered in and out of the room and Elijah made futile attempts to force his sister to walk the length of the tatty carpet. During a lull in the chatter, Theresa yawned loudly, flushing with embarrassment as the other two women stared at her.

'Sorry, I don't know where that came from. I've been feeling so tired lately.'

Maku stared at her through narrowed eyes and the sensation that something was amiss grew more intense. Then, she smiled. *Of course!* For once Theresa had come without her customary bottle of wine in hand as if arriving for a posh London dinner party. And wasn't that the second glass of Coke she'd polished off since she'd arrived without her usual whinge that the amount of sugar in a single bottle was enough to rot an entire set of teeth? And who better than Maku could recognise what sudden bouts of exhaustion and deeply shadowed eyes signalled?

Well, well, this isn't exactly great timing. Only too aware of Theresa's ambitious business plans, Maku felt a pang of sympathy. The sentiment immediately evaporated as her eyes fell on the large, sparkling stone nestled against the platinum wedding band on Theresa's left hand. *Tee should have my problems – at least she has a big house, a rich husband and house help.* She glanced at Lyla who was leaning down to tickle Abra's tummy, a wide smile on her face as the baby chuckled helplessly. *She* clearly doesn't know what's going on. This time the ache Maku felt was for her cousin. Lyla would make *such* an amazing mother. What the hell was the point of all those years of churchgoing and praying if the poor woman was still unable to conceive? In her shoes, Maku would have given up on God and his unfulfilled promises long ago.

'Theresa, if you really want to know what tired looks like, then come and take my place for a day.' Maku's smile robbed her words of any sting. 'At least you've got Auntie Sisi to do your cooking and cleaning – I can't find a house girl to stay with us who doesn't drive me, the kids or Nortey crazy.'

'Well, why don't you get someone to help out with just the cooking, then?' Theresa suggested, ignoring the dig. 'Between your job and looking after the children, you've got a lot on your plate, and I know a woman who might be able to help. She offered to cook for us before we hired Auntie Sisi and I've still got her number if you want to call her.'

Maku scoffed at the prospect. 'I suggested that to Nortey once and he looked at me like I was mad. Then he started ranting about how he'll only eat food that I've prepared and that he didn't marry me to put up with another woman's cooking. Look, even if I prepare large portions of food so I can freeze some for later in the week, he starts whining, "*You know I like my food freshly cooked*". Honestly, he's worse than the children.'

She tossed back the last drops of cola in her glass. 'I blame his mother for pampering him so much. Can you believe he actually went and told her what I'd suggested? So then, of course, *she* started on at me. It's bad enough that her little prince ended up marrying a village girl, but instead of being grateful, I'm not even prepared to be serviceable and cook for her son. I swear she went on for at least twenty minutes.' She adopted a high-pitched, nasal voice: *'Eh, you want to let another woman cook for your husband? Are you stupid? She will put poison in the food to bind him to her and force him to leave you!'*

Lyla laughed. 'That's what comes of marrying the youngest child in the family. In Nortey's case, he's also the only boy, so completely spoilt, I'm afraid.'

Theresa shook her head in irritation. 'It's really just as well Tyler's mum isn't alive to get on my case because I've got absolutely no time for these ridiculous traditions. Women work just as hard as men, and a lot of us earn more than our husbands, so why is it down to us to take care of everything else as well? You've got your own ambitions, Maku, and you can't keep doing it all by yourself. Don't you want to start your accountancy training now you've got Abra in full-time nursery?'

'Of course, I do,' Maku sighed. 'My boss has even put my name forward for one of the training bursaries the company gives out to staff every year. But I don't see how I'll be able to fit studying in with my job and taking care of the kids, not to mention cooking every day, cleaning – don't look at me like that, Lyla, I *do* clean!'

Maku's frustration was so palpable that her cousin bit back the mocking words that had been hovering on her lips and said gently, 'Look, Maku, Tee's right; don't give up on your dreams. You're going to have to figure out a way to get ahead, with or without Nortey's support. Whatever we can do to help, just ask. We love you and, quite honestly, you deserve better than *this*.'

She waved a dismissive arm around the dingy sitting room with its faded patch of carpet and once-white walls stained with children's fingerprints. 'Just think about it, that's all.'

* * *

It was all Maku *could* think about as she sat in the office a few days later. Along with the news Nortey had brought home with him that night, accompanied by the stench of beer from Jake's Joint. It was one thing to enjoy the benefits of being the spoilt youngest child, she brooded, but it was quite another to pass its burdens on to your partner. Not that any such consideration had appeared to bother Nortey when he carelessly pushed aside his half-eaten plate of freshly cooked jollof rice to make his big announcement.

Only days before departing for a nine-month executive programme in Paris, his sister, Adoley, had begged Nortey – which basically meant Maku – to look after her six-year-old daughter Isabelle while she was away. Adoley's husband George, the country manager of an international development agency, was frequently away on business which, she'd claimed, made it impossible for him to care for Isabelle on his own. As Nortey and Maku had children of the same age, it made sense for her younger brother to take in his niece while she was away in France.

Maku's instinctive response to Nortey's halting explanation had been a loud shriek of angry disbelief.

'What the *hell* are you telling me? You've got to be kidding – I can barely manage with the three kids we have already!'

Her protest had been quickly followed by a feverish clutching at straws. 'Why can't your mother look after Isabelle? She doesn't have anything else to do!' *Apart from criticising me.*

But Nortey had stubbornly refused to budge. 'I'm sorry, but Adoley was panicking. She's leaving in less than a week and she wouldn't stop going on about it. I *had* to say yes. Maku, I promised her we'd do it, so let's just make the best of it. Look on the bright side, you're always saying Adoley hates you. Once you've taken care of her child, you'll get bonus points and she'll have to be nicer to you.'

Looking furiously at his smug, unrepentant expression while the stale smell of Jake's beer filled her nostrils, Maku hadn't known whether to wring his neck, slit her wrists, or both.

'Do you think this is *funny*? If you honestly think that smiling at me like that will change my mind, you don't know me. And if, and I mean *if*, we do take Isabelle, is your sister going to contribute to the cost of her daughter? We're struggling enough with our own children without you volunteering another mouth for us to feed.'

'Isabelle's a good kid; she won't be any trouble.' His attempts to soothe her had fallen on deaf ears as she frantically thought up even more reasons why the idea was impossible.

'Nortey, that child eats cornflakes and sausages and

God knows what else just for *breakfast*. I can't afford food like that!'

'Okay, okay, fine. I'll talk to George and ask him to buy some of those things and bring them with her. I'm sure he won't mind.'

When she scowled in reply, he'd added impatiently. 'Look, I know this isn't the best, but Adoley is my family and I have to help her out. Maku, it's only for a few months, for God's sake. Come on, it's not the end of the world – what difference will one extra child make?'

With that, he'd returned to wrestling with his sons on the living room floor, skilfully forestalling any further discussion. Thirty minutes later, glaring at his prone figure lounging on the sofa watching football on the bulky, old-fashioned TV they still couldn't afford to upgrade, Maku reluctantly rounded up her overexcited children for their baths. After herding them into bed, she had disappeared into her room and pointedly ignored Nortey's attempts to reach for her when he finally came to bed.

Replaying Nortey's words, Maku once again felt the intense outrage at being taken for granted. She stared in frustration at her computer and bit down hard on her lip, the sheen of angry tears making the numbers on the spreadsheet dance across the screen. She was running out of time. Today was the deadline to tell Mr Danso if she wanted the training bursary. She knew her manager had earmarked one of the awards for her and had even delayed making the announcement of this year's recipients to give her time to decide. After Lyla's pep talk and before Nortey had dropped his bombshell, Maku had made up her mind to seize the opportunity and find a way to fit studying in with her childcare duties.

While she was the first to admit her social limitations, Maku knew she had a gift when it came to numbers. She could quickly master the most complicated Excel macros and interpret columns of data that left qualified accountants scratching their heads. But no matter how good her analytical and numerical skills, she was painfully aware she wouldn't climb any further up the ladder without at least an accountancy diploma. Eagle Enterprises was a reputable company and wouldn't risk promoting unqualified employees into professional grades. Continuing with the status quo was simply not an option and Maku desperately needed a promotion, not only to satisfy her ambitions, but also because she needed the money.

As much as she loved Samuel, Maku still cursed the broken condom which had led to her first pregnancy when she was only nineteen and had nothing more to her name than an IT certificate. She tried not to extend the curse to cover her first meeting with Nortey at her graduation ceremony, a ridiculously overblown label for the thirty-minute event when certificates were distributed to the twenty students on her course followed by refreshments in the form of stale biscuits and tepid cartons of fruit juice. Nortey had strolled in halfway through the presentations, and at first glance he had appeared to be the answer to any woman's romantic prayers. And even though she hadn't been praying, Maku had found it impossible to tear her eyes away. Tall, attractive, and with a bright smile that used every feature on his face, he had charmed her from the moment his sister Adorkor, a fellow student, introduced them. Maku had made a good show of pretending not to notice the gleam of interest in his eyes, having decided long ago that men, unlike her career, could wait. But Nortey's teasing whisper that he was only there to bag a free drink had left her giggling helplessly, allowing his cheeky insouciance to slip past her street-smart defences. Before she realised she had said yes to his invitation, they were sitting in a coffee shop and chatting away like old friends.

'Maku, did you hear me?' Rita's gratingly high-pitched voice jolted Maku out of her thoughts.

'What did you say?'

Rita pouted and tossed back her braids with an exaggerated sigh that irritated Maku even more than the woman's voice.

'I *said*, can you hurry up and check the spreadsheet I gave you this morning and put it into a PowerPoint slide. My boss wants to go through the presentation, so he can be well prepared for tomorrow's board meeting.'

Maku bit her tongue hard. Although she had almost finished, she still resented Rita's request. As the Finance Director's PA, Rita should have been the one checking the figures and putting the presentation together instead of handing over the task to her. Just because Maku was good at something didn't mean that everyone had the right to dump their work on her.

'Fine,' she said dismissively. She had too much on her mind to let the woman get to her.

'So how long will it take you to finish?' Rita persisted.

'I just *said* okay, didn't I?' Maku barked, her annoyance spilling out unchecked. Rita's face darkened in offence, but Maku stared back unrepentantly. If the woman was expecting an apology, she'd be waiting a long time. Rita appeared to draw the same conclusion and she tossed her braids once again and left without a word.

Maku tapped the keyboard listlessly, her thoughts a million miles away from the columns of figures on the screen in front of her. Why had she been so stupid as to let Nortey persuade her into bed so easily? With Lyla at university in England and no one else to confide in, she had allowed her heart and, if she were honest, her ego to take the lead. Knowing that a handsome, educated man like Nortey was in love with her had been a heady rush. After all, how many girls from her background found themselves being chased by a man from a good family and with a postgraduate degree, no less, not to mention a job that he swore was a stepping stone to bigger things? Importantly for Maku, Nortey never made derogatory remarks about her village origins or her lack of sophistication. Charmed by his carefree, relaxed attitude to life, which was so different from her own obsessive single-mindedness, Maku had swept aside Auntie Pat's warning not to lose her focus. Instead, she found herself going out on frequent dates with Nortey and agreeing with him that she had plenty of time to start the Finance course that topped her to-do list. Three months and one ruptured condom later, that dream had been deferred indefinitely.

At that point, neither Lyla's outraged phone calls from her university campus in rural England nor Auntie Pat's reproachful 'I told you so' had hit her harder than the realisation she'd have to abandon any chance of studying accountancy if she decided to have the baby. Without a job and a place of her own – continuing to live with Auntie Pat once she had a child would be impossible – any money she earned would have to be spent on rent and food, always assuming she could find work when even university graduates were struggling for jobs. Numb with fear, and too petrified to tell Nortey, even her mother's furious phone call peppered with insults and finishing up with '*You stupid girl!* Is this what I sent you to Accra for? If you were going to get pregnant at your age with no husband, you might as well have stayed here!' had washed over her.

And yet, no matter how badly it would derail her planned career, no one could persuade Maku to contemplate getting rid of the baby. She ignored her mother's abuse and pretended not to understand Lyla's carefully veiled suggestion to pay for her to 'sort it out'. Because even greater than her pain and frustration at seeing her professional dreams move out of reach was a quiet, secret longing she had never voiced to anyone – her overwhelming desire for the recognition and, yes, the *respect* marriage would bring. Because, surely, with a baby on the way, Nortey would marry her? And when she was a married woman with a successful husband from a decent family, Maku reasoned, she would at last be *somebody* and not just the village girl everyone disparaged. As Nortey's wife, she would finally fit in, finally receive the deference she craved from all those who looked down on her.

To his credit, Nortey had immediately stepped up to take responsibility for his part in the pregnancy. Only moments after she had tearfully broken the news and watched his wide grin shrink into a dismayed 'O', he had gamely recovered and immediately suggested they get married. His version of getting married, not hers.

'Don't worry, Maku. It will be fine. I'll speak to my mother and we'll come and see your aunt and uncle and then organise everything,' he'd said confidently.

'Everything' had turned out not to be the perfect white wedding she'd secretly hankered after since attending a plush ceremony in Accra Cathedral years earlier with Auntie Pat while Uncle Sidney was away. Maku could still remember every detail of that day. The bride whose big, puffy white gown had transformed her from an average-looking woman into a beautiful fairy princess and the reception at a posh hotel with waiters in uniform serving dinner on gleaming white china plates.

To Maku's disgust, Nortey's idea of marriage was a simple traditional arrangement with guests consisting of his furious mother, disgruntled sisters and a motley collection of relatives who trooped to Auntie Pat and Uncle Sidney's house with a couple of crates of drinks, a few uninspired rolls of fabric and a ring with a diamond so small, it was barely visible. Instead of the usual lavish engagement ceremony – which, Nortey had earnestly reminded her, was also a customary marriage – the event had been conducted with so little fanfare that once the drinks and gifts had been handed over and the necessary exchanges between the two representatives for her and Nortey's families had been concluded, Nortey's relatives had dispersed with gloomy sighs which showed more plainly than any words, their repugnance at what their only boy had been reduced to. Any suggestion on Maku's part to follow the traditional event with a church or even a registry office wedding had been met with a stony refusal by his family and vague, awkward excuses from Nortey which usually included the words 'cost' and 'priorities'.

Maku gnawed at her lower lip, feeling the stubbornly dry patches against her tongue. With the children growing up so fast, their finances were becoming more strained by the day. Nortey's stepping stone of a job hadn't led anywhere beyond the Economics department of the local university where he earned a very modest salary as a lecturer, an income rendered even more modest by his frequent visits to Jake's Joint.

To make matters worse, Maku had yet to find the money to pay off the dressmaker. What the hell had possessed her to take the yards of white lace and imagine that she could keep up with the repayments? She tapped the keyboard impatiently and suppressed the bitter laugh threatening to escape. Who was she kidding? It didn't take much soul searching to know why she hadn't been able to resist the material. The beautiful white fabric was exactly what she had imagined for the wedding dress of her dreams and, having seen the roll of glittering pale lace on the counter at the dressmaker's, Maku could no more have left the material behind than she could have left Abra.

Maku sniffed disconsolately. With a single blow, pregnancy had put paid to both her dreams of a white wedding and her chance for a career. And now, *now* that she finally had the opportunity to take a step towards that second goal, Nortey's high and mighty sister, who barely gave her the time of day, was about to ruin that for her, too. Yet again, a child was going to mess up her plans. Her eyes brimmed over, her chest tightened in pain and her breath failed her. For a wild moment, Maku felt like she was drowning. When would this ever end? When would it be *her* turn to have a better life and give her children more than a drab bungalow and second-hand clothing?

Lyla's words swirled around her head yet again. *You're going to have to figure out a way to get ahead.* A surge of energy suddenly swept through her and she sat up straight and pushed the keyboard away, swiping roughly at the tears on her cheeks with the back of her hand. *Enough!* No man had ever made her cry – unless seeing Samuel's face for the first time when he was born counted – and she was damned if she was going to let it happen now. There was no alternative if her life was ever going to improve. She *had* to take that training bursary. Whatever it took.

With a cautious look around to check that no one could hear, Maku snatched up the battered mobile phone on her desk and punched out a number. As soon as she heard the crisp greeting, she spoke without hesitation.

'Theresa, it's me. What's the name of that woman you were talking about – you know, the one who offered to cook for you? What do you mean, *why am I asking?* Because I need her number, and I need it now. That's why!'

Nortey

'Okay, my man, I'll see you later. I should be there by six.'

Nortey ended the call and stared at his handset for a moment, still slightly shocked by the turn the conversation had taken. After being rebuffed so often, he hadn't expected Tyler to accept his half-hearted invitation to go to Jake's Joint for a drink. And with such enthusiasm.

He shook his head and a grin spread across his face. *I wonder what's going on in yuppie paradise.* Maybe Maku's theory was right and Theresa really *was* pregnant. In which case, no wonder the poor guy wanted the chance to escape and knock back a few drinks – the guys at Jake's understood how crazy and hormonal women became when they were expecting. Whatever the reason for his change of heart, it was high time Tyler got it through his head that, in Ghana, real men didn't hang around with their wives all the time. A guy could get laughed out of town for a lot less.

Nortey grimaced at the pile of papers stacked on his desk. Marking fifty essays analysing the impact of economic theories on global financial markets in a poky airless office held about as much appeal as going home did these days. Isabelle had been living with them for a week and it was safe to say that it wasn't going well. As Maku had predicted, the child was set in her dietary ways and, on her first morning with them, had refused point blank to eat the spicy, sweetened *koko* his boys were used to gulping down for breakfast. After two days of not-so-silent protests, and with no financial contribution from George forthcoming, Nortey had gritted his teeth and driven to Swanson's to hand over a wad of notes in exchange for a packet of Kellogg's Corn Flakes. Threatening his sons with an instant beating if they dared to touch their cousin's breakfast cereal, he had avoided Maku's accusing gaze and left early for work that day – and every day since.

He glanced at his watch. Only four-thirty. Even he couldn't justify leaving the office so early. He was fast running out of plausible excuses for cutting short his work day and he shifted uncomfortably as he recalled Professor Ghartey's recent warning. Spotting Nortey rushing towards the lecture hall, the Prof has stepped squarely into his path, his gaze travelling with undisguised scorn over Nortey's navy polo shirt and grey chinos and down to the scruffy Adidas trainers scored with stripes once white and now an indifferent shade of grey.

'Mr Quarshie, please don't think you can continue to use this university as a base while you dabble in ventures that take up the time you should be using to, dare I say it, actually *teach* your students?'

The pontificating old fool hadn't been moved by Nortey's protests that he had never failed to deliver any of his lectures. Stroking one of the pretentious bow ties he'd adopted after a year's sabbatical teaching at Oxford University, Professor Ghartey had glared at Nortey with such ferocity his bushy eyebrows had merged into an undulating furry line.

'We are *not* in the business of providing the bare

minimum to our students when their parents are parting with significant sums of money to see their children educated to the highest possible standards. As it is, you make little attempt to research and publish in reputable journals or engage in community service like your peers in other facilities of higher education. If you don't believe you can add any more value to enriching these young minds than simply trotting out the same tired old notes every year, then perhaps it's time for you to reconsider your vocation as a teacher and your place in our institution.'

With a deep sigh, Nortey reached for the essay at the top of the stack and flipped through the first couple of pages, willing himself to concentrate on the convoluted argument the student had set out. He scratched at the itchy dry skin on his forearm and tried his best to focus, but within minutes his mind had drifted back to Tyler and the alacrity with which he had accepted his drinks invitation.

Theresa must *really* be getting on Tyler's nerves if he's ready for a night out with the boys, and who could blame him? Nortey frowned as he recalled Theresa's first visit to their house and her look of distaste as she'd walked into the small bungalow, a look she had quickly masked when she'd caught him watching her. Christ, that woman was such a *snob!* And so full of herself with all her big plans to start a PR agency. So maybe his house wasn't one of those fancy Labone mansions and, yes, living so close to the industrial area wasn't exactly the smartest neighbourhood in Accra, but he provided for his family, didn't he? Just because Theresa had grown up in the UK, she thought she was something. Maku might not wear fancy clothes and visit expensive salons, but at least she knew how to treat her man and not make him feel like a failure, one of the many reasons why he loved her.

Nortey grinned as he thought of another good reason. Despite her frequent complaints about the weight she'd gained since having Abra, Maku's wide hips and heavy breasts never failed to excite him and when she smiled at him with those teasing dark brown eyes, there was little he could refuse her. Maku might have her faults, but along with her cracking sense of humour, she was straightforward and easy-going – or at least she had been until he'd stupidly said yes to taking in Isabelle.

His grin faded, and he scratched his head and flipped through the essay, his thoughts everywhere but on the neatly typed words in front of him. He could only hope that now Theresa had moved to Ghana, she wasn't going to start putting ideas into Maku's head. The woman never missed a chance to tell anyone who would listen that she had no time for Ghanaian traditions, and the last thing he needed was his wife thinking she could call the shots. It was bad enough Maku had decided to resume her studies – a stupid idea in his opinion, and he *worked* in education.

Not that Maku had taken any notice when he'd pointed out that an accountancy course was hardly a priority. His protests that they wouldn't be able to afford the course fees had been rebuffed by the news about her company's bursary and, with the cornflakes incident still fresh in both their minds, he'd felt it prudent to hold his tongue.

Nortey's red pen skittered across the page as he boldly scribbled a mark at the bottom of the essay. Feeling a little guilty at not including any feedback to guide the student, he tossed it aside and reached for the next one. Glancing through the first page, he paused and sucked thoughtfully on the end of his biro. Maybe he should have a word with Lyla about Maku's burgeoning ambitions. Maku had a lot of respect for her cousin and might well listen to her. And Lyla was a nice girl – a little too skinny for his tastes, mind you – but still very kind. But then, being so *Chrife* and going to church all the time probably meant she had to love everyone, whatever their faults.

Lyla was all right – and at least she didn't judge him. Whenever Lyla asked him about his career and when he might get promoted, she sounded interested and encouraging and didn't have that sceptical expression he'd caught on Theresa's face more than once. So maybe he wasn't as rich as Tyler just yet, but it was only a matter of time. The pineapple farming project the Frimpong brothers had briefed him about at Jake's was likely to generate a massive return and, if he could get his share of the capital together, making that kind of money would be life-changing. Maybe he should try talking to Jeff Parnell again. After all, he was the one who'd introduced Jeff to Tyler, and if the man could lend such a huge sum to Tyler Brew who'd only been in the country for five minutes, why not invest in Nortey who knew everyone worth knowing in this town?

The stifling heat of his office felt oppressive and Nortey rolled up his sleeves and mopped his forehead with a crumpled handkerchief. The air conditioning had broken down yet again and the sluggish air filtering in through the open louvre windows only served to circulate the stale heat around his office. Reluctant to complain and invite another discussion with Professor Ghartey, he made a mental note to slip a sweetener of a few cedis into Seibu's pocket. It was the old scoundrel's job to maintain the building and yet Seibu always acted as if he was doing you a favour whenever something needed fixing, blatantly refusing to lift a finger unless 'a little weight' was added to his wallet.

Nortey moved speedily on to the next essay, his red pen absently striking out the occasional word while his mind raced off in different directions, already spending the fortune his pineapple exports would yield. He could just see Maku's broad face alight with joy as he walked her into one of those large, detached red-brick houses in the new development near Achimota, the ones with green lawns at the front and back. The boys would have a decent space to play football instead of the cracked, weed-infested strip of concrete behind their rented bungalow, and his little Abra would be able to wear pretty, flowery dresses like the babies on the TV adverts. With that kind of money, Nortey dreamed, he could fix up his mother's house and buy her a new polytank, one which held at least a hundred gallons, and put an end to her constant complaints about the lack of running water in her area and the snide comments about his sister's husband taking better care of her than her only son.

With his mind on the wealth that could soon be his, the grin never far from Nortey's face returned as he raced through the pile of papers. He would have a word with Tyler when they met up at Jake's that night and persuade him to put in a good word on his behalf with Jeff. The farm deal was a sure thing, and with just a bit of persuasion, Jeff would realise it, too.

Lyla

Lyla bit hard on her lip to suppress a groan as another shaft of pain shot through her lower abdomen. Despite the faint kernel of hope she nursed every month, the familiar cramps that once again proved her unfitness to be a mother were really no surprise. Head bowed, she sat motionless on the ornately carved wooden stool and waited for the spasm to ease before attempting to stand up. Not content with trumpeting her ongoing infertility, the cramps were often so intense that she was in danger of fainting.

'Low blood pressure, Mrs Amoah,' had been the opinion of the doctor she'd reluctantly consulted after almost keeling over during an afternoon meeting with her sales team. 'Your menstrual cycles are very heavy and have caused a deficiency in your iron levels.'

Another deficiency to add to the others, Lyla thought bitterly. Her polite smile had vanished when the doctor added, 'If you don't mind me saying, Mrs Amoah, you are extremely slim. Perhaps we should arrange for you to have a full check-up? It will help if we can investigate this a bit more thoroughly to see how we can help make that pregnancy happen.'

If 'deficiency' was bad, then 'investigate' was even worse and Lyla had barely suppressed a shudder. She didn't need any investigating, thank you very much, no matter how well intentioned. That was the last visit she'd paid to the doctor and she had no plans for another.

The pain slowly subsided and she sat up and pushed the tangle of braids away from her face. A quick glance at her watch confirmed that it was time to start making dinner. Kwesi would be home in an hour – or not. Predicting her husband's behaviour was an exercise she really should have given up long ago. As the General Manager of the largest retail store in Accra's central shopping mall, Kwesi could cite an abundance of excuses for why he was regularly late home from work; from awkward customers who needed soothing – apparently for hours on end, in some cases – to incompetent staff in need of additional training. And if it wasn't his workers that kept him busy after hours, it was one or other of his numerous suppliers demanding to be entertained at one of Accra's popular nightclubs, or insisting on personal visits at the oddest times – all of which, Kwesi assured her, formed a vital part of his relationship-building responsibilities. Whatever relationships were being cultivated, Lyla thought as she trudged upstairs to change into one of the simple caftans she preferred to wear at home, they certainly weren't with his wife.

She tried, and failed, to remember the last time Kwesi had come straight home, and she winced as another dart of pain stabbed at her stomach and slowed her footsteps to a shuffle. Pushing open the door to the bedroom, she sank with relief onto the corner of the bed. Even with no guarantee that her husband would appear, she had to cook dinner. It would be just her luck not to bother and then have to deal with his heavy sighs and reproachful silence at finding no warm pot of rice and stew waiting for him.

Kwesi was firmly in the I'm-a-traditionalist-and-I-don't-do-the-cooking camp when it came to preparing meals, ignoring the fact that Lyla's demanding senior managerial job often had her working long hours. His love of tradition, however, stopped just short of taking on the role of sole provider and foregoing the healthy salary and bonuses Lyla's job brought home.

She fell back against the pillows and stroked the silky quilt covering the huge mahogany-framed bed Kwesi had insisted they invest in with a wry smile. *A bed*. It was almost laughable given how little time he managed to spend in it, at least with her. Who knew what he got up to when she wasn't in the house? If their former housemaid's stories – before Kwesi had peremptorily sacked her – were to be believed, the master of the house wasn't averse to bringing female guests home in Lyla's absence.

The vast expanse of mattress seemed to mock her, and she stood up and slowly stripped off the navy suit and plain white shirt she had worn to work. The skirt had once fitted like a glove but now slid past her narrow hips effortlessly, the fabric barely touching her skin.

Lyla, you really need to eat, she berated herself as she hung up the suit jacket and tossed the blouse into the wicker hamper by the door. How could she hope to fall pregnant when her body had barely enough sustenance to look after itself, never mind a growing foetus? Trying to ignore the stabbing pains, she slipped into a long cotton caftan and tied her hair back with a headscarf before descending gingerly down the stairs and into the silent kitchen.

An hour later, spicy grilled chicken pieces warmed in the oven and a fresh pot of rice sat waiting on the cooker next to Kwesi's favourite rich tomato gravy. Retreating to the living room, Lyla stretched out on the oversized black sofa, another piece of furniture that had found its way from the store into their home, tuned the television to her favourite Christian channel, and tried to relax.

High overhead, the ceiling fan whirred efficiently, its faint rhythmic whumps drowned by the strident preaching from a stocky evangelist minister on the TV screen. Feeling slightly groggy from the powerful codeine tablets she'd swallowed while she was cooking, Lyla watched him pace up and down a brightly lit stage in what appeared to be a huge auditorium, and with a headset clamped around his head that looked more suited to a rock star than a pastor.

Her mobile buzzed loudly, and she reluctantly picked up the handset. Kwesi's name flashed across the screen and she grimaced and mentally braced herself.

'Lyla?'

'Kwesi,' she echoed dryly, her eyes flicking towards the black and white clock on the wall. Eight-thirty.

'I've had to stop by my mother's house, so I might be a bit late. I'll have dinner here, so don't bother cooking anything for me.'

She gritted her teeth and sighed silently. 'Fine. So what time are you coming home, then?'

'We–ll I'm not sure. She wants to discuss some family matters, which means I could be here for some time. It might be quite late by the time we're finished, so don't wait up.'

'Give her my greet—' He ended the call before she could

finish her sentence and she shrugged, unconcerned. *I was only being polite anyway – it's not like I have anything to say to the old bat.*

She tossed the phone to one side and reclined against the cushions, ignoring the TV and letting her eyes wander aimlessly around the spotless living room. Something about Kwesi's call didn't quite add up and she struggled through her drug-induced haze to remember what it was. *Ah yes!* An irritated Kwesi unable to reach his mother on the phone and grumbling loudly about her annoying practice of refusing calls and visitors after nine o'clock, no matter who they were.

The trouble with telling so many lies was that it was almost impossible to keep track, Lyla mused. She wondered idly why she couldn't be bothered to work up any righteous indignation at her husband's blatant untruths. She'd be better off reviewing the last month's sales figures which were showing a worrying downward trend, and with the reduction in tourist bookings resulting in a correspondingly sharp drop in revenues. It was hardly surprising, Lyla thought. Who in their right mind would want to holiday in a country with power cuts every other day, not to mention the chaos the government's latest exchange rates fiasco had caused? Her team would have to find creative ways to attract new customers until things stabilised.

A jolt of energy for the task ahead banished thoughts of Kwesi and helped clear the haziness, and she reached for her briefcase. The cramps were subsiding, and her stomach growled hungrily, reminding her that it had been hours since lunchtime. Slipping her feet into soft leather slippers, she headed to the kitchen where the sight of the cooling saucepans on the cooker recalled her absent husband and she felt her resurgent appetite slide away. Reminding herself that she had to eat, Lyla put aside three pieces of grilled chicken and stacked the rest of the food into containers in the fridge. Turning off the light, she returned to the living room clutching a small plate and gnawing on a chicken wing.

A couple of hours later, her team strategy presentation was finished, but there was still no word from Kwesi. She replayed the excuse he had offered, and a sudden surge of fury took her by surprise. Her face burning with rage, she took deep breaths and forced herself to stifle her racing emotions. *Calm down, Lyla. Stay focused on what really matters.* It took several minutes before she felt in control again and hauled herself up to bed.

Propped up against a stack of pillows in her bed, Lyla stared at the ceiling and listened to the gentle hum of the air conditioner. *So much for married life.* She gently rubbed her tender belly and spread her legs wide to stretch out her cramped muscles. The ship. That was how Maku had described this huge bed and it struck Lyla as almost funny that her cousin envied her for the life she thought she had. If only she knew. Nortey might be light years away from winning a husband of the year award, but Lyla would have chosen his good-humoured, sociable banter, his endless supply of corny jokes and – if Maku was to be believed – his incredible sexual abilities any day over her sterile, empty marriage. Maku was so caught up in her world of imagined slights that she would never have believed that she, Lyla, envied *her*. In fairness, it was hard to argue that having a great career, a handsome husband with a good job *and* a beautiful house in a safe gated community wasn't enough for any woman. And yet, after years of trying, she still didn't have a child. While most people reacted to her situation with a sympathetic shrug or a comment that she was young enough to keep trying, a couple of well-meaning friends had hinted strongly that she consider adopting a baby.

She curled up into a ball and rolled back on to her side of the bed, thumping the pillows with frustration. Adoption wasn't the answer, at least not for her. If God wasn't giving her a child of her own, it was because He knew she didn't deserve one. Adoption would be trying to cheat her way into something she hadn't earned. Even as the logical, sensible part of her brain scolded her for being ridiculous, the other part – the part that couldn't forget – continued its strident condemnation.

The codeine eventually soothed the pain in her abdomen, but sleep continued to elude her. Finally, with an exasperated groan, she sat up and stared at the neon green numbers on her bedside clock. *Eleven-thirty!* She was sorely tempted to call Ma Abena and ask to speak to Kwesi. That would put the cat among the pigeons, assuming of course that Kwesi's mother would even answer her phone. She slumped back against the crumpled sheets. In any case, what would be the point? Her mother-in-law would only find a way to make it Lyla's fault that her husband was missing in action.

When she eventually heard the familiar thud of the front door, instead of bringing relief that her husband was home, the sound caused every nerve in her body to jangle. For a moment Lyla was tempted to close her eyes and pretend to be asleep, but the fury that had seized her earlier in the evening returned with a vengeance and she sat up and waited, her heart beating furiously.

A few minutes later, the door opened quietly and Kwesi tiptoed in with his shoes clutched in one hand. Lyla switched on the bedside lamp and watched his startled expression quickly rearrange itself into an apologetic grin.

'Are you still awake? Sorry – I hope I didn't disturb you when I came in.'

He didn't appear to expect a response and he dropped his shoes and undid his belt, smoothly yanking his shirt loose before stepping out of his trousers and tossing them carelessly over the nearest chair.

'How's your mother?' As much as Lyla wanted to sound cool and unconcerned, she couldn't disguise the halting tremor of anger in her voice.

If the question took him by surprise, it was hard to tell. Shrugging out of his shirt, he rolled it up into a ball and dropped it in the hamper before replying.

'She's very upset about the state of the house in Tema and wanted me to look over the tenancy agreement. She insists the tenants should pay for the repairs, but I've told her to let the managing agents deal with it. It's really not good for her to get worked up at her age.'

With his head kept firmly down, there was no danger of his eyes meeting hers as he rummaged through a heavy chest of drawers and pulled out a white T-shirt, and Lyla watched in silence as he headed into the adjoining bathroom. Then, as quickly as it had arrived, she felt the heat of her anger dissipate. She slipped down into the bed, turned off the light and didn't say a word when he finally climbed into the ship.

For the rest of the week Kwesi returned home later and later each day, sorely testing Lyla's efforts at maintaining a stoic silence in the face of such blatant provocation. By the weekend, her willpower was failing fast. Her husband's increasingly weak excuses for staying out late enraged her, not only because he lied so easily, but also because he made no effort to make them even remotely plausible. The previous night, she had gritted her teeth while he smoothly explained how he had to personally supervise the delivery of a new sofa to the Minister of Finance's house, before hanging up the phone and venting her frustration on the cooked yam congealing in the pot. Slowly and methodically, she had removed each slice and cut it into small neat squares before tossing it into the kitchen bin. One part of her was disgusted at herself for wasting food, but it was so cathartic to imagine it was Kwesi's heart she was quietly dicing, just as he was doing to hers, that she couldn't stop herself.

Metaphorically hacking her husband into pieces had also helped to quell the raw, burning sensation that had taken root in her chest after Theresa's phone call earlier that evening. *Pregnant.* Her best friend, who had absolutely no desire to start a family, was expecting a baby.

'Lyla? Are you okay?' Theresa had sounded anxious and guilty, leaving Lyla flooded with remorse. This was Tee. *Of course,* she was happy for her.

'I'm just stunned, that's all,' she'd replied, even forcing a laugh into her voice, particularly impressive given the tears sliding down her cheeks. 'Congratulations! I'm so happy for you. What did Tyler say?'

'Oh *God*, you know what he's like. There I was, still trying to get my head around the whole thing and persuade myself that it wasn't a total disaster, and then he comes in with his '*Let's look on the positive side*'.'

Theresa had ground to an awkward halt, followed by another anxious, 'Lyla? Please don't feel bad. It will happen for you, too. Soon – I promise.'

* * *

At the end of a Saturday morning spent cleaning her already spotless house, Lyla stripped the sheets from their bed the minute Kwesi left for his weekly tennis game and stood under a hot shower, her tears mingling with the powerful jets of water.

She moisturised her skin and slipped into her underwear and then pulled open the wardrobe door. Glancing at the clock, she sighed and tried to curb her resentment. It would be so nice not to spend her Saturday rushing around doing other people's bidding. The harsh, berating voice that had taken up residency in her head promptly reminded her that no one had forced her offer to sing at Andrea's wedding. Just because Andrea occasionally helped with Lyla's youth group didn't mean that Lyla owed her anything. But remembering Andrea's excitement at her suggestion made Lyla feel guilty for being churlish.

It also didn't help that the contents of her wardrobe were so uninspiring. She pulled out and then discarded one dark suit after another. *It's a wedding, Lyla, not an office meeting.* Her standard church attire of knee-length skirt, plain white blouse and a silk scarf simply wouldn't do for today. *What the hell has happened to you, Lyla? You've turned into an old woman.* She rummaged through the farthest recesses of her wardrobe to find some of her traditional African clothes but, having lost so much weight, she knew that the made-to-measure *kabas* and skirts would hang off her. Right at the back, almost hidden from view, she spotted a flash of scarlet and jerked the hanger off the rail, almost losing her balance in the process. She'd forgotten all about the sexy scarlet wraparound dress and she stared at it for a long moment trying to remember what on earth had induced her to buy it. Probably an attempt to get Kwesi's attention, back in the days when that still mattered. She held it up against her in front of the full-length mirror and an impish grin slowly formed as she imagined the shock she would cause if she found the nerve to wear this to church.

She scrutinised the dark shadowed eyes looking back at her. Without a scrap of make-up, her skin looked sallow and lifeless. *Is this all you want for yourself, Lyla?* The question reverberated around her brain and suddenly, feverishly, she pulled the silky dress over her head, adjusting the deep plunging vee that exposed the swell of her breasts and tying the belt to pull the fabric in to her slim waist. She smoothed down her braids and looked in the mirror, turning to the side and running a hand over her bottom. Well, at least *that's* still there, she thought with relief, although it could do with a bit more padding. She turned to face the mirror again. Could she really go to church in this very bright but incredibly gorgeous dress that clung to

77

her body and softened her frame from angular to slender? Wouldn't she just be drawing attention to herself?

Dress soberly and don't be so vain, Lyla, The Voice scolded. *You're a married woman. Besides, why would you even care about attracting anyone at church?* Unbidden, the picture of a tall, bearded man flashed across her mind. She suddenly felt unable to look herself in the eye and instead set about rummaging in the bottom of her wardrobe for the spiky-heeled black slingbacks she kept for special occasions. You might as well do this properly, she told herself, as she slid her feet into the shoes.

The dress deserved make-up and Lyla scrabbled in the drawer for the palette of eyeshadows and a blusher she hadn't touched in months. She applied a light foundation and smoothed a pearly copper shadow over her eyelids. A second picture flashed through her mind – this time of a pair of golden-brown eyes with a deep, penetrating stare. Taking a deep breath, Lyla stroked the mascara wand over her long lashes, willing her hand to control its sudden trembling. *Stop behaving like a silly schoolgirl. Reuben is off limits and so are you, so take your mind somewhere else.* She slicked a bronze tinted gloss over her lips and ran downstairs before she had time to come to her senses and tear off the dress.

The sun was high in the sky and there was barely a hint of breeze to cut through the humidity. Solomon had been lounging at the far end of the verandah enjoying the shade instead of standing by the gate guarding the property as he was paid to do. When Lyla emerged from the house, slamming the door behind her, he jumped to his feet and his eyes widened in shock as he took in the low-cut neckline and the long shapely legs revealed by the wrap skirt.

Lyla felt herself flush. *Have I really become so dowdy that my own security man doesn't recognise me?*

'Solomon, open the gate please.'

'Yes, madam.' He remained rooted to the spot seemingly unable to tear his eyes away and she sucked her teeth loudly in annoyance. The wedding service was set to begin at two and she had less than half an hour to be in the church.

'I mean, *now!*'

Without stopping to check he'd followed instructions, Lyla strode over to her car and slipped into the driver's seat, clicking the seat belt into place and kicking off her heels. She reversed skilfully, the tyres crunching loudly over the loose gravel, and manoeuvred the car through the narrow gate and out on to the street. She slowed down ahead of the barriers that kept the residents of the Marula Heights gated community safe from opportunistic burglars and waited until the lone guard on duty raised the security gate, returning his salute as she drove through to the main thoroughfare.

The traffic was relatively light and, suddenly eager to reach her destination, she pressed down hard on the accelerator while keeping her eyes peeled for the potholes that had grown in both size and number after the recent floods.

A green minivan, little more than a rust bucket on wheels, pulled out in front of her as she approached the traffic lights, forcing her to swerve sharply and narrowly miss hitting a woman selling tomatoes by the side of the road. Lyla bit back the curse trembling on her lips and offered the shaken trader a weak smile of apology before moving off, relieved Theresa wasn't there to launch into another tirade about Ghana's reckless drivers.

The car park of Christ the Redeemer church was packed, and Lyla had to circle the whitewashed building twice before finding a space. She slipped on her sandals and stepped out into the blazing sunshine, noting with relief that Andrea's wedding limo had yet to arrive. Another member of the choir emerged from his car and Lyla smiled in greeting, only to flush deeply when he instantly emitted a piercing wolf whistle. She reluctantly stepped away from her car feeling horribly self-conscious and deeply regretting her impulsive decision to wear such a revealing dress.

'Sister Lyla, you look *be-yootiful!*'

'Thank you, Brother James.'

She squirmed with embarrassment as James leaned in to kiss her warmly on the cheeks, a marked departure from his usual impersonal handshake, and the sharp scent of his cologne made her nostrils prickle.

'Shall we go inside? I'd like to have a quick word with the organist about my solo before the wedding party gets here.'

With that she pulled away and hurried out of the car park, sensing him following close behind. Several men in dark suits stood by the door handing out service books to the guests and she smiled as one of them rushed forward.

'Welcome, Sister Lyla.' He pressed a book into her hand, his grin exposing gleaming white teeth, and looked her up and down making no attempt to hide his admiration. In a flash, her self-consciousness disappeared and was replaced with a rush of confidence which acted like a shot of adrenalin to her spirits. Her dramatic change of appearance was clearly having an impact and Lyla straightened her back, revelling in the sensation of feeling like an attractive woman again. The mischievous spirit of the old Lyla widened her smile and she walked confidently down the aisle, stopping only to greet the organist.

'Sister Lyla,' he murmured, handing her a sheet of music. Pretending not to notice his eyes bulging in shock as they travelled up and down her dress, Lyla quickly talked through the treatment of the song and went to join the rest of the choir, giving a small encouraging wave to the visibly nervous bridegroom pacing up and down.

Engrossed in reviewing the lyrics to the solo she had elected to sing during the wedding service, Lyla's attention was diverted by someone gently pushing their way through the row to stand next to her. She didn't need to look up to know who it was, and her skin tingled despite the coolness of the church.

'Good afternoon, Sister Lyla.' The deep voice sent a tremor through her and jolted her heart into a rapid tattoo of beating. Without warning, her body was flooded with a heat so intense that she could feel the prickle of moisture on her top lip.

'Good afternoon, Brother Reuben,' she murmured, reluctant to look at him in case he picked up on the internal havoc his presence was wreaking. She quickly wiped her lip with the back of her hand and kept her head down while she tried to calm her accelerated pulse.

'I was worried about being late, but of course the bride isn't here yet and I could have taken my time. But, then,

I suppose it's the prerogative of you ladies to keep us men waiting, isn't it?' His voice was low and amused.

Lyla laughed and forced herself to look up, praying her face didn't reveal the emotions jangling inside her. 'It certainly is! But I really hope Andrea gets here soon – poor Leon is wearing the floor out with all that pacing.'

Reuben's laugh rumbled deep in his chest and she felt the tremor shoot through her again. Although he wasn't touching her, even standing next to him in the confined space was creating a disturbing intimacy. At around six feet four, Reuben had always struck Lyla as a giant of a man. Today, his broad shoulders and barrel-like chest were draped in a long, pale-blue linen shirt that fell loosely over matching trousers. As Reuben flipped through the service book, his muscular arm brushed against Lyla's and she felt a sudden mad urge to lean into him and burrow under his arm like a neglected puppy.

She flinched as the unexpected crash of the organ signalled the bride's arrival and she had to gulp hard to regain control of her frayed nerves before joining in with the choir for a medley of praise songs. Lyla sang along, making herself concentrate on the words in front of her instead of the deep baritone emerging from the man beside her. As she surrendered to the music, her taut nerves slowly began to ease.

The wedding service followed, and Lyla watched intently as Andrea and Leon took their vows, the bride's face shining with trust as she repeated the priest's words in a clear, confident voice. Lyla felt a lump settle in her throat. *Did I look like that on my wedding day? Does she really know what she's letting herself in for?*

Lyla and Kwesi's expensive society wedding had been the talk of the city. Theresa had gamely agreed to be her maid of honour despite struggling to understand Lyla's decision to marry a man she had been seeing for a matter of months. Maku, on the other hand, had flatly turned down Lyla's invitation to be a bridesmaid. Heavily pregnant with Elijah, she'd made it clear that she had no intention of humiliating herself with a bulge that, according to her, would make her the ugliest bridesmaid in history.

'Sister Lyla, your solo is next – you should go forward.' The woman standing to her left hissed the words under her breath and nudged a sharp elbow into Lyla's side.

Lyla reluctantly pried herself away from the pressure of Reuben's arm to slip out of the pew and walk to the microphone. She quickly adjusted the height of the stand, intensely conscious of the curious eyes of the congregation shifting over to her. This was always the worst part of a solo – that moment when everyone turned their attention on to her – and she took a deep breath to clear her mind of everything but the words she was about to sing. She forced herself to forget her nerves, to blank out the room full of people in front of her and Reuben in the choir stalls behind her. With a nod to the organist, she launched into her solo, her voice pure and high.

'... How great thou art!' As the last note died away and the music stopped, there was a moment of electric silence in the church. Andrea sniffed and wiped a tear from her eyes, and then began to clap vigorously. Within seconds, the room was filled with thunderous applause and Lyla bowed her head, trying to keep her composure. After a moment she moved back to her place, trembling with the euphoria that singing always brought.

'That was beautiful, Sister Lyla. So very filled with the Spirit. And may I say how lovely you look today?' Reuben whispered, his soft beard tickling her ear as he leaned down.

Despite herself, Lyla grinned. *You may, indeed.* But with that, The Voice was back. *Woman, you are in church and you are married!* But whether it was the dramatic red dress and the rarely worn high heels or simply the long-lost spirit of the old Lyla back for a visit, she ignored The Voice and her smile widened happily. It had been so long since she'd felt this good that she made no effort to shift away from Reuben, instead relishing the strength of the muscles she could feel against her.

After the newly married couple had signed the register, Pastor Jeremiah climbed up into the pulpit to deliver his sermon.

'Marriage, my brothers and sisters, marriage is ordained by God for the procreation of children...'

Lyla's smile faltered. The pastor's words were like accusatory blows aimed specifically at her but there was no way to tune out the voice amplified by the microphone and reverberating around the church walls. Her brief euphoria dissolved into resentment. *Great. So, what about those of us who don't have children? What is the purpose of our marriage?* Resentment turned into frustration followed by impotent rage, and she bit down hard on her lip to stop herself shouting out the words. As if sensing her turmoil, Reuben laid a calming hand on her arm. Although he removed his hand almost immediately, the heat from his palm lingered, setting off a different type of frustration altogether. Pastor Jeremiah's voice dimmed into the background and Lyla remained lost in her thoughts until the choir stood to lead the hymns that ended the wedding service.

As the other choir members made their way out of the stalls, Reuben turned to Lyla and gently grasped her arm, and for once there was no sign of his smile.

'Sister Lyla, are you okay? You seemed upset during the service.'

She looked up into his warm brown eyes and sighed inwardly at the concern reflected in their depths. How was it that he always seemed to see her? Not just look at her, but really *see* her, when the man she was married to didn't have a clue? She stared at him trying to summon up an answer. Up close, his eyes were so clear that she could see the radiating edges of his pupils. Although Reuben almost invariably had a smile on his face, Lyla had always thought that he had sad eyes – as though at some point in his life he had experienced great pain. It was the same sadness she saw in her own eyes when she dared to allow herself more than a brief glimpse in the mirror, and perhaps why she had felt such a strong and immediate connection to him when he'd joined their church the previous year. *So, nothing to do with his handsome face, muscular body and warm smile then, Lyla?*

Touched by his solicitude, she forced a smile. 'It's nothing really but thank you for asking. I'm not feeling very well but I'd promised Andrea I would sing today, and I didn't want to disappoint her.'

Whatever he planned to say was cut off by a loud

greeting from a well-built man in a flowing white lace *agbada* standing at the end of the pew.

'Reuben! Long time no see, my friend. How are you?'

The men shook hands warmly and Lyla took advantage of the diversion to mutter a quiet goodbye and slip away. Her earlier elation had disappeared, and all she wanted now was to return to the sanctuary of her house. She hurried down the aisle towards the door, exchanging polite greetings and shaking outstretched hands as she slipped past guests dressed in a mix of traditional and Western-style clothing.

When Lyla eventually made her way out of the church, she was momentarily dazzled by the bright sunshine. Shielding her eyes from the glare, she spotted Andrea and Leon and made her way across to join the line of people waiting to greet the newly-weds.

When it was her turn, she hugged the bride warmly. 'Congratulations, Andrea. You look *so* beautiful.'

She turned to smile at Leon who was busy mopping at his forehead with a large handkerchief. 'Well done, Leon. You did very well in church.'

'Sister Lyla, thank you so much for singing,' Andrea said earnestly. 'Your voice was so moving and—' she broke off and scanned Lyla's dress before adding with a cheeky grin, 'you are looking *very* sexy today.'

Lyla took a deep breath and tried to ignore the deep flush of embarrassment she could feel creeping up her face. 'Look, Andrea, I'm so sorry but I won't be able to stay for the reception. I've been a bit unwell and it's probably best if I go home.'

The woman behind her in the line was growing

impatient at the delay and she pressed forward, ramming the wide brim of her feather-trimmed hat against the back of Lyla's head. With an apologetic smile, Lyla stepped aside and made her way to the safety of her car.

Driving home, she could feel the tension that had built up during the service begin to drain away, and she hummed along distractedly to the music playing on the radio. Waiting at a set of traffic lights, she watched a woman cross the road holding tight to two toddlers and her thoughts wandered back to Pastor Jeremiah's sermon. But his discomfiting words about marriage and children were quickly replaced by the even more disturbing memory of Reuben's hand on her arm and she sighed deeply, allowing herself a moment to relive the sensation of his fleeting touch.

Reluctantly pushing thoughts of Reuben aside, she pondered for a moment on what to do about dinner before deciding to do nothing. Thanks to Kwesi's late nights, the fridge was packed with leftovers from meals that had barely been touched and there was no point cooking yet more food to go untasted.

Lyla turned on to the dual carriageway that led to Marula Heights and felt her spirits droop at the thought of another lonely evening. She shivered as the chilled air in the car penetrated the thin fabric of her dress and, as she approached her house, the sight of a taxi parked a few feet away from her gate, with its driver slumped over the wheel and clearly asleep, did nothing to improve her mood. She could see no sign of Kwesi's BMW in their driveway and took a deep breath to prepare herself for what was coming.

Lyla had just stepped out of her car when the front door opened, and a dark-skinned woman stood framed in the doorway. Small – not much taller than five feet – she wore a long traditional *boubou* in a purple print, and open-toed black sandals. Her hair was covered by a tightly wrapped scarf and, as she watched Lyla approach, not even the hint of a smile lightened her severe features.

'Good afternoon, Ma Abena.' Lyla made no attempt to embrace her mother-in-law and instead stood in silence while the other woman raked her over from head to toe with narrowed eyes. Her inspection complete, Ma Abena inclined her head in a slight nod.

'Good afternoon. I was on my way to the hairdresser's and decided to visit you and my son.' She spoke with a dry and faintly accusatory tone and continued before Lyla could respond.

'I came here first because the girl who does my hair is so slow that, by the time she finishes, I'm too tired to do anything except go home. Your boy,' she glanced over at Solomon who was standing to attention by the gate, 'said you were at church. I don't understand why you go to church on a Saturday – what kind of religion is that?' She looked pointedly at Lyla's dress and raised an eyebrow. 'And is *this* how people dress in your church?'

'It wasn't a regular church service, Ma Abena. I went to a wedding.' Lyla forced an even tone into her voice and tried not to sound defensive. The last thing she needed was a lecture from Kwesi's mother about the impudence of her generation who dared to contradict their elders instead of respectfully listening to advice.

'I'm sorry there was no one here to welcome you,' she

added humbly. 'I, um, wasn't expecting you.'

'Do I have to make an appointment to visit my own son's house?' Ma Abena snapped, her eyes flashing with annoyance. 'I don't understand young people. In my day you didn't question when family members came to visit you – you were just grateful that they took the trouble at all!'

Lyla held her tongue and stood her ground until the older woman reluctantly stepped aside to let her through. She squeezed past her mother-in-law and walked into the house, her high heels tapping against the terrazzo-covered hallway. Relieved to escape the humidity outside, Lyla dropped her handbag onto the hall table and slipped out of her shoes before turning back to her guest.

'Please, Ma Abena, may I bring you some refreshments?'

'I looked in your fridge but there was nothing to drink except iced water. Is that all you have to offer your guests?' Ma Abena sniffed, her disdain almost palpable.

If you had warned me you were coming over instead of just showing up, maybe I would have thought to get some drinks. Lyla clenched her jaw tightly and willed herself not to rise to the bait.

'I wasn't able to go shopping today because of the wedding,' she said levelly. 'We have fruit juice in the cupboard and there's plenty of ice in the fridge.'

Ma Abena shrugged indifferently and, without waiting for an answer, Lyla walked into the kitchen with the other woman following close behind. Ma Abena watched silently as Lyla twisted the cap off a carton of pineapple juice and depressed the button on the ice maker in the fridge to release a torrent of shaved ice into a tall glass. The fridge door was still open as Lyla turned to hand over the drink and she caught the other woman's pointed stare at the containers of food stacked on the shelves.

'Is this how you people live these days?' She took the glass of juice without a word of thanks and stared accusingly at Lyla. 'Why is there so much food sitting in the fridge? Are you telling me you can't even cook fresh food for my son?'

Stung by the unfairness of the accusation, Lyla stared in silence at the plastic containers as if seeing them for the first time. To the uninformed eye, she could see why it might look like the results of a cooking bonanza rather than evidence of a husband with no appetite for eating at home. Struggling to hold in the words straining behind her lips, she gazed down at her bare feet and wriggled her toes against the cool floor tiles. *Just shut up, Lyla. Don't say a word; she'll leave once she's had her fun.*

She shut the fridge firmly and gestured towards the door. 'Why don't you take a seat in the living room? I'm not sure when Kwesi is coming home, but I'll call him now.'

Clutching her drink, and with little choice but to comply, Ma Abena swept out of the kitchen and into the living room, settling herself comfortably on a leather sofa.

'I don't understand why you haven't got house help,' she grumbled, setting her glass down after taking a long draw of the cool drink. 'This is a big house and since you insist on going to work instead of looking after your home and your husband, the least you could do is bring in a girl to help you.'

If your son would stop sacking and/or propositioning any decent help I find, I might stand a better chance of holding on to my staff. 'I have a woman who comes in

90

to clean during the week,' Lyla murmured, biting back the retort and taking a seat across from Ma Abena. She crossed her legs beneath her and dialled Kwesi's number and then pressed the speaker button. The call went straight to his voicemail, earning another testy glare from his mother.

Buoyed by the knowledge that the waiting taxi signalled a short visit, Lyla enquired politely after the other family members and tried to look attentive as the older woman launched into a litany of complaints about her unhelpful children and their noisy offspring.

Ma Abena drained the last of her juice and deposited the glass on the side table with a final thump, her mouth working vigorously as she sucked on the remaining slivers of ice. Her eyes darted around the room and Lyla braced herself for whatever parting shot was on the way.

'Ah, this place is so quiet! When are you going to give me grandchildren, eh? Both of my girls have two children and even with that foolish wife of his, Papa Kwame already has three sons. Kwesi is the only one who hasn't given me grandchildren. Why is that?'

'Ma Abena, you know we've been trying—'

'Pah! What do you mean, *trying*?' Ma Abena spat the word out in disgust. 'Is this something you need to take lessons for? If you are having problems, you should see a doctor. Look, Lyla, I'm a plain-spoken woman and I must be honest. You have been married for years now, so let me warn you. Every man wants a child, and up until now my son hasn't seen any baby coming from you. Do you know how weak that makes Kwesi look to other men?'

Without waiting for an answer, her gaze raked Lyla's

slender frame with contempt. 'But, then, look at you and how thin you have become. You don't eat, so how will you get pregnant and carry a child?'

Despite her best efforts, Lyla's eyes flooded with tears. Before she could speak her mobile rang, and the sound shattered the tense silence. Kwesi's name flashed up on the screen and she cleared her throat and put the call on speaker.

'Hello?'

'Yeah, hi. I just saw your missed call. What's wrong?'

Why does something have to be wrong before I call you, Lyla wondered, discreetly wiping away the solitary tear that had spilled onto her cheek.

'Your mother is here and I – we – wanted to know if you were on your way home.'

Kwesi sounded both annoyed and evasive. 'I won't be back for a few hours. I've got a meeting with one of our new suppliers at their factory out in Aburi. Tell my mother I'll come by hers on my way home.'

The line clicked off before she could say another word and Ma Abena snorted and gathered her *boubou* around her before hoisting herself to her feet.

'He has been promising to visit me for the past two weeks. What did I do to deserve children who are so ungrateful they can't pay attention to their own mother?'

She picked up her handbag and marched towards the front door, her back stiff with irritation. Following close behind, Lyla stopped to slip on her shoes before tailing outside after her.

She bit back a smile as Solomon sprinted ahead to open the gate. Ma Abena's temper was legendary and, her diminutive size notwithstanding, Solomon was terrified of her.

The creaking of the gate roused the taxi driver from his nap, and he rubbed his eyes and switched on the ignition. Solomon opened the car's back door and backed away respectfully as Ma Abena lowered herself onto the shabby leather seat and wound down the window, fanning herself ostentatiously with a handkerchief.

'When my son returns, tell him I want to see him as soon as possible – and I don't want any excuses.'

With a flap of her handkerchief in Lyla's direction, she barked an order at the taxi driver who slipped the car into gear and drove off without a word.

* * *

'So, what are your plans this evening?' Kwesi sounded unusually cheerful as he pulled on his jacket.

'Theresa and Maku are coming over,' Lyla said evenly, watching Kwesi spray a blast of cologne on to his hands and pat his cheeks before taking a final look at himself in the full-length mirror. The sickly-sweet scent drifted across to the bed and she crinkled her nose involuntarily at the cloying fragrance. He was certainly going to a lot of trouble with his appearance for what he claimed was a simple business meeting with a supplier.

'At least, I'm hoping Maku can make it,' she added. 'Nortey's promised to stay in with the children this evening.'

Kwesi slipped a clean handkerchief into his pocket and snorted with derision. 'She'll be bloody lucky if she can tear him away from Jake's Joint long enough for that to happen. Nortey should buy shares in the place with all the time and money he spends in there. By the way, I meant to tell you. Bob Kessie mentioned he's seen Tyler at Jake's a couple of times – I really hope the man isn't allowing Nortey of all people to influence him.'

You can talk! You're hardly up for husband of the year yourself, Lyla thought resentfully, but she said nothing. She was looking forward to seeing her best friends and didn't want to start the evening with an argument. After their quarrel following his mother's visit a couple of weeks earlier, she didn't have the energy to get into another slanging match with Kwesi. And most importantly, she needed to stay calm for this to work.

'What time are you getting back?' From where she lay on the bed, Lyla saw his face reflected in the mirror and didn't miss the familiar hunted look that descended on his handsome features whenever he was called to account. He ran a finger around the inside of his shirt collar and straightened the lapels of his navy linen jacket before answering.

'I don't know – it all depends on how the meeting goes. In any case, if you girls are getting together, you don't want me hanging around to spoil your fun.'

He spoke quickly, his words bumping up against each other in a sure sign he was lying, she noted. He thrust his wallet into his jacket pocket and strode towards the bedroom door.

'I'd better be off, or I'll be late. Tell Theresa and Maku I said hello and that I'll see them another time.'

Lyla watched him walk out without a word of farewell. *Like mother, like son.* Shrugging off her irritation, she pushed aside the pillow that had been propping up her hips and lowered her legs to sit up slowly, her fingers automatically smoothing the ruffled bedcovers. *Was it half an hour or forty-five minutes that you were supposed to keep your legs up for after sex?* Well, since it had taken Kwesi at least an hour to shower and get dressed, she had definitely exceeded the recommended time. She grimaced at the memory of the rapid fumbling that had passed for lovemaking and fought down the torrent of disgust threatening to bubble up into her throat.

Taking a deep breath, she clasped her hands together and bowed her head, praying that her eggs didn't feel as hostile towards his sperm as she felt towards him. *Father in Heaven, please forgive me. I know he is my husband but...* she bit her lip, unable to continue. How could God forgive her when she went from one sin to another? And besides, how could it be forgivable to hate your husband and still want his sperm? But then if marriage was for the procreation of children, she countered, what she was doing wasn't so wrong, was it?

She waited until the nausea subsided and then walked slowly down the stairs and into the living room. *Please God,* she prayed, *please forgive me and let it work this time.*

She plumped up the bronze silk cushions on the armchair and straightened the embroidered throw draped across the back of the sofa where Ma Abena had planted herself during her last visit. After years of snide comments and half-audible asides, that afternoon had been the first time her mother-in-law had openly confronted her about her inability to bear children, and she shivered at the memory of the unconcealed malice glittering in the older woman's eyes.

The light toot of a car horn at the gate carried into the silent room and instantly brought a bright smile to Lyla's face. Dismissing all thoughts of Kwesi's disgruntled mother, she hurried to open the front door to her friends.

Kwesi

With a final handshake, Kwesi jumped into his car and turned on the ignition, barely able to restrain himself from rubbing his hands with glee. Conscious of the man waiting on the pavement to see him off, he quickly reversed out of the tight parking space and sped off before allowing himself a loud chuckle of satisfaction.

This time around, after Kwesi's smooth assurances that their arrangement would once again remain strictly between the two of them, the furniture supplier had needed little persuasion to adjust his company's invoice. Once the Finance department had paid for the consignment of furniture awaiting delivery to the store, Kwesi would be back to pick up his share of the sweetener. He could practically feel the golf clubs he'd been eyeing for the past six months between his hands. With a bit of luck, he should have enough left over to buy Nadia a small piece of jewellery – although knowing that girl's tastes, small probably wouldn't cut it.

His smile faded, but even the worried frown that took its place and puckered up his forehead didn't mar his good looks. With a face just on the right side of masculine to avoid the tag of pretty, Kwesi didn't need the admiring glances he received from women to know the effect his looks had on the other sex. His brother's jealousy-fuelled cracks and his sisters' exasperated comments bemoaning the unfairness of his smooth brown skin that had never been visited by adolescent acne and eyelashes longer than either of theirs had been the soundtrack to his life.

Kwesi would have been the first to admit that his brother's bitterness was understandable. After years of losing his girlfriends to his stunning younger brother, Papa Kwame had been left with little choice but to select a plain wife who would not only count herself lucky to have married him but would also be in no doubt she was out of Kwesi's league. Yet, even now when the three children Violet had borne in quick succession had left his wife considerably heavier and even more homely, Papa Kwame made a point of never leaving Violet alone with Kwesi.

Having witnessed at first-hand his brother's track record with women, no one had been more surprised than Papa Kwame when Kwesi had first announced that he was getting married.

'Are you sure about this?' Papa Kwame had enquired dubiously, once he had recovered from the stunned silence brought on by the unexpected news. 'Aren't you the one always saying there are too many women in the world and too little time to get around to all of them?'

'And aren't *you* the one who always complains I need to grow up, find a good woman and settle down?' Kwesi had countered. His conviction that this time he had found the one woman who could tame him and keep his interest for more than a few weeks was met with equal scepticism by his sisters – both of whom had long experience of comforting women about whom their brother had once thought the same. While they all acknowledged smart, elegant Lyla Blankson was a good catch, not a single member of Kwesi's family was under any illusion she would be able to hold on to him for more than six months.

In the event they had been proved wrong, and six years later Kwesi was still by Lyla's side. But whether this was because marriage had presented no obstacle to him continuing life as before, or because he was still unsure why the elusive Lyla had agreed to marry him in the first place, Kwesi didn't know and he rarely spent time worrying about it. What *did* disturb him was that after six years there was no sign of a son and heir. His concern was less because he loved children; he was fond enough of his numerous nephews and nieces but had little interest in the sleepless nights and domestic duties children brought and dreaded their drain on the income he needed to maintain his lifestyle. Furthermore, having witnessed Violet's ballooning shape after her spate of childbearing, he had no wish to see Lyla's body deteriorate in the same way. No, if he were honest with himself – an activity Kwesi avoided unless strictly necessary – the problem with his childless marriage was the doubt it cast on his virility, particularly annoying given his reputation with the ladies. Almost worse was that it invited his mother to weigh in on what she considered to be an intolerable situation and cause him even more stress.

Arriving at the main highway, Kwesi drew up behind a long line of cars waiting to cross the traffic lights into central Accra. He drummed impatiently on the steering wheel and glanced at his watch. There was little point getting stressed with traffic in the city and he forced himself to breathe in and out slowly. The cars would eventually move and at least his air conditioning was counteracting the unbearable humidity.

He beckoned to one of the young street hawkers milling around the stationary cars selling merchandise. Tossing a couple of notes in the boy's direction, he reached for a copy of a tabloid newspaper and snorted in amusement at the headlines. Another church leader caught having an affair with a parishioner's wife. He must remember to show the article to Lyla – he was fed up with her constantly citing one or other of her pious born-again Christian brothers and sisters. He was also increasingly exasperated by the amount of time she spent at church. If he'd known this was how things would pan out, he'd have thought twice about marrying her.

Even as the thought flitted through his mind, Kwesi knew it was a lie. He had been mesmerised by Lyla since their early teens at boarding school and would have married her even if she'd lived in a church. In school, Lyla had been the girl that every boy, Kwesi included, wanted to date. Quick-witted and fun and with a teasing smile that always promised far more than it delivered, she had been the first to wear the latest fashions from abroad and her long, lean figure had been the perfect frame for every style. Lyla was also fiercely intelligent, passing all her exams with top marks and easily winning a full scholarship to study at one of Britain's leading universities. Regrettably, unlike the hordes of girls unable to resist Kwesi's long-lashed soulful eyes and his endearingly crooked grin, Lyla had remained immune to his charms. Instead, in their last year of school, she had dated the far less attractive but undeniably brilliant Martin Lane, now a prominent physicist living in Chicago.

The traffic lights changed and by dint of jumping the red light and ignoring the angry toots from the drivers coming from the other direction, Kwesi was able to cross the junction. On the other side of the highway and once again caught in slow moving traffic, his mind drifted back to his wife. Hopefully she would be too busy entertaining her friends to notice he was going to be very late home tonight.

Life with Lyla hadn't always been like this, he sighed, thinking back to their chance meeting at a former classmate's wedding soon after Lyla's return to Ghana. Seizing the opportunity to lay on the charm, Kwesi had nonetheless been taken aback when Lyla had readily agreed to his dinner invitation. Admittedly she seemed quieter and far more reserved than the girl he remembered from school, but he had been so euphoric at finally cornering the hard to get Lyla Blankson that it had made little difference.

Although she was a bit too serious sometimes and had a rather disconcerting habit of drifting off into her own world, Lyla was still smart, ambitious and entertaining, not to mention stunning. Gratified by the envious looks from other men when he took her out, Kwesi was keenly aware that they made an extremely attractive couple. Lyla was a prize he was only too happy to show off to the world and, for the first time ever, he truly believed he was in love and that finally this was the woman who would be enough for him. Kwesi knew his reputation with women was poor and at times he felt frustrated by his own lack of self-control. But even when he was determined not to flirt, the women he came across rarely demonstrated the same willpower. If anyone could make him break this pattern of behaviour, he reasoned, it would be Lyla. And yet when he impulsively popped the question during a dinner date only six months after their first, it was hard to tell who was more surprised – he for asking the question, or Lyla for accepting without hesitation.

Ignoring the astonished and openly sceptical reaction from family and friends alike – and pretending not to see the relief on Papa Kwame's face once he realised his brother was serious – Kwesi moved swiftly to plan a spectacular wedding to showcase his beautiful bride. Standing before the altar of the huge cathedral making his vows and then dancing with Lyla later in front of over five hundred guests at their lavish reception, Kwesi had been truly convinced this was it. Lyla was the only woman in the world for him.

Still basking in the gushing compliments about his extravagant wedding, Kwesi had been blind to the flirtatious receptionist at the hotel during their honeymoon in Cape Town and had barely made eye contact with the pretty new secretary in the Merchandising department when he returned to work. He'd even resolutely ignored the advances of the attractive and deeply frustrated second wife of Alhaji Jintora, the elderly and infirm Minister of Mining, despite her oblique hints at the possibility of spending a small fortune at his store.

The taxi driver behind him honked his horn aggressively and Kwesi pressed down on the accelerator, his luxury car moving forward smoothly to close the gap in the traffic. It had taken at least three months, he calculated, before the persistent demands of Hajia Zeinab Jintora had proved more than his willpower could withstand. After that first breach, it had been harder to justify saying no to the other contenders for his attention. As he slowly returned to his favourite pastime, Lyla increasingly turned to her church. By their first wedding anniversary, the Church of Christ the Redeemer had become his wife's second home, while his own house saw progressively less of him. When he occasionally asked himself why his highly intelligent wife appeared to believe his excuses – some of which sounded totally implausible even as he uttered the words – he could find no answer for her excessive tolerance. Having heard her on the phone laying into any of her sales team who tried to pull a fast one, Kwesi knew Lyla had no problem asserting herself when she wanted to. Which led him to the uncomfortable conclusion that perhaps Lyla simply didn't care enough to assert herself as the only woman in his life.

Free at last from the static line of traffic, Kwesi turned off the highway and down a narrow road, steering cautiously around the potholes while avoiding the open gutters on both sides. He cursed angrily as the car bounced over a concealed block of broken concrete and slowed to a crawl, muttering furiously under his breath. He pulled up in front of a tall building with flaking pink paint and a rusting corrugated metal roof. Outside the side door, which was framed with naked multicoloured bulbs, stood a small blackboard with the words '*Nadia's Boutique*' scrawled in barely legible writing.

With the engine still running, Kwesi scoured his surroundings. While there wasn't much chance of being seen by anyone he knew in this part of town, it didn't hurt to be cautious. Across the road, some elderly men on wooden stools were huddled around a radio blaring the commentary to a soccer match, while a few feet away a group of boys in shorts and faded football jerseys kicked a somewhat deflated ball around a patch of hard-baked ground.

Kwesi turned off the engine, and the car instantly felt stuffy. He slid down a window and immediately regretted it when the acrid stench from the open gutter choked with discarded plastic bags and God knows what else hit him hard. He hastily closed the window again, preferring to swelter in the heat rather than subject himself to the foul smell.

A quick glance at his Rolex confirmed it was six-thirty, half an hour after Nadia usually closed shop. He observed the ramshackle building that housed Nadia's family and her salon with distaste. Nadia knew only too well that he hated coming here but any complaints only triggered sulking and not-so-subtle hints for a house across the highway in highly sought-after Kanda.

'If you don't like coming to see me here, find me a decent house, then,' she'd demanded when he'd picked her up from the salon not long ago and been forced to bribe a boy to watch his car while he came in to fetch her.

'I mean, look at this place! Why should your girlfriend have to live somewhere like this?' she'd grumbled, and he had silently agreed. Why indeed *would* anyone want to live in Nima with its teeming gutters and ramshackle, squalid houses? But where the hell was he supposed to get the kind of money needed to rent property in an area like Kanda? His side deals at the store helped to pad his income, but expensive houses were a world away from his budget.

He was reluctant to leave his BMW unattended in the rundown neighbourhood and after a moment's hesitation he pulled out his phone and dialled her number. Nadia answered on the second ring and plaintively demanded he come in to wait while she finished tidying up.

The air in the car was growing steadily staler and Kwesi rubbed his hand over his low-cropped hair in exasperation. He should have insisted she meet him at the hotel and then he grimaced as he remembered the last time he'd made *that* suggestion and she'd flown into a rage, accusing him of treating her like a prostitute. He sighed. All in all, Nadia was becoming far too demanding. With anyone else he would have walked away long ago, but Christ... the *things* the girl could do to his body! He almost groaned aloud as his mind flipped back to their last encounter. Kwesi was no slouch in the bedroom but when it came to sex, Nadia was in a league of her own.

Trying not to think about how she had developed her enviable skills, he took a cautious look around and stepped out of the car, locking it securely before striding into the salon.

MAY

MARRIAGE: THE PERFECT ANTIDOTE TO MY CHILDHOOD POISON

Theresa

'*Tyler*! What the f—? Tyler, *wake up!*'

Standing in the doorway of the spare bedroom, Theresa stared at the figure lying prone on the bed, torn between relief her husband wasn't dead in a ditch somewhere and fury she'd spent half the night needlessly worrying that he was. When he didn't stir, she moved towards the bed and prodded him hard in the back.

'Wake *up!*'

Tyler groaned and rolled over, rubbing his jaw as he squinted up at her blearily. Shielding his eyes from the bright sunshine streaming through the thin curtains, he struggled up and Theresa recoiled at the scent of stale beer. Her pregnancy had brought with it a sensitivity to smells that had never bothered her before. The aroma of frying onions that used to have her mouth watering now made her stomach churn unpleasantly and she had recently banned the pungently smoky salted fish that liberally flavoured their soups and stews.

'Why are you sleeping in here?' Theresa tried – and failed – to keep the accusatory tone out of her voice. Having woken up in the middle of the night to an empty bed, her initial annoyance that Tyler was still out drinking had turned into panic when her repeated calls to his phone went unanswered. After several anxiety-fuelled hours, she had been on her way downstairs to instruct Joseph to call the police when she'd heard the snores emanating from the guest bedroom.

Do you have any *idea how scared I've been?* Her pride wouldn't let her voice what she really wanted to say, so instead she pointed out coolly, 'Joseph has been waiting outside to take you to the office for almost an hour now.'

Yawning widely, Tyler shrugged off the light bedspread and swung his legs onto the ground. He avoided her eyes as he leaned across to snatch the phone lying on the bedside table and scowled as he took in the time.

'Okay, *okay*! Give me a break, will you? I must have forgotten to take the phone off silent after my meeting because I definitely set the alarm before I fell asleep.'

'Fell asleep or passed out?'

'Very funny. I had two drinks last night, tops. And the only reason I slept in here is because you're always complaining the smell of beer makes you feel sick.'

Theresa bit her lip and tried to control her anger at his attempt to shift the blame on to her. 'Well, maybe if you stayed at home you wouldn't smell of beer in the first place. Tyler, this is the third time this week you've been out drinking and—'

He stood up and brushed past, cutting her off in midstream. Picking up his discarded shoes and the trousers carelessly tossed across the chair, he sounded impatient as he headed towards the door.

'Seriously, stop nagging, Tee. It's not like I'm going out drinking for the sake of it. I told you a million times that I need to build up my network in this town. I've got a luxury building going up and the only way to reach the people with deep pockets is to get out there and connect with the movers and shakers.'

'Fair enough – but does that mean you have to be out *every* single night?' she snapped. 'I thought we were supposed to be doing this together.'

He turned, and she noted with a frisson of alarm the puffiness around his face and the tiny lines of exhaustion radiating from his bloodshot eyes. Tyler had never been a heavy drinker and the weeks of constant socialising were clearly taking their toll. His once muscular stomach protruded beneath his white sleeveless vest and she tried to remember when he had last visited the gym.

He laughed mirthlessly and looked her straight in the eyes, his expression a blend of defiance and accusation. '*Together*? Let's be honest, Theresa, it's not as if you ever want to go anywhere with me, is it? Any time I suggest doing something, you're either too tired or you've got a meeting with some client or other.'

She glared at him angrily and he lifted a conciliatory hand. 'Tee, I don't want to fight. I admit I've been out a fair bit, but you need to understand that it's one hundred per cent for business. Look, it's late and I need to take a shower and get out of here. I'm sure you've got plenty to do yourself – isn't Margaret here yet?'

Theresa took a deep breath and tried to sound calm. 'No. She sent a text saying she's running late. Something about organising a food parcel to send to the boys' school.' She hesitated for a second, her face troubled, and then putting aside her pride, she blurted out, 'Ty, I know you're under a lot of pressure, but it feels like we're going in two different directions and…'

She tailed off as he doubled back to silence her by pressing a gentle kiss on her lips.

'Hey, it's *okay*. No one said moving here was going to be easy, but we're fine. It's taking a while for things to settle but we've got to stay positive. It will all work out – I promise.'

She nodded reluctantly, trying not to grimace as the stench of alcohol hit her once again. She watched Tyler leave and then sank onto the corner of the unmade bed, her hand reaching down to stroke the soft swell of stomach concealed by her cotton dress.

'It's okay, Bump, there's nothing to worry about,' she murmured. According to one of the pregnancy blogs she'd stumbled across, it was vital to communicate frequently with a developing infant. 'Your dad's just being a bit of a pain in the you-know-where, that's all. By the time you're ready to come out, we'll all be just fine.' Hoping the baby felt reassured, Theresa straightened the bedcovers and headed for her office.

On her way down, she heard the familiar toot of a car horn at the gates and hurried to open the door, her thoughts moving from Tyler to the working day ahead. She stood inside the doorway and smiled warmly at the woman striding easily along the pathway and up the terracotta tiled steps.

Margaret returned the smile, revealing perfect white teeth that lit up the smooth dark-chocolate of her skin. Tall and slim, she invariably wore clothes made from vibrant African prints. Today's outfit was a long skirt in a vivid pattern of cobalt blue with a fitted, scoop-necked top.

Theresa stared at her admiringly, marvelling at the

deftness with which Margaret had wrapped her matching blue headscarf.

'Good morning! You look *amazing* – are you absolutely sure you're not twenty-five?'

Margaret laughed and wiped her sandals briskly on the mat before stepping over the threshold. 'Thanks for the compliment but I'll be forty-four on my next birthday and I have two teenage sons to prove it.'

Stepping aside to let Margaret through, Theresa followed her business partner into their converted office. Overriding Tyler's protests that she was getting ahead of herself, she had insisted on an extra desk and planned to recruit a junior executive as soon as their workload warranted it. Judging by the business already flowing into TB Communications, Theresa had a feeling that might be sooner rather than later.

'Do you want tea or coffee or anything before we get stuck in?' Theresa watched Margaret switch on her laptop and settle herself at her desk.

'Hmm? No, I'm okay for now. How are *you* feeling today?'

Margaret looked up from the sheaf of papers she had begun sifting through to study her partner. 'Are you getting any sleep or was that little one in there doing gymnastics all night?'

Theresa smiled weakly. 'The Bump isn't what keeps me awake.'

Margaret looked puzzled, and Theresa shrugged. 'Sorry, I'm just a bit fed up with all the late nights Tyler's been keeping lately. I can't sleep properly until I know he's safely back at home.'

Margaret sighed and put down the papers, her

attention now fully engaged. 'Theresa, I know it's easy to say but you really need to put yourself first and stop worrying about what Tyler's doing. Your baby needs you to be healthy and rested.'

'Now you sound just like my mother,' Theresa protested, forcing a laugh although she felt more like crying. 'Tyler's never at home when she rings, and she's threatening to come over because she's convinced he's neglecting me. Now, *that* would be stress I don't need – there's no way I could cope with her and Tyler in the same house.'

'It might not be as bad as you think. We all need support when we're pregnant,' Margaret said gently.

'Yes, but that's supposed to be my husband's job, not my mother's!'

'Believe me, Theresa, when you're expecting, you take help wherever you can get it,' Margaret said wryly. 'And don't think for a moment that it's only African men who don't get it – you should have seen Giles when I was pregnant with the twins. He was absolutely hopeless and in the end I literally begged my mother to move in with us until after the boys were born.'

Theresa giggled, the threat of tears receding. 'I'm sorry, but I honestly can't get my head around the idea of *Giles* feeding babies or changing nappies.'

Giles Hutchinson, Margaret's British husband, was probably the most traditional old-school person Theresa had ever met. An ex-military commander, he had met his wife while on a contract in Ghana as a security adviser and, despite their fifteen-year age gap, had married a year later. Giles had since set up an international security advisory firm, making him extremely wealthy but also ensuring he was frequently away on business.

When a mutual friend had introduced Margaret and Theresa, they had hit it off immediately. Within days, Margaret had invited Theresa to lunch, spending most of the meal pleading for the chance to help her build the PR agency.

'It makes perfect sense,' Margaret exclaimed, barely pausing for breath. 'I know a lot of business people in Accra who could use a good public relations firm and I've still got contacts at the media houses from my days working in advertising. I'm an excellent copywriter *and* I know how to negotiate buying media space. My boys are in boarding school for most of the year and Giles is always travelling – Theresa, I've got so much time on my hands I'm going *crazy!*'

In truth, Theresa would have begged *her* if Margaret hadn't offered, and since that day Margaret had been true to her word, brazenly using her network of contacts to set up meetings for Theresa and inviting prospective clients to dinner at the imposing mansion Giles had built in the plush airport residential area.

Initially bemused by the idea that his wife would want to work after more than a decade as a full-time wife and mother, Giles had eventually been persuaded that sitting around a huge house while their sons boarded at one of the country's top schools wasn't the best use of the skills Margaret had gained from almost a decade of working for the country's leading advertising agency.

It had been Margaret who'd thought up TB Communication's new slogan – '*Building Brands, Protecting Businesses*', found them a lawyer to help navigate the red tape involved in registering the firm and an accountant to take care of the books. Sooner than Theresa would have believed possible, her days were a whirlwind of meetings with journalists, media agencies and influential local bloggers, while most of her evenings were spent dealing with the endless administration involved in running the business. Within weeks, TB Communications had landed three major clients in quick succession and Theresa and her new partner were swamped with requests to develop PR plans, create campaigns, draft press releases and set up media interviews. Only a few days earlier, they had been invited by a well-known telecoms company to pitch for a lucrative national awards contract.

Despite the ongoing nausea and the physical discomfort which Dr Owusu had assured her was perfectly normal, Theresa was relishing the challenges of seeing her dream become a reality. The only fly in the ointment was the increasing strain their respective new ventures was placing on her relationship with her husband. Despite Jeff Parnell's investment, Tyler was struggling to get his project off the ground and had come up against unforeseen barriers at every stage. The moment the landowners had scented new money in the air, the original price agreed for the lease of Sycamore House had suddenly become the subject of protracted negotiations. With discussions threatening to drag on for weeks, Tyler had been left with little choice but to pay almost a third more than the agreed amount to secure the property. With his profit margin slashed, he had been forced to revisit the terms he had previously fixed with the building contractor and suppliers, several of whom at first refused to play ball. Reluctant to seek additional financing and further increase his debt, Tyler had used every ounce of charm and goodwill to persuade his reluctant partners to stick with the project, promising that it was only the start of many more to come.

Theresa flushed with embarrassment at Margaret's continued scrutiny. 'Sorry, I was a bit lost in thought there. Forget what I said about Tyler – it's still early days for both of us and it'll take time to find our feet. Anyway, enough about me! I've drafted a pitch for the awards show, but I'm not sure it's strong enough. Can I email it to you to look at?'

The conversation moved on to work matters and Theresa was reaching for her phone to return a client call when the door opened and a freshly shaved Tyler in a smart grey suit appeared. She noted with relief that his eyes were clear, and he looked perfectly sober.

'Morning, Margaret, how are you?'

Without waiting for an answer, Tyler turned to his wife. 'I'm heading off now. I don't have any meetings outside the office today, so I'll send Joseph back with the car once he's dropped me off.' With a brief wave, he disappeared before she could utter a word.

Charming! Theresa fumed silently. So now she didn't even merit a goodbye kiss! Conscious of Margaret's eyes upon her, she took a deep breath and picked up the phone, quickly dialling the number and forcing her mind away from her marital troubles.

* * *

Later that afternoon, as Joseph drove her to the printers to check the initial proofs of a client's annual report, she impulsively dialled Lyla's number. Anxious not to be overheard Theresa glanced at Joseph, but her driver's attention was on the talk radio station he invariably tuned into when he was behind the wheel.

'Hi, Tee. What's up?' Lyla sounded distracted.

'Are you busy or can you talk for a few minutes?'

'Sorry, but I'm trying to sort out a slide deck for a presentation to my boss and I've only got a few minutes before the meeting starts. Can I call you back a bit later?'

Theresa's sigh must have sounded more forlorn than she realised as Lyla immediately added, 'Better still, if you're at home this evening, why don't I come over? It seems like ages since I last saw you and that bump. Are you huge yet?'

Cheered by the thought of seeing her best friend, Theresa smiled. 'I really don't think it's grown much in a week, but I'd still love to see you. Come for dinner – I should be home by six.'

She switched off the phone and patted her tummy, resisting the impulse to tell the baby Auntie Lyla was coming for a visit in case Joseph thought she'd lost her mind. It would be good to see Lyla and get her take on Tyler's inexplicable change of attitude. She certainly couldn't ask her mother, given the antagonism between Tyler and Clementyne, who didn't need any further ammunition to rail against her son-in-law, as their phone conversation the night before had proved.

'Why is that husband of yours never there when I call, Theresa? Doesn't he realise you're expecting a baby? I knew he couldn't be trusted!'

Theresa sighed. Playing peacemaker between her acerbic-tongued mother and increasingly wayward husband was far from the calm and serene pregnancy she had hoped for.

* * *

By the time Joseph had navigated the heavy rush-hour traffic to bring Theresa home, it was well past five o'clock and Margaret had gone for the day, leaving post-it notes with scribbled reminders all over her desk. Theresa peeled off a note Margaret had stuck to her monitor – *'Write Twitter tweets (ask the twins??) for JHB new product launch'* – and grinned at her business partner's ongoing attempts to master social media.

Unplugging her laptop, Theresa tucked it under her arm and went in search of Auntie Sisi. Thank God for domestic staff. They might cost a fortune but, after stewing in traffic for over an hour, she was grateful to put her feet up for a few minutes before Lyla arrived, and leave the cooking to someone else.

Theresa walked into the kitchen and grimaced at the strong aroma of frying onions. 'Good afternoon, Auntie Sisi. What are you making for dinner?'

Wearing a pair of fluorescent lime leggings that did her chunky thighs no favours, Auntie Sisi looked up from the contents of the saucepan she had been stirring vigorously. She swiped a heavy forearm across a face damp with perspiration and looked dubiously into the pot as if she hadn't yet decided.

'I froze some spinach leaves last week so I'm using them to make *kontomire* stew. You didn't say anything this morning about what I should cook, so I thought this would be okay.'

The smell of the onions combined with the fragrant vapours escaping the saucepans simmering on the cooker was overpowering, and Theresa nodded and clutched her laptop tightly to her chest, trying not to breathe in too deeply.

'No, that's fine. My friend will be joining us for dinner so please make enough for everyone.'

Without comment, Auntie Sisi tipped a pile of diced tomatoes on the chopping board into the pot and Theresa hastily backed out as a loud hiss of steam rose into the air. Making for the safety of the living room, she stretched out on the sofa, for once not caring about placing her feet on the expensive cream fabric. *How ridiculous to live in a house where you can't put your feet up without feeling guilty.*

Opening her laptop, she logged on to her emails and immediately spotted a message from Melanie, her best friend at her former employers in London. Curious, she clicked it open and shook her head slowly as she read Melanie's litany of complaints about Cromwell McIntosh. Not only were there no pay rises on the horizon, but also several jobs were likely to be at risk if business didn't pick up. '*You definitely made the right decision to leave, Theresa,*' the message ended. '*It's incredible that you have your own PR business out there, not to mention all that lovely sunshine.*'

Melanie's email signature – Account Manager – brought a smile to Theresa's lips. After all the promotions she'd deserved and yet been consistently denied while at Cromwell McIntosh, here she was today, the Managing Director of her own business.

Trying not to sound too smug, Theresa dashed off a sympathetic reply before responding to the slew of

122

enquiries from prospective clients that was becoming a regular feature. Who would have thought she would be running a thriving operation so quickly, she marvelled, experiencing a surge of pure happiness as once again she thanked her lucky stars for Margaret. Without such an influential and well-connected partner, she might still be struggling to find her first client instead of wondering how to manage those they already had. Making a mental note to speak to Margaret about accelerating the recruitment of an Account Executive, Theresa logged off and snuggled into the expensive silk cushions for a nap.

The sound of the gate scraping open penetrated through the half-open windows and jolted Theresa awake, earning her a reproachful kick from the Bump. She sat up and took a moment to steady herself before going to open the front door. Lyla scooted up the steps, elegant in spiky-heeled grey shoes that were a perfect match for her fitted linen dress.

'Quick, come in!'

Almost pulling Lyla through the door, Theresa slammed it shut and turned to her friend who seized her in a warm, tight hug. Without warning, the baby landed a kick of protest and Theresa exploded into laughter.

'Did you feel that?'

Lyla's eyes widened, and she stepped away and reached out a tentative hand, placing it against her friend's rounded belly. 'Oh, my goodness, that's *incredible!* How weird is it to actually have something alive inside you?'

'If you want the truth, it's a bit like carrying around an alien that's taken over your body,' Theresa said briskly. 'Come on, let's get you a drink. If Tyler's not back in the next half an hour – which wouldn't surprise me in the slightest – we'll start dinner without him.'

Lyla raised an eyebrow but made no comment. Following Theresa into the living room, she dropped into an armchair with a happy sigh and crossed her long legs, grinning widely as her eyes took in her surroundings.

'This room is so beautiful I don't even dare walk on the rug.'

Theresa snorted. 'Just as well. If I told how much that stupid thing cost, you'd have me put away. What would you like to drink? I'm going to see how Auntie Sisi's getting on with dinner.'

As if on cue, the housekeeper appeared in the doorway. She nodded politely to Lyla and gave a little bob, the gesture straining the seams of the shimmering green Lycra. 'Good evening, madam.'

'Good evening, Auntie Sisi. How are you today?' Lyla smiled warmly at the older woman.

'By His grace, madam, I am very fine. Please, what can I bring you to drink?'

Lyla requested a Coke and her lips twitched in amusement as she watched the woman leave the room. 'Where the heck does she buy her clothes? I had no idea you could even *get* leggings in that colour.'

'That makes two of us. I've given up asking her to wear normal clothes – it's actually quite exciting to see what she turns up in each morning. So, how did the meeting with your boss go?'

Lyla rolled her eyes in exasperation. 'Not well. Our numbers have been hopeless this quarter. I've had – let's call them frank conversations today with a couple of the team who've been slacking off and hoping I wouldn't notice. I think I've heard every sorry excuse in the book for why they aren't doing what they are supposed to do.'

Theresa chuckled. 'Well, if anyone can keep them on their toes, it's you.' She hesitated and then blurted out, 'I just wish you were as tough on Kwesi as you are with your team.'

Before Lyla could respond, Auntie Sisi bumped the door open to deposit a small tray with bottles and two glasses on a side table. Theresa winced as the metal tray scraped against the polished marble top.

'Thanks, Auntie Sisi. You can leave it – I'll pour the drinks. Is dinner ready yet?'

'The rice is cooked, but the stew will take some more time. Should I fry some plantain?'

'Mmm – yes, please,' Lyla interjected. 'With plenty of pepper and ginger.'

Theresa stroked her stomach. 'God, I envy you. This little one hates every one of my favourite foods and doesn't stop kicking when I eat something spicy.'

'Ignore it – the child is African, and the sooner it gets used to pepper, the better,' Lyla retorted with a dismissive wave of her hand.

The housekeeper left the room and Lyla smiled mischievously. 'Am I hearing things or has Auntie Sisi's accent changed? I'm sure I caught a bit of a twang going on.'

Theresa shook her head with a sigh and picked at a loose thread on her sleeve. 'I'm glad you noticed – I thought it was just me.' She looked up with a rueful smile. 'At first, I thought she was mimicking me, but I don't think she realises what she's doing. Still, I suppose it's better than people having a go at me because of my accent. You know, like that stuck-up cow whose party you dragged me to – do you remember?'

'Oh, yes, Mercy Peterson. I remember her trying to show off to her crowd with some dig about you not being anything special because you have an English accent.'

Theresa laughed. 'I mean, *seriously*? I stick out like a sore thumb whenever I open my mouth and somehow that's supposed to make me feel superior?'

'If anyone's got a complex, it's Mercy. I don't see much of her any more. It's a shame because she used to be quite sweet but then her husband had an affair with her best friend a couple of years ago. The whole thing is pretty messy, and it's left her very bitter.'

Theresa was shocked into silence and Lyla pondered for a moment, *her* expression *pensive*. 'Tee, if I tell you something, do you promise not to judge me?'

'That sounds ominous. What is it – are you having an affair too?' She giggled, but Lyla didn't join in and Theresa's laughter gurgled to a halt. '*Lyla?*'

'*No!* Of course, I'm not having an affair. At least, not really...' Lyla's voice trailed off and she kept her eyes fixed on the thick ice-blue rug in the centre of the room.

Theresa stared at the troubled frown creasing Lyla's smooth forehead, totally flabbergasted at the idea of her hyper-religious friend having *any* kind of affair, real or not. Out of all of them, she was the good one – the one who'd left her Anglican faith for the evangelical Christian church because, as she maintained, in her new church people didn't just talk about God, they *did* God.

'It's not. I'm not—' Lyla came to an abrupt halt and

exhaled as deeply as a long-distance runner after crossing the finishing line. 'Look, it's not like I'm actually *doing* anything. It's just that there's this man at my church and—'

'*At your church?*' Theresa squeaked, her voice high with disbelief. 'Lyla, I thought you people were supposed to be the moral guardians setting an example for all of us.'

Lyla flushed and returned her gaze to the rug. Neither woman spoke and, as the silence grew, Theresa's initial incredulity gave way to curiosity as she tried to absorb the idea that Lyla of all people could entertain even the hint of an adulterous thought. She gnawed at her lip thoughtfully. But if Lyla, who was so obsessed with doing the right thing that she tolerated Kwesi's appalling behaviour, *was* drawn towards another man, he had to be something special. And, as far as Theresa was concerned, unless the guy was a psychopath, almost any man was an improvement on the womaniser who had rushed her best friend into marriage.

Theresa cleared her throat and kept her tone neutral. 'Well, if you haven't done anything, can I suggest you stop looking so guilty? Quite honestly, even if you *were* having an affair, I wouldn't blame you in the slightest. As far as I'm concerned, it would damn well serve Kwesi right after all his—'

Theresa broke off her sentence at the sound of the gate opening swiftly followed by the powerful roar of Tyler's car and sighed with irritation. *Typical!* Just when she and Lyla needed time to talk, Tyler decided for once to come home on time. Lyla didn't look any happier about the intrusion and with a helpless shrug Theresa quickly rearranged her scowl into what she hoped was a welcoming smile as her husband strode in.

'Good evening, my lovely wife,' he murmured as Theresa lifted her face for him to plant a dutiful kiss on her cheek. 'How was your day?' He leaned over to give her stomach a gentle rub. 'How's Bump doing?'

Lyla stood up to greet Tyler with a kiss on both cheeks. 'The poor child is going to be stuck with that name if you two keep this up.'

Tyler sank into the neighbouring chair and tugged at his tie before pulling it off in one swift movement. Unbuttoning his shirt collar, he slumped back and rubbed his eyes wearily.

'Hard day?' Theresa's crisp tone didn't convey much sympathy and Lyla looked at her sharply.

'You could say that,' Tyler said. 'We were supposed to break ground at the site tomorrow and clear the outhouses, but now the contractor says they can only get hold of one digger instead of the three he promised.'

'Will that delay things?'

'Hopefully not too much. He reckons they'll have the rest of the machines by the end of the week and his men will work on Saturday to make up the time.'

'But didn't you check that he had the equipment when you agreed the job?'

'Of course, I did – I'm not an idiot!' Tyler snapped, clearly peeved at the insinuation. 'He had everything in place when we agreed the project. He had to sublease the diggers to get some extra cash because of all the delays with getting the lease signed.'

'Are you getting compensation for the hold up? You're the one losing money if it's going to extend the time until the project pays.' Theresa sounded less than impressed.

'Look, I'm just glad he's still on the job and agreed to compromise on the money. Juggling things in construction isn't as easy as your line of work.'

Theresa bristled, and her lips tightened in anger. 'For your information, PR *isn't* easy. We work to deadlines just like everyone else, which makes it even more important to be organised and plan ahead and not just leave things to chance.'

Tyler jumped to his feet. 'I need a drink. What time is dinner?'

Theresa rolled her eyes at the mention of the word drink and then shrugged and tried to sound indifferent. 'If you're going to the kitchen, you can ask Auntie Sisi yourself.'

'Can I get either of you anything while I'm there?'

Lyla and Theresa shook their heads in unison, and without a word, he dropped his tie onto the chair and walked out.

The minute the door shut behind him, Lyla asked bluntly, 'What's going on?'

'What do you mean?' Theresa tried not to sound defensive at the clear accusation behind Lyla's words.

'Oh, come on, Tee, you could have cut the tension in this room with a knife! That certainly wasn't the loving couple I know. What's wrong?'

Theresa pursed her lips and propped a cushion behind her lower back.

'I wish I knew. He's changed since we moved here. He was really excited about the building project at first, but lately...' She shook her head and twisted the rings on her finger distractedly, then threw a surreptitious glance at the closed door and lowered her voice.

'Lately, he just comes and goes as he pleases. He's never around to talk to and when he's here all he does is constantly pick on me. I feel like I can't do anything right as far as he's concerned.'

'It's not easy getting started in business in a new country—' Lyla broke off as Tyler returned carrying a frosted green bottle. He took a sip from it and then deposited the bottle on a marble-topped table, paying no attention to his wife's irritated tut.

'For God's sake, Tyler, at least use a coaster!' she exclaimed, tossing a small woven mat at him. 'Those tables cost a small fortune.'

As if she hadn't spoken, Tyler turned to Lyla with a grin. 'Auntie Sisi is frying a mountain of plantain in there, so I hope you're hungry. Theresa eats like a bird these days which means it's down to you and me to get through it.'

Lyla smiled and maintained a diplomatic silence, but Theresa was incensed at being ignored and sniffed. 'If you were nearly six months pregnant, you mightn't feel like eating massive quantities of food either. But then you'll never have to worry about that, will you?'

'Oh, really? So now it's *my* fault I can't be the one who gets pregnant?'

Auntie Sisi's entrance to announce that dinner was ready put a stop to the bickering and they moved into the dining room with their drinks and took their places around the mahogany table without a word. Lyla peered into the ceramic serving dishes and clapped happily, her excitement breaking the tense silence.

'*Kontomire and* plantain! I'm so glad I came over.'

Theresa smiled at her affectionately. 'You are so

ridiculous about fried plantain. Auntie Pat used to get so annoyed with you when we were kids for always eating more than your fair share.'

'Excuse me, but I remember *you* as the one who hogged the plantain at mealtimes,' Lyla retorted. Putting aside all decorum, she reached out to pick up a piece of the crispy hot plantain with her fingers. Popping it into her mouth, she immediately began to pant, flapping her hand in front of her open mouth.

Theresa burst into peals of laughter and Tyler shook his head with a wry smile. 'I meant it when I said there's a lot of plantain, so you really won't need to compete with Tee tonight.'

He picked up a heavy glazed serving bowl and spooned a generous helping of white rice onto his plate. Passing the bowl to Theresa, he reached for its twin and inhaled with satisfaction as he piled the rich meaty spinach stew glistening with palm oil over the rice.

'This looks great! Auntie Sisi's taste in clothes might be a bit suspect, but there's no denying the woman can cook.'

Theresa stared at the small pile of rice on her plate and pushed a few grains around with her fork. 'You mean, unlike me?'

Without waiting for an answer, she reached for the platter of plantain that Lyla reluctantly offered and speared a few onto her plate.

Tyler refused to rise to the bait and instead tucked into the food in front of him. Making no further comment, Theresa filled her glass and Lyla's with water from the crystal jug on the table and was reaching for her husband's glass when he stopped her.

'It's fine. I've got a couple more beers cooling in there.' He nodded towards the small fridge concealed in the cabinet against the far wall.

'What a surprise,' Theresa muttered sarcastically and set the jug on the table with a thump.

Lyla took one look at Tyler's darkening expression and jumped in hastily.

'Tee, didn't you mention last week that Belson International are one of your new clients? I read in the papers this morning that they've been fined for fixing prices. What's going on there?'

Theresa shrugged. 'I don't know all the details yet, but I've got a meeting first thing tomorrow with their head of communications to discuss how to deal with the fallout. Once I've got the facts, we can come up with a story for the media.'

'You mean, spin the truth and say, "No comment"?' Tyler said dryly, taking a long swallow of his beer to finish the bottle.

'Actually no, I don't. It's our job to protect our client's reputation but we don't do it by lying or hiding facts, particularly when it comes to the media.'

Lyla swallowed another mouthful of the spicy fried plantain. 'But what if they're guilty – surely you have to put some kind of spin on it?'

'Well of course, some organisations try to lie their way out of a crisis, but we always advise our clients to be as ethical as possible.'

She ignored Tyler's snort of derision. 'Look, the media is the most powerful tool we've got to influence how the public sees our clients, and by being truthful and not hiding any facts from them, we're much better placed to turn the story to Belson's advantage and show they're taking the matter seriously. It's rarely the actual dirty deed which gets a company vilified; it's the cover-up that's the kiss of death to their brand reputation. Like we say in PR, tell it all, tell it fast and tell the truth.'

'I've never thought about it that way,' Lyla remarked. 'So, go on then. What else do you guys do?'

Theresa pushed her plate to one side impatiently. 'Oh my God, where do I start? Okay, so our main goal is to give our clients visibility, but we also need to protect their brand and reputation, right?'

Lyla nodded, her mouth too full to speak.

'Good. So that means we need to stay on top of their business, and whatever's going on in that sector. When I worked in London, we'd always conduct research into public opinion so we could plan the best way to get our messages out to the right audience.'

Theresa stabbed at a few grains of rice and chewed quickly and then laid down her fork. 'I think that's what I've always loved about PR, you know? The sheer variety of the job – some days we can do fun things like planning corporate events but then we also get to handle media coverage if there's a crisis, like right now with Belson. That's why it's been so important for me to spend time building relationships with the right journalists, because it's the only way they'll trust me to give them a good story they can use.'

'So, basically, what you're saying is you know how to manipulate the media.' Tyler had left the table to retrieve a bottle of beer from the fridge and was already almost halfway through its contents.

As if he hadn't spoken, Theresa looked pointedly at Lyla. 'Then there's the basic stuff like churning out press releases and writing thought pieces and articles about our clients – essentially anything that gets the word out on digital media.'

'And here I was thinking that it was all long lunches and fashion shows,' Lyla said wryly.

'I wish!' Theresa laughed. 'The business is only just taking off and it's already hectic. We've got so much on our plate that I don't know when I can stop long enough to have this baby.'

Tyler swallowed the last drops of beer and sat back with a soft belch. 'You won't need to worry about that if my project goes belly-up. I'll stay at home with the baby and you can pull in the big bucks.'

'If it means you'll actually stay in your house for a change, then maybe it's worth considering,' Theresa shot back.

Tyler picked up the mobile phone lying beside his plate and stood up abruptly, and the sound of his chair scraping across the floor made both women flinch.

'Excuse me – I have to make a phone call.' His comment was directed at Lyla and, without so much as a glance in Theresa's direction, he left the room.

Lyla's fork was still suspended in mid-air as the two women looked at each other in shocked silence. Then Theresa heaved a deep sigh, not bothering to hide her frustration, while Lyla chewed thoughtfully and observed her friend without comment.

After a moment, Theresa sighed again and raked her hands through her long dark curls, her brown eyes deep pools of misery. '*Now*, do you see what I mean? He's always sniping at me.'

'Tee, I don't know what to say. From where I'm sitting, it looks like you're both pushing each other's buttons. Tyler's always so upbeat and positive. I've never seen him so touchy and irritable. Is he under a lot of pressure with this—?'

'Hold on a minute! What do you mean, is *he* under pressure? What about *me*, for God's sake? I'm trying to run a business here, not to mention being pregnant!'

Lyla put down her fork while looking longingly at the small pile of plantain remaining in the serving dish and patting her stomach regretfully. 'I'm so full, even I can't force another bite.'

She wiped her mouth with the white linen napkin on her lap and turned to face Theresa squarely. 'Look, how can I put this without you getting upset? From what I've seen this evening, neither of you can resist taking potshots at the other. No – wait, hear me out.'

Theresa's expression was mutinous, but she didn't interrupt as Lyla continued. 'You came to Ghana to start a new life together and surely the most important thing is that you stay united. Yes, you're doing well and right now everything's going your way but try and look at it from Tyler's perspective. He's always been very successful and, whether they admit it or not, I'm afraid African men are a bit chauvinistic and like being top dog when it comes to their women. It sounds like he's struggling with his project and, with your business taking off so quickly, how do you think that might make him feel?'

'So, what? I'm supposed to pretend that I'm not doing

well so he can feel better about himself?' Theresa pushed her chair back and tossed her used napkin on to the table. 'This is *Tyler* we're talking about, Lyla. He wasn't brought up here – well, not really. I mean, he went to a British public school, for God's sake! Neither of us has ever been bothered about stupid gender stereotypes – we've always been equal partners.'

'Yes, but that was when you were both successful and living in London where people are far less judgemental about whether a woman earns more than her man. This is Ghana, where everybody wants to know your business, and if the guy isn't doing as well as his wife, well – then, sorry, but he just looks weak.'

Theresa couldn't hide her incredulity. 'Are you *serious*?'

'Absolutely. I know it's not what you're used to or what you want to hear but things are still a lot more traditional here. If you want to make your marriage work, you've got to—'

'I've got to *what*? Stroke his ego, even when he's being a pain in the arse? Pretend everything's perfect when it isn't? Just like you do?'

The words were out before she could stop them, and Theresa gasped and seized Lyla's arm. 'Oh my God, I'm sorry! Really, Lyla, *I'm so sorry!* I shouldn't have said that – you're only trying to help and I'm being an absolute bitch.'

Lyla stared without expression at Theresa's hand clutching on to her and then looked directly at her. 'It's okay. I know you think I'm a fool for sticking with Kwesi, but I've got my reasons.'

Her tone changed, and she lowered her voice urgently. 'Theresa, this isn't about me. It's about you and Tyler.

You've got to figure out what's going on between the two of you and fix it before things get worse.'

'I know, I *know*. You're absolutely right, and I need to learn to keep my mouth shut. It's just the more scared I get that he's drifting away from me, the more I say the wrong things and push him even further! I don't mean to be so impatient with him and I know it must be eating him up inside that his plans have become so messed up.' She paused and took a breath. 'To be honest, Tyler's always been strong and it's really worrying to see him struggle like this. We took such a big risk coming here that sometimes I get overwhelmed by it all and just lash out and say horrible things.'

Lyla gently patted Theresa's hand. 'I know it's not easy dealing with so many changes at once. Adjusting to a new country and starting a new business with a baby on the way is bound to drive anyone crazy – even if you were already halfway there!'

She grinned, and Theresa sighed in relief, still mortified to have turned on her best friend. Lyla was right. She needed to be more supportive and do better at taking Tyler's feelings into account.

'Thanks for always being there for me, Lyla,' she said. 'At least you really listen. I can just imagine what Maku would say. "He's a man for God's sake. Put on a sexy nightie and remind him what he's been missing."'

Lyla burst into giggles. 'Yeah, I know.' Then she added with a teasing glint in her eye. 'Although, maybe it's not such a bad idea to remind him of what life was like before?'

Theresa narrowed her eyes and then gave a dreamy smile as she mulled over the suggestion. 'Well, it's been a while since either of us has dragged the other into bed, so you might have a point there.'

'Right, that's my cue.' Lyla rose to her feet, ignoring Theresa's protest. 'Thanks for a lovely dinner but I'm going home. I'll leave you and your husband to get up to whatever's going on in your mind.'

Theresa was still laughing and tugging on Lyla's arm when Tyler walked back into the room, fastening his top button. Her smile faded when she realised he was back in his suit jacket.

'I'm going to meet Jeff,' he said briskly. 'He's not happy with the speed of progress on the project and I need to get him on side. I'll see you later.' With a brief nod in Lyla's direction, he turned on his heel and moments later the front door slammed shut behind him. The finality of the sound made Theresa's heart ache with a pain so sharp it felt physical.

Lyla spoke first, clearly baffled. 'What just happened?'

Theresa responded with a half-hearted smile, reluctant to speak in case her voice cracked, and far too ashamed to admit to her best friend her dread that this time she had pushed her husband too far. Having trumpeted their perfect love story for years, Theresa was too proud to admit that Tyler's increasing alienation had brought to the surface her deepest fear that the man she loved and trusted would one day, just like her father, decide that leaving was better than staying.

So instead, she changed the subject and smiled at Lyla and said nothing, letting her fear that this time her husband would not return home wrap itself around her heart and turn it into a frozen core of ice deep inside her.

The ice froze her emotions and allowed her to listen without judgement to Lyla's stumbling explanation about her complex feelings for Reuben, allowed her to give Lyla the reassurance she needed to hear, allowed her to hug her friend goodnight and then stumble upstairs to lie in bed. It allowed her to drop into a fitful sleep for a couple of hours, and then wake up abruptly at the imagined sound of the gate swinging open.

Only then, as she lay there alone, did her fear unravel and the ice thaw. Disbelief gave way to an anger she nursed for a few moments until that too faded, leaving in its place an unexpected and vicious hatred of Tyler for putting her through this. And then came a sadness so piercing, she could only stroke her swollen belly and weep. *Why did you let us come here to do this to me?*

Tyler

'Sir, please come this way.' With a deferential smile, the waiter turned to lead Tyler to the far end of the club where Jeff had secured a table.

Despite the sullen mood that had descended upon him since slamming out of the house a couple of hours earlier, Tyler's curiosity was piqued by the activity taking place around him. The club was jam-packed and in near darkness with multicoloured strobe lights sporadically illuminating the heaving crowd on the dance floor. The heat in the venue was overwhelming, and he unfastened the top button of his shirt and followed his guide through the bodies massed around the bar. Most of the people there appeared to be in their late teens and twenties, and he couldn't have named the artist belting out the Hip-life track thumping at an almost unbearable volume if his life had depended on it. Why Jeff had chosen this venue to meet was a mystery which was instantly solved when he spotted his host sitting in a booth at the far end of the room with a young woman pressed up against him. She wore a red strappy dress that skimmed the top of the slender thighs draped over Jeff's, and her hair cascaded in black silky curls over one bare shoulder.

'*Tyler*!' Jeff bellowed, making no effort to stand up as Tyler approached. The booth was lined with padded leather seats and the table in the centre covered with used wine flutes, a collection of shot glasses and a half-empty bottle of champagne. The girl gave Tyler a barely perceptible nod and made no effort to disentangle herself when Tyler shook Jeff's hand and sat down opposite them.

Jeff picked up the glass in front of him and took a swallow of the dark yellow contents. He gestured towards the young woman whose slim arm, weighed down by silver bangles, was draped around his neck. 'Meet Mariama.'

Mariama's hooded eyes gave no hint to her thoughts as they roved over Tyler's dark suit, pale blue shirt and navy tie and Tyler forced a quick smile of greeting, trying to hide his distaste at the middle-aged man sitting across from him preying – there was no other word that came to mind – on a young girl who was probably still a student. Despite the heavy make-up, he would have sworn that Mariama was no more than nineteen or twenty. She was also quite clearly drunk.

Feeling awkward at seeing Jeff in this setting and highly uncomfortable at the behaviour of his financial investor, Tyler wondered what Theresa would have done. Knowing his wife, she would have refused to condone Jeff's sleaziness by her presence and would more than likely have walked out without a word. Not that she was exchanging many words with him either these days, Tyler thought with a pang, unless you counted accusations and insinuations.

Just as his building project was progressing, albeit slowly, his relationship with Theresa was speedily deteriorating and he badly missed their once easy banter. Communication between them now ranged between poor and awful; arctic silences that lasted for days and endless sniping followed by petty quarrels. Even when he made a point of staying in to try and put things right, Theresa would lock herself away, appearing happier to be in her office than in his company, and heightening his fear that his wife simply didn't care that their marriage was spiralling towards disintegration. This morning, when she'd found him in the spare room, was the first time in months that Tyler had seen in Theresa's eyes not just resentment but genuine anxiety about what was happening between them. Although he had played down her fears, the sheer relief of knowing that she still wanted their relationship to work had spurred him to come home early, eager to see how they could turn things around and make their new life work.

But now as he sat across from a clearly hammered Jeff Parnell, Tyler soberly questioned the wisdom of their move to Ghana. If anyone had told him six months ago that he would soon be spending most of the week out drinking with the boys and fielding sarcastic comments and/or glacial silences from a disenchanted wife, he would have laughed them out of the room. Some of the stories from the regulars at Jake's Joint about their stale, joyless marriages were incredibly depressing, but Tyler had never imagined that a similar fate could befall the famously joined at the hip 'Two Ts'.

From the day they had exchanged their vows, Tyler had been in no doubt that marrying Theresa was the smartest decision he had ever made. His parents, who had met an untimely death in a car crash during his early twenties, had never been particularly good role models for marriage. Despite his mother's attempts to shield

142

him from the truth, Tyler had always known about his father's affairs with other women. But having witnessed how wounded his mother had been by her husband's persistent infidelity, Tyler had sworn to himself that when he married, it would be exclusive and for life. And so, it had been. In London, despite their busy schedules and demanding jobs, he and Theresa had been each other's best friends and champions, placing their marriage above everything and anyone. Clementyne's relentless attempts to shoehorn her disapproval into a rift in their relationship had consistently missed their mark, and the irony that Ghana would succeed where Clementyne had failed left a bitter taste in his mouth.

'What're you drinking, man?' Jeff slurred, leaving Tyler wondering what kind of business the man proposed to discuss in his state and in these surroundings. As it was, he could barely hear himself think, never mind conduct a discussion while his chief investor was sprawled on a banquette with a girl wrapped around him.

'I'll have a beer,' Tyler mouthed, not bothering to raise his voice enough to compete with the music. He gestured to the waiter who'd escorted him to the table, pulling him close to give his order.

With a nod, the young man took off, returning a few minutes later with a glass and a large bottle of beer. He uncapped the bottle and poured out the drink and they both studied the white foam until it settled. Slipping a note into the waiter's hand, Tyler picked up his glass and raised it to Jeff in a silent toast.

This was their second meeting in a week and Tyler had been surprised but not unduly concerned to see Jeff's name flash up on his phone earlier that day. Despite the last-minute hiccups, the project was on course and the builders had promised to make up for lost time. Once the apartments were sold as planned, both he and Jeff stood to make a significant profit, which made Jeff's unexpected invitation to join him for a drink and a general catch-up that evening more than a little awkward. Tyler's instinctive reaction had been to refuse, but he'd also been wary of sounding too curt. Whatever his personal feelings about the man, he still needed the additional tranche of money Jeff had agreed to put up and offending him needlessly made no sense. To Tyler's relief, Jeff had accepted his excuses with good grace, allowing him to leave Patience to lock up the office while he raced home to build bridges with his wife before it was too late. Although he hadn't expected to see Lyla, his initial disappointment at not having time alone with Theresa had been nothing compared to the humiliation he'd felt at her unconcealed disdain towards him. Theresa's open hostility and the verbal jabs she'd aimed at him in front of her best friend had become so unbearable that in desperation he'd called Jeff, and then killed time at a bar before making his way here.

'*Move over, man!*' his host shouted, gesturing with his free hand towards a young woman standing silently beside him. Startled by her sudden appearance, Tyler dutifully shifted along, and she slid into the booth and sat so close he could feel the heat from her body.

'Saba, this is my man, Tyler!' Jeff leaned across the table, almost spraying the words into the girl's face. 'Tyler, this is Saba – Mariama's room-mate.'

So, they *were* university students, Tyler thought

resignedly. He'd heard of students who chose to supplement their income by heaping attention on to wealthy sugar daddies, but he still hated the idea.

Saba turned towards him and Tyler, seeing her eyes light up, wondered how to gently break it to the baby-faced, curvy young woman that her glittery halter-necked top didn't make look any older than her years, and that he had zero interest in anything she had to offer. Hanging out at Jake's with the boys was one thing, taking up with teenagers was quite another.

Saba picked up one of the wine glasses on the table and sipped from it with a flirtatious smile, deliberately pressing against him when she leaned forward to set her glass down. Tyler's arm was draped across the back of the banquette and she brazenly shuffled along the seat to close the small gap between them and increase his discomfort.

'*Hey, Diaspora!*'

Tyler looked up sharply and suppressed a sigh. Johnnie Fernandes, a frequent visitor to Jake's, was waving a half-empty beer bottle in Tyler's face with a knowing smile.

'Johnnie,' Tyler acknowledged curtly, grateful that the loud music prevented any real conversation. He had known Johnnie since school and the adult version was even more annoying than the fourteen-year-old boy he'd left behind. He also didn't appreciate Johnnie's nod towards Saba, followed by a sly wink as if they were in on some big secret together, and Tyler pointedly inched along the leather seat to put some space between him and the girl.

'*Chale*, maybe I should stop calling you Diaspora, huh? You look like you've acclimatised pretty well.'

Ready to protest his innocence, Tyler bit back the words, knowing Johnnie wouldn't believe him whatever he said. In Johnnie's shoes, he probably wouldn't have either. After all, why would a grown man be sitting next to a pretty young girl in a barely-there outfit and buying her drinks if he had no intention of taking advantage?

With another suggestive grin, Johnnie waved his bottle in farewell and moved off towards the crowded dance floor. Tyler turned back to Jeff, but his attention was on Mariama's breasts which were only inches from his face. Watching the older man's stony grey eyes brazenly fix on the pert swell of exposed flesh and the erect nipples visible under the flimsy dress, Tyler sighed deeply and wondered what he was doing there.

The next hour crawled by as Jeff grew drunker and more uninhibited, stroking Mariama's arms and face in a way which left no doubt about his intentions when the evening was over. The unrelenting thud of the music was giving Tyler a headache and the tension was made worse by Saba's persistent efforts to engage his attention by pressing up close to whisper intimately into his ear at any given opportunity. The pressure continued to build in his head until Tyler was unable to endure it for a second longer. Well beyond caring whether Jeff would be offended, Tyler stood up and abruptly took his leave.

Driving down the deserted highway, he shook his head sadly. How had it come to this? Instead of their great adventure, here he was driving around aimlessly on his own at two o'clock in the morning. The eagerness with which he'd listened to his old school friends urging him to return to Ghana now seemed laughable. But his intense desire to add to the many success stories of returnees making good – Ato Johnson who'd left his management job in Ohio to set up a thriving cashew nut business a few miles outside Accra, or Perry Kotei who'd been in his MBA class in London and was now the Managing Director of a local consulting firm – had made moving here sound like perfect sense. Once he'd taken the plunge and landed in Ghana ready for the challenge, however, it had been a different story. Friends were suddenly too busy to meet up, and instead of the once-promised offers of support and investment capital, he was lucky if anyone answered his phone calls. Accidental meetings in town usually generated shifty glances followed by excuses to hurry away while tossing out assurances and sympathetic phrases such as *'Man, we are all suffering; it's not easy here!'* or *'Chale, don't worry, things will fall into place soon'* or – worst of all – *'You had it so good in London, man – why did you leave that place to come back here?'*

And yet, in the same way his old friends had disappeared, Tyler knew that success would see them return without any sense of embarrassment. Indeed, since word of the deal with Jeff Parnell had started to circulate, several people had already made overtures towards him, hinting at how to use his connection to Jeff for lucrative deals that he had no doubt would only benefit them.

The headache was getting worse. He rubbed his eyes wearily with the heel of his hand, holding the steering wheel firmly with the other in the knowledge that a pothole concealed by the dim street lighting could easily send the car into a spin. He turned off the highway and headed down the Ring Road, now mercifully clear of its usual traffic. As he passed Jake's Joint, he briefly considered stopping and then, remembering his encounter with Johnnie, changed his mind and carried on driving. He didn't have the energy to sit down with guys like Johnnie who gathered at Jake's uninspiring watering hole to drink their fears away.

It was probably the attitude of his so-called friends that had driven him to spend time with Nortey at Jake's Joint in the first place, Tyler mused. At Jake's, no one ran away from a man who was struggling, as if his failure would somehow taint or infect you. Seated around the scarred wooden tables with uneven legs, the camaraderie and beers quickly transformed disappointments into optimism and a conviction that a lucky break was just around the corner. Everyone at Jake's agreed that success was simply a matter of time and persistence, and it was this ethos that made the bar a seductively irresistible refuge for men who needed both company and reassurance.

Without warning, a searing band of pain like an elastic band being yanked savagely around his head bit into his skull and forced out a groan. Almost immediately, he was hit by an intense feeling of fatigue. The band around his head tightened and throbbed as if multiple darts were jabbing inside his head and stabbing him from behind his eyes. He had just passed the junction which led to his office and he pressed down hard on the brakes. Hit by such overwhelming exhaustion that even his bones felt like rubber, Tyler gripped the wheel and shivered from the pain drilling through his skull. It was too dangerous to stay where he was and risk a speeding car crashing into him, and he tried to slow his jagged breathing and calm the surge of helpless panic. Forcing himself to focus, he put the car into reverse and took the turning.

A few minutes later, Tyler unlocked the door to his suite of offices. With the air conditioner turned off, the air felt stale, and he stumbled past the leather sofa opposite Patience's desk almost blind with agony, clutching on to the back of the seat to keep his balance. The pain from the migraine overcame any guilt at invading his PA's space, and he scrabbled around for the pack of extra-strength ibuprofen he knew she kept tucked in her desk drawer. Tossing back three tablets, he retrieved a bottle of water from the fridge in his office and swallowed half its contents in one gulp. He stretched out on the sofa and kicked off his shoes, whimpering at the pain from the sudden movement. Then, reaching blindly for one of the soft throw cushions, he jammed it under his head and prayed for sleep.

Maku

Pursing her full lips, Maku smoothed out the dress and swivelled round to inspect the view. The fabric was stretchy enough to accommodate her curves, and if she held in her stomach she could just about get away with it, she decided. An image of the neatly folded white lace stashed in the walnut chest of drawers flashed through her mind and she sighed gloomily as she wondered if she would ever be slim enough for her dream wedding dress – not that there was much chance of a wedding to wear it to.

Trying not to let resentment spoil her mood, Maku carefully applied the dark plum lipstick Lyla had insisted on buying her during one of their shopping expeditions. Exclaiming that it would suit Maku's complexion perfectly, Lyla had brushed away her protests – 'Can't I give my cousin a gift if I want to?' – and refused to take the crumpled cedi notes Maku had half-heartedly tried to press into her hand. The lipstick was normally hidden away to avoid the risk of the boys using it as a crayon, but tonight it was the perfect accessory for their long-overdue girls' night out.

For once, Nortey had kept his promise to stay in, allowing Maku a rare opportunity to escape the four children. She finished off her make-up and ran her fingers though her freshly braided hair, irritated at the sight of the silver threads glinting among the dark locks. It really wasn't fair that Nortey's hair was still jet black when he was five years older than her. On the other hand, it made perfect sense, she thought sourly, seeing as she was the one carrying the stresses of a full-time job, not to mention studying *and* taking care of four children – five, really, the way Nortey behaved.

The sound of the gate opening spurred Maku into action. Quickly seizing the black handbag which served for both day and evening use, she switched off the fan, trying not to look at the broken air-conditioner unit Nortey had promised to repair and which eight months later still sat in reproachful silence, and hurried out of her bedroom. Pausing only to yell, *'Lyla's here, I'm off!'* in the general direction of the living room, she slammed the front door behind her and scooted into the passenger seat of her cousin's car before anyone could stop her.

The restaurant where they'd agreed to meet Theresa was fitted out in the style of an American diner. Framed monochrome prints of 1950s movie stars and old-fashioned posters of adverts for Campbell's Soup and a variety of condiments covered walls painted a stark white. A shiny jukebox sat in the corner was apparently only for decoration as the tinny country music playing in the background came through speakers fixed into the corners of the ceiling.

Maku followed Lyla into a booth near the front of the half-filled restaurant and took the laminated menu handed over by a bored-looking waitress. While they waited for Theresa, Maku skimmed through the menu and wrinkled her nose at the food on offer. She usually enjoyed anything she hadn't had to cook herself, but even she couldn't get excited about the uninspiring variations of hamburger and fried chicken. A quick glance at Lyla's expression suggested she wasn't alone.

Wait until the bourgeois princess gets here. Maku cast a look around and grinned at the thought of her fastidious friend's reaction to this second-rate diner. Right on cue, Theresa appeared in the doorway. As Maku watched her scan the restaurant and register the garish posters and Formica-topped tables, she could almost feel the effort Theresa made to keep her expression neutral. The mask slipped for a moment when one eyebrow rose involuntarily at the sight of the fake jukebox, and Maku beckoned her over with a resigned wave. At least Tee was consistent in her snobbery.

After ordering their drinks the conversation bounced back and forth across the table while they settled in for the evening.

'I kept expecting you to call and say you couldn't make it tonight, Maku. Did you have to bribe Nortey to get him to stay with the children?' Theresa teased. Her dark eyes were dancing with merriment, and Maku sniffed.

'Don't get me started on that man. He thinks he's doing me a favour by taking care of his own kids! I made dinner and left him to it – he can see for himself what it's like trying to feed a baby and two boys who refuse to sit still when they eat. And as for Isabelle,' she gave a wicked chuckle, 'just wait until that little madam tells him she doesn't eat kenkey.'

'Is she still living with you?' Theresa frowned. 'Why can't her father look after her – they have house help, don't they?'

They fell silent as the waitress arrived and deposited

three brimming glasses on the table. She reached into the pocket of her red-and-white-checked apron for a note pad and Maku stared enviously at her narrow hips and a waist so tiny she'd had to wind the apron strings around twice before looping it into a bow at the front.

The waitress took their orders and left, and Theresa picked up her glass and eyed her drink for a moment before taking a tiny sip and repeating her question.

'Of course, they have house help,' Maku retorted. 'You should see Adoley's nails – I swear that woman never lifts a finger at home.' She leaned forward with an impish smile. 'And let's just say that her husband is having the time of his life while she's away. I didn't tell Nortey, but I saw George in town last week with a woman sitting in the front seat of his car looking *very* comfortable. Now I know why he didn't have a problem with us keeping Isabelle – he obviously doesn't want the child around to cramp his style or report back to her mother.'

Lyla gave a wry chuckle and shook her head resignedly. Instead of joining in the laughter, Theresa frowned and traced a finger lightly across the condensation on her glass.

'Well, I think it's despicable. Is it just *our* men who can't be faithful to one woman? And why is everyone so blasé about it?'

'Because half the men don't think they're doing anything wrong,' Maku shrugged. 'I'm serious – if you challenge them, they'll just tell you that having more than one woman is traditional, and they're only doing what their fathers did. Don't look like that, Tee, it isn't only African men that cheat, you know. I was watching a TV programme the other night about the British royal family and how Charles even *admitted* he'd had a mistress!'

Lyla looked at her thoughtfully. 'Nortey goes out an awful lot, Cuz. Don't you ever worry that he's fooling around?

'Nope,' Maku said decisively. 'Why would he even need to look elsewhere when he's got *all this*.' She ran her hand up and down her body with an exaggerated leer, causing the other two to burst into laughter.

'What?' she pouted, trying to look offended.

'Excuse me, Miss Ghana, but looks have nothing to do with a man straying. Beautiful women still got cheated on,' Theresa remarked. 'Just look at Beyoncé – and you know she's seriously gorgeous.'

'Yeah, well I know Nortey doesn't try his luck with other women,' Maku said confidently.

'How?' Lyla challenged.

'Firstly, he's too damned cheap and lazy to chase a girl and then have to take her out and buy her gifts. And secondly, he knows I would find out, and he also knows I would kill him *after* cutting off his *hoo-hoo*. Trust me, he's more afraid of me than you know.'

Lyla choked on her drink and Theresa thumped her hard on the back until she protested. '*Ow!* It's okay, I'm fine now. Tee, your hands are *hard*!'

The return of the waitress with their orders brought a moment of silence while they explored the food on their plates, the reality a far cry from the glossy pictures on the menu. Maku poked dubiously at the bowl of drooping leaves masquerading as a side salad before spearing some of the brittle French fries heaped onto her plate and cramming them into her mouth. Swallowing hard, she reached for the bottle of tomato sauce in the middle of the table and poured it liberally over the pile. So far, her diet had been spectacularly unsuccessful and there wasn't much point in depriving herself of the food on offer. After all, how often did a girl get to eat out – even if the food wasn't exactly haute cuisine?

Theresa took one look at her food and quickly reached across to snatch a chip from Lyla's plate. 'Your fries don't look as burned as mine.'

'*Hey!* Eat your own food!' Lyla protested, lifting her arm to block another attempt. 'Try that again and I'll smack you – pregnant or not.'

'Surely you wouldn't do that to the mother of your soon-to-be godchild?' Theresa wheedled.

Lyla snorted. 'You don't get to use that line whenever it suits you. Eat your own meal.'

But despite her spirited defence of her food, Lyla took only a couple more bites of her burger before dropping the rest onto the plate and settling back in her seat. Sitting across from her, Maku tucked into her portion and mentally shook her head. If this was all her cousin intended to eat, it was no wonder the woman was so skinny!

'Maku, are you sure you don't want to be my baby's godmother, too?' Theresa's low-pitched voice in full persuasion mode intruded into Maku's thoughts.

'Thanks, but the answer is still no,' Maku said bluntly. 'Sorry, but I've already got three kids – and that's not including that little diva, Isabelle. I can't be responsible for any more children.'

Theresa nibbled on a French fry thoughtfully. 'If I end up as a single parent, you'll have to pitch in anyway.'

'Oh, come on, Theresa!' Lyla remonstrated gently. 'Things aren't that bad.'

'They absolutely are! Tyler barely even looks at me these days.'

Maku mopped up the river of ketchup on her plate with the last of her fries and chewed vigorously. Fork in hand, she turned to Theresa and narrowed her eyes. 'You know, maybe it's not his fault,' she speculated. 'I saw a Nigerian movie last week where the man was cursed by his mistress and couldn't have sex with his wife but didn't know how to tell her.'

Lyla sighed. 'When do you have time to watch so much TV when you're forever complaining about all the coursework you have to finish?'

'It was on while I was getting my hair braided. Is that okay with you?'

'Don't get huffy with me, Cuz. I'm just trying to look out for you and make sure you pass those exams. I can't wait for you and Nortey to move somewhere decent.'

'Hear, hear!' Theresa raised her glass.

'Why's your drink that funny colour?' Lyla asked curiously.

'Because I've added in some water – do you know how much sugar there is in fruit juice?'

Lyla and Maku both rolled their eyes, but Theresa simply shrugged. 'I'm deadly serious. If I don't watch my sugar intake, I'll end up with gestational diabetes.' She prodded the limp burger cooling on her plate. 'How do they get away with calling this a hamburger – and why did we come to this crappy diner, anyway? I still don't understand why we didn't go to the Italian restaurant that's just opened up in Osu.'

'Because *I* can't afford it and it wouldn't hurt you to try places where normal people eat for a change,' Maku retorted. 'You can be so *bougie* sometimes.'

'You do know that's not an insult, right? Do you have any idea how fast the middle class is growing in Africa, and how much demand there is for world-class restaurants and services right here in Ghana? I've just finished writing a press release for a study by The National Economics Institute and they reckon there's going to be—'

Lyla raised a hand and cut her off hastily. 'Yeah, alright Tee, we get it. And we agreed there'd be no work talk tonight. So, if you don't give us chapter and verse about economics, I won't bore you both with the details of my annoying deputy manager who has another job on the sly and keeps calling in sick and hoping I won't find out.'

'Well, if we can't talk about work, that just leaves talking about our husbands, and I'd rather not,' Theresa rejoined, before immediately launching into an extended rant about Tyler.

Maku groaned inwardly and pretended to listen as she picked at the leftover fries on her cousin's plate. She briefly considered calling Nortey to check on the kids and then dismissed the thought. *It's not as if he rings home from Jake's Joint to tell his children a bedtime story.*

'Not only did he not come home all night, but you should have *heard* the way he spoke to me the next day when I pulled him up on his pathetic excuse.'

Maku tuned back into Theresa's tirade and tried not to show her irritation. As much as she loved Tee, the girl really didn't know when she had it good. As far as Maku could tell, Tyler treated her like a queen. Just look at the wedding he had given her! From Lyla's reports and the evidence in the framed pictures adorning Theresa's living room, their marriage ceremony had been spectacular. Despite all her moaning, at least Theresa could refer to herself as *Mrs* Brew, Maku brooded. She'd taken care of Nortey for years, and given him three children, and yet she still had to wear the indignity of being called 'Miss'.

'At least you've got a husband,' Maku broke in, unable to contain her bitterness at the unfairness of it all.

'Don't be so silly, Cuz,' Lyla said impatiently. 'You've also got a husband.'

'Yeah, Maku,' Theresa chimed in, 'will you *please* change the record? I honestly don't get what your problem is. Traditional marriage ceremonies are just as valid as church ones, you *know* that. For God's sake, you've been with Nortey for years and you're just as married as we are, if not more so!'

'So how come both of you have two rings on your finger and I only have this one, then?' Maku stretched out her left hand to eye the thin gold band on her finger with undisguised contempt. 'And it's such a rubbish ring too – you need a microscope to see the diamond.'

She sucked despondently on her straw, letting Lyla and Theresa's well-rehearsed double act wash right over her. Lyla went first with a reassuring *of course*, traditional marriages were considered legal in Ghana, and then Theresa jumped in to add that *of course* while traditional ceremonies didn't confer the title of Mrs, Maku had every right to think of herself as a married woman.

As if they hadn't spoken, Maku pulled the straw out of her mouth and said, 'Maybe it's because I grew up in a village. That must be why Nortey thinks I'm not worth a proper wedding.'

Lyla's patience was clearly wearing thin. '*Maku!* How many chips can you fit on your shoulder at one time? You've lived in Accra for more years than you were ever in Biorkor!'

'Yes, but Nortey's family still act as if I came to town last year.'

'You're more than able to stand up for yourself with that lot. I thought you said village life is what made you feisty.'

'True,' Maku agreed gloomily. 'There wasn't much to do in that place except fight. Biorkor is the swinging capital of absolutely nowhere.'

'You know, if you want a white wedding that badly, then insist on it,' Theresa said wearily. 'But trust me, a big wedding doesn't guarantee a great marriage – ask Lyla.'

Lyla gave Theresa a warning look and took a slow sip of her drink, and Maku narrowed her eyes at her cousin. 'Why? What's going on, Cuz?'

'No more than the usual,' Lyla replied calmly. 'Tee's just exaggerating. Anyhow, we were talking about you, not me. How's it going with Auntie Lizzie? Is she still cooking for you on the sly?'

Maku brightened. 'I swear that woman's an angel. There's no way I could fit in all my revision without her help. I have to keep reminding her to go easy on the pepper since Nortey can't handle it, but honestly, she's been amazing. I just give her the money and she quietly brings the food to the house every week.'

Theresa looked incredulous. 'Does Nortey really not suspect anything?'

'Trust me, I would know about it if he did!' Maku laughed grimly. 'One good thing about him going to Jake's so often is that I can defrost Auntie Lizzie's food and cook some fresh rice or yam to go with it long before he ever gets home.'

Theresa dissolved into helpless giggles. 'I can't believe the charades women here are forced to go through for men.'

Maku watched Theresa wipe away her tears of laughter and broke into a reluctant chuckle.

* * *

A week later, the last thing Maku felt like doing was laughing. She sat behind her desk and stared down at her payslip, her mind whirling around the list of expenses that the paltry sum had to cover. She had already blown this month's budget after being forced to hand over two hundred cedis to Nortey to cover his contribution towards some ridiculous scheme to import mobile phone accessories. Even when she'd reminded him that Abra's nursery fees were overdue, his mouth had set stubbornly. Knowing she would get no peace until she gave in, an exasperated Maku had handed over the money, hoping she could pick up some overtime at work to make up for the loss.

Maku bit hard on her lip in frustration as her thoughts scampered around her head like angry rats. How the hell was she going to manage? She had to budget for Abra's childcare costs as well as Auntie Lizzie's cooking out of this – this *pittance*! On top of that, Isabelle's relentless demands were costing them far more than the meagre contributions Nortey had been able to prise out of that stingy bastard, George. And then, of course, there was the monthly instalment owed to the dressmaker for the white lace cloth.

She sighed deeply at the thought of the fabric she had so rashly taken on credit for a wedding she had suspected would never happen, and which a blazing row with Nortey had now confirmed. Fired up by the conversation with the girls at the diner, the minute Nortey had walked into the house the following evening, accompanied by the ever-present aroma of Jake's Joint, Maku had launched her attack.

'Look at Lyla. She hasn't even given Kwesi a child and he *married* her. I've given you three children and you can't even do the right thing by me!' she'd yelled.

Clearly emboldened by the beer he'd consumed, Nortey had argued forcefully, albeit somewhat incoherently, about the need to focus on their priorities, an argument that left her almost spitting with fury. Eventually ending the bitter slanging match by pinning the blame squarely on his family, Nortey had staggered off to bed.

Just remembering the conversation made Maku boil with anger all over again and she crushed the flimsy slip of paper in her hand, wishing it was Nortey's head.

'Maku?'

She looked up sharply as Rita's voice pierced through the heavy fog of emotions threatening to overwhelm her. Rita was with a young man whom she recognised as the new intern in the Finance department. Having been given the task of supervising his induction, Rita sounded even bossier than usual as she performed the introductions.

'Maku, meet Clement Hagan. He's going to be working with us for the next three months. Clement, this is Maku Tetteh.'

Clement nodded with a polite smile. 'Nice to meet you, Mrs Tetteh.'

Clearly tickled, Rita slapped Clement's arm playfully. 'She's *Miss* Tetteh, not Mrs,' she tittered. With that, she swept Clement away to continue their rounds, leaving Maku burning with embarrassment.

She lowered her head to avoid meeting anyone's eyes and took several deep breaths to calm her ragged breathing. Smoothing out the crumpled payslip, she stared at it once again, trying to read the printed figures through the shimmer of her tears.

Nortey

Slamming the door of his ageing Toyota, Nortey shook his head back and forth as if to physically expel his mother's words from his mind. It was at times like these that he desperately wished he had a brother. Another boy who would take the pressure off him to be the perfect son and the primary object of his mother's suffocating attention. Being the youngest of six children had brought some perks, including five older sisters who had cooed over him and treated him like a prince from the day he was born. But it had also imposed the duty of turning up whenever his mother wanted help from 'my only son'.

The sun was blazing overhead and even with his windows down the car felt stifling. He turned the key in the ignition, breathing a sigh of relief when the temperamental engine turned over, and sped down the road past the neat town houses that made up the quiet residential estate. His sisters had clubbed together to buy their mother's two-bedroom house – all Nortey's savings had been ploughed into a pig farming project at the time – and free his sister Naa from the daily maternal interference that came with having the old lady live with her. By prudently installing a distant cousin in the spare room of the new house to act as a companion, Nortey had hoped to be spared the frequent summonses, but after three years it was clear that his mother had no intention of loosening her hold.

Wiping his forehead with a handkerchief already damp from use, Nortey fell in line behind the cars queuing up to the main intersection. He glanced at his watch and cursed silently. With all this traffic, it would be a miracle if he managed to get back to campus in time for his three o'clock lecture. Once again, he berated himself for letting his mother walk all over him. Why the hell had he succumbed and allowed the old lady to persuade him round to her house on a weekday afternoon – and to fix her crooked wardrobe door, of all things! *Am I a bloody carpenter?*

He banged on the steering wheel in frustration and inched the car forward until it almost touched the bumper of the sleek Audi in front. Of course, the wardrobe door wasn't the issue – otherwise why dismiss his suggestion to send round a handyman? His mother had summoned him simply because she knew she could. And just like everyone else in his family, he knew it saved time to give the woman what she wanted as she always got her own way in the end. Unfortunately, time was the one thing he didn't have to spare today.

Finally crossing the junction, Nortey turned on to the main highway leading to the university campus. His relief at seeing the traffic thin out was soon dissipated by the memory of his mother's fury after he'd been stupid enough to repeat Maku's words. His mother was the most opinionated woman ever, which was precisely why he should have known better than to mention the row with Maku. The fact that things between them still didn't feel right and it was unsettling him, was no excuse to break the cardinal rule of *never* asking his mother for advice, Nortey thought grimly. He knew better than anyone how

Mama operated when she was asked her opinion. Not content with simply stating her viewpoint, she would invariably take control of the situation, thereby making an independent decision impossible.

What made his lapse even more idiotic was that it concerned his wife and predictably, as happened whenever Maku was the subject, his mother had exploded.

'Is she *mad?* That girl is an ungrateful *bush* girl! She is lucky we are a decent and honourable family who allowed this marriage to go ahead in the first place. Who does she think she is to complain now? Doesn't she appreciate the number of educated and beautiful girls you could have chosen to marry instead of her?'

Nortey pressed down hard on the accelerator and smiled wryly at the notion he had ever been a man with his pick of the best girls in town. Beautiful, educated girls did not trample over themselves to attract lowly lecturers, and meeting Maku had been a relief. Dazzled by his qualifications, she had fallen for his charms and never questioned his assurances about his future success. Later, her easy acceptance of his patent lack of drive had bolstered his self-esteem and removed the stress of having a partner with career ambitions for him that exceeded his own. Whenever Nortey considered it, the very idea of the kind of pressure a man would face were he married to someone like Theresa Brew invariably produced a shudder.

The line of cars approaching the university gates had slowed to a standstill and he tapped his fingers anxiously against the steering wheel. Faculty rules required all lecturers to be in situ at least ten minutes before class started and the thought of facing Professor Ghartey's disapproval if he was late again brought Nortey out in a cold sweat. His boss's last warning had been crystal clear, and the last thing Nortey needed was to be suspended from his job or, even worse, to lose it altogether.

Still no movement. Nortey pressed his horn sharply, but to no avail. The vehicles ahead of him didn't budge and the bumper to bumper queue lined up behind him made it impossible to back his car out. Even if he could have moved, there was no other route to enter the campus and he had no choice but to wait.

Nortey's thoughts returned to his mother's harsh comments about Maku. He had immediately leapt to his wife's defence and pointed out how helpful she was being with Isabelle, but his mother had simply snorted in disgust.

'Adoley is her big sister so why should I praise her for looking after her sister's child. Are we not all one family?'

'Yes, Mama, but to be fair, she already takes care of our three kids and—'

'And *what*? Didn't I bring up *six* children?' his mother cut him off, contempt dripping through her words. 'Do you hear me complaining?'

Nortey tactfully avoided pointing out that his mother had never worked outside the home and had also enjoyed the services of two maids, a garden boy and a cook throughout his childhood. As soon as his sisters reached puberty, his mother had put them to work around the house and dished out chores he'd never been troubled with. In Mama's world, men held a distinct and privileged status which excused them from many of the demands placed on women.

'In any case, George is a very busy man and shouldn't be expected to look after a child when he has such an important job,' she'd snapped. 'Your foolish wife should stop complaining and do what any woman is expected to do for her senior sister.'

The mid-afternoon heat beating down on his car wasn't the cause of Nortey shifting uncomfortably in his seat. It wasn't even the unmistakable malice in his mother's eyes or the acid tone she reserved for Maku. What had really unnerved him were her parting words as she escorted him to the front door.

'Tell that girl to get on her knees in gratitude that we permitted even the traditional marriage. After all these years, who has the time or money to waste on a foolish church wedding? You will do nothing of the sort and *that* is my final word on the matter.'

Nortey sighed wearily, feeling battered from all sides. Now his mother had staked her position, it would be impossible to cross her. It wasn't so much that he objected to a church wedding, although he frankly didn't see the point as he and Maku were already married. What he did baulk at was spending money he didn't have on expensive suits and dresses, not to mention the cost of a reception for family and friends. Even a modest wedding was well beyond his means, and he had yet to pluck up the courage to confess to Maku that the money he'd invested in the mobile phone deal would never yield a return. He fully intended to tell her at some point, but she could be very scary at times – he really should have known better than to trust the Osei boys and their big talk at Jake's about the huge demand for mobile phone accessories. But who could have known their Chinese partner would disappear with the goods they had paid for in advance?

It was five minutes to three when Nortey finally arrived at the faculty car park, his heart pumping furiously at the prospect of running into Professor Ghartey. Grabbing his briefcase from the back seat and without stopping to lock the car, he sprinted down the path behind the building, praying Seibu hadn't yet repaired the emergency fire door. Nortey's chest heaved painfully at the unaccustomed exercise and he could feel the sweat dripping down his back.

He stopped to mop his face before pushing open the heavy door and glanced at his watch once again. Two minutes to three. Patting down his tufty hair, badly in need of a trim, Nortey gave his face an ineffectual swipe with the now sodden hanky and strode towards the lecture hall. He had just grasped the door handle when, from behind, he heard the unmistakable sound of a throat being cleared.

Damn it! Nortey froze and closed his eyes as he felt the weight of his heart sink deep into his chest.

'Mr Quarshie?' The deep voice with its clipped accent sounded furious.

The sweat clinging to Nortey's face felt like beads of ice-cold water as he slowly turned and reluctantly pried his eyes open to face his boss. *Why, why, why* had he gone to his mother's house?

'Professor?'

The word remained suspended in silence as Professor Ghartey's dark piercing eyes glared at him from a face that could only be described as grim. Just as the tension clawing at Nortey's chest became unbearable, the older man dipped his head in a brief nod of acknowledgement and smoothed the navy polka-dot bow tie at his throat.

'When you've finished your lecture, I'd like to see you in my office.'

Lyla

Lyla cast a worried glance up at the dark clouds gathering overhead as she hurried back to her car. After the intense heat and humidity of the past few days, there was a strong likelihood that the moist, heavy air would produce a violent thunderstorm. Choir practice had continued for longer than usual, and she still had to prepare her notes for her team's appraisal meetings the following day. She was fumbling in her bag for her car key when the sound of gravel crunching behind her stilled her hand. She didn't need to turn around to know who it was because her stomach was already catapulting inside her with all the friskiness of an excited puppy. What in heaven's name was it about this man that caused her body to react so strongly whenever he approached her?

'Sister Lyla – are you in a hurry?' She trembled involuntarily at the sound of his rich baritone voice, and her legs suddenly felt wobbly.

Pull yourself together, woman! Her silent self-admonishment in the seconds it took to swivel around to face him didn't stop the smile she directed at Reuben from looking decidedly shaky. In her flat pumps, he towered over her and she craned her neck upwards, almost squinting as her eyes sought his.

'I'm running late, I'm afraid. It's almost seven o'clock and I have to finish some work this evening.'

She crooked an eyebrow, and Reuben chuckled in response to her unasked question. 'Singing is thirsty work and I just wondered if you would care to join me for a quick drink before you head home?'

His eyes were serious despite the gentle smile curving his lips and taken aback by the request, Lyla gulped silently. He tugged at his full beard and his expression was quizzical as she continued to stare up at him, her brain suddenly lacking the ability to form a coherent sentence. Although they chatted frequently during choir practice, she and Reuben had never spent any time alone, and she wasn't altogether sure they should. Her first instinct was to decline – going anywhere with a man whose voice wreaked such havoc with her nerves and whose proximity had her silently whimpering for his touch was surely playing with fire. On the other hand, he was only asking to share an innocent drink in a public spot, so what would be the harm?

Before she could talk herself into it, Lyla took a deep breath and said as decisively as she could manage, 'I'm so sorry, Brother Reuben, but I have a pile of work to finish before tomorrow morning, and I'll have to stay up late into the night as it is.'

It was hard to tell if he was disappointed as his smile didn't waver. He nodded slowly and stepped back, allowing her to open her car door and then shutting it for her with a gentle thud once she had settled into the driver's seat. She switched on the ignition and rolled down the window and Reuben bent low, his face so close to hers that she could feel the warmth of his breath on her face.

'Maybe another time then, hmm?'

Despite the solid barrier of the car door between them, Lyla felt herself quiver. When she nodded, he straightened up and gave a brief wave before walking towards a dark-blue Range Rover.

Exhaling deeply, Lyla put the car into gear and shot out of the car park, her chest thudding as if she'd run a mile. Any concerns about thunderstorms disappeared as she sped away from the devilish temptation to turn back and follow Reuben wherever he wanted to go. *Lyla, you've just left church – what's wrong with you?* The harsh voice inside her head was back with a vengeance and she felt like weeping. Why was she so drawn to this man and why was God tempting her so badly? She was trying hard to be a good Christian and a faithful wife, so why was He testing her this way? *Maybe God just wants you to be happy.* The idea floated through her mind and was immediately banished by The Voice. She had no right to happiness; she simply didn't deserve it. *No, Lyla. You've made your bed, so lie in it.*

As she approached the gates to Marula Heights, the security guard jumped to his feet to raise the metal barrier, his eyes not quite meeting hers as he returned her greeting without his usual cheery smile, and Lyla continued up the wide avenue towards their cul-de-sac. It was sufficiently cool to dispense with the car's air conditioning and she slid down her window, relishing the sweet, sticky scent of the tropical evening. Although the rain had held off, the air still felt heavy and she suddenly yearned for a long, cool shower to calm her thoughts and soothe her restless body.

Pulling up to her house, Lyla's eyes widened in astonishment at the sight of Solomon standing behind the

172

closed gates and embroiled in a heated argument with a woman on the other side. Ignoring his forceful gestures to go away, the woman was shouting and gesticulating wildly while banging an oversized handbag against the gates in evident frustration. The sound of Lyla's car engine and the beams from the powerful headlights brought an abrupt end to the commotion. Pulling up the handbrake, Lyla stared at the woman who had turned to face her, taking in her waist-long hair and heavy make-up. She was more of a girl, really, probably no more than in her early twenties, Lyla decided. The stranger walked slowly towards the car and Lyla's gaze wandered over the low-cut black vest that stretched across full breasts, the tight black leggings and dizzyingly high red stilettos.

Conscious of the scrutiny, the girl clasped her bag tightly against her body and stared back defiantly. Lyla's eyes dropped first. She knew who this was. She had no idea of her name, where she lived or what she did, but she knew – had always known – that one day, she would find herself face to face with one of Kwesi's indiscretions.

As if that knowledge had prepared her for this moment, Lyla shifted the car into gear. Solomon threw his hands in the air in disgust and reluctantly opened the gates, stepping back as she inched the car into the compound. In her rear-view mirror, she could see the girl following her inside and pushing Solomon aside when he attempted to hustle her back behind the gates.

Lyla sighed and reached for her handbag and the bulging briefcase full of employee files before stepping out of the car and locking the door. She kept her movements deliberately slow in the faint hope the girl would lose patience and leave. But, instead, she marched up to Lyla, her gait unsteady as her high heels navigated the fine gravel, and stuck her chin in the air, her heavily outlined eyes flashing aggression and trepidation in equal parts.

Lyla said nothing, silently marvelling that although she was standing almost toe to toe with her husband's mistress, she felt only a slight curiosity about this girl/woman. She certainly hadn't invited her here, so whatever this person had to say, she would have to do so unprompted.

The message seemed to have been received as the girl finally stated flatly, 'You know who I am.'

She sounded even younger than she looked, and Lyla felt a quiver of revulsion at the thought of her husband pursuing this – this *child*! As if infuriated by the spasm of pity Lyla couldn't hide, the girl's face hardened.

'Why are you not surprised?'

The fleeting sympathy Lyla had experienced vanished, and she suddenly felt bone-numbingly weary. She had work to do, and more importantly she had no interest in spending any time with this girl. This was Kwesi's world, not hers. Without uttering a word, and painfully conscious of Solomon wringing his hands in agitation, Lyla moved towards her front door. She had barely taken three steps when the girl reached out and grasped her arm with a hand that was small, but strong enough to force Lyla to turn back.

'Do you think you can just walk away and ignore me?' she spat out furiously. 'You know who I am, don't you? You *know* I'm Kwesi's girlfriend?'

Lyla looked down at the hand gripping her and absently noted the long red fingernails. How obvious, she thought dismissively, I'd have hoped my husband would have gone for a bit more class. She shook off the hand and raised a cool eyebrow. 'If you're looking for Kwesi, he's not at home.'

'I know. It's you I wanted to see.'

Lyla laughed, a harsh bark that sat awkwardly in the tense silence. 'You want to see *me*? Why? Has Kwesi dumped you? That's usually why girls like you would come here.'

The girl flinched as the import of the words hit home. Lyla narrowed her eyes, suddenly enjoying the chance to inflict a little pain of her own.

'Oh, do you really think you're the only one he fools around with?' She laughed again and advanced a step, feeling a momentary flash of reward as the girl instinctively retreated.

'Well, my dear – what's your name?'

'Nadia', the girl muttered, clutching her bag across her body as if defending herself from an impending attack.

'*Nadia.*' Lyla lingered over the word for a moment and then said slowly, her words savage in their deliberateness, 'Well, *Nadia*, hear me well. You are only one of many foolish girls who believe every word that Kwesi tells you and who buy the idea that he's crazy about you. So, let me tell you something. If you seriously think Kwesi is prepared to give up all *this*,' – she flung a careless hand in the direction of the stately white house behind her – 'for a life with *you*, then you are deluding yourself.'

'*You're lying!*' Nadia shouted angrily, jabbing a scarlet-tipped finger at Lyla. 'Kwesi loves me – you're the one who won't face the truth!'

Solomon dropped his head into his hands with a loud groan, but Lyla simply laughed. 'He *loves* you. Is that what he told you?'

Nadia gave a sullen nod and Lyla studied her curiously, her expression akin to a scientist contemplating a test result.

'So, why is he still living here with me?'

Nadia tightened her lips and tossed back her hair. 'He's going to leave you. He promised to marry me, and I believe him.'

Solomon shook his head in anguish and moved to the far end of the compound, clearly unable to take any more.

Lyla shifted the weight of the heavy briefcase she had still not set down. 'Then you're a fool. Kwesi's already married – and believe me, you are not the one who will change that.'

Lyla breathed in deeply, inhaling the heady fragrance from the luxurious beds of flowers blending into the night air. She began to walk away and then turned back, her voice weary, 'Go home, Nadia. There's nothing for you here.'

Suddenly desperate to get inside her house and escape the unwanted intrusion, Lyla marched towards her front door, her purposeful strides making it clear that the discussion was over. But she had taken only a few steps when Nadia called out.

'I can't go home!'

Keep walking, Lyla – don't stop! But there was something about the sound of Nadia's voice that halted Lyla in her tracks. An underlying desperation that somehow managed to pierce the shell of indifferent fatalism that had formed around her the moment she spotted the girl at her gate.

As if encouraged by the fact that Lyla had stopped, Nadia repeated, 'I can't go home. I *have* to see Kwesi.'

Lyla closed her eyes and inhaled sharply. Then she turned around, holding her body firm against the blow she instinctively knew was coming. Nadia came a step closer, her vivid blue eyeshadow shimmering in the porch light.

'I'm *pregnant!*'

* * *

The ice cubes clinked against each other as Nadia took another long sip before setting down her drink on the glass-topped table beside her. She put a hand over her mouth and emitted a quiet burp, and then glanced across warily to where Lyla sat, clearly not sure what to make of her. Which was understandable, Lyla thought, as the only words she'd uttered since Nadia's announcement had been *'You'd better come in'*, followed by *'Have a seat'* and *'I'll get you a drink'*.

'Why do girls like you do this?' Lyla watched Nadia flinch; the unexpected question surprising her as much as the girl. 'You knew Kwesi was married, so why did you get involved with him?'

Nadia traced a squiggly pattern on the frosted glass with the tip of her nail, and then she pulled her finger away and shrugged.

'Did you ever stop to think about his wife – or his family?' Lyla persisted.

'Why are you asking me that? Shouldn't you be asking your husband if *he* was thinking about you?' Nadia glared at Lyla with stormy, kohl-lined eyes.

Lyla nodded thoughtfully. 'So, what do you want?'

'What – what do you mean?'

'I mean, what *exactly* do you want? You said you came here to see me, so what did you want to happen when you decided to come to my home this evening to tell me you are carrying my husband's child?'

For the first time since Lyla had met her, Nadia looked uncomfortable. She shifted restlessly in the spacious armchair and kept her eyes fixed on the polished wooden flooring. After a few moments, she raised her head and looked directly at Lyla.

'I want what Kwesi promised me. I want a house in Kanda, and I want him to take care of me and our child.' She set her jaw stubbornly as if waiting for Lyla to contradict her.

Although she had asked the question, Lyla's heart contracted as she listened to Nadia's words. It would be easy enough to blame the girl in front of her but didn't she, of all people, know how easy it was to succumb to the seductive power of easy promises and lose every ounce of common sense? Until, of course, it was too late to turn back and change your actions – or their consequences. Brutally slamming the lid on her own memories, Lyla forced herself back into the present.

'And what does Kwesi want?'

Nadia bit her lip and dropped her eyes again. Lyla watched the different expressions flitting across the girl's features and was convinced that her initial instincts were correct.

Resignation settled on Nadia's face and she reached for her glass and drained the juice. 'Okay, so you were right – he *has* been avoiding me,' she conceded before adding defiantly, 'but I know that's only because he thinks you won't let him go. Once he knows about the baby, he'll realise he doesn't have to stay here any more and—'

'And what?' Lyla probed, sounding almost clinical.

What the hell is wrong with me? It suddenly struck her that she was sitting in her living room calmly conversing with a strange, aggressive girl who was not only laying claim to her husband, but also was carrying the child that she, Lyla, had struggled so hard and endured so much humiliation to conceive. Why wasn't she screaming at her, attacking her, slapping her – doing what she had no doubt Maku would have done had she been in this situation? How on earth could she sit here having a civilised chat as if this defiant intruder in front of her was a welcome and invited guest? Did she love Kwesi so little – or hate him so much – that she couldn't summon up an ounce of real passion or emotion to protest what was happening, Lyla marvelled? Or had Nadia's bombshell acted like an injection of anaesthesia into her veins and numbed her against any feeling? Nadia's incredulous expression suggested that the girl was wondering the same thing. Oddly, though, Lyla *was* now curious. Who was this girl? Suddenly, she wanted to know everything, to understand how Nadia had met her husband and why she stubbornly believed that Kwesi was ready to change his life for her when she had clearly become dispensable?

Nadia tossed back the water from the melting cubes and sucked on the last slivers of ice. Then she set the glass down carefully and scrutinised Lyla in turn.

'You are not what I expected, you know,' she pronounced a few moments later.

'And what was that?' Lyla sounded almost amused.

Nadia shrugged. 'Kwesi always said that you are a very tough woman. I had to fight with the security man at the main gate before he let me come inside the estate alone, and when I told your watchman I was here to talk to you, he kept shouting, "*I beg, you have to go before madam dey come house!*" I thought he meant that you would beat me, but now I rather think that it was you he was trying to protect.'

'Why – do I look as if I need protecting?'

Nadia gave a short, humourless laugh. 'You see, you are even mocking me instead of being angry.' She sat bolt upright and stared at Lyla with piercing eyes. 'Why *aren't* you angry? Do you not love him? Don't you care about Kwesi and me?'

Lyla stared at her thoughtfully. 'Tell me about… Kwesi and you. Where did you meet?'

Nadia shook her head, clearly deciding Lyla had lost her mind. But when it became obvious Lyla was expecting an answer, Nadia sighed and slumped back into the chair.

'He saw me first. I'd walked past him in the lobby when I went into a hotel shop to buy a magazine. He waited for me to leave the shop and then stopped me and told me I was very beautiful and introduced himself. I don't normally waste my time with men who approach me like that, but he was so handsome that when he offered to buy me a drink…'

She tailed off and her face softened, a tiny smile crossing her lips as if telling the story had transported her back to that first encounter. One drink had turned into several, and Kwesi had punched his number into her mobile, suggesting she call him if she was interested in meeting again. Already wildly attracted to him, she had waited all of three hours before making the call. The next day, they met for a lunch which turned out to be the first of many. Nadia described their subsequent meetings in hotels, the money he'd given her to buy supplies for her salon, the gifts of clothes and jewellery, and even the trip to Cape Coast where they'd spent most of the weekend in bed.

It felt surreal to hear her husband's proclivities described by another woman in such a clinical fashion, and Nadia spared no details. Despite everything Lyla had suspected about her husband, listening to the persuasive battle Kwesi had waged to seduce Nadia and hearing in such stark terms just how *predatory* he could be, made Lyla feel physically sick. Not only for the silly young woman in front of her, but also for herself and the stupid, *stupid* fool she, too, had once been.

The sound of the front door slamming caused them both to freeze. Nadia's eyes widened, and suddenly she looked terrified. In an instant, all her earlier bravado seemed to desert her, and she shrank into the expensive leather chair looking as if she wanted nothing more than to disappear.

Once again Lyla felt an unexpected pang of compassion. This frightened girl was no woman. Nadia might be unsophisticated and poorly educated, but she was still someone's child. And now, she was going to have a child of her own.

'Solomon says we have a visitor,' Kwesi announced from the hallway, his footsteps sounding closer as he approached the room. 'Is Theresa here?'

'We're in the living room,' Lyla called out.

As her husband strolled in, the broad smile that never failed to charm twisted almost comically when his eyes came to rest on the silent figure dressed in black and sitting in his favourite armchair.

Kwesi

Driving up to his house, Kwesi drummed his fingers on the steering wheel impatiently while Solomon fumbled with the gates. Raising his hand in a cursory greeting, Kwesi steered the powerful car into the compound and parked alongside Lyla's Audi. He hummed cheerfully under his breath as he sat for a moment weighing the pros and cons of asking out Jessie, the new Marketing Officer with the pretty dimples and seductive smile. He normally maintained a strict policy against dating his staff members, but damn it, the girl was *sexy*.

As he thought about the phone call he'd received just before leaving the office, Kwesi couldn't help the grin that spread across his face. Jessie's query could have been handled easily by her line manager and it had clearly been a ploy to get his attention. He had to admire her audacity, though – he certainly wouldn't have had the guts to phone his General Manager when he was a new joiner.

Thinking about guts brought Nadia to mind, and he mentally patted himself on the back for finding the courage to get rid of her. Even her extraordinary bedroom skills hadn't been enough to counter her constant nagging and the increasing demands on his wallet. How could she possibly have imagined he would buy her a house and a new life? He shrugged away the memory of his promises to do just that; after all, any man being ministered to in the way only Nadia knew how was permitted to say things without having them held against him afterwards. He was just thankful that the initial avalanche of texts and bitter, threatening voice messages after he'd stopped taking her calls had ceased, and that she'd finally taken the hint. She's probably moved on to another sucker by now, he thought, and then frowned, not entirely gratified by the idea that he could be so quickly replaced.

'Please, sir.' Solomon approached him, looking apprehensive.

Feeling slightly irritated at the thought of Nadia in someone else's bed, Kwesi bounded out of the car, locked the door and started towards the house.

'Sir, please.'

'Yes, Solomon, what is it?'

Almost running to keep up with his boss's long strides, Solomon stammered, 'Please, sir, you dey get visitor. Madam dey inside and—'

Kwesi suppressed a groan. Was Theresa here *again*? That would be the third time in less than a week. Didn't the woman like eating in her own house?

'Okay, thanks.' Abruptly cutting off the halting words the security man was trying to get out, Kwesi waved Solomon away and pushed open the front door, shutting it firmly behind him.

'Solomon says we have a visitor,' he announced from the hall, dropping his briefcase on the table and heading towards the living room. 'Is Theresa here?'

'We're in the living room,' Lyla called out.

Instantly switching into charm mode, Kwesi arranged his smile and rubbed his hands together as he strolled into the room. His gaze fell on a figure dressed in black sitting in his favourite armchair and, as their eyes met, Kwesi stopped dead in his tracks. Somewhere in his consciousness, he could feel his grin freeze and he stared in stunned disbelief at the girl, his stomach churning violently and turning his insides into liquid as he willed his legs not to collapse beneath him.

'What the *hell* are you doing here?' The words emerged in an outraged whisper before he could help himself.

Nadia, her hands clasped between her thighs, seemed to have shrunk into the spacious armchair. But, as if spurred on by the horror on his face, she sprang to her feet with eyes blazing scornfully.

'I warned you that you couldn't just throw me away like some – some used toilet paper, didn't I?'

Lyla! Suddenly aware that his wife was sitting on the sofa observing him in silence, Kwesi quickly tried to gather himself. He turned to her with a chuckle that even to his own ears sounded forced.

'Lyla, I don't know what this girl has been telling you, but you need to understand that she is a liar. I fired her from the store a few weeks ago for stealing and she threatened to make my life hell—'

He broke off as Nadia gasped aloud and took a step back, her eyes wide with disbelief. '*Kwesi!* Are you serious? Can you hear what you are saying? Me – *Nadia* – a thief? And when did I ever work in your store when I have my own beauty salon? What lies are you telling your wife?'

As if she hadn't spoken, Kwesi's eyes remained fixed on Lyla. 'You can't possibly believe anything happened between me and this girl? I mean, *look* at her!'

With a howl of outrage, Nadia hurled herself at him and Kwesi was forced to hold her wrists to prevent her from raking her nails down his face.

As if shaken out of her reverie, Lyla raised a hand and shouted, '*Stop!*'

They froze. Kwesi's hands were still clamped around the girl's wrists as Lyla stood up from the sofa and advanced towards them. He released his grip on Nadia and watched nervously as his wife slowly and purposefully walked right up to him.

'Stop,' she repeated coolly. 'Kwesi, just stop it. Stop lying, stop insulting her, stop treating me like a fool. We all know she's telling the truth, so leave her alone.'

Kwesi looked from Nadia's face, contorted with hurt and fury, to Lyla's, and he swallowed the words bubbling in his throat. Lyla didn't appear as furious as he had feared and maybe it wouldn't be too hard to talk her round. Pushing away the unwelcome question of why his wife wasn't livid about having his transgressions thrown in her face, Kwesi focused on his predicament and moved swiftly from attack to defence.

Releasing a deep sigh to indicate how wretched he was feeling, he gazed deeply into Lyla's eyes with an earnest expression. 'I'm so sorry – you don't deserve this. I've messed up, but I swear it's not what she says.'

He shook his head, his look now one of abject sorrow. 'Yes, we flirted, and I'll admit that we've kissed a couple of times, but honestly that's all that happened. I swear!'

Nadia gave a bitter laugh and raised her chin in defiance. 'Eh, Kwesi, is that how you use people? We didn't just kiss, and you know it. Aren't you the same one who said you couldn't get enough of my body and that the things I do to you drive you crazy, huh? Is that what you call *flirting*?'

Ignoring Nadia's shrill voice reverberating around his elegant living room – *God, the woman sounds like a twelve-year-old child! What the hell did I ever see in her?* – Kwesi kept his eyes on Lyla, alarmed by her eerily calm expression.

'Lyla, please don't listen to her. She's only angry because I didn't want to take things any further with her. That's why she's here trying to cause trouble. I promise you that I've never given her any reason to think what happened was going anywhere.'

Nadia gasped in fury. '*You never*—? *O*h, Kwesi, you are unbelievable! I was such a fool to listen to you and all your stories about your wife being barren and unable to give you a child, and how you were going to buy us a new house so we could have a big family together...'

Nadia tailed off and turned to Lyla, shamefaced. 'I'm sorry. I don't mean to hurt you, but that's what he told me.'

She rounded on Kwesi again, but this time her voice was husky with raw emotion. 'Why did you come after me, Kwesi? Look at your wife – she's *beautiful!* Why did you tell me all those things and make me want you?'

Kwesi flinched, but then quickly recovered himself. This was no time to let Nadia get to him; he had to save his marriage.

'Lyla, I love you,' he said gently, taking his wife's hands in his and desperately willing her to listen to him and believe his words. 'You *know* you're the only woman for me. I can be a fool sometimes, and I overstepped the mark with this girl, but I swear it didn't mean a damned thing.'

With that, Nadia howled and launched herself on him again in an uncontrolled frenzy, slapping furiously at his head with her bare hands. In a frantic attempt to protect his face from her ferociously sharp nails, Kwesi pushed her aside roughly, causing the girl to stagger backwards. Her pencil thin heel slipped against the polished floorboards and she lost her balance, screamed and then fell, landing heavily in a tangled heap. She whimpered piteously from where she lay sprawled against the armchair, her long hair extensions flung back to expose the heavy make-up smeared across her face like a drunken clown.

With a loud exclamation, Lyla rushed over to help Nadia, gently hoisting her up into the chair before turning to face a shocked Kwesi. Lyla's passively cool demeanour had vanished and her face was contorted with rage as she glared at him with her fists clenched, looking ready to attack him if he took a step in Nadia's direction.

Trembling with rage, she screamed, 'Leave her alone, you *bastard!* She's *pregnant!*'

AUGUST

MARRIAGE IS THE PERFECT INSTITUTION

Theresa

Theresa heaved herself up with an audible groan and stood still for a moment to regain her balance. It felt like half her time these days was spent either going to or leaving the little washroom by her home office, and she winced as another kick landed just above what used to be her waist. *Christ!* Wasn't it enough that this little creature had turned her world upside down without throwing in the constant kicking?

Dear God, when will this end? she muttered under her breath. Her slim hips ached constantly with the weight of the nearly full-term baby, her ankles were perpetually puffy, she waddled rather than walked, and had started to leak involuntarily if she laughed too hard. Not that laughing was a frequent occurrence these days, she thought bleakly.

'*It is what it is*', as Mama would say. Although, thankfully, Mama was currently in no position to say very much. Two days before setting off for Ghana to support her daughter through her first experience of childbirth, the indomitable Clementyne Curtis had slipped on the kitchen floor and broken her foot, making any travel impossible, according to her doctor, for at least eight weeks. Once she'd been assured that her mother was in no danger, Theresa had felt mostly relief at having been spared the role of referee between her domineering mother and increasingly difficult husband.

She lingered at the washbasin, lathering and rinsing her hands over and over as she pondered the state of her marriage. *For richer, for poorer, for better and for worse –* weren't those the vows they had taken? Well, they were certainly living through the 'for worse' part now. And had it not been for Margaret's expertise and help to build TB Communications, they might also have been experiencing the 'for poorer' part. Foreign exchange rates had been shaky for months, and Tyler had yet to generate any off-plan sales on the luxury apartments under construction in the redeveloped Sycamore House. Worse still, rumours were circulating about a new tax that was intended to dampen the country's rapidly rising property prices and make housing more affordable to local people, but which would inevitably make the sector much less attractive to investors. But, of course, she had heard none of this directly from Tyler.

Theresa grimaced and rinsed her hands a final time before reaching over to pluck the soft peach towel from its holder. What passed for communication between her and Tyler had deteriorated so badly that they scarcely spoke to each other. Indeed, silence was often the safest bet as any exchange of words almost invariably led to an argument. It wasn't always Tyler's fault, Theresa acknowledged with a sigh, recalling her bitter response that morning to his polite enquiry about the baby.

'If you're so keen to know how the baby's doing, how about forcing yourself to come with me to my doctor's appointment for a change?'

Predictably, this had drawn an angry riposte. 'If you bothered to tell me when you set up these appointments,

I could plan my schedule to come along. It might surprise you to learn that you're not the only one who's busy!'

Theresa examined her face in the mirror and frowned at the deep shadows under her eyes. Whoever said babies didn't give you sleepless nights until they were born didn't know what they were talking about. Although the nights were cooler, she insisted on making use of the air conditioner to counter the hot surges that constantly assailed her. Even with the bed to herself, she was so heavy that it was difficult to get comfortable. Tyler had moved into one of the spare bedrooms without any discussion, and Theresa had studiously refused to give him the satisfaction of commenting. She hated sleeping without his comforting presence beside her and oddly, given how irritating it could be, she even missed his gentle snoring. But what she certainly didn't miss was Tyler stumbling in at all hours of the night, or the pungent aroma of beer and spicy meats from Jake's Joint that drifted off the clothes he would toss carelessly in a heap on the bedroom floor before climbing into bed and falling into a dead sleep, while she lay wide awake burning silently with anger.

Any hope, after her conversation with Lyla, that saving her marriage was within Theresa's control had vanished one morning three months earlier. The morning when she'd stood in the open doorway of the guest room staring at an empty bed whose undisturbed covers proved that, this time, her husband had not returned home. From that day, when she had been far too angry and upset to give any credence to Tyler's stumbling explanation as to how a drink with Jeff had resulted in a night's absence, Theresa had lived on an emotional roller coaster. The memories of her past short-lived romantic relationships and the fears she'd convinced herself that marrying Tyler had buried, all resurfaced with a vengeance. Riddled with the chronic insecurities which had been the legacy of her parents' relentless feuding, she'd found herself swinging between bouts of optimism that she and Tyler could resuscitate their ailing marriage, and resentment that she even had to try. And, through it all, the unvoiced fear persisted that even Tyler, the one man who had always strived to understand and calm her anxieties, would one day stop trying.

With another sigh, Theresa dragged her mind away from her painful thoughts. She wet a finger and ran it across her eyebrows to restore some semblance of shape. Their fast-growing list of clients had taken precedence over manicures, pedicures and facials, and her regular beauty routines had fallen by the wayside along with her figure. She inhaled sharply as another kick landed, and quickly smoothed down her hair. Joseph was waiting in the car and if she didn't leave soon, the heavy city traffic would make her late for her doctor's appointment.

* * *

'Everything looks excellent, Mrs Brew, and Baby is sitting exactly where we want!' Dr Owusu beamed at her from across his desk, looking so pleased that Theresa wondered if he was about to announce an award to Baby for good behaviour.

Although both the ceiling fan and the upright fan behind his desk were whirring briskly, the room was stifling, and Theresa couldn't wait to get out of the stuffy surgery.

Back in the car, she immediately instructed Joseph to switch on the air conditioner for the drive home. Despite this being the coolest season, it was still the tropics, and the combination of pregnancy, heat and humidity far exceeded her level of tolerance. She debated ringing Tyler to report Dr Owusu's comments but, remembering their earlier argument and his hurtful words, she pushed the phone back into her bag. He obviously didn't care enough to cancel his meetings to come with her so why bother, she decided, rejecting any possibility that she was being unfair, and leaning back against the leather seat to give free rein to her resentment. After rehashing the morning's bitter exchange a few times, the resentment turned to self-pity and an intense feeling of loneliness.

She suddenly felt a desperate need to talk to someone who would take her side and comfort her. Lyla and Maku were both at work and she impulsively leaned forward to tap her driver's shoulder. 'Joseph! I've changed my mind – let's go to East Legon. I need to see Mrs Blankson.'

Having spent so many summers with Lyla's family when she was growing up, Auntie Pat, Lyla's mother, had become like a second mother to Theresa, and one she found far easier to get along with than her own. Indeed, Theresa had never quite understood how warm, open-hearted Auntie Pat had grown so close to her hard-nosed, judgemental mother during the short period when Clementyne had reluctantly tried living in Ghana. The two women had maintained their friendship, even after Clementyne's insistence that her family return to London, and it was this unlikely bond that had allowed Theresa to continue visiting Ghana after her father's abrupt decision to return alone to his homeland. Throughout Theresa's adolescence, the carefree summers with the Blanksons had been her lifeline, with the long holidays bringing a welcome respite from Clementyne's suffocating attention and the trauma of being held hostage to the bitter exchanges between her warring parents. Having spent so much time with the Blanksons over the years, Theresa had always felt like an integral part of Lyla's family, and she made a point of seeing Auntie Pat, now a widow, whenever she could.

Joseph turned through a narrow entrance into a pebbled driveway and the sight of the whitewashed, two-storey house with large ceramic planters flanking the front doorsteps brought an immediate smile to Theresa's face. This big old house with all its nooks and crannies felt as familiar as her own home in London. Her smile widened at the memory of their end of holiday ritual, when she, Lyla and Maku would solemnly measure themselves against the heavy wardrobe still to be found in the guest bedroom, the marks that had tracked their growth gouged along its length.

Joseph came around to help Theresa out of the car just as a slim, dark-skinned woman opened the front door. Wearing a loose, off-the-shoulder cotton dress, Auntie Pat looked exactly as Theresa imagined Lyla would in another thirty years. With the same high cheekbones, clear skin and twinkling eyes, only her short, naturally styled hair now liberally sprinkled with grey, set the mother apart from her daughter.

Auntie Pat also gave the same warm lengthy hugs as Lyla, and she flung her arms exuberantly around Theresa who returned the embrace, closing her eyes to better soak in the loving tenderness.

'What a wonderful surprise! I heard the gate and I was *so* happy to see your car – isn't it lucky I stayed at home today to finish my accounts,' Auntie Pat burbled animatedly, clasping Theresa's hand in her own as they walked into the house.

'Let's get you a cool drink and then you can tell me how everything went at the doctor's – it *was* today you had the appointment, wasn't it?'

Auntie Pat continued her stream of chatter as she led Theresa into a huge kitchen and extracted a bottle of iced water from a large, old-fashioned fridge. Filling a tall glass, she led the way into a light and spacious living room dominated by an imposing suite of leather furniture. She set the drink on a side table and turned to help Theresa lower herself into an oversized armchair.

'It's so nice to take the weight off my feet.' Theresa exhaled with relief as she settled back against the soft cushions. 'This chair is ridiculously comfortable.'

'I must admit I thought the suite was a bit much when Kwesi and Lyla gave it to me for Christmas,' Auntie Pat said with a rueful smile. 'But the leather is so soft that I fall asleep if I sit down for too long.'

She perched on the edge of the sofa and leaned forward eagerly. 'Enough about the furniture – what did the doctor say? Is there any change in your due date?'

Theresa shook her head with laughter at her aunt's unbridled excitement. 'Nope, but the good news is that the baby's in the right position. Dr Owusu says first babies often come early, so I should be ready for it to make an appearance at any time.'

'*It?*' Auntie Pat teased. Much to everyone's amusement,

Theresa had been adamant from the start that she didn't want to know the baby's gender.

'Yes, *it*!' Theresa grinned. 'The doctor keeps calling it Baby, so he doesn't give the game away.'

Auntie Pat kicked off her sandals and settled back on the couch, tucking her legs beneath her. It's hard to believe she's over sixty, Theresa marvelled, as she took in the older woman's beautiful unlined face, and the graceful shoulders exposed by the dropped neckline of her dress. It irritated Lyla immensely that men flocked to her mother like bees to the proverbial honeypot, and once when she and Theresa had stopped by for a visit, she had been infuriated to find a distinguished older gentleman looking very much at home in her mother's living room. On the way home, when Theresa had laughingly suggested that one of Auntie Pat's suitors might persuade her to marry again, Lyla had greeted the suggestion with horror.

'Oh, come on, Lyla! Auntie Pat is gorgeous *and* she's still young. You've got your own life so you can't get upset if she decides to share hers with another man. I know you adored Uncle Sidney, but your mum must feel lonely sometimes.'

But Lyla had categorically rejected the possibility that any other man would be good enough for her mother. 'I'm not saying it can't happen. I'm just hoping it doesn't, because no one can match Daddy, and I don't want some clown trying to take advantage of her.'

Auntie Pat had never been a woman any man could take advantage of, Theresa thought wryly, as the conversation bounced between her aunt's rapidly expanding clothing business, now up to three boutiques across the city, and arrangements for Baby Brew's imminent arrival. Theresa recited the list of things in place for the delivery, ticking each item off on her fingers. The puffiness brought on by water retention had forced her to remove her rings, and her eyes lingered on the bare third finger, a symbol of the yawning distance between her and her husband.

'And how does Tyler feel about becoming a father soon?' Auntie Pat asked curiously.

Wondering if her aunt had a gift for reading minds, Theresa hesitated and tried to choose her words carefully. Despite having come here for sympathy, she felt unexpectedly guilty about slagging Tyler off, so instead she shrugged and tried to sound non-committal.

'It's hard to tell. He's been really busy at the site, so he's not at home very much and – and my work has become so intense that—' To her horror, her voice cracked, and she buried her face in her hands feeling absolutely mortified.

'*Theresa!*' Auntie Pat's features clouded with concern and she moved quickly to crouch by Theresa's chair and rub her back gently.

'What's going on? You really shouldn't be upsetting yourself, my dear. This is the time to take extra special care of you and your baby. It sounds to me like you're doing far too much just when you should be cutting down your workload. You must let Margaret and the girl you hired take over for now.'

Theresa sniffed and wiped her eyes with the back of her hand, annoyed at herself for losing control. She raised her head to meet Auntie Pat's probing stare and once again felt the sting of her husband's parting words that morning. Why *should* she protect Tyler? His behaviour was unacceptable and she shouldn't have to let people think he was the good guy when he was neglecting her. He didn't deserve it.

'It isn't just the business, Auntie Pat, although you're right that it's probably time for me to ease up a bit. It's Tyler. He – he—' she struggled to put her frustration into words. There were so many things her husband was doing to upset her that it was hard to know where to start. 'It's been going on for a while, but I've been too embarrassed to say anything to you. Tyler's changed since we've been here. He's hardly ever at home these days – if he's not at the project site, then he's off drinking with the boys. I honestly think he spends more time with Nortey than he does with me.'

Auntie Pat raised an incredulous eyebrow and Theresa nodded insistently. 'Yes, Nortey, of all people. Tyler could hardly bring himself to say more than hello to him before, and now he's his new best friend!'

Auntie Pat returned to the sofa, looking perplexed. 'But where is all this coming from? I knew Tyler had some problems getting his project off the ground, but I thought since that British man had loaned him the funds that—'

'That everything was fine,' Theresa finished off. 'Well, it isn't. He's always stressed, and he snaps at me constantly. We're either fighting or ignoring each other and then this morning, he refused to come to the doctor with me.'

She gulped as the tears coursed down her face, and impatiently pulled out a crumpled tissue from her bag to wipe them away. 'Coming to Ghana was supposed to be an adventure, not a nightmare! I don't know how it happened but being here has made my husband mean and selfish and at this rate, baby or no baby, I don't think we'll last!'

'*Theresa!* Don't say such a thing!' Auntie Pat exclaimed in distress. 'Tyler loves you very much. Listen, you are both dealing with so many changes in such a short time that it's not surprising there's some tension between you. But you have to talk to him and tell him how you're feeling.'

Theresa blew her nose vigorously and cleared her throat, trying hard not to sound pathetic. 'I've tried, but then he accuses me of attacking him and being totally unsupportive just because *my* business is going well. I'm really scared he can't handle me being successful and that—'

She broke off abruptly and took a deep breath before continuing shakily. 'Honestly, Auntie Pat, it's one argument after another these days. It's just as well Mama isn't coming to visit.'

Allowing Theresa a few moments to compose herself, Auntie Pat changed tack. 'And how is Clementyne? I spoke to her just after her accident, but I haven't had a chance to catch up with her since.'

'She sounds fine, although from the way she goes on you'd think it was her back she'd broken and not just a foot,' Theresa said acidly, and then sighed. 'I shouldn't be mean. She's normally so active that she's finding it tough not being able to get around. Still, I'm glad she's not coming just yet – I couldn't deal with her constant criticism and the way she snipes at Tyler all the time. We've got enough problems without adding more fuel to the fire.'

'It's a shame that Clementyne hasn't given Tyler a chance,' Auntie Pat said mildly. 'He's such a lovely man.'

'Mama says he's weak, just like my father.' Theresa

looked her aunt squarely in the eye. 'Did *you* think my dad was a weak man?'

'Clementyne is such a strong woman that most men probably seem weak by comparison,' was the wry response.

Theresa fell silent for a moment. 'So, if he wasn't weak, why did he abandon me?' she said. The bitterness still buried inside her seeped through the words and brought a shocked expression on to Auntie Pat's face.

'Is that what you think happened with your father?'

Theresa shrugged defiantly. 'He made the decision to leave, didn't he? If he really loved me, he could have stayed and stood up to Mama.'

'And is that what scares you about Tyler – that he's weak?'

'Yes,' Theresa said baldly. 'We're going to have a baby any minute now and I always thought I could rely on him, but I'm not so sure any more. What if he can't cope with *this*' – she gestured towards her rounded belly – 'or make a success of his business? What if he decides he's had enough and wants to go back to England? I don't ever want to think about him the way Mama thinks of my father.'

'Tyler isn't your father, and you aren't Clementyne,' Auntie Pat said sternly. 'You two are facing very different challenges, but you'll need to work together if you want your relationship to succeed. You've invested time and love into building a life together, so don't give up on that investment. Marriage can be wonderful, but it isn't easy – it takes a huge amount of compromise and sacrifice on both sides.'

Auntie Pat hesitated and then looked directly at Theresa. 'My darling Tee, you have every right to expect your husband's support, but be honest with yourself. Are you giving him the support *he* needs or are you expecting more from him than you yourself are prepared to offer? You're his wife, and in the same way you're asking yourself if you can rely on him, perhaps he's also wondering the same about you.'

For a moment the two women sat in silence, and then Auntie Pat continued, her usually cheerful voice sounding surprisingly stern, 'Marriage is supposed to be for better and for worse, isn't it? Shouldn't Tyler be able to count on your support if he's struggling?'

Theresa's lips tightened, and she raised her chin. 'It's not that I don't support him. It's—'

'Just that he isn't the same confident and successful man you married, and you're afraid of how you'll feel if he fails and is no longer your Prince Charming? You've always said that you and Tyler are equal partners in your marriage, so prove it. If he's in trouble, maybe it's time you rode to *his* rescue.'

Open-mouthed, Theresa stared at her aunt. Where was the no questions asked, take-my-side-support she had come in search of? Instead of the soothing reassurance of her rightness that she craved, she was being told in no uncertain terms that she had to share the blame for the state of her marriage. Auntie Pat, just like Lyla, was making Tyler's behaviour *her* responsibility. Why did *no one* seem to appreciate what she was going through? She winced as the baby, who had been resting quietly, suddenly aimed a kick high into her tummy.

Theresa took a deep, slow breath and Auntie Pat gave a sympathetic grin. 'You see? That little thing in there is your priority now. And I wouldn't worry about your mother. So long as you and Tyler are united, she won't be able to come between you. It was always going to be difficult for Clementyne to let you go; she'd grown accustomed to being the centre of your world, and she would never have thought any man good enough for you. Believe me, I get the same attitude from my daughter – look how ridiculous Lyla gets any time a man so much as takes me out to dinner.'

Theresa rubbed her tummy gently as she tried to absorb Auntie Pat's words. Their baby was due almost any day and, one way or another, she and Tyler had to sort themselves out. They simply couldn't carry on like this.

'Tee, have you seen Lyla recently?' Absorbed in her thoughts, the anxious note in Auntie Pat's voice caused Theresa to look up in surprise.

'We spoke on the phone yesterday, but I haven't actually seen her for – gosh, probably a couple of weeks now. I'm finding it harder to get out and about these days. Why?'

'Has she mentioned anything about – well, is there something that's troubling her? She came over at the weekend and she looked terribly thin, even for her. She insisted nothing's wrong, but to tell you the truth I'm really quite worried about her.'

Theresa felt a flush of guilt rise to her cheeks. Lyla *had* seemed quieter in recent weeks, but she'd been so caught up in her own dramas with Tyler that she hadn't probed. *Oh God! What if*—? She gnawed anxiously at her lip. How could she have been so self-absorbed? 'She didn't say anything out of the ordinary when you spoke, did she? You – you don't think maybe she's had another—?'

'Miscarriage?' Auntie Pat shrugged in bemusement. 'She hasn't said so, but it might explain things. I lost two pregnancies before Lyla was born, and each time the experience left me in pieces. It would be just like Lyla not to tell me, so I wouldn't worry about her.' She furrowed her brow thoughtfully. 'Maybe I should call Kwesi?'

'I can't imagine *he* would be much help,' Theresa said tartly, just managing to stop herself from blurting out the truth about Kwesi's constant philandering to her unsuspecting aunt. 'No, I'll go over and see her myself.'

For an instant, her mind flashed back to the conversation she'd had with Lyla a few months earlier when Lyla had confessed to having a crush on a man at her church. *What was his name? Ah yes, Reuben!* Was Lyla's changed demeanour something to do with this man, Theresa wondered?

Looking a little puzzled but nevertheless satisfied that a plan of action was in place, Auntie Pat clucked impatiently. 'I'm so sorry, I haven't even offered you something to eat! Are you hungry? I bought some very ripe plantain yesterday – should I ask Agnes to fry some for you?'

Theresa laughed at the persuasive tone and slyly raised eyebrow. Hands down, Auntie Pat's favourite hobby was feeding people.

'Thanks, but no. Can you believe fried plantain gives me heartburn these days?'

Amused, Auntie Pat shook her head. 'When I think of the fights I had to referee between you and Lyla any time fried plantain was on the menu; for all her feistiness, poor Maku didn't get a look in.'

With a sudden clap of excitement, Auntie Pat jumped

to her feet. 'Speaking of my niece, I *must* show you this beautiful dress I got for Abra before you go. She'll look so sweet in it.'

'Well then, let's hope Maku agrees; you know how proud she is. She'd rather stick to those horrible cheap imports she buys from the market than take anything she thinks is charity.'

Auntie Pat sucked her teeth forcefully as she headed for the door. 'If I want to give my own niece's daughter a dress, I will give her a dress! Maku can be so stubborn. We all need help sometimes, but that young woman always feels she has something to prove.'

* * *

Later that evening, overcome with exhaustion and fed up of waiting up for Tyler, Theresa slipped into her roomiest nightshirt and was padding towards her bed to call Lyla and invite her over for dinner the following day, when Tyler rang. Mindful of Auntie Pat's advice, she took a deep breath and pressed the button.

'Theresa?' Tyler sounded so curt that she immediately bristled.

'Yes. Where are you?'

'At the office – and I'm going to have to stay late tonight. There's a German company that's interested in buying one of the units for their country manager and they want to see a proposal first thing tomorrow.'

She twisted a strand of hair around her finger and tried to keep her tone neutral. 'Can't you work on it at home?'

'There's a lot of information I need to access here, so it's easier for me to do it in the office. I'd better get on with it – I just wanted to let you know.'

'Okay,' she conceded reluctantly. 'By the way, the doctor said—'

The rest of her sentence fell into empty space as the click on the line confirmed he'd hung up. She stared at her handset in angry disbelief, fuming at the peremptory end to the call. Her good intentions vanished as anger and resentment frothed up again, drowning the brief spark of desire for reconciliation. *Bloody cheek!* He hadn't even had the courtesy to ask about the doctor's appointment! *Thanks for showing so much interest in your child, Tyler!*

Boiling with rage, she stormed off to bed, all thoughts of calling Lyla forgotten.

Tyler

With a weary sigh, Tyler clicked off his computer and leaned back against the padded leather chair he had once thought so stylish, and which he no longer gave a crap about. Any more than he cared about the other overpriced office accessories his overpriced stylist had insisted were essential to his image of a successful businessman. Feeling utterly spent after a long and gruelling day, the only image in Tyler's mind was that of his large, comfortable bed, although even that was now denied him thanks to his own impulsive decision to change his sleeping arrangements. With the guest suite having been commandeered by Theresa for the baby's nursery, he was confined to the rarely occupied small bedroom and its lumpy single bed which barely accommodated his six-feet frame.

After several hours in front of the screen, his eyes were burning. He rubbed them hard and blearily surveyed his deserted office. Patience had reluctantly left for home several hours earlier, looking as guilty as a mother hen abandoning her chick. Even in the face of all the evidence that the luxury apartments he was developing would be a hard sell, his assistant's enthusiasm for the business showed no sign of flagging. If his own wife had exhibited a fraction of the faith Patience showed in him, they might be in a better place, Tyler thought sadly.

Theresa. How the hell had it come to this? He corrected

himself – how had he *let* it come to this? The hot words and cold silences, the quarrel trembling on the lips of every exchange. For years, he had understood Theresa and her demons better than she had herself – and accepted them. But the woman with whom he shared a house today could have been a stranger. Like any couple, they'd had their ups and downs over the years, but the very idea that he and Theresa would be unable to have a decent conversation – or indeed, any kind of conversation these days – was simply laughable. Not that he felt like laughing. Far from it.

Theresa had sounded so bored and uninterested when he'd phoned to tell her he was working late that he couldn't wait to end the call. He'd finally finished the proposal for the Germans, but the thought of going home brought a spasm to his stomach not unlike acid burn. The idea of another evening of accusatory glares reminding him of yet more things he'd done wrong was simply unbearable. He didn't need Theresa to tell him he was a failure – the list of unsold units pinned to the office noticeboard was a daily rebuke that he was way behind target on his projected revenues. To make matters worse, he was running out of time to pitch to Jeff for the second tranche of the loan. He had procrastinated for as long as he could, but he needed to access the money now to complete the units, and none of his tentative approaches to his contacts had led to alternative sources for additional capital. He was under no illusion that persuading Jeff would be easy – the loan from JP Investments had been expressly structured as two instalments so, as Jeff had bluntly phrased it, 'if you fuck up the first lot we lend you, we don't have to throw good money after bad!'

Too agitated to sit still, Tyler stood up to pace around the office, slightly unnerved by the eerie silence broken only by the low hum of the air conditioner. Given the current state of sales, Jeff was likely to see any further investment as bad money and cut Tyler loose. Without the funds to finish the interiors to a standard high enough to attract his high-end target market, Tyler could kiss goodbye to his business, as well as the personal savings he and Theresa had sunk into it.

Unable to bear the confines of his office any longer, he grabbed his jacket from the chrome-plated coat stand, apparently another essential accoutrement of a successful business, and headed for the door, switching off the lights and air conditioning on his way. It was bewildering how the electricity bills increased steadily each month despite the periodic power cuts and the extensive reliance of the businesses occupying the building on the fuel-powered generator, the costs of which were also charged out to them. With a mental shrug he left the office: that was Ghana for you. Yet another reality to which he had to adapt.

Tyler backed his car out of its designated space in the empty parking lot and turned on to the main road. It was just after 10 o'clock. Theresa would probably still be up to greet him with either a sullen silence or heated accusations, depending on her mood, and Tyler promptly turned his car in the opposite direction to home. His wife's use of sarcasm over recent months was strongly reminiscent of her mother's, although she hadn't quite reached the level of Clementyne, the ultimate mistress of the cutting comment. Thinking about Clementyne brought on another stomach-clenching turn. Although he took no pleasure in her injury, he was mind-numbingly grateful that his unbeloved mother-in-law had cancelled her visit – observing the current state of his marriage would have given her acid tongue free rein to exploit the distance between him and Theresa.

He raised the volume of the melodious jazz flowing through the car speakers and kept driving with no destination in mind, wanting only to clear his mind and let the sweet sounds of the saxophone soothe his frazzled nerves. His thoughts drifted to the impending new arrival and his heart lifted at the thought that his son – despite Theresa's insistence on not knowing the baby's gender, he was convinced it was a boy – would soon be a real, live person he could hold in his arms and love. Any time now, the Bump would become a breathing, crying bundle of demands on his time, sleep and wallet, and he couldn't wait. Whether it was spurred by the plaintive notes of the music flooding the car, the accumulated grind and stress of his lonely days, or the emotional exhaustion that reached deep into his soul, Tyler felt an unexpected prickling behind his eyes. *God, what a nightmare!* This was so not how he wanted his kid to enter the world. Instead of being by Theresa's side loving her, laughing with her and planning their lives together, he was driving on a semi-deserted highway to nowhere, his once unfailing optimism now a distant memory.

The car behind him flashed its lights impatiently, and Tyler blinked and increased his speed. He was close to Jake's Joint, but he felt no inclination to make his way there. It had been weeks since he had set foot in Jake's, having finally tired of the same crowd of underachievers congregating around beer-soaked tables to reinforce each other's delusions of imminent success. Knowing he would never find a credible investor among the die-hard drinkers there, he had quietly detached himself from the alcohol-fuelled sessions, preferring instead to spend time at the local jazz bar to avoid going home.

Spotting a flickering neon sign a few metres ahead, Tyler slowed and turned into a wide entrance leading up to a building set back discreetly from the main highway. Informally known as The Embassy, the hotel was a popular venue for the foreign diplomats assigned to the consular offices and embassies in the heart of the city. Unusually for a Thursday night the car park was only half-full, and Tyler steered his car into a vacant space. Perhaps a quiet drink at the bar would help him compose his thoughts and figure out a way to save his rapidly disintegrating marriage. He desperately missed his wife and best friend and with their first child expected any day, he simply had to fix things between him and Tee.

Tyler walked through the marble-tiled lobby of the luxurious hotel and into the bar. He perched on a high stool and ordered a drink, sipping the ice-cold lager the waiter placed in front of him with appreciation. The combination of soft lights and the classical music playing quietly in the background already made him feel better, and he surveyed his surroundings curiously. The lounge was styled like a traditional English gentlemen's club, with padded maroon leather armchairs arranged around low tables and booths along the wall for more private conversations. As Tyler glanced around, his eyes met those of an elegantly dressed blonde woman seated a few stools away. Holding his gaze, she swung one slim leg over the other, drawing his eyes down the length of her shapely limbs to the nude stilettos on her feet. The invitation was unmistakable, but Tyler's blank expression offered no reciprocity.

Irritated rather than flattered by the less than subtle come-on, he was keen to escape before she embarrassed them both by approaching him. Picking up his glass, he made his way over to a booth towards the back of the bar, positioning himself at the edge to make clear his desire to be left alone. The lounge was deserted, other than two men in quiet conversation in the booth behind his, and when the woman at the bar made no attempt to follow him, Tyler relaxed and was soon lost in his thoughts.

'... beaten to a *pulp*, I tell you!'

The urgent tone of the man sitting behind him roused Tyler from his contemplation on the best strategy for wooing his wife, and he listened idly as the other man peppered the first with questions.

'So, what's going to happen to him?'

After a pause followed by the thump of glass on wood, the first man replied. 'We persuaded the family to hush things up in the end, but the High Commissioner had to deal with it pronto before the press got hold of the story. He was in a bloody foul mood after meeting the Minister yesterday – from what I heard, the man gave the HC a real earbashing about Brits who come here and behave like this is still their colony.'

Tyler took a long swallow of his beer, mildly amused by the man's aggrieved tone. He examined the remains in his glass and wondered if he should order another. He hadn't eaten since the lunch Patience had ordered in for him just after midday, and two beers on an empty stomach might be pushing it. His attention was suddenly caught by a word in the conversation taking place behind him that wiped away any interest in another drink.

'But what in God's name was Parnell thinking?' The incredulity in the questioner's voice came through loud and clear, and Tyler's heart quickened. *Parnell*?

'I doubt he *was* thinking, old chap,' was the grim response. 'Seems the girl's a university student. Nineteen, according to the Police Commissioner. Looks like he took her out drinking, and then tried it on. When she turned him down, the idiot completely lost the plot! Left her face a mangled, bloody mess, apparently.'

Tyler's heart thumped violently in his chest. *Please God, surely they're not talking about Jeff?* But even as the plea ran through his mind, he knew as certainly as if he'd spoken to the police himself that it was *his* Parnell the two men were picking apart. His investor, the only remaining saviour of his business, and now apparently the perpetrator of a brutal assault. Thinking back to the evening months ago when he'd witnessed an openly lecherous Jeff plying young students with alcohol, it was all too easy to imagine him guilty of a drunken assault.

Tyler pressed against the wood panelling dividing the two booths and strained to listen in on the conversation. Before long, he received the answers to his unspoken questions.

'Parnell paid the girl's family twenty thousand dollars to stop them prosecuting, and we managed to get him out on a flight last night. If it wasn't for the fact any bad publicity at this point could bugger up the trade deal we've been working on with the government, the HC would cheerfully have thrown that arrogant, entitled bastard into jail himself,' the man groused. 'Parnell's been a royal pain in the arse since he came to this country – acts like his money can buy anything!'

Noting with bitterness that Jeff's money certainly appeared to have bought him his freedom, Tyler tossed back the dregs of his beer and slid out of the booth, his face set grimly at the thought of the innocent battered teenager. As the other implications of Jeff having been spirited out of the country sank in, anger and panic warred for supremacy in Tyler's mind. He strode back to his car and slipped behind the wheel, the beer he had drunk earlier now feeling sour in his stomach. Why the hell hadn't he approached Jeff earlier for the second instalment of the loan instead of prevaricating? If he'd listened to Patience's gentle suggestion and gone to Jeff sooner, he might have secured the money he desperately needed before the stupid, reckless *imbecile* decided to go on a drunken rampage and find himself summarily deported.

Tyler took a deep breath to steady his jangling nerves. This was a disaster, and he had no idea how he was going to break the news to his wife. But then, what if he'd got the wrong end of the stick – it was always possible that the men in the bar had been talking about another Parnell? He'd call Jeff right now and prove it was all a horrible misunderstanding. He fumbled in his jacket pocket for his phone and scrolled down to Jeff's number in his list of contacts, his heart thumping as he punched the number with a trembling finger and pressed the phone against his ear.

There was no mistaking the long, high-pitched tone of a phone line no longer in operation, and Tyler dropped his head onto the steering wheel in despair.

Maku

With a final wave to Joanna, Maku clutched the heavy textbook to her full bosom and bit her tongue hard to stop herself from squealing with excitement. She left the college grounds and hurried to the main road to catch her bus, wishing she was Isabelle and could skip along without caring what anyone thought. After all, how often did she get anything for free, never mind an expensive textbook on accounting which their tutor had described as the most comprehensive resource on the subject. Having asked only to borrow it for an evening to take some notes, the last thing Maku expected was that her classmate would casually gift it to her.

Joanna had been more concerned with examining her freshly manicured nails, and breezily dismissed her classmate's stammered thanks. 'My sister, you can keep it. I've told you – as soon as this semester is over, I'm applying to beauty school. I don't even know why I'm wasting my time doing this course, Maku. I've told my father a hundred times that I'm hopeless at accounting, but does he listen? He didn't even ask me before he went and paid for these stupid classes!'

When Maku tentatively asked why Joanna was still attending the college, the reply had been blunt. 'The school refused to give him back his money, so he's making me take the course. Because he's paid, I come here every week. And when I fail, he can't talk.'

Classes at the private college had ended earlier than usual today and Maku stood on the dusty verge running alongside the highway, ready to hail one of the overcrowded minivans that would take her close to home. Beaming with excitement, she ran her fingers reverently over the book, marvelling at its pristine glossy cover and the crisp pages that showed no signs of having been turned. With a final lingering stroke, she slipped it into the blue dinosaur-embossed backpack she had borrowed from Samuel. Maku was usually far too proud to accept gifts unless it was Christmas time, immediately bristling if she even suspected she was an object of pity. But this present was different. Although the company scholarship included a contribution towards purchasing books, it didn't stretch to cover the cost of an imported textbook like this one.

For a moment, Maku wondered what it would be like to be Joanna and to have enough money to give away expensive items on a whim as well as a rich father who paid for unwanted courses. Between Maku and her family's monthly outgoings, and with Isabelle still weighing on their finances, life was far from easy. Comparing the casually rich like Joanna to her own daily struggles to make ends meet brought a bitter taste of jealousy that temporarily overrode the sweetness of gratitude. Willing herself not to allow her euphoria to turn into despondency, Maku slung the heavy backpack over her shoulder. Wasn't the whole point of taking this course to gain a qualification so that one day she would also have the luxury of wasting money, she asked herself? That said, no matter how rich she grew, she would never be foolish enough to pay a school for the privilege of simply showing up.

Her thoughts were interrupted by strident hooting from a sporty red Mazda that came to a screeching halt inches away from where she stood. Joanna poked her head out of the window and shouted impatiently, '*Maku!* Didn't you hear me calling you? Quick, *get in!*'

Maku hesitated, but Joanna was blocking traffic on the single lane highway and the impatient drivers behind her were already leaning on their horns to signal their displeasure. She hurried round to the passenger side and scrambled in, barely slamming the door shut before Joanna shot off, pausing only to lean out and hurl a curse at the driver behind her. Sliding up her window with a smirk, she glanced across at Maku.

'My sister, what were you thinking about so hard you couldn't hear me?'

For once tongue-tied, Maku squirmed uncomfortably on the low-sprung leather seat. Her views on Joanna's wastefulness were certainly not for sharing, and she swiftly changed the subject.

'Your car is very nice.' Her eyes wandered over the fancy dashboard and immaculate cream interior with envious admiration. Clearly Joanna didn't have children, Maku decided, mentally comparing the sports car's butter-soft leather seats to the ripped and stained upholstery of Nortey's old Toyota.

Joanna grunted distractedly. She was clearly bent on jumping the traffic lights at the busy crossroads and she hurtled through the amber light, only just making it through before the traffic surged across. Maku inhaled sharply and instinctively tightened her grip on Samuel's rucksack. Joanna appeared to have paid as little heed to her driving instructor as she did to their accounting lecturer, Maku thought grimly. The car might be beautiful, but she didn't want it for a coffin. Fortunately for Maku's nerves, the long tailback at the roundabout forced Joanna to slow to a crawl.

'Where do you live? I can take you home if you like,' she offered cheerfully.

It was hard not to respond to the girl's infectious smile and, despite the adrenalin coursing through her from Joanna's hair-raising driving, Maku couldn't help but grin. Her initial assumption when Joanna had first approached her that the girl would be as snobbish as her expensive clothes suggested, had evaporated at Joanna's whispered plea for a simple explanation of what the lecturer had meant by double-entry bookkeeping. The query had turned out to be Joanna's final attempt to keep up with the technicalities of the course, and she had focused her efforts thereafter on catching the eye of the only single man in their class.

Joanna raised an enquiring eyebrow and Maku tried to gather her thoughts. There was no way she was going to ask Joanna to drive her home and risk shredding her swanky tyres on Maku's rough, stony road. They were almost at the Ring Road and Maku had a sudden brainwave.

'Can you drop me in Labone? I've been promising for ages to visit my friend.'

With a shrug, Joanna sped down the dual carriageway, braking sharply at the roundabout before veering off towards the quiet residential area. Maku breathed a silent sigh of relief when they finally roared up to the gates of Theresa's house – she had never imagined she would prefer the sweaty occupants of a *tro-tro* to riding in a luxury car. She waved goodbye to Joanna and shook her head in wonder as she watched the red car screech off, stirring up a cloud of dust in its wake. Muttering a quiet prayer for her classmate to reach home safely, Maku pressed hard on the bell and waited for the gate to be opened.

Dressed in a loose cotton caftan that failed to disguise the enormous bulge of her stomach, Theresa slowly waddled out of her home office to where Maku stood in the hallway, failing miserably to stifle a grin.

Theresa scowled. 'Don't you dare laugh at me – do you have any idea how fat and uncomfortable I feel? I can't even see my feet any more. I'm so exhausted all the time and if this baby doesn't come soon, I swear I'll lose my mind!'

Maku sniggered unrepentantly. 'I've had three children, Tee. I know exactly what it's like. Anyway, I'm not laughing at you, I'm laughing *with* you.'

Theresa giggled at the familiar phrase they had used as children to torment each other to the point of tears. She gave Maku a quick hug and led the way into the living room, lowering herself laboriously onto the sofa.

'Sit, sit!' She gestured impatiently towards one of the armchairs and Maku dropped Samuel's rucksack on the floor and sank into the chair, glad to be out of the afternoon heat and free to enjoy the cool elegance of her friend's beautiful house. Theresa rang the small bell on the side table and within moments Auntie Sisi ambled in, her rubber flip-flops slapping rhythmically against the floor. Maku winced at the housekeeper's lilac leggings, which clashed mercilessly with her orange T-shirt and neon-pink sandals, and trying to control her twitching lips, she quickly asked for a Coke.

As soon as the woman had left the room, Maku exploded into laughter, and Theresa responded with a resigned smile.

'I know. The colours are horrendous, but there's no point trying to get her to smarten up. I'm just grateful she cooks well and does a good job of taking care of the house. As Mama always says, you can't have everything.'

Maku had never met Theresa's mother but, from everything she'd heard, not only was the woman formidable, but she also dispensed advice even more freely than the opinionated Chief of Biorkor.

'I'm sorry I didn't come over last week like I promised,' Maku confessed with a guilty smile. 'I managed to get some overtime at work, and between the kids and the coursework we had to submit—'

Theresa shushed her quickly. 'Maku, it's okay. I know it's not easy getting around without a car, and since it was me and Lyla who pushed you to do the course in the first place, I can't blame you for not having enough time to trek across town to visit.'

They both fell silent as Auntie Sisi shuffled back in carrying a tray, and they waited for her to deposit their drinks and leave the room.

'Cheers!' Theresa raised a glass of water.

Maku followed suit before taking a long sip of her chilled, sweet drink. 'Did I interrupt your work? I got a lift from a friend on my course, and I wanted to come and see you instead of ringing with more excuses.'

Theresa smiled. 'No, it's fine. We're all done for the day.'

Maku took another sip of her drink and settled back into the comfort of her chair. Her eyes circled the familiar spacious room with its elegant curtains, expensive furnishings and stylish knick-knacks, and fell on a large framed photo of a veiled Theresa smiling confidently at Tyler as a cloud of white confetti swirled around them. The professionally shot close-up of a couple so clearly in love was a world away from the snapshot Adoley had grudgingly taken of Maku and Nortey standing stiffly side by side at their traditional marriage ceremony, and which was the only picture she had to mark the occasion. Staring at this image of a stunning bride with her adoring groom, the envy that never really went away bubbled up inside Maku with such force that she could almost taste the bile.

Theresa had been following her friend's gaze and shrugged. 'Things aren't always as they appear, you know.'

Maku wrenched her eyes away from the laughing couple in the silver frame to examine Theresa's flawless skin and doll-like features, still beautiful despite the weight gain from her pregnancy. She shook her head, baffled by the woman's attitude. Why do some people never appreciate what they have? How did Theresa manage to have all of *this*, and yet still claim to be unhappy? What more did she want? Maku forced herself to swallow the bile rising in her throat.

'You mean you and Tyler are still having problems?'

Theresa shrugged and looked down at her hands and Maku's eyes lasered on to the bare finger. The diamonds that normally twinkled brightly, tormenting Maku by their very presence, were nowhere to be seen and she sighed heavily and wondered whether ditching her rings was some kind of symbolic protest. As much as she loved Theresa, Maku was sick and tired of having to commiserate with someone fortunate enough to have her own business, live in a huge house with servants and – yes – a husband who had bothered to marry her properly. What did it matter if Tyler no longer acted like some fairytale Prince Charming? This wasn't London, it was *Ghana*! If your man went out drinking with his friends, you put up with it because that's what the men here did. If Tyler had started beating Theresa up or refusing to pay his share of expenses, *then* she would have something to complain about. As it was, Maku struggled to find any sympathy or even to understand what Theresa's problem was.

'I bet you're thinking I'm just a spoilt princess with totally unrealistic expectations about marriage,' Theresa said pointedly.

As that pretty much summed up her thoughts, Maku held her tongue. Better just let the princess say what was on her mind and, hopefully, it would give Maku enough time to come up with something diplomatic to say.

Undeterred by Maku's silence, Theresa jabbed a finger into the sofa to underline her point. 'What you don't seem to understand is that my relationship with Tyler was very different before we moved here. If Tyler had always been this – this distant and unsupportive, I wouldn't like it – not that I would have married him in the first place, mind you – but at least it would be consistent. But, I *promise* you, before we came to Ghana, he was always—'

'Yeah, I know, considerate, caring, always spending time with you, blah, blah, blah!' Maku cut in impatiently, unable to endure another litany of complaints about a man whose only mistake, as far as she could see, was choosing to adore a woman who was never satisfied. Maku's irritation at Theresa's constant stream of grievances, already sharpened by jealousy at her friend's lifestyle, was fast eroding the restraints on her self-control.

She leaned forward and cocked her head to one side curiously. 'Theresa, you've been complaining about your husband for months now. If he's so bad, why don't you just do yourself a favour and leave him?'

Theresa gasped, clearly not expecting the sharp retort, and her hand moved to rest on her swollen belly as if to protect her child from Maku's hostility. The instinctive gesture made Maku feel guilty, but not quite enough to hold back.

'I understand that you're going through a lot,' – *although if you think you've got it bad, you should try having my life!* – 'but I have to be honest. If you really think that *Tyler*, of all people, is a bad husband, you don't have a clue!'

Clearly stung, Theresa glared at her. 'I'm not saying he's a *bad* husband. Not exactly, anyway. What I'm trying to get across to you—'

Quick as a flash, Maku jumped on her words. 'Just because I didn't go to university like you doesn't mean that I don't understand English! If you're complaining about the man, then you're saying he's a bad husband – otherwise, what are you talking about?'

'No one said anything about you not going to university! Why do you always have to make everything about you and your – your total inferiority complex?' Theresa said heatedly.

Maku gasped in outrage. '*I* make everything about me? Don't make me laugh.' Unmoved by Theresa's dumbfounded expression, Maku's words spilled out, propelled by a long-suppressed resentment that stunned her as much as it obviously seemed to shock Theresa. 'You are the most self-absorbed person *ever!* Right from when we were kids, it's *always* been all about you. If you weren't whining to Lyla and everyone about your mother being too overprotective, you were crying for attention because you wanted your daddy.'

Having started, Maku couldn't control the torrent of angry words spilling from wounds she had long thought healed, or at least safely plastered over.

Maku's withering reference to her father snapped Theresa out of her stupor. 'Shut the hell up about my dad, Maku! You have *no* idea what it's like to lose a parent.'

Her eyes flashed pure fury, and for a moment Maku hesitated. Then, spurred on by a fresh burst of frustration, she yelled back, 'At least your father *died!* Mine is still alive, but do you think he ever asks of me? Or that my own mother even bothers to come to Accra to see her grandchildren? Auntie Pat has been more of a mother to me than mine ever was.'

'Well, that isn't my fault, is it?'

Maku's chest heaved with the pressure of forcing back the sourness she could feel pushing up inside her chest. It was almost as if she was standing outside of herself watching the scene and hearing the bitter accusations she was flinging at Theresa. Deep down, she knew it wasn't Tee she was angry with – but if she didn't blame her, then who could she blame?

Her agitation was too great to remain seated and Maku jumped to her feet. 'Isn't it? Who else here is complaining because they have a husband who goes out to work every day and helps to pay for all *this*?' She gestured around the living room with a sweep of her hand. 'Do you know how many women would be happy to take your handsome husband off your hands? But then, since you say he's never at home, maybe someone already has?'

'That's an ugly thing to say!' Theresa snapped.

Without Lyla to take on the role of peacemaker, the two women glared at each other, neither prepared to concede anything but an unwavering conviction of their own rightness.

Maku planted her hands on her broad hips. 'You think your life is hard? Don't make me laugh! You wouldn't last five minutes in Biorkor.' She glanced around at the expensive ornaments on the gleaming chrome and glass shelving and her nose crinkled into a contemptuous sneer. 'You have everything any woman would want, and you are still not grateful.'

Goaded into retaliation, Theresa said scornfully, 'Oh really? *I'm* the whiny one? Don't you think we get fed up of you constantly bitching because you didn't have a wedding? I mean, who the *hell* cares about a crappy wedding? It lasts one day and then it's all over! If I were you, I'd be less bothered about walking down the aisle and more concerned about the kind of man you married.'

Maku froze. 'What exactly do you mean by that?' she demanded. 'No, don't bother, I get it. You're such a *snob*! You think I don't see how you look down your nose at Nortey? But, you know what? Unlike you, *I* don't need a man to be perfect before he's good enough for me. All I need is someone who's good enough for me to believe in. Just because Nortey's not a rich businessman like Tyler doesn't make him any less of a man.'

'If he's such a man, why is it always you that supports your family while he spends half his salary at Jake's Joint?' Theresa shrugged, sounding triumphant at piercing Maku's self-righteous shield. 'And how come you're secretly paying another woman to cook because Nortey's too bloody spoilt to eat food that's been in the freezer? And, if he's so great, why is he forcing you to look after his sister's kid instead of standing up to her?'

Theresa laughed, but there was no humour in her face. Only the look of someone who had been deeply hurt and was desperate to strike back. 'Or maybe it's not just Nortey. Maybe *you're* the one enabling him to be so selfish. And why would you do that? Is looking after Isabelle your way of sucking up to his family, hmm? Are you hoping that they'll finally think you're good enough for him?'

She ignored Maku's indignant wail and pressed on relentlessly. 'Is that it, Maku? Do you honestly believe that if you're nice to Isabelle, they'll give you their blessing and arrange a lovely white wedding for you? Good luck with that idea! Oh, and if Nortey isn't *weak*,' she added viciously, 'why does he *allow* his family to dictate whether or not you get to have a church wedding?'

The last barb hit home with the force of a jackhammer. Stricken, Maku stared at Theresa, her lips unable to form a single word. With a suppressed sob, she snatched Samuel's rucksack from the floor. Looking appalled,

Theresa struggled to her feet. Not waiting to force her swollen feet into her sandals, she padded across the floor towards Maku, but before Theresa could stop her, Maku stormed out of the room.

Clutching the rucksack in one hand, Maku wrenched open the front door and slammed it shut behind her. Tears flooded her eyes as she marched towards the gate, her heavy footsteps angrily grinding the gravel into submission.

'Maku!' A brief glance over her shoulder revealed Theresa hopping in agitation on the top step, her bare feet clearly no match for the sharp stones on the pathway.

Undeterred, Maku pushed past Joseph who had been standing by the half-open gate, her tear-filled eyes barely registering his mouth open in O-shaped shock.

'*Maku – wait!* Please don't go. *I'm sorry!*'

She could hear Theresa calling her. But despite the audible anguish and fear in her friend's voice, Maku was too far gone to turn back.

Nortey

Nortey scribbled a lengthy comment below the 55% mark he'd awarded the student's essay and tossed the paper onto the pile. The plastic end of his red biro was ragged from the marks his teeth had inflicted as he powered through the stack of turgid essays on Applied Macroeconomics. Finally reaching the bottom of the pile, he scrawled a few words on the paper, dropped the biro into his desk drawer and pushed his chair back to reach for his briefcase. He had no intention of taking home any papers, but, should he be unlucky enough to run into Professor Ghartey, a briefcase would signal that he was taking his boss's caution seriously. Although after that fiasco last term with Tony Tagoe, the Prof was in no position to sack him.

It had been three months since Professor Ghartey had pounced on him just before his lecture, but the panic that had seized Nortey that afternoon was so fresh in his mind that it felt like three days. After the encounter, and convinced he was about to lose his job, Nortey had struggled to teach his class, instead mentally rehearsing his excuses and preparing to prostrate himself before his boss, if needed. If he had known that the Prof was going to *promote* him – being landed with additional classes was hardly a promotion, but it had sounded good when he explained it that way to Maku – instead of fire him, he could have saved himself the trouble.

When he'd walked into the old man's office, it had almost been worth the ninety minutes of agony to witness his boss's pained expression as he haltingly explained how Tony Tagoe's insistence his students purchase his self-published lecture guides if they wanted to pass his module had led one of them to file a complaint against the lecturer. The student's outraged parents had demanded action, forcing Professor Ghartey to suspend Tony pending further investigations. His boss had also been compelled to transfer Tony's course module on to Nortey's teaching schedule – along with a salary increase.

Nortey slipped his jacket from the back of his chair and grinned at the memory of his boss's discomfiture at having to reward Nortey for what he'd tartly labelled 'unacceptable tardiness'. But his smile faded as he recalled Professor Ghartey's parting shot.

'I would caution you not to take these current circumstances for granted, Mr Quarshie. If my investigation into Mr Tagoe's conduct necessitates that I relieve him of his employment, I will have to recruit a new lecturer into the faculty. Please don't give me cause to recruit *two* new lecturers. I hope I make myself clear?'

With a quick glance at his watch to confirm that it was after five-thirty – the Prof had made it clear that just because the university students were on holiday, it didn't mean the faculty could slack off – Nortey left his office, relieved to be out of his airless prison. He glanced around warily, but there was no sign of his boss and Nortey whistled merrily as he strolled to his car. He tossed his briefcase onto the back seat and had just opened the driver's door when he remembered Maku's instructions.

Retrieving the case, he lobbed it into the boot instead. It would be asking for trouble to leave valuables in full view of a supermarket car park.

Driving off, he stopped at a set of traffic lights and wondered once again what had upset his wife. Maku had been unusually quiet over the past week, failing to respond to his banter and burying her nose in her thick textbook whenever he asked what was wrong.

As he drove off, he debated calling Lyla to find out what Maku clearly didn't want to tell him. *Jesus! What if she was pregnant again!* Nortey swerved dangerously as the horrific thought crossed his mind. No, surely not! They were both so careful these days, knowing there was no way in hell they could afford another child. He concentrated on his driving and forced his breathing to return to normal. Maku would most definitely have told him if that was the problem. *Told* him? Knowing her, she'd have thrown something very heavy at him if he'd impregnated her again. Maybe it was just her hormones and he should take her word that there was nothing wrong. He sighed heavily at the puzzle that was the opposite sex. *Why the hell can't women just say what's on their minds?*

As he sped down the dual carriageway into the centre of town, Nortey mentally calculated how much he could afford to spend at Swanson's. He'd promised Samuel some of the American sweets advertised on TV on his next shopping trip for Isabelle, for despite his best efforts to convert his niece to the cheap, nutritious *koko* that his boys enjoyed for breakfast, Isabelle still insisted on cornflakes every morning. George's sporadic contributions in no way matched the cost of his daughter's upkeep and Nortey's complaints to his mother had fallen on deaf ears. George's strategy of giving his mother-in-law frequent gifts to keep her sweet had worked a treat, Nortey thought sourly as he turned off the roundabout into Osu.

Damn it! He slammed the brakes and pressed hard on his horn as a blind beggar walking alongside the busy road stumbled and almost fell into his path. He waited for the boy guiding the older man to pull him back to safety before moving forward to join the static line of traffic. He hated the congestion of Oxford Street with a passion and coming to this part of town drove him crazy. Everything from the cacophony of car horns disturbing his thinking to the persistent street hawkers knocking on his windows for attention, and then trying to sell him some useless piece of hardware, irritated him beyond measure. Even more annoying were the women who approached his open window with steel bowls loaded with pungent dried fish for sale or, even worse, freshly caught fish that reeked after hours in the hot sun. He honked in annoyance at a taxi driver who had cut in front without so much as a glance in his direction and narrowly missed scraping his bumper. *Bloody idiot!* Fuming, Nortey ignored the angry toots from the drivers in the other lane and swiftly executed a U-turn. He bumped his beaten-up old Toyota over the pavement and grunted with satisfaction as he manoeuvred his way through the narrow entrance into Swanson's car park.

Feeling rather more cheerful after finding a parking space in the busy lot, Nortey locked his car and sauntered into the store. The blast of frigid air as he walked in brought a welcome respite from the late afternoon's humidity, and he paused for a moment to enjoy the sensation of coolness against his skin before walking purposefully towards the back. Until Isabelle's arrival, he could have counted on the fingers of one hand the number of times he'd patronised Swanson's, and yet now he knew precisely where to find the items he needed. He winced at the sight of a new price label on the shelf displaying the cellophane-wrapped cereal boxes; cornflakes were clearly not exempt from the recent currency fluctuations. Unfortunately, the unexpected price hike also meant no treats for his boys. Nortey stared at the bright yellow sticker and chewed on his lip in frustration as he pictured the look of disappointment on Samuel's face when he returned empty-handed. Silently cursing himself for caving in to his sister's demands, he grabbed a box from the pile and turned back towards the checkout.

Lost in his gloomy thoughts about how to break the bad news to his son, it took Nortey a moment to register the familiar face walking towards him. It was the sound of the man's chuckle that snapped Nortey to attention and brought him to a standstill. While the sight of his dour brother-in-law with a smile on his face was noteworthy in itself, Nortey's immediate attention was focused on the attractive woman who had slipped a proprietary hand into the crook of George's elbow.

Although what happened next took less than thirty seconds, when Nortey later replayed it in his mind, it felt considerably longer. As the couple approached, George looked up and his eyes instantly locked on to Nortey's. Under different circumstances, watching his brother-in-law's laugh instantly freeze into a grimace would have been comical. As it was, humour was the last thing on Nortey's mind.

George's companion was oblivious to the silent drama, and she tugged on his arm to point out an item on the shelf, forcing George to turn his attention back to her and momentarily break eye contact with his brother-in-law. As though the brief interruption had restored his equilibrium, George picked up his pace and scooted past Nortey without so much as a nod of acknowledgement, almost dragging the woman along with him.

Stunned at the colossal rudeness of the man married to his sister and whose child currently lived under his roof, Nortey stood rooted to the spot. Then, fuming, he swung round and set off after the couple. Turning into the adjoining aisle, his gaze fell on to the full basket George was carrying, and Nortey's jaw fell open. *What the hell!* While he was depriving his own children of a handful of sweets so this man's daughter could have her luxuries, George was strolling around this overpriced supermarket buying fresh steak and wine for a woman who was most definitely not his wife!

Nortey charged forward, but after a couple of paces he came to an abrupt stop. Swallowing hard, he tried to calm the raging emotions threatening to overwhelm him. *Think, man, think!* This was a small town and making a scene here would only embarrass them both, not to mention Adoley. He was also painfully aware that George's standing with his mother was much higher than his own, and she wouldn't thank him for showing up her beloved son-in-law by upbraiding him in public. And yet George's contemptuous attitude *burned*! The way his brother-in-law had so blatantly dismissed him made it clear he saw Nortey as no threat whatsoever, and if Nortey didn't challenge him right now wouldn't he be giving George the green light to cheat on his sister?

Nortey stood in the aisle of Swanson's, torn between rescuing his dignity by confronting George or risking a major rift with his family, and slowly, like air seeping from a tired balloon, his sense of purpose faded.

Angry with George and furious at himself for backing down, he ducked his head and strode to the checkout. Pulling out the last few notes from his wallet, he threw them onto the counter and waited while the girl behind the till calmly counted the money and rang up the purchase. Almost snatching his change and the receipt from her fingers, he grabbed the brightly coloured box of cereal and stormed out of the store.

Driving out of the car park, Nortey's chest heaved with indignation as he relived the humiliation of his encounter with George. He burned with mortification at letting his brother-in-law summarily dismiss him as a man to contend with, and the affront to Nortey's pride only began to dull as he turned into the car park of Jake's Joint.

Lyla

'You can't be serious!' Lyla gasped.

She stared in disbelief at the diminutive figure standing before her, but Ma Abena stood her ground and returned the look with an implacable glare.

'What have I said that isn't serious? Isn't the child for my son? Then, it's only natural that it should live here with the father. Think about it – is it right that a grandchild of mine should grow up in *Nima*?' She spat the word out like a bitter seed.

Unable to stand the spiteful expression on her mother-in-law's face, Lyla turned away and moved closer to the open window. There was only a hint of breeze coming through into the living room, but even that felt better than the fetid air surrounding this venomous woman and her contemptible son. How had she allowed herself to be drawn into this family? *Dear God, do I really deserve this level of punishment?*

From the corner of her eye, Lyla could see Kwesi shifting uncomfortably and she folded her arms tightly to resist the overwhelming urge to slap him with the same ferocity that Nadia had displayed that fateful evening. *Was it three months already?* It felt like yesterday. She still grappled with understanding that the baby she had longed for was on the way. Only it wasn't her baby, it was Kwesi's. *Kwesi and Nadia's baby*. She rolled the names together in her mind, almost savouring the unfamiliar combination. He was *her* husband, but now he was forever linked to another woman by *their* child. A woman – or a girl, really – who was probably coping far better with her changed circumstances than Lyla, who still couldn't accept the reality of what had happened.

After Nadia had left their house that evening, Lyla had somehow managed to finish the notes for her staff appraisals and had even slept for all of three hours until the awful memories flooded her slumbering consciousness and banished further respite from the full truth of Kwesi's betrayal. But knowing what had happened didn't mean she had to accept it and the following morning, and every day thereafter, Lyla had stubbornly refused to acknowledge the situation, peremptorily cutting off Kwesi's attempts to discuss his pregnant mistress. She had emerged from her stoic silence only once, when Kwesi had offered to persuade Nadia to terminate the pregnancy, unleashing a savage torrent of abuse at him and threatening him with all manner of hell if he even *suggested* an abortion to Nadia.

In the ensuing weeks, she made only two changes to her daily routine: refusing to share a bed with Kwesi, and not cooking a single meal unless she herself was hungry and wanted to eat. The second decision had forced Kwesi to spend time in the kitchen because, for almost the first time in their marriage, he now came straight home from work – the irony of which was not lost on Lyla, who now wished him anywhere but in her house.

But what made things so much worse for Lyla was the isolation that came with keeping the truth from everyone around her. Whether through some twisted sense of loyalty to Kwesi or because telling people meant admitting her failure to keep her husband faithful or to perform the simple task of bearing his child which even Nadia had accomplished, Lyla simply couldn't bring herself to tell her mother or her friends. Secrets. At least *that's* something I'm good at, she would remind herself bitterly when the loneliness of her situation threatened to overwhelm her.

Lyla knew her mother was worried about her – their frequent phone calls often ended with the plea *'Tell me what's wrong, Lyla!'* But there was no way she could bring this shame of Kwesi's – and of hers – to the door of the woman she loved so dearly. Ma had been through so much after losing Daddy; Lyla simply couldn't do this to her. She longed to tell Theresa, who was clearly concerned by Lyla's continued weight loss, but her friend's heavy pregnancy had left her practically confined to the house, and she already had enough to deal with. Maku, who under normal circumstances would have shaken the truth out of Lyla, was so swamped with her studies and her children that she barely knew what time of day it was. Which was probably just as well, Lyla thought. Her fiercely protective cousin would have likely raced over to slap Kwesi and insult him to his face. All of which left God as her only support. And these days, even He didn't seem to be listening.

And if the past few months hadn't been hard enough, here was her insane mother-in-law making the bizarre suggestion that she, Lyla, take Nadia's baby – correction, *Nadia and Kwesi's baby* – into her own home and bring up the child together with Kwesi. Had the world gone mad or was Lyla the crazy one?

Clearly offended by Lyla's reaction to her suggestion, Ma Abena picked up her handbag to leave. The sudden movement broke into Lyla's chaotic thoughts and without a word she followed the older woman as she marched towards the front door, itching to shove her over the doorstep and out of her house. Making no attempt to see her off, Lyla stopped at the entrance while Kwesi walked his mother to her waiting taxi. But instead of climbing in, the older woman doubled back, pushing her son aside to march up to where Lyla stood leaning against the door frame.

'Whether you like it or not, I thank God that my son will have a child at last.' Ma Abena's eyes glittered with malice. 'Since you have not been able to do your duty and give him one, the least you can do is to welcome this child into its father's home and treat it as your own!'

Lyla held her gaze for a long moment, and then slowly and deliberately stepped back into the house and slammed the door in the woman's face. Shaking with rage, she raced up the stairs to her room and banged the door violently behind her. She muttered vile curses she had no idea she even knew as she stripped off her caftan and flung her wardrobe door open, tugging at a clothes hanger to drag out a pair of trousers. She pulled them on, grimacing at the waistband that sagged against her flat stomach, and snatched a plain white T-shirt from the heavy chest of drawers. Slipping on the top and a pair of flat pumps, she grabbed her handbag and car keys from her dressing table and flew back down the stairs.

Ignoring Kwesi's startled enquiry, she slammed out of the house and jumped into her car, intent only on getting as far away as possible from this disgusting man and his even more loathsome mother. With an effort, she resisted her immediate impulse to drive straight to her mother's house. Ma didn't need the upset of seeing her in this state. Similarly dismissing Theresa, who didn't need any more stress in her condition, Lyla fled to the only sanctuary she knew.

* * *

Half an hour spent kneeling was causing Lyla's legs to cramp. Assuring herself that God would listen – or not – just as well if she sat rather than knelt, she shifted up on to the wooden pew and bowed her head. It was late on a Saturday afternoon and with no services scheduled until later, the church was deserted. Asking God's forgiveness for breaking the fifth commandment to honour one's parents after the abuse she had viciously hurled at her mother-in-law had been relatively easy. Praying for strength not to break the sixth commandment by killing her husband had been somewhat harder. She still couldn't wrap her mind around what Kwesi had brought upon them or, more importantly, decide what she was prepared to do about it. Burying her head in the sand hadn't served her well for the past six years and it wasn't doing her any good now.

She stared at the altar, her eyes on the ornate crucifix hanging overhead. The tortured face of Jesus in torn robes and with bloodied feet felt like a silent rebuke: *You think you have it bad? Look what happened to me.* She dropped her gaze in shame. Having a cheating husband whose mistress was expecting his child was nothing compared to the suffering of the man up on that cross. How dare she complain about a situation that half the women in the country had probably confronted at some point? And yet, was it wrong to feel so wretched that there would be visible proof in a few short months that the vows she and Kwesi had taken before God had been decisively trampled upon? Just because other women tolerated and even welcomed the fruits of their husband's adultery, if Ma Abena was to be believed, did that mean she had to do the same? But then, what was the alternative? *Divorce?* Even thinking about the word made her shudder. Yet another failure to add to her impressive track record. Failure to marry the right man, failure to give him a child, failure to atone for—

'Sister Lyla?'

The deep voice broke into her mental self-flagellation and she froze. Of course, it was him! Despite her inner turmoil, Lyla almost smiled. With her past, why would God *not* want to punish her even further by allowing her to run into this man when she was in such a state?

She turned and watched him approach, his soft-soled sandals almost soundless against the terrazzo flooring inside the church. No wonder she hadn't heard him come in. She craned her neck to meet his eyes and forced a tight smile. Of all the days to flee her house in unflattering clothes and without a scrap of make-up, she thought wryly.

'Brother Reuben. What brings you here at this time?'

He nodded down at the pile of books in his arms. 'I promised Pastor Jeremiah I'd bring along some books for the children's library. I've been clearing up all afternoon and decided to do it today before I lost my nerve.'

She dropped her gaze on to the colourful books before her eyes returned to find his. Were these precious mementoes from his childhood? Puzzled by his words and the unusual melancholy in his voice, she blurted out, 'Why would you have a problem with giving away picture books?'

Reuben hesitated and then nodded towards the space next to her. She slid along the pew, allowing him to squeeze his big frame in beside her. He carefully placed the books on the seat and, as his arm bumped up against hers, she felt once again the instant zing of electricity between them. Ignoring the insistent voice in her head, her body refused to let her shuffle further along and break the contact. Since turning down his request to go for a drink, an invitation that had not been repeated, Lyla had exchanged only a few words with Reuben during choir practice. Yet something was clearly upsetting him and, putting aside her own troubles, she twisted round to face him.

'You look sad, Reuben,' she said softly.

His smile held no trace of humour, and he tugged gently at his soft, thick beard. 'I feel sad, Lyla, but it will be well. Isn't that what God promises us – that all will be well?'

Reuben's eyes were like deep brown wells of pain. Lyla had rarely seen him without a smile, and she felt a surge of compassion and wondered what could have caused such anguish.

'Do you want to talk about it?' she ventured, uncertain about intruding on his privacy.

He nodded. 'Yes, but not here. Wait for me while I put these in the back room.'

He stood up abruptly and picked up the pile of books, stepping out of the pew without waiting for an answer.

She didn't move a muscle and a couple of minutes later he was back.

'Come with me,' he said.

His tone was neither a question nor a command, leaving it up to her to agree. This time she didn't hesitate, standing up and reaching for the outstretched hand he offered. They walked down the aisle of the church in silence and out to the car park. When they reached his Range Rover, she made no comment when he opened the passenger door, taking his hand again as he helped her navigate the high step. Once she was safely inside, he shut the door with a decisive thump and walked around to slide behind the wheel.

Firmly quashing The Voice inside her head wailing in alarm, Lyla pulled the seat belt across her slender frame and stared straight ahead, seeing but not seeing the deep orange streaks radiating from the setting sun into the darkening sky.

Reuben steered the heavy vehicle out of the car park and on to the main road, only then breaking the silence.

'We can go to a coffee bar or I can take you to my house. You choose.' His flat tone gave no indication of his preference and she turned to study his profile. But other than a brief glance in her direction, he kept his eyes fixed on the road ahead.

She shrugged lightly, tired of pretending. 'Let's go to your house.'

He nodded but made no comment. Instead, he tapped on the steering wheel to turn on the radio, and a sweet chorus of gospel music flooded the car. Lyla smiled to herself and rested her head against the cushioned backrest. This was exactly the kind of music she would have expected Reuben to listen to: positive, uplifting and melodious. He hummed along to the music as they drove along the highway and, after a few minutes, she joined in.

Reuben smiled and reached across to briefly squeeze her hand and she relished the momentary feel of his fingers, missing its warm strength the instant he moved it away. *Why am I not feeling guilty?* Even as the words of praise filled her ears, Lyla had no difficulty in silencing the harsh Voice that never failed to remind her of her religious duty. Sitting in this car with Reuben and going wherever he was headed didn't feel wrong. Finally, she would learn the mystery behind this man who had intrigued her for so long. Because Reuben *was* a mystery. Although her social life had steadily shrunk to the occasional family festivity and spending time with Theresa and Maku, she'd still never come across Reuben outside church. The unwelcome whispers by well-meaning friends about Kwesi's extra-marital activities had made it awkward to attend the kind of parties where the gossips in her network might have shed some light on Reuben, while Christ the Redeemer was hardly the place to go digging into other church members' personal lives.

Almost twenty minutes later, Reuben turned into a driveway and tooted his horn and within seconds a burly guard appeared as if from nowhere. With an unsmiling salute, he opened the gate and stood back to let the car through. Lyla blinked hard as she took in the mansion at the end of the driveway. She had grown up in a big house, but this was something else. The glass-fronted house was beautiful in its simplicity. Its white walls had clean lines, and shallow white stone steps led up to a solid mahogany front door flanked by two miniature orange trees.

Stunned into silence by the sheer beauty of her surroundings, Lyla hopped off the passenger seat as soon as Reuben brought the car to a stop, and walked slowly up the steps on to a broad, sweeping verandah studded with graceful columns and filled with colourful plants in glazed ceramic pots. Reuben, following close behind, gave her a reassuring smile and then fumbled in his pocket for the keys, unlocking the door and standing back to let her through.

After a moment's hesitation, she crossed the threshold and her flat ballet pumps glided over smooth black and white floor tiles. The interior of the house was just as impressive as the exterior promised. White walls and a circular entrance hall, along with a curving staircase that led up to the next floor. In the hallway, silver framed African-themed art adorned the walls, the bright splashes of colour warming the stark whiteness. But the most striking feature was the light. The huge windows allowed in so much that it felt almost as if she was still outdoors.

'May I get you something to drink?'

Reuben had been watching her expression with a half-smile playing on his lips, and she flushed with embarrassment at being caught staring.

'Um, yes, please. Water will be fine,' she stammered.

'Come and take a seat,' he invited, opening a door and walking through into what was clearly a well-used living room with comfortable looking grey armchairs and a huge corner sofa with a large footstool. An impressive collection of vinyl records and CDs filled the shelving built into one wall, while a sleek chrome stereo deck took up the shelves on the adjoining wall. Reuben clearly enjoyed his music and art, she thought, as her gaze travelled around the collection of abstract paintings on the walls.

Reuben left the room while Lyla perched on the edge of the sofa and marvelled at the size of the mounted TV screen. He was back within a couple of minutes holding two small bottles of water and a crystal glass. Twisting open the top, he poured the contents of one of the bottles into the glass which he placed beside her, and then sat down in the armchair opposite.

He unscrewed the top and then raised the bottle in his hand with a brief smile. 'Welcome to my home, Lyla. It's good to have you here.'

She held her glass aloft for a moment and murmured something non-committal before taking a long swallow. The cool liquid ran down her throat, reminding her of how parched she was, and she took another sip. This was proving to be the strangest day ever. First a blazing row with Ma Abena, and now sitting here alone with Reuben in his luxury fortress. The house felt like a haven from the noise and bustle of the city only a few metres away from its impressive front door. If this was my house, Lyla thought dreamily, I don't think I'd ever feel the need to go out.

She watched Reuben pick up a small gadget, and seconds later the room was filled with the sound of classical music. She raised an eyebrow; okay, so this was a surprise. Studying her expression, Reuben burst into a rich chuckle of laughter, his first proper laugh since his sudden appearance at the church. She smiled back tentatively, suddenly feeling unaccountably shy. She had followed him willingly, but what did he want from *her*? She lacked the confidence of the old Lyla Blankson, and with her skinny frame and tired eyes, it was hard to believe that any man would find her attractive. Thinking of church brought Lyla back to her mission.

She put down her glass and sat forward, her eyes earnest. 'I think God wanted us to meet each other today and I want to understand why,' she said hesitantly. 'Reuben, I've always thought you have some inner sadness and it hurts me to see that.'

Reuben looked pensive and then set down his bottle of water.

'I also think God wanted us to meet today, but not because of my sadness. Lyla, I'll tell you whatever you want to know about me, but I want you to be equally honest. Can you do that?'

He was asking her to trust him. Lyla knew that, and she desperately wanted to. But she also knew if she told him the truth, he would turn away from her in disgust and that she couldn't bear. She opened her mouth intending to deflect and change the subject, and then closed it, experiencing once again the same sense of fatality as when she had stepped into his car.

'Que sera sera', as Auntie Clementyne would say. Whatever will be, will be, wasn't that right? She was so tired of pretending, of hurting. If God had brought Reuben to her today, then He *had* been listening. So, whatever the outcome, however this man might despise her afterwards, she needed to trust that God had brought her here for a reason.

So instead of protesting, she simply nodded. 'You can

ask me anything, too, and I promise I'll tell you the truth.'

Reuben nodded. Then his eyes moved to the wall behind her and she turned to follow his gaze to a large framed black and white picture of two young children: a girl and a boy, clearly twins. It was the only picture on that wall, and she knew instantly from their eyes, identical to Reuben's, that they were his.

'Max and Leah,' he said softly. 'They were three when that picture was taken.'

'Where are they now?' Even as Lyla asked the words, she knew the answer. The children's books he had brought to church hadn't been souvenirs of his childhood. They had belonged to his twins, to his children who, for whatever reason, were no longer with him.

'They died two months after that picture was taken,' he said flatly. He picked up the bottle and swallowed the rest of the water in one go, and then set it down. 'We were living in Chicago when it happened. My wife had been suffering from severe depression for some time, but she was seeing a therapist and we thought we had it under control.'

Lyla felt a cold hand squeezing her heart and her eyes widened in shock.

'Did – did she…?'

Reuben finished the words she couldn't say. 'As I said, we thought we had her illness under control – until the day she drove her car through the barriers and over the side of the road into the river. She wasn't wearing a seat belt and, according to the coroner, she would have died on impact. Max and Leah were strapped in the back seat and didn't stand a chance.'

Shaken to her core, Lyla gasped aloud and then covered her mouth with her hand, her eyes flooding with tears. *'Oh, God, no!* Oh, *Reuben.'*

Lost for words, she shook her head silently from side to side. How could he, how could *anyone*, bear such a tragedy? Without thinking, she scrambled off the sofa and knelt at his feet, her hand reaching for his in an instinctive desire to bring comfort. His eyes glistened, and he stroked her hand where it rested on his. For a few minutes there was silence between them, the sweet strings of the classical violin playing in the background expressing the searing emotions his explanation had stirred far better than any words would have done.

'When did it happen?' she whispered eventually. His hand stilled, and he gave a deep sigh. 'Exactly four years ago today,' he said. 'Although I'd lived in the United States for almost fifteen years, I didn't have the heart to stay after it happened, so I decided to come home. A year after the funeral, I hired a manager for my company, packed up the contents of our house and moved out. It took another year or so to build this house while I went back and forth to keep an eye on the business, and the rest, as they say...'

He tailed off and looked down at Lyla who was still crouching beside him.

'Thank you for listening – I haven't spoken to anyone about it for a long time.' He laughed without humour. 'I decided today was the day I would take the children's clothes to the orphanage, and their books into church. You know, so something positive could come out of their lives having been cut short so suddenly.'

His gaze suddenly seemed to pierce right through her.

'I think something positive did happen today, Lyla. Don't you?'

Caught unawares, she tried to pull her hand away, but he held on to it. Standing up, he helped her to her feet and, without loosening his hold, led her back to the sofa. He sat alongside her, the L shape of the couch allowing him to see her face.

'I've told you my secret, Lyla, so now please tell me what troubles you so? From the first moment I saw you, I knew there was something special about you. Even the short conversations we have at church have shown me how bright, intelligent and caring you are. I joined the choir just so I could spend more time around you,' he added with a rueful smile.

Lyla laughed nervously, longing to hear more about his feelings for her and yet deeply afraid of where his honesty was leading them.

Reuben leaned forward. 'I promised to be honest with you, so I'll say it. There's a special connection between us. I feel it whenever I'm near you, and something deep in my heart tells me that you feel it too. Lyla, I know you are married, and I respect that, but it's obvious you are very, very unhappy and that is why I'm saying all this to you now. I've watched you literally shrinking away over the past few months and I can't hold my peace any longer. Seeing you in church today was a sign, and I need you to trust me enough to let me help you.'

Overwhelmed by the tide of emotions flooding through her, Lyla covered her face and burst into loud, racking sobs that shook her thin frame. All the pent-up anger, hurt, sadness and guilt – oh, *so* much guilt, poured out in the river of tears soaking through her hands and into the giant hanky that Reuben quietly slipped through her fingers. She didn't know how long she cried, but when she finally raised her head, despite her reddened, puffy eyes, she felt a sense of lightness steal over her. It was that feeling, one she couldn't remember experiencing before, that gave her the confidence to finally start speaking.

As the shadows lengthened across the room, the only sound above the quiet music playing in the background was that of Lyla's soft voice. At first hesitant, it grew stronger as she opened her heart to the giant of a man sitting beside her. The truth about her marriage and Kwesi's philandering, her fruitless attempts to fall pregnant, the abuse she suffered from Ma Abena's vicious tongue, and then Nadia, and the final straw. *Nadia and Kwesi's baby*.

Reuben placed a comforting arm around her shoulder, and she leaned against him gratefully. He felt as warm and as solid as she had always imagined, and she yearned to stay forever within the shelter his body offered her. She felt the vibration against her ear of his voice rumbling deep in his chest as he asked the question she knew she couldn't avoid.

'You've been through hell, Lyla, and I'm so sorry. Your husband doesn't deserve you. But you know that, too. It doesn't sound to me like you ever really loved this man, so why did you marry him – and why have you stayed?' He gently moved his arm away and turned her to face him.

Disregarding her promise to Reuben, she shrugged defensively. 'Like you said, I'm married. The church—'

'The church, the *true* church, doesn't believe in needless suffering,' Reuben broke in, shushing her attempts at justification. 'God wants us to live life to the full; to love and to be loved, and if your marriage isn't giving you love, then you are in it for another reason.'

He hesitated, his eyes probing her tear-stained face before gently reminding her, 'You promised me the truth, Lyla.'

She drew in a deep, shuddering breath. *Que sera sera, Lyla.*

'I can't leave my marriage. Being unhappy is my punishment for what I did.'

Baffled, Reuben took both her hands in his. 'Punishment for what? What did you do?'

She couldn't bear to look at him, but she had promised. Dropping her head, she whispered in shame, 'Punishment for having an abortion.'

Another deep sigh shook her to the core. *There! She'd said it.* After all the years of silence, she had finally said the words. The tears she thought she'd exhausted dripped on to the hands holding hers, and she steeled herself in readiness for him to pull away from her in disgust.

'I'm so sorry,' Reuben said sadly, holding her hands even tighter. 'That must have been very hard for you.'

She stared at him in astonishment, fresh tears streaming unchecked down her cheeks. 'Did you hear what I just said? *I killed my unborn baby*! After what happened to you, how can you even stand to *look* at me?'

Reuben pulled her into his arms and rocked her gently while she sobbed uncontrollably. 'Lyla, Lyla,' he soothed, repeating her name until she calmed down. Raising her head, he gently wiped away the tears, his fingers warm against her cold, damp face.

'There's a world of difference between the two situations. Eva was very unwell and what she did was – well, it was devastating and truly awful, but her actions were those of a deeply troubled mind. Deciding to terminate a pregnancy isn't something I imagine any woman does lightly. So, I can only assume that you had very good reasons for doing so.'

She sniffed and blew hard into the damp handkerchief on her lap. 'I wish I could be as generous as you, but I hate myself for what I did. I was only twenty at the time.' She took a deep ragged breath and swallowed hard.

'I met Ravi at a concert on campus at the start of my second year at university in England. He was studying engineering and we loved the same music. He was funny and smart, and pretty soon we were inseparable. I was crazy about him and he said he felt the same way.'

She hesitated, and then plunged on. 'Until the day I told him I'd missed my period and that I was terrified I was pregnant. He swore we'd figure it out together and that it didn't change anything. So, I took the pregnancy test and it was positive. At first, he'd come over after lectures to the house I shared with three other girls just as he'd always done, and honestly, he was so sweet. He reassured me we would make it work with our baby and we wouldn't be the first couple to become parents so young. But, after a couple of weeks, it was painfully obvious he was pulling away from me. Then—'

Lyla took another deep breath. 'About three weeks after I'd taken the pregnancy test, he showed up at my house with a wad of money and told me I had to get rid of the baby. He said his parents had always planned to arrange his marriage to a Hindu girl and that they'd never accept an African.'

Lyla sighed and smoothed back her hair. 'The doctor at the clinic said there wouldn't be any side effects and I could have children whenever I was ready. At the time, losing Ravi hurt far more than a child who never got to be, and I convinced myself that what I'd done was no big deal. I carried on with my degree, and I even – God forgive me – encouraged Maku to consider a termination when *she* fell pregnant.'

She gave a humourless laugh and shook her head slowly before continuing. 'But then one day I went to church and it began to dawn on me that I had done something really, really wrong. It started eating me up inside, but I felt too ashamed to tell anyone. I came back to Ghana after I graduated – my father wasn't well, and I hated the idea of Ma being on her own. But after Daddy died, I realised that God hadn't chosen to save him because I had taken someone else's life. However hard I tried, I just couldn't let go of my conviction that my actions had damaged us all and that it was up to me to seek atonement. When Kwesi first asked me out, I knew all about his reputation – we'd been at school together and from everything I'd heard, he hadn't changed – but by then I didn't think I deserved to be happy. I was desperate to have a baby to make up for what I'd done and as proof that God had forgiven me. And that's when God *really* began to show how angry He was with me. Every time I fell pregnant, I lost the baby – every single time.'

Reuben shook his head. 'God isn't angry with you, Lyla. God *loves* you. You know that from everything we understand about our faith.'

'I know, Reuben, and I've tried so hard to believe it, but when it comes down to the – the tussle between my faith and my guilt, it seems guilt always wins. God, Reuben, *look at me* – I'm such a mess!' she said wretchedly.

'Oh, Lyla,' A wealth of sadness flooded his deep baritone voice. 'I'm so sorry you've lived with such guilt for so long. God isn't punishing you, my darling – you've been punishing yourself.'

For a moment she tried to take in and process what Reuben had said. And then, hot on the heels of her maelstrom of emotions, came another. Had Reuben just called her *darling*?

He leaned forward and cradled her face between his hands, resting his forehead against hers.

'It's time to let go of all these negative feelings and start allowing yourself to be happy, because *that's* what you deserve. Nothing more, and nothing less.'

It had been months since she'd felt the touch of any man, including her husband, and her body instinctively melted into his. Suddenly his hands had moved from her face to her shoulders and before she knew it, his arms slipped behind her to fold her against him. She raised her head and her lips met his in a kiss so sweet that neither of them could stop. Lyla moaned from the sheer nearness of him, the sound causing him to ravage her mouth with his and pull her tighter against him, leaving her in no doubt what her body was doing to his.

He pulled back, his breathing ragged, and his eyes asked hers a silent question. *Stop this madness, Lyla, and leave now!* The harsh Voice tried to force its way back into her head. For once, The Voice was right, and she knew what she was doing was wrong. But she couldn't deny what she felt for him, and neither reason nor logic nor faith could stop what was about to happen.

So, instead, she stroked Reuben's beard, relishing the feel of its texture between her fingers. It felt even softer than in her countless fantasies about this beautiful man. Then, she raised her arms to pull his head down and bring his lips back to hers. Slamming a mental door against The Voice and knowing full well she was about to break the seventh commandment, Lyla moved back into Reuben's arms.

Kwesi

Jessie's smile unleashed her adorable dimples, and Kwesi couldn't help returning her grin. By rights he should have been rebuking her for presenting herself at his office uninvited, but he had to admire the sheer brazenness of the young Marketing Officer. From her first day on the job, Jessie had made no secret of her crush on the store's top boss, scandalising the older managers by piping up out of turn at staff meetings and artlessly directing questions to Kwesi with an innocent air that fooled no one. Her impromptu visit to his office this afternoon was the latest salvo in her ongoing campaign to make him take her seriously; a battle which, Kwesi conceded, she was getting very close to winning. His reticence about getting involved with a subordinate employee had weakened with each encounter, and Jessie was wasting no time moving in for the kill.

Kwesi leaned back in his chair and crossed one ankle over his knee before directing the full force of his soulful brown eyes on to his willing captive. She looked considerably less prim than at the morning staff meeting. Having undone the top two buttons of her long-sleeved white blouse, the curve of her breast cradled in a lace bra was on display whenever she leaned forward. The black pencil skirt she wore appeared modest, until the split it revealed when she crossed her legs made it anything but.

A quick glance at his watch showed that it was just

past closing time. For weeks he had made a point of going straight home after work, but it was now starting to get rather tedious. It wasn't as if Lyla had shown any signs of a thaw in her cold war against him, and she continued to freeze him out of their bed. He was also heartily sick of cooking his own food. What kind of life was it for a man to come home after a hard day's work and find his wife on the sofa watching TV and leaving him to go into the kitchen and fend for himself?

'So, I was wondering if you wanted to discuss my ideas for improving our marketing plan somewhere a bit more – you know, comfortable, sir?' Jessie said, putting a demure emphasis on the 'sir' as if to support the fiction that work had anything to do with what she had in mind.

'Don't you think you should be running your ideas past Anselm before coming to me?' Kwesi asked mildly, playing along to see just where she would take this.

Jessie pouted prettily. 'Mr Asiedu is a very old-fashioned marketeer. He's not interested in how we can use digital campaigns to reach new markets for our products and promote our brand – all he cares about is print and radio.'

She uncrossed her legs and crossed them again in the other direction, forcing her skirt to ride up higher and reveal curvaceous thighs, and Kwesi reluctantly dragged his eyes away from the open invitation. 'I'm sure you would appreciate what I'm trying to do here if you gave me a chance – to explain.' She paused deliberately before tagging on the last two words.

Oh, I know exactly what you're trying to do here, young lady! The thought flashed through Kwesi's mind at the same time as the sudden surge of lust that took him by surprise.

When it came to women, he preferred to do the chasing, but for some reason Jessie's less than subtle tactics were getting to him. It must be the months of abstinence, he decided, and shifted his chair forward so the desk would conceal his obvious desire. Maybe he could take Jessie for a drink, he thought, suppressing the rational part of his brain that warned him not to create a mess on his own doorstep. The other part of his mind argued back forcefully: what the hell else was he supposed to do? It wasn't *natural* for a man to live in this state of enforced celibacy his wife was putting him through! He'd apologised countless times, and he had no idea what else he could do to pacify her. Besides, the more time that elapsed, the more convinced he became that Lyla had to accept some of the blame for their situation. By not taking more interest in what he'd been doing during his frequent absences and accepting everything he'd told her, however ridiculous, she'd allowed him too much freedom to stray. Her silence had effectively condoned his behaviour, and if she had *really* loved him...

Jessie gave him a penetrating stare that dissolved any other thoughts, and he felt his insides turn to liquid. He glanced at his watch again, his mind whirring as he mentally calculated his chances. Even if he was late getting back, Lyla was unlikely to be home. She'd suddenly taken to disappearing to her mother's house in the evenings and not returning until late in the night, but he was in no position to voice his annoyance, particularly when they had yet to resolve the problem of Nadia and her – he carefully skirted around using the word 'our' – baby. His mother's constant bellyaching was also getting on his nerves, and it wasn't helped by his brother's triumphant crowing that he had always known Kwesi would make a mess of his marriage.

Trust Papa Kwame to back Ma Abena's suggestion about taking in the baby – neither one of them had to live with Lyla! After her reaction last week, he hadn't dared to broach the subject again, but he was slowly coming around to the prospect of fatherhood, and maybe having it live with them wouldn't be as ridiculous as his mother's suggestion had first sounded. In fact, given Lyla's history of miscarriages, she should be grateful for the opportunity to mother a child – and at least the kid was his rather than a stranger's child they might otherwise have been forced to adopt. And maybe, Kwesi wondered, spurred on by the force of his own argument, maybe Nadia would be *relieved* to hand over the kid. After all, it wasn't as if she had room in her crowded family house for yet another occupant. But he had to be sure she would go for it before promoting the idea to Lyla, which reminded him of the text he had sent Nadia that morning suggesting they meet after work to discuss the situation. Kwesi sighed. Any assignations with Miss Jessie here would just have to wait. Instead of flirting with the young woman in front of him, he needed to see Nadia and put forward his proposition.

Suddenly the door to his office slammed open and the subject of his thoughts marched in, closely followed by Kwesi's PA.

'*Boss, I'm sorry!* I tried to stop her—' Vera's voice was high with indignation.

Nadia took in the scene and then glared rudely at the older woman. 'I thought you said he was busy! Is this what you people call busy?'

Kwesi stood up and raised a calming hand. 'Vera, it's fine. I'll deal with this. It's late – you can go home now.'

After a moment's hesitation, Vera threw Nadia a dirty look and walked out with a pointed sniff.

Kwesi stepped out from behind his desk. 'Nadia, I sent you a message that I would come over later.' He kept his voice measured but, declining to take his cue, Nadia took a step towards him, tossed her long curls and stared up at him scornfully.

'Oh, excuse me if I don't believe a word that comes out of your mouth – which I *don't*, because we both know that you are *full of shit*!' She raised her voice, mimicking his frigidly polite tone, and Kwesi's lips tightened in anger.

Undeterred, Nadia swung around and zeroed in on Jessie who had been cowering in her chair as if hoping not to be noticed and pounced without hesitation. 'Whatever he tells you, trust me he's lying! So, if I were you, I would carry yourself and your fat legs back to wherever you came from.'

Kwesi winced as Jessie stared dumbly at Nadia. He turned back to Nadia, suddenly seeing her through Jessie's eyes, and cringed at the idea that the attractive young executive would picture him spending time with this – this cheap tart! Nadia's pregnancy had thickened the tiny waist which had once so enticed him, while the short, tight dress she had squeezed into was doing her no favours. Her skin looked sallow, and even the heavy make-up couldn't conceal an angry rash around her mouth. Kwesi shuddered inwardly. *What the hell was I thinking?*

Jessie scrambled to her feet. There was no sign of her dimples, and it was clear from her expression that she was terrified of confronting this madwoman.

'Um, I'll see you tomorrow, boss,' she muttered. She slipped past Nadia, avoiding even the slightest contact, and bolted from the room.

Kwesi watched her leave, and then turned on Nadia furiously. But, just as he was about to explode, he remembered his mission. Ma Abena would give him no peace until he'd persuaded this girl to let him take the child, and the thought of his mother's ire was like a cold shower damping down his fury. Signalling to Nadia to take the seat Jessie had just vacated, Kwesi perched on the edge of his desk and folded his arms. Digging deep, he dredged up a smile and lowered his voice to the seductive tone which had always worked with her.

'Did you come here to fight with me? I was planning to pick you up and take you to dinner so we could sit down and have a proper talk.' He batted his thick eyelashes for good measure.

Nadia curled her lip and sniffed, but made no comment, leaning back in the armchair and swinging one leg over the other. Kwesi averted his gaze from the garish blue dragon tattoo on her thigh that he had caressed more often than he cared to remember and wondered why he had ever thought it sexy.

He shook his head and said dolefully, 'Nadia, believe me, I didn't want things to get out of hand the way they did. I really care about you, but it was all becoming so complicated with my wife that I had to, you know, slow things down a bit until—'

'Until when, Kwesi?' Nadia cut in bitterly. She leaned forward, her expression combative. 'Until you were ready to leave your wife and buy us a house so we could start a family together? Well, here's your chance!' She pointed to her stomach with a scarlet-tipped fingernail. 'We have the baby, so where is the house you promised me?'

Cursing his weakness for blurting out whatever it took for Nadia to work her extraordinary bedroom magic, Kwesi scrabbled for a response. With nothing else coming to mind, he settled for the truth.

'Nadia, I know what I said, but I don't have the kind of money to buy you – us – a house. I only manage the rent on my house because Lyla pays half of it.'

Nadia narrowed her eyes, scepticism written all over her pinched features. 'You're trying to trick me. I know you're rich – look at the car you drive!'

Kwesi sighed. 'It's a company car, Nadia. It comes with my job.'

He stood up straight and pushed his hands into his trouser pockets defensively. He wasn't enjoying having to destroy the mystique she had built up around him, but there was no alternative. 'You're right, I *was* a liar. At least about getting you the house, but that's in the past. We need to talk about what's happening right now.'

'You mean my baby?'

'I mean *our* baby,' he corrected her.

Nadia shrugged. 'If you can't afford to buy me a house, then it's *my* baby.'

Kwesi eyed her shrewdly. 'Okay, so what if I offered to look after the child? Since I can't afford a second house, it makes sense to let it live with me. Between Lyla and me, we could give it a good home and send it to the best schools and—'

266

He broke off as Nadia leapt from her chair, her face contorted with rage. Kwesi hastily stepped aside, the memory of the slaps she had given him before still fresh in his mind.

'*It! It! It!* Is that what our child is to you, eh? An "*it*"?' She spat the words out savagely. 'And what makes you even *dream* I would give my child to you and your wife? Do you think you have enough money in the world to buy my baby?'

Kwesi blanched and glanced towards the door, frantically gesturing to her to lower her voice, and enraging her even further.

'What? Are you afraid there are people out there who will hear? That your employees will find out their posh, handsome boss is just a dirty liar who thinks he can buy anything?'

'Nadia,' Kwesi pleaded, 'I'm *begging* you! At least consider it.'

Ignoring his agonised expression, Nadia marched to the door. She gripped the handle and then swung round to face him and spoke slowly and deliberately in a voice as cold as the eyes she turned on him. 'There's nothing to consider. I will never give up my baby to you and your wife. In fact, *you* consider this.'

She jabbed a forefinger in his direction. 'Either you keep your promise and provide for me and our child, or I will make sure everyone in this company, in fact everyone in this *town*, knows exactly what a lying, cheating *idiot* you are!'

* * *

A little later, still reeling from the ferocity of Nadia's attack, Kwesi returned to Marula Heights. He powered his car up on to the forecourt of his house and jumped out, pausing only to toss a word of greeting to Solomon before heading up the path to the front door.

After the brutal encounter in his office, he was desperate to see his wife, even if she wasn't prepared to speak to him. He needed Lyla, and for the first time he wondered whether he had pushed her too far, and if the life they had built and the marriage he had displayed so proudly to the world could be saved.

Forcing himself to calm down before he went in, he took a deep breath and inhaled the sweet aromas coming off the floral bushes Lyla had planted, chiding himself sternly for the rare moment of self-doubt. *Of course, everything will work out.* He fixed a cheerful smile on his face to underline his conviction and pushed open the front door. But even before crossing the threshold, he knew what to expect. The empty spot in the driveway had already signalled his wife was not at home and just as he'd feared, it was dark inside, and he was alone.

NOVEMBER

**THE RING WAS PERFECT
(BUT NOT THE SUFFERING)**

Theresa

Theresa buttoned up her blouse and watched with a smile as Auntie Sisi bustled away with Ben, leaving her free to finish the PR campaign strategy urgently awaiting her attention. Her smile deepened at the sound of Auntie Sisi loudly kissing the baby's plump, satiny cheeks as she carried him off, and Theresa returned to her laptop feeling renewed gratitude for her housekeeper and self-appointed nanny.

Despite the looming deadline for the campaign presentation, Theresa clicked open the document with the guest list for Ben's baptism and scrolled through the names, wondering how to break it to her husband that the tally of guests had risen to sixty. Tyler's redevelopment project had come to an abrupt standstill, and with no word from Jeff nor any other financing on the horizon, he had been adamant they keep the ceremony small and simple.

'You mean cheap!' Theresa had mocked. TB Communications was thriving, and to her mind there was no reason why she should scrimp on the baptism of her first child just because his daddy was feeling sensitive. But, to her intense irritation, Tyler had yet again refused to rise to the bait and had simply turned and walked away.

Ben's arrival had brought something like a truce to the hostilities between them. Tyler was proving to be a doting, hands-on father but, despite his enthusiasm for his new role, there was a distance between him and Theresa they couldn't bridge. Instead, they lavished the love they had given up showing each other on to the new addition to their family. Whenever Theresa threw in the odd barb to provoke a reaction, Tyler remained unfailingly stoical and would either not respond or simply leave the room. This strange new dynamic meant that, although there was none of the open fighting of the past, there was no love either. And there was certainly no lovemaking.

Scanning through the list yet again in a fruitless attempt to see who she could cut without causing offence, Theresa tried to contain her growing frustration at the state of her marriage. The careful veneer she and Tyler had learned to paint over their emotions, in order to keep the peace, had created a deeply unsatisfactory stalemate. *A stale mate indeed – with the emphasis on stale!* She was so fed up with the polite, soul-destroying rut in which they had become mired that she sometimes wished for the raging arguments of before, when at least they had cared enough to fight.

Tyler's refusal to engage would have been even more infuriating had she not been so preoccupied with her bouncing three-month-old baby boy. To Theresa's annoyance, Tyler had been proved right about the gender. Although Ben had arrived a few days after his due date, his surprisingly easy delivery confounded her fears that her narrow hips wouldn't permit the huge bump to pass through. Putting aside their differences, Tyler had remained by her side throughout the entire experience, squeezing her hand in encouragement and gently coaxing her through the pain and an unexpected panic attack that gripped her shortly before the baby emerged. Ben's appearance had also ended his father's self-imposed exile to the spare room, and Tyler loved nothing better than to give his son his midnight bottle and rock him gently back to sleep in the pine cot next to their bed.

Theresa sighed and clicked off the Excel sheet. It was no use; she simply had to invite the extended relatives on the list to the baptism. Tyler would probably be furious she'd disregarded his feelings about a costly event when his finances were so uncertain, but there was no way she could leave out the friends she had made over the past year in Ghana, or exclude her key clients when so many of them had sent generous gifts after Ben's birth. Tyler would just have to accept that this wasn't London where such an occasion was considered an intimate and private event, and that celebrations here invariably involved a large gathering. One name, though, was conspicuously absent from the list. Although her mother's broken foot was now healed, Theresa had persuaded Clementyne that as she and Ben were due to visit London in a few weeks, it made no sense for her mother to come all this way simply to attend the baptism. Clementyne had acquiesced without argument, partly swayed by her irritation that Theresa had chosen to name her son after her late ex-husband, even if was only as his middle name.

The next few days came and went in a blur of broken nights, hectic workdays and endless breastfeeding. Theresa's creative strategy presentation won the company a lucrative new client with a generous PR budget, giving Theresa and Margaret the perfect excuse one afternoon to leave Clara, their Account Executive, to man the office while they relaxed over a long, leisurely lunch of freshly grilled seafood at a beachside hotel. After lunch, Theresa slipped on her sunglasses and snoozed in a deckchair under the shade of an umbrella until her painfully swollen breasts forced her to return home and feed her son.

Up in her room getting ready for another girls' night out – or rather in, as she had insisted on hosting it at home to avoid leaving Ben – Theresa rifled through her wardrobe and pulled out a cotton caftan with a vibrant rose-splashed design and three strategically placed studs that allowed for easy breastfeeding. She slipped the roomy garment over her head and pulled the fabric in under her bust, fastening the velvet ribbon into a secure knot.

Much to her disappointment, Maku had cried off at the last minute to revise for an important test. With her accountancy exams only weeks away, she was spending every available minute poring over her copious handwritten notes and thumbing through her precious and now well-worn textbook. Brushing off Theresa's protests that she must know the entire syllabus off by heart, Maku had insisted there was no room for complacency.

'I'm determined to pass these exams, Tee. I can't carry on like this!'

The rift caused by her vicious quarrel with Maku a few months earlier had taken several weeks to heal. As much as Theresa had been horrified by the pain she had caused Maku with the cruel remarks she'd hurled at her, she had, in turn, been deeply hurt by her friend's callous dismissal of her childhood traumas, and her forthright comments about Theresa's attitude to marriage. What had stung her most about the latter was Maku's accusation that Theresa expected Tyler to be perfect to be worthy of her – a charge which, after much self-reflection, Theresa had fiercely rejected. She knew she had high expectations of people – after all, what child of Clementyne Curtis's wouldn't? – but, she reasoned, she held herself to the same high standards she expected of everyone else.

After extensive coaxing from Lyla, Theresa and Maku had eventually exchanged grudging apologies and over time they had both put the wounding words and accusations behind them. If Theresa occasionally sensed some unresolved tension between them, she had also now made her peace with Maku's ambivalence towards her. She and Maku were as close as sisters and, however fiercely they fought, they nonetheless loved each other dearly.

The sound of Lyla's car horn cut short her contemplation and Theresa hurried downstairs, hoping Auntie Sisi had been able to resist playing with the baby long enough to make dinner. From the moment he'd arrived home from hospital, Auntie Sisi had been smitten by Ben's velvety skin and lush, silky hair, and she wasn't alone. Both the security guard and Amos, the young garden boy, cooed over him whenever they got the chance, while Joseph seized any excuse to hold the baby during their visits to Dr Owusu's clinic for Ben's weigh-ins and vaccinations.

Theresa opened the door to Lyla and stood back to let her in, noting with approval her friend's bright eyes and glowing skin. Although she was still slender, the gaunt skinniness that had gripped Lyla was no longer in evidence. Theresa returned her friend's loving hug, breathing in the floral bouquet of her perfume. When Lyla finally released her, Theresa stepped back and whistled at the combination of Lyla's fitted aquamarine dress and strappy navy sandals.

'You're looking seriously sexy tonight, my friend! Are you sure this is all for my benefit?' she teased, giggling as Lyla thrust her hip forward in an exaggerated pose.

'Of course, it isn't for you,' Lyla retorted, striding into the hallway and peering into the living room. 'I wore it to charm Ben – where's my little prince?'

'I never realised that becoming a mum was going to make me invisible,' Theresa grumbled. 'No one wants to talk to me any more – they'd all rather cuddle the baby!'

'Well then, you'd better learn to deal with it. Where *is* he?'

'Auntie Sisi has kidnapped him, which means we'll probably end up eating dinner at midnight.' Theresa shook her head resignedly and headed past the kitchen to the den, where she found her housekeeper leaning over Ben's basket and softly crooning a song in her native tongue. With a sheepish grin, she straightened up and wiped her hands on her Harlequin-print leggings before greeting Lyla, who promptly scooped up the gurgling baby, leaving a wistful Auntie Sisi to reluctantly make her way back to the kitchen.

The two women returned to the living room with Theresa carrying the Moses basket while Lyla cradled Ben gently against her chest.

'Where's Tyler this evening?' Lyla looked up from nuzzling the folds of the baby's neck to quiz Theresa, who shrugged non-committally.

'He knows it's girls' night, so he's made himself scarce.'

Planting a soft kiss on the baby's cheek, Lyla looked

at her sympathetically. 'How's it going with you two? I thought things had improved since this little one came along.'

'Well, we're not fighting any more, if that's what you mean. Although sometimes I think I'd prefer it.'

'Why would you say that?' Lyla looked shocked.

Theresa shook her head, once again feeling frustrated by Tyler's passivity. 'I know it sounds awful, but it's almost like he doesn't *care* enough to fight. He was really sweet and supportive when I was in labour, but now it's as if we're both trying so hard to give Ben a calm and healthy environment that we tiptoe around what we really want to say, paste on bright smiles and talk to the baby rather than to each other. I know I don't want my son to go through the awful experiences I suffered with my parents quarrelling all the time, but this... You know, sometimes I'll say something evil just to provoke a reaction – *any* reaction – but then he'll just go quiet or walk out.'

Lyla stroked Ben's soft curls and kept her voice low as his head began to nod. 'I'll put him down so he can nap properly.'

She laid him gently on his back in the basket and moved back to the sofa, tucking her legs under her. 'Okay, it looks like dinner is going to take a while, so talk to me. Sometimes another person's perspective can help.'

Theresa sighed, unsure of where to begin. How could she explain her anxiety that this relationship would go the same way as those in her past, and her deep-seated fear that her marriage wouldn't withstand the strains of their new life? Or that much as she and Tyler were no longer fighting each other, neither were they fighting *for* each other? Hesitantly she tried to spell this out to Lyla who listened intently and without interruption.

After a long pause, Theresa added haltingly, 'God, what if Tyler gets fed up with this – this sexless, monochrome marriage, and decides to cheat on me?'

Despite Theresa's distress, Lyla's almost imperceptible wince at the word 'cheat' didn't escape her notice. Any more than Lyla's new-found verve and the brightly coloured, sexy clothes she suddenly favoured after years of dressing like a retired nun. Was there something going on with Reuben, she wondered? It had been ages since *that* conversation, and Lyla had deflected any subsequent attempts to raise the subject.

Lyla shifted her position on the sofa to face Theresa squarely. 'Is this really a mystery? You know where all this comes from, don't you?'

Theresa screwed her face into a grimace. 'For God's sake, stop trying to psychoanalyse me. Not *everything* is about my childhood!'

Lyla tilted her head to one side. 'Isn't it?' she challenged.

But even as Theresa's mouth set stubbornly, she knew only too well that Lyla had witnessed this cycle more than once. The impact of her parents' turbulent marriage had lasted far beyond Theresa's teenage years. Attracting men had never been her problem; it was always what came afterwards. The light-hearted banter and laughter that accompanied the first, second and even third dates, invariably evolving into relationships that were soon stifled under the weight of Theresa's chronic insecurities. Feeling happy would trigger intense anxiety about the new man in her life, and constant questioning as to whether they had a future together. The questioning inevitably led to the stomach-churning fear that either he had no ambition – a deal breaker, as Clementyne had constantly drummed into her – or was *too* driven and ambitious to pay her enough attention. Crippled by her fears, any disagreement, no matter how slight, was instantly magnified in Theresa's mind into a major rift. The inevitable arguments and break-ups that followed would then reinforce the pattern. Tyler had been the first man who'd understood how her mind worked and had steadfastly refused to let her push him away. But even Tyler had his limits.

Undeterred by Theresa's mutinous expression, Lyla sighed in exasperation and pushed back her heavy braids.

'So, there's no pattern here of you sabotaging your relationships by creating problems, or by finding fault with inconsequential things. Is that what you're saying? So, what happened with Roy, then – you know, the lovely man you left because, according to you, he was too argumentative?'

'That's *one* person!'

'You dumped Mario after he confided his dream to become an artist, which *you* decided meant he was always going to be broke. Oh, and if by some miracle he happened to succeed and make a load of money from his art, he would travel around the world and abandon you.'

'What's your point, Lyla?'

'My point, *Theresa,* is that between Clementyne's impossible standards and your mixed-up feelings about your dad, you always put way too much pressure on your relationships,' Lyla said heatedly. '*No* man is perfect or likely to measure up because you're always scared they're going to let you down. I know Auntie Clementyne really loves you but, honestly, all her bitching about men has really screwed you up!'

Theresa stared open-mouthed at her friend. *Where the hell was all this coming from?*

Lyla clearly hadn't finished. 'Has it ever occurred to you that Tyler might be having a hard time living on that pedestal you placed him on when you got married?'

'What on earth are you talking about? I didn't put him on any pedestal. I know he's got faults – lots of them!'

'Perhaps he does, but then we all do, and maybe you need to stop punishing him for that. Besides, don't you think it's time you stopped focusing less on his issues and more on your own?'

'*What* issues?' Theresa said coldly. Lyla was supposed to be on her side, not sitting here attacking her in her own home!

Lyla didn't back down. 'Tee, not everyone is going to do to you what your father did.'

Without warning, Theresa's face crumpled. With a sigh, Lyla moved over to touch her shoulder and the reassuring warmth from her fingers seeped through Theresa's thin cotton dress, helping her to regain her composure.

Lyla spoke softly. 'Tyler's made mistakes, and I'm not excusing them – or him. But it's as if you're just willing him to let you down, the same way you did with those other guys.'

'Lyla, it's hardly the same – Tyler and I have been married for years!' Theresa protested with a sniff as she carefully wiped under her eyes. 'I thought I knew him, but he's changed since we've been here, so yes, in that way he *is* just—' She broke off, putting a hand over her mouth.

'Like your dad?' Lyla finished the sentence with another deep sigh. For a moment the only sound in the room was the muted ticking of the clock high on the wall and the gentle snuffling of the sleeping baby.

'You know, Ma always says that, as women, our fathers are the first male relationships in our lives, and that it sets the tone for how we deal with men forever afterwards.'

'Well, that doesn't bode well for me then, does it? I loved my dad so much, and look how well that turned out,' Theresa retorted with a humourless laugh.

Lyla looked at her thoughtfully. 'Do you remember what you said when Tyler proposed to you?'

'What do you mean?'

'Do you remember how you described his proposal when you were telling me about it?' Lyla persisted. Theresa looked at her, puzzled, and Lyla continued impatiently, 'You were having dinner at his flat, he went down on one knee and said some really romantic things and then asked you to marry him. Right?'

Theresa smiled faintly. 'Yeah, and?'

'Instead of saying yes right away, what did you say?'

'I – I said he had to promise… Lyla don't look at me like that! I wasn't going to say yes until I was sure it was going to be for keeps. I couldn't – can't – bear the idea of divorce.'

Lyla nodded. 'I know. But if I'm picturing this right, a man proposes marriage and declares his undying love, and you give him a cold-eyed, fishy glare and demand that he swears to be by your side forever before you even say "yes"?'

Theresa shrugged defensively. 'Well, what's the point in marriage if you're not convinced it's going to be forever?'

'True, but there's also something a bit off-putting about demanding that commitment just as someone is offering it to you, don't you think?' Lyla pointed out. 'Look, Tee, I'm only trying to make you see that the more you focus on the possibility of Tyler leaving you, the more you're driving him away. You're making this a self-fulfilling prophecy by the way you're treating him.'

'So, what are you suggesting? That I should just go along with the way things have become for us? And that if he feels like – like *living* in his office or shutting me out or screwing up his life with stupid business decisions and losing all our savings, that I shouldn't have anything to say about it?'

Theresa's voice rose in anger, and she stood up and walked across the room to avoid waking the baby. Swinging round, she added fiercely, 'I'm sorry, Lyla, but I'm not you! I can't just stand by and allow my husband to get away with doing whatever the hell he likes, and not say a word!'

As if the words were physical blows, Lyla bowed her head and her slim frame hunched over itself. Theresa bit her lip as a wave of remorse swept away the anger that Lyla's words had generated.

'Sorry,' she whispered. 'I didn't mean that.'

'Yes, you did. And you're right,' was the muffled response. Visibly pulling herself together, Lyla looked up with weary eyes. 'But we're not talking about me – at least not right now. I've seen with my own eyes how good you and Tyler used to be, and if living in Ghana is ruining that, then maybe you need to think again about whether this is the best place for you.'

'You *are* joking, aren't you?' Theresa's eyes widened with incredulity. 'After everything we've gone through to move here! You do realise that selling our flat and giving up our jobs wasn't meant to be a temporary move. And never mind Tyler, what about *me*? After finally getting my own business off the ground, you actually think I should turn around and go back to London? What the hell *for*?'

'For the sake of your marriage?'

'*What* marriage?' Theresa was almost howling in her frustration. 'If Tyler isn't the man I thought he was, then there's no marriage to go anywhere for!'

'Tee, do you hear what you are saying? Is your business more important to you than Tyler? Is having a perfect husband more important that having no husband at all?'

'Maybe it is,' was the defiant response.

Lyla shook her head, her face sombre. 'Well, then, unless you really do want to end up alone, it's time you grew up and got real. Instead of criticising your man, *help* him! Yes, I've put up with a lot of crap as far as Kwesi is concerned, but I don't have a man who loves me the way Tyler does you. So, if you're really prepared to lose him because he's a bit lost right now, then that's up to you – but let me remind you that it took you a long time to find someone like him. He might have his faults, but he's a *good* guy.'

'Well, if he's so good, you try living with him then,' Theresa replied bitterly.

A soft knock at the door was followed by Auntie Sisi's entrance to announce that dinner was ready. As if on cue, Ben began wailing, and Theresa lifted him out of the crib to soothe him. She rained kisses on his cheeks, and he wrinkled his tiny nose and sneezed, causing her to break into helpless giggles.

'Okay, my little tiger, let's all eat together.' She smiled at Lyla, her good humour restored. 'I'm sorry. You're the last person I want to fight with. Come on, let's go and see what Auntie Sisi's made for dinner – believe me, I'm used to breastfeeding and eating at the same time!'

* * *

Oh my God! This has *to be Lyla's Reuben!* Trying not to gape, Theresa shook the hand extended by the strapping giant standing in front of her. Lyla had described him as tall, but she hadn't mentioned his soulful brown eyes or the lustrous full beard that framed *extremely* sensual lips. No wonder her friend had found herself attracted to him – you'd have to be blind not to be! Theresa's mind was whirring so fast, she could barely concentrate on the introductions her business partner was making.

Margaret had set up the meeting, explaining that the Ghanaian founder of Watts Industries, a US technology firm that had made millions from a revolutionary piece of software for the finance industry, was looking for publicity for a business incubation scheme he planned to set up in Ghana. Distracted by a cold Ben had picked up and knowing the man was an old friend of Margaret's, Theresa's preparation for the meeting had comprised of little more than a brief skim through Watts Industries' website.

She snapped to attention as her partner stood up with a cheery, 'I'd better go, or I'll be late picking up the boys. They're coming home for the weekend, and I'll be stuck in traffic if I don't leave now. Reuben, I'll leave Theresa to go through the details with you and we'll come back to you with a full proposal.'

Reuben walked Margaret to the door, kissing her warmly on both cheeks before saying goodbye. Turning back to Theresa, he gestured towards a massive polished-oak conference table that took up almost half of his vast office.

'Let's sit over there, shall we? I find these office chairs so small and uncomfortable – entirely my fault for letting people who've never met me pick out my furniture!'

His laughter was infectious, and she grinned and moved to sit across the table from him. She forced herself to concentrate as Reuben swiftly outlined his plans for a foundation to support early-stage companies in Ghana, and which would be funded from a share of the profits of his American business.

'There's a whole lot of talent in this country and we need to create more opportunities to harness all this incredible creativity and energy. You know, Theresa, I meet a lot of entrepreneurs with great ideas, cutting-edge even, that can really help shape the future of this country, and even the world,' he said, his deep voice vibrating with passion. 'But for the most part, they're struggling to get funding or support to take them to the next level. And that's where the foundation comes in. I want to use it to invest in the right people and, more importantly, give them guidance and some *real* partnership. I'll never forget how lonely I felt when I first started my company, and how hard I had to fight to get anyone to believe in my business idea.'

Theresa bit her lip. Reuben's words were an uncomfortable reminder of her own response to Tyler's business challenges. She had been so caught up with running her new enterprise that, other than her fears for their hard-earned savings, she'd shown little patience for Tyler's predicament since Jeff's disappearance or, if she was brutally honest, even before then. While she had been immensely fortunate in finding a talented and dedicated business partner, Tyler had been forced to rely on the mercy of Jeff Parnell, whose lack of scruples had cost both men dearly. If she hadn't been lucky enough to meet Margaret and benefit from her extensive network, Theresa thought soberly, would she be feeling as overwhelmed and as lonely as Tyler must be now?

Suddenly, Theresa felt overcome by a sense of deep shame. For months, her concerns had centred on her own dissatisfaction with Tyler and her irrational fears of him turning into a failure or bailing out on her. Despite Auntie Pat and Lyla's pleas, not to mention Maku's blunt warning, never in all that time had Theresa given any real thought as to how to help her husband.

'I'm so sorry, Theresa, forgive my terrible manners. I haven't even offered you a drink!' Reuben exclaimed, jumping to his feet. 'I always get so carried away when I'm talking about this project that I completely forget myself.'

He went over to a tall cupboard which turned out to be a concealed fridge stacked with bottles of water and assorted soft drinks. As she nursed a tall glass of cold water, ostensibly taking notes while Reuben outlined the foundation's investment criteria, Theresa peeked up at him through her lashes. There was something really *solid* about him, she decided, and not just because of his impressive physique. His eagerness to do something positive for his country after making what was obviously a substantial fortune overseas was unmistakably authentic. Theresa hadn't met many multimillionaires, but she suspected very few of them came armed with Reuben's heavy dose of humility or felt the genuine empathy that resonated in his voice as he described his desire to help people get their start in business.

After an hour of peppering him with questions and suggesting promotional ideas, Theresa stood up with a smile and pushed her leather-bound notebook into her bag.

'I think I've got all the information I need, Reuben. What you want to do with your foundation is truly groundbreaking, and I'm confident we can find creative ways to help get your message out there to entrepreneurs and potential funders. I'll go through some ideas with Margaret and we can get a proposal to you by the end of next week. Would that work for you?'

Reuben shook her hand warmly and escorted her to the door. 'It's been great meeting you, Theresa, and I'm really looking forward to working together. Margaret says wonderful things about you. I must admit I'm pretty impressed by your courage in leaving London to start up in business here.'

Theresa grinned back. 'Well, luckily I wasn't on my own or I certainly wouldn't have been brave enough to do this. Both my husband and I felt that Ghana would be a great place for us to get our business ideas off the ground as well as make a difference. I still get the occasional bitchy comment suggesting we won't stick it out, but we didn't come here on a whim – both Tyler and I are really committed to making it work.'

With a final goodbye, she walked to the lift and pushed the button for the ground floor. As the elevator slowly descended, her mind wandered back to something Reuben had said earlier. The lift doors slid open, but instead of walking out Theresa hesitated, and then firmly pressed the button to return to the second floor. This time when the lift came to a halt, she stepped out quickly.

Taking a deep breath, she retraced her steps to Reuben's office, and knocked on the door.

Tyler

Tyler jogged down the tiled steps towards the far corner of the bank's car park. The outstretched branches of the acacia tree had provided a measure of shade from the afternoon sun, but the door handle was still hot to the touch. He switched on the ignition and waited for the air conditioner to cool the stuffy car while mulling over the bank officer's parting words: 'We'll contact you when our Credit Committee has reviewed your financials, sir.'

Why can't people simply say what they mean? It was obvious from the banker's thinly veiled impatience that Tyler's loan application would be tossed into a filing cabinet before he'd even driven off their grounds. After all, he was only one of thousands seeking loans that the banks seemed increasingly reluctant to offer, and with no proven track record of enterprise on his side, there was every chance that the Credit Committee – assuming they even considered his submission in the first place – would consider him too high a risk. Without people like Jeff taking a punt on a newcomer with no prior experience of entrepreneurship, he wondered, how the hell was anyone supposed to build a business?

Tyler clicked his seat belt into place and manoeuvred his way out of the car park. Waiting to enter the whizzing stream of traffic on the busy highway, he contemplated his lack of financing options and twisted his lips into a humourless smile. He really couldn't have chosen a worse time to start a property business. The recent government announcement that the Ministry of Finance was to extend the consultation period for the proposed controversial property tax law had done nothing to help his case. So long as the law remained a possibility, no one was willing to risk investing in the sector, and he could only hope the outcry from the industry would be enough to persuade the government to backtrack.

After a moment's hesitation, and suddenly gripped by the urgent need to visit the site of his abandoned project, Tyler decided to head south rather than return to the office. Not that there was much to see at Sycamore House. Six weeks earlier, with no further money forthcoming, the crew had been instructed to down tools until they could be paid.

The project manager had been sympathetic, but firm. 'Look, boss, you're a good man and I like you, but my workers need to eat and look after their families. As soon as you have the funds, we'll get the job done. Call me when you're ready.'

The situation was clearly not new to the contractor and, Tyler reflected, it was probably the reason why the man had insisted on inserting monthly advance payments into the contract.

There had been no word from Jeff Parnell since the night of his ignominious flight, and neither Tyler nor the other companies in receipt of money from JP Investments had any idea where to find him. But while Jeff's disappearance had removed some of the immediate pressure to repay the loan, it had also left Tyler without the additional financing he needed to finish the project.

The main roundabout was choked with traffic and it took him a few minutes to weave in and out of the congested lanes. Powering down the dual carriageway towards the coast, he turned off the air conditioner and slid down the windows to let in the bracing sea breeze. He pushed away the dark thoughts about his failing business, wanting only to relive the moment, a few days earlier, when an unexpected ray of sunshine had broken into the desolation that had become his life.

He had been lying on the bed next to Theresa, the two of them exhausted after a long day and several attempts to get Ben to sleep. Only half-listening as his wife announced yet another name to add to the crowd of people invited to his son's baptism, Tyler had responded with a non-committal murmur, which Theresa had taken to be an objection. Turning towards him to argue her case, she closed the gap between them, and he felt the warmth of her body against his. Instead of the immediate recoil he had grown used to, she remained pressed up against him. Neither one of them spoke, allowing the connection between their bodies to replace words that might quickly drive them apart.

When, after several moments, Theresa still hadn't moved, Tyler hesitantly reached out his arm to encircle her shoulders. The tentative gesture seemed to release a hidden tension within her, and she dropped her head against his chest and wrapped her arm around his waist.

'I miss us.' Theresa sounded wretched, but her words brought a stab of relief so intense that it pierced through the fog of pain and hurt that had blanketed him for months. Like a hot air balloon cut loose from its moorings, Tyler's spirits soared above the despair that had dogged him for what felt like an eternity. Theresa hadn't disappeared. Despite everything, his wife was still here, and she still loved him.

Wary of saying anything that would shatter the moment, he kissed the top of her head and gently whispered, 'Me, too'.

That night, for the first time in many lonely months, they had made love – with a hungry passion, but also with a tenderness that was sweeter than he could have ever imagined. Losing himself in the arms of his partner as they explored each other's bodies, Tyler had caressed her feverishly, all the while whispering the words of love he had left unspoken for so long.

But now, as he turned into the short driveway leading to Sycamore House, Tyler felt his slowly burgeoning optimism begin to fade. He parked and stepped out of the car, grimacing at the relentless heat that immediately assaulted him. The soles of his polished shoes crunched against loose gravel as he approached the deserted building and walked around it slowly, his eyes taking in the newly installed windows and doors, the rich beds of earth that had been cleared for flowering shrubs and now sprouted weeds, and the wooden fencing around the back still waiting for its coat of varnish.

The sun beat down mercilessly, and he could feel sweat trickle down his back as he picked his way carefully through the stacks of concrete slabs behind the partly constructed car parking area. He finished his tour of the site and walked back around to the front. Shielding his eyes from the glare of the sun, he squinted up at the abandoned three-storey edifice and marvelled at the desolate silence around him – a remarkable shift from the frenetic activity, only a few weeks earlier, to transform the building into luxury apartments.

The words SYCAMORE HOUSE were proudly stencilled in gold lettering into the graphite marble tiles above the smoked glass doors, but behind the stylish whitewashed exterior and the brand-new windows, the interiors were still far from complete. Sycamore House had become a visual metaphor of his hollow charade of a business, Tyler thought bitterly.

A pair of vultures flew out from the leafy branches above him, and he watched them circle the building before settling on the guttering beneath the new red roof tiles. From their perch, the birds flapped their huge black wings as if marking their territory, and with raspy, drawn-out hisses they fixed him with a proprietary glare that dared him to scare them away. Even the bloody birds were mocking him now, Tyler thought despondently. Unable to bear it any longer, he turned tail and trudged back to his car.

Back at the office, he climbed slowly up the short flight of stairs, and forced his face into a jovial expression he was nowhere close to feeling. Luckily, the first year's office rent had already been paid, but he still had to find the money for his devoted PA's wages at the end of the month. The initial capital from Jeff's company was locked into the redevelopment project, and Tyler's own savings were dwindling fast.

He pushed open the glass door to the office suite, already picturing Patience's sympathetic smile as he updated her on the abortive bank meeting.

'Sir, *sir*! Where have you been?'

Patience jumped to her feet the instant Tyler walked in, her grip on her mobile phone so tight that her knuckles were white. 'Sir, I've been calling you for the past one hour!'

Her dark eyes were almost bulging out of her face, and Tyler's genial expression vanished as a jolt of fear darted through him. He had never seen his placid assistant so agitated, and belatedly it dawned on him that he had forgotten to switch his phone back on after leaving the bank.

'What's wrong?' he barked. 'Is it Theresa? Has something happened to my son or—?'

Patience cut him off with an impatient shake of her head. 'You had a call. A company by the name of Watts Industries.'

The name meant nothing to him, and he stared at her, puzzled. 'Patience, I'm sorry, but I've never heard of Watts Industries. What did they want?'

She took a deep breath, clearly struggling to regain her composure. 'They want a meeting to talk about Sycamore House.'

Tyler stared at her in stunned silence. Then, as her words began to register, he stammered in disbelief, '*What*? Are – are you serious? They want to buy a unit?'

It had been weeks since anyone had shown an interest in the redevelopment, and his mind raced feverishly at the possibility of offloading one of the apartments. A sale would bring in enough money to finish off at least two more units and give him enough breathing space to keep the project alive and save his business.

Patience smiled gleefully, a broad, happy smile that showed each one of her even white teeth. 'No sir. They want the *whole building!*'

Maku

Kicking off her rarely worn high heels, Maku sank into the sofa with a sigh of relief. To forestall any grumbling from Theresa, she had abandoned her comfortable leather sandals and crammed her wide feet into narrow white stilettos for the church service. What she hadn't taken account of was having to stand throughout the garden reception that followed. She carefully massaged each foot in turn, cursing under her breath as the blood flowed back painfully into her crushed toes.

There was really no need to keep her voice down. The house was empty, with the children having been dispatched to their grandmother's while she and Nortey attended Ben's baptism. Following the cocktail reception in Theresa and Tyler's beautifully landscaped garden, Nortey had dropped Maku at home and then left almost immediately to pick up the children, shaking his head ruefully when she'd called out to his retreating back, 'Don't rush back with them – take as long as you like!'

With any luck, Maku thought, his mother would hold him hostage for a few hours, boring him with family gossip and throwing in a few of her many gripes for good measure. Leaving her shoes to join the discarded toys scattered across the living room floor, she walked barefoot to the kitchen, flexing her liberated toes along the way. She filled a glass with cold water from the fridge, and her thoughts returned to the beautiful church service. Theresa had looked radiant in a fitted white lace dress with a tiny matching jacket, and it was incredible how she had snapped back into shape so quickly after giving birth to Ben. Maku smoothed the folds of her flared navy and white skirt, letting her hands skim over the contours of her broad hips, and sighed. Although Abra would soon be two, she wasn't even close to shedding the extra weight from that pregnancy.

She sipped the chilled water slowly. Theresa had looked fabulous, but she really couldn't say the same about her husband. Tyler had appeared gaunt, his expensive suit hanging loosely against his normally muscular frame. Still, it wasn't surprising he was under stress; anyone would go crazy if their main – or in Tyler's case, their only – investor had run off. Had Tyler's jovial smile when she'd engaged him in conversation during the reception been genuine? Or was he trying a bit *too* hard to be brave? She sincerely hoped he wasn't about to have a breakdown. Life was weirder than fiction sometimes, Maku reflected, her mind flicking to the film she'd caught on TV about a man who'd been swindled out of his fortune by his best friend. Hopefully, Tyler wouldn't follow that character's example and stalk and kill Jeff Parnell – but then you never really knew how someone would react if they were desperate. Even Nortey, who had been annoyed at Tyler for abandoning Jake's Joint, had sounded genuinely sorry about the other man's troubles, reserving his snarky comments for Theresa, who always seemed to rub him up the wrong way.

Maku sighed again and pictured herself back in the church with Nortey. But, this time, walking up the aisle towards him in a long dress made from the silky lace hidden in her bedroom drawer. She could hear the organ playing the wedding march and smell the fragrance of the colourful flowers she would choose to decorate the church. In her dream scenario, Nortey would look handsome in an expensive suit like Tyler's – except his would fit properly – and the children would be dressed up and watching the ceremony from the front pew. Best of all, the priest would be waiting at the altar to recite the vows she and Nortey would repeat before pronouncing them man and wife. *Mrs Quarshie, at last!*

The strident ringtone of her mobile crashed into her fantasy, and Maku deposited the empty glass next to the sink and padded back to the living room. Picking up her phone, she glanced at the screen and pulled a face before taking a very deep breath and accepting the call.

'Maku? Is that you?'

The voice on the line sounded both irritated and impatient. But then again, Adoley always sounded like she'd been forced to interrupt something far more important to speak to you.

'Hi. Yes, it's me.'

Only mildly tempted to ask after her sister-in-law, Maku decided to remain silent. *She called me, so she can begin the pleasantries.* But in typical Adoley fashion, social niceties were in short supply.

'How's Isabelle? Is she there?' The peremptory tone immediately raised Maku's hackles. This is *exactly* why the woman should phone her brother instead of me, she fumed silently, and clamped down her teeth hard on her tongue to prevent her instinctive reply.

She inhaled, counted to five, and exhaled. Then, enunciating her words slowly, she replied, 'No, she's at Mama's house with the other kids. Nortey and I went to my friend's baptism, so—'

Adoley cut her off without ceremony. 'I'll call Mama, then. I haven't spoken to her for a few days, so I might as well kill two birds with one stone.'

Briefly relishing the mental image of her mother-in-law being felled by a large rock, Maku was about to hang up when she heard Adoley's voice squawking through the phone, and she reluctantly brought the handset back up to her ear.

'... trying to reach George, but I'm not getting through. Has he been coming over to see Isabelle? He promised me he would spend time with her while I'm over here. Oh, and by the way, I hope you are giving her plenty of vegetables and making sure she takes her multivitamins every day. I told Nortey to keep a close eye on that – I know you're not worried about these things when it comes to your own children, but I've always been very particular about Isabelle's nutrition.'

If you're so particular, why don't you get your cheating husband to cough up some cash, then? Don't you know *how little your brother earns?* Exasperated beyond measure by the patronising tone, Maku fought the overwhelming desire to relay exactly what Adoley's precious George had been up to in her absence and knock her off her arrogant high horse. But, instead, Maku gritted her teeth and swallowed down hard on the words bubbling up into her throat. Whether she liked her or not, Adoley was her sister-in-law – well, sort of, she qualified silently – and that called for some degree of solidarity. Although Adoley still hadn't quite accepted Maku as part of her family, the one thing village life taught you was that you don't live alone. Whatever your views about them, your family came first.

Ending the conversation as politely as she could manage, Maku tossed her phone onto the dining table to join the motley collection of used plates, dirty bibs and half-read newspapers, and wandered back to the kitchen to excavate the last remaining container of soup from the freezer for dinner. Auntie Lizzie's home-cooked food was in dangerously low supply, but thankfully she was bringing a new batch in the morning. Who would have guessed there would be benefits to having a husband who was so chauvinistic that he never opened the freezer, Maku wondered drily, as she placed the pot of chicken soup on the counter to defrost and headed to the bedroom to change out of her party clothes. Her final exams were less than two months away, and with no rowdy children to distract her, she had time for some revision. Relishing the peace, she curled up on the bed and flicked through her accounting book in search of the topics her tutor had hinted might come up in the next test.

All too soon, the sound of the gate scraping open, followed by Nortey's sputtering car engine, brought an end to her study session. Maku pushed her book to one side with a sigh of regret and slipped her feet into the worn flip-flops by her bed. Just as she reached the front door, Samuel and Elijah burst in and raced past her, screaming at the top of their lungs all the way down the corridor towards the living room, jostling furiously to grab the TV remote. Isabelle offered Maku a polite smile and a mumbled 'Good evening, Auntie', before following the boys at a more sedate pace. Seconds later, a harassed-looking Nortey strode in, clutching Abra in his arms.

'Have they eaten?' Maku nodded towards the living room from where the sound of a cartoon soundtrack was blaring.

Nortey handed over the child and shrugged. 'I think so. I didn't ask, but Mama always feeds them so I'm sure they're fine.'

He remained hovering by the door, and Maku raised an eyebrow. 'Are you going somewhere?'

She narrowed her eyes at the guilty look that flashed across his face. She knew that look, and she was in no mood for it. 'Don't tell me you're going to Jake's tonight? We've already had a nice day out – can't you just stay at home for once?'

But even as she said it, she knew she was wasting her breath. Once Nortey had made up his mind, nothing would dissuade him.

'I won't be long, I promise! I *really* need to get hold of Leslie Koranteng. We're working on a project together.' He gave her his sad-puppy-dog look and injected a note of extra wheedling into his voice, 'Just think about it, Maku. If it comes off, we'll make a load of dough. Now, isn't that worth me going out for a couple of hours?'

Maku gnawed at her lip in frustration. She had been hoping to revise for the upcoming test, but without Nortey at home to watch the children, it would be impossible to study until after they'd gone to bed. She opened her mouth for a last-ditch attempt at persuasion, and then closed it again as her hand brushed against Abra's forehead.

Frowning, she looked up at Nortey. 'Abra has a temperature – how long has she been like this?'

His blank expression told her that he hadn't even noticed, and she gave an impatient tsk and hurried towards the bathroom, barely registering the sound of the front door shutting firmly behind him.

Stripping off Abra's light cotton dress, Maku soaked a small towel in cold water and pressed it gently against the drowsy child's face and upper body. Abra squirmed but didn't protest as Maku gently coaxed a small syringe with liquid paracetamol between her lips and wrapped her in a light muslin cloth. A couple of hours later, with the boys and Isabelle changed and ready for bed, Maku tiptoed across to where Abra lay sleeping in her cot. To her horror, instead of the baby's usual gentle snuffling, Abra's breathing was harsh and her small chest heaved feverishly.

Terrified by the sound of her baby's raspy wheezing, Maku's face tightened with fear, and she raced to the living room to find her phone. Punching Nortey's number, she tried to force down her rising panic while the phone rang and rang. It clicked to voicemail, and she suppressed a whimper. Still clutching the phone, she hurried back to the cot and stared intently at the child stirring restlessly in the confined space. When she gently touched her skin, Abra was burning hot.

Oh my God! What the hell am I meant to do? She had three other children in the house, and she needed to get Abra to the hospital immediately! She redialled Nortey's number and, once again, it went to voicemail. Biting her lip, Maku picked up the child and wrapped her in the soft white blanket Lyla had given them as a christening gift, wincing as Abra's hoarse gasps grew even louder. Gathering her daughter against her, Maku seized her handbag from the floor by her bed and hurried to the living room where Isabelle and the boys sat transfixed in front of the television. Far too scared for her daughter to issue her usual threats against sitting too close to the screen, Maku took a deep breath and tried not to let the children sense her panic.

'Boys, Isabelle! Abra is sick and I have to take her to the hospital right now.'

The boys barely broke eye contact with the screen, while Isabelle stared pointedly at the well-worn rubber flip-flops on Maku's bare feet, her expressive features revealing her incredulity at her aunt's choice of footwear.

Maku ignored the unspoken criticism and directed her words at her older son. 'Samuel – are you listening?' she persisted. 'Your father will be home soon, and Qasim is outside by the gate. Lock the front door when I've gone, and don't open it again until Daddy comes. Do you hear?'

Dragging a protesting Samuel down the corridor, she waited until she heard the click of the lock behind her before leaving hurried instructions with the drowsy security man stretched out on his mat. Once outside, she hastened towards the junction to hail a taxi, her thin sandals offering scant protection against the sharp stones studding the untarred road. As the taxi bounced along the road in the dark, Maku anxiously cradled Abra between the folds of the blanket and stroked her forehead to soothe her feeble cries. The air trapped inside the rickety taxi was so stale she could almost taste it, but she didn't dare open a window and risk exposing her child to the sticky humidity of the night.

Why in God's name was Nortey not answering his phone? What if he'd been in an accident while speeding to get home to his family, Maku wondered? Her heart thudded painfully at the thought, and she whipped out her phone and punched Nortey's number with trembling fingers. This time, much to her relief, he answered, his voice almost drowned out by the music playing in the background, and a cacophony of voices raised in laughter.

Shaking her head impatiently, she hissed into the handset, '*Nortey!* You need to go home now!'

'Why, what's wrong?' She heard the sulkiness in his tone, but she couldn't have cared less.

'Abra's *really* sick.'

'Maku, stop overreacting. She probably just has a bit of a cold. She'll be fine.'

'No, she won't!' Maku choked, as her eyes darted towards the flushed face of her swaddled baby. 'We're in a taxi on the way to the hospital. Nortey, I'm deadly serious – go home now and watch your kids! I'll call you when I know what's wrong with her.'

By the time the taxi pulled up in front of the public hospital, Abra's breathing sounded even more laboured, and Maku was trembling with terror from the dark thoughts swirling around her head. She dropped some notes onto the seat next to the driver and broke into a near run up the short flight of steps. Pushing through a set of double doors, she dashed towards the front desk.

The reception area was spartan, illuminated by stark fluorescent strip lighting set against an anaemic green ceiling. A good number of the plastic chairs arranged in cramped rows were occupied, and yet the place was eerily silent. It was hard to tell who was sick as the people waiting appeared to bear their suffering with a stoic quietness. Maku frowned as her eyes fell on an old man sitting in the front row. Although he was doubled over and clearly in agony, he barely made a sound.

Suppressing her panic at the number of people ahead of her, she marched resolutely to the reception desk.

'My baby is sick and needs to see a doctor!' Trying not to sound as scared as she felt, Maku glared at the heavy-set woman with short grey hair sitting behind the counter.

With the weary air of someone who had heard it all before, the woman sounded almost bored as she pushed a white card across the counter towards Maku. 'Fill the form and take a seat. A doctor will call you when it's your turn.'

Incensed by the receptionist's jaded attitude, Maku angrily swept the card aside. 'I *said*, my daughter is very sick. I don't have time to fill in a form. She's hardly breathing – look at her! She must see a doctor immediately!'

The woman gave a short, bitter laugh. 'Madam, look around you. Everyone here is sick and needs to see a doctor. Please, fill in the form and take a seat. A doctor will see you as soon as they can.'

Maku snatched the card and the proffered pen and rocked Abra with one hand while she tried to write down the information with the other. The words swam before her eyes in a blur of tears of fear and frustration, and she blinked them away and scribbled as fast as she could before thrusting the card back at the woman.

Frantically kissing Abra's hot little face, Maku pulled out her phone and dialled Lyla's number. It went instantly to voicemail. Trying hard to keep calm, Maku left a hurried message and immediately dialled Theresa's number. She sagged against the counter with relief when her friend's clear voice came on the line.

Theresa listened without interruption and then spoke briskly. 'I'm on my way. Lyla left here quite a while ago, so keep calling her. Try not to worry, Maku.'

Unwilling to join the people sitting on the worn plastic chairs, Maku paced up and down the reception area cradling her daughter and trying to keep her jangled nerves under control while people were called into the doctors' rooms at what felt like agonisingly long intervals.

Although it felt like twenty hours later to Maku, it was a little over twenty minutes when Theresa hurried through the front doors and made a beeline towards her.

'Come on, let's go – Joseph's outside with the car. I asked Margaret, since she knows everyone in this city, and her friend's a doctor at the Metropolitan Hospital. She rang him, and he says we should come right away.'

Maku stared at her in stunned disbelief. '*Seriously*?'

Theresa gave her a reassuring smile and bent to stroke Abra's face gently before answering. 'Yes, seriously. If we go now, we can be there in ten minutes.'

Maku spun around and stared angrily at the receptionist. 'You see? *That's* what should happen when someone has a seriously sick baby. The doctor should be told to see her right away!'

The woman met Maku's glare with a look of indifference, and Theresa tugged urgently at her friend's arm.

'*Leave it!* It's not her fault the system is under so much pressure. Let's just get Abra to the doctor.'

A minute later, Maku was strapped securely into the back seat of Theresa's air-conditioned car. She pressed an ear against Abra's chest and gnawed at her lips to stop herself from wailing in anguish. Abra's breathing had turned into a long painful wheeze that was agonising to hear.

'We'll be there soon, and they'll take good care of her.' Theresa squeezed Maku's knee gently. 'My doctor always says kids are tougher than they look.'

Maku sighed. 'I just hope Nortey's back at home. I keep thinking about the trouble those boys will get into without an adult in the house.'

'They'll be fine,' Theresa said firmly, and Maku decided to believe her. She had enough on her mind without adding the nightmare scenario of Samuel and Elijah on the loose. She glanced apologetically at Theresa's lace suit. 'I'm so sorry for dragging you away from your guests. You've already had such a busy day without me adding to it.'

'Don't you dare apologise for calling me!' Theresa fixed her with a steely glare. 'I'd have been furious with you if you hadn't, and I'm glad that for once you had the sense to ask for help.'

Chastened, Maku fell silent. After a moment, Theresa reached into her bag for her phone, muttering impatiently as she dialled a number, 'Where the *hell* is Lyla? She left my house ages ago!'

Lyla answered the phone immediately, and Maku listened with half an ear to Theresa's summary of events while she gently rocked her child.

'Okay, then, meet us at the hospital. We're literally just driving in now,' Theresa added.

From the shrub-lined pathway to the steel-framed glass doors and cool, air-conditioned vestibule, Accra Metropolitan Hospital was a world away from the medical facility they had just left. As they walked in, Maku clasped Abra against her breast and looked around in awe at the cream walls, thick carpets and comfortingly subdued lighting. A large television flickered from its stand high on the wall, and soft music played quietly in the background, creating a reassuringly serene atmosphere. Unlike the scuffed plastic seats in the public hospital, the waiting room chairs were padded and had armrests, and Maku sank into the nearest one, leaving it to Theresa to approach the receptionist.

After a short discussion, the woman behind the counter picked up the phone and placed a call. After a few moments, Theresa hurried over to Maku, her voice thick with relief.

'It's fine. They were expecting us, and the doctor is on his way.'

Moments later, a tall, light-skinned man in a white coat strode towards them. Theresa stood up to greet him, and they shook hands before he turned to place a comforting hand on Maku's shoulder.

'I'm Dr Eshun,' he said softly. 'Is this our little patient?' Without waiting for an answer, he whipped off the stethoscope that had been dangling around his neck and pushed the buds into his ears, before gently prising Abra from Maku's hold and peeling back the folds of the blanket. He listened intently and then looked down at Maku who, now her hands were free, was chewing on her thumbnail and making no attempt to conceal her abject terror.

The doctor gave her a reassuring smile. 'I'd like to take your daughter to the examination room and run a few tests. Please try not to worry. I'll come out and see you as soon as we know what we are dealing with.'

Maku nodded, her eyes fearful as she watched him carry her child away. She knew Abra was in safe hands, but her relief was tempered by the fear of what the doctor would find. What if she'd left it too late, or wasted too much time at the other hospital? Far too scared to cry, she was only vaguely aware of Theresa taking the seat next to hers and reaching for her hand.

They sat in silence, listening to the soft strains of the classical music playing in the background, and the different tracks sounded indistinguishable to Maku. Despite the lateness of the hour, staff were coming and going, and hospital porters could be seen wheeling the occasional trolley bed into and out of the lifts.

By the time Lyla arrived almost half an hour later, Maku was visibly agitated. There had been no word from Dr Eshun, and Theresa's soothing assurances were falling on deaf ears.

As soon as she saw Lyla, Maku jumped to her feet. 'Where've you *been*? I've called you a hundred times!' she demanded accusingly.

Lyla looked mortified and quickly held out her arms to wrap Maku in a long, loving hug.

'I'm *so* sorry, Cuz. I didn't hear my phone – where's Abra? What did the doctor say?' Dropping into the empty chair beside Maku, Lyla directed her questions at Theresa.

'We're still waiting to hear. He's examining her now and

doing some tests.' Theresa leaned across Maku to look squarely at Lyla. 'How could you *not* hear your phone – I called you at least three times?' she quizzed.

Even shrouded in her fog of worry, Maku noticed Lyla ducking her head as if to avoid Theresa's stare. 'Look, I'm here now, and Abra is all that matters.'

The conversation came to an abrupt halt as Dr Eshun appeared from a side room and made his way towards them, his white coat flapping against his trousers. Maku rose to her feet shakily, almost wringing her hands in her distress.

'How is she, doctor? How's my daughter?' she pleaded.

The doctor couldn't have been much more than in his early to mid-thirties, but his warm eyes and reassuring voice projected the calm assurance of someone far older.

'Mrs—'

'*Miss* Tetteh,' Maku interrupted earnestly, and Theresa and Lyla exchanged exasperated glances.

'Miss Tetteh, we've checked blood samples and run some tests, and thankfully we've been able to eliminate any serious infections. I'm pretty sure it's the same virus we've been seeing quite a lot recently. Is Abra asthmatic, by the way?'

Maku shook her head in confusion. 'N-no – but what kind of virus does she have? She was fine this morning before she went to her grandmother's house. Is it very bad, doctor? Please tell me she'll be okay!'

'Unfortunately, the virus can sometimes cause quite severe respiratory deterioration—' Maku's face crumpled and he added hastily, 'but please don't worry, she's in good hands here. In general, these things come and go quite quickly, and I know it's a little frightening to observe when it strikes, but, hopefully, she'll be back to herself in a few days. In the meantime, she's quite dehydrated, so we've put her on a drip and administered some steroids to help reduce the wheezing.'

'How long will she need to stay here?' Theresa broke in as the doctor's explanation appeared to have stunned Maku into silence.

Dr Eshun scratched his chin and his eyes darted between Theresa and Maku. 'We'll need to keep her overnight to monitor her temperature and manage the hydration. If she improves, there's no reason why she can't go home tomorrow to recuperate. We try not to keep patients in hospital unless it's absolutely necessary.'

Maku's knees sagged in relief and she had to restrain herself from leaping on to the man and hugging the life out of him. She nodded and sank back into her seat without a word.

Theresa hadn't finished. 'Doctor, do you have a room where Maku can stay with Abra tonight?'

The doctor hesitated. 'Ye-es, but I'm afraid we'd have to charge—'

Theresa brushed aside the rest of his sentence. 'That's not a problem. If you could please arrange it for us, we'd be very grateful.'

With a nod, Dr Eshun strode over to the reception desk. The minute he was out of earshot, Maku looked up at Theresa in alarm. 'Tee, what do you mean it's not a problem? I can't afford a room in this place!'

Theresa gave a tsk of annoyance. 'No one's asking you to,' she hissed under her breath. 'I'll take care of the bill –

you just worry about Abra.' She hesitated, 'I mean, don't worry about Abra – oh, you know what I mean.'

Lyla broke the escalating tension by swooping down to squeeze Maku tightly. 'Honestly, the pair of you. God is good, Cuz. Our little girl will be just fine.'

Maku nodded, and moments later the doctor was back. 'One of our nurses will come for you as soon as the room is ready, and we've transferred Abra. I'm on duty tonight, so I'll keep monitoring her.' With a final reassuring pat of Maku's shoulder, Dr Eshun walked away.

The women sat in silence in the almost deserted waiting area until a young nurse in a starched white uniform approached them with a shy smile.

Maku turned to Theresa, her eyes brimming with unshed tears. 'Tee, I'm so grateful to you for everything you've done. You can't—'

Her voice cracked, and Theresa silenced her with a tight hug. 'Isn't that what sisters are for?' she said softly. 'Just remember the next time you need help that we're always here for you. I'll ring you in the morning, and Joseph and I will come and pick you up when the doctor gives Abra the all-clear.'

Maku nodded with an inelegant sniff, and hugged Lyla goodbye before following the nurse. At the end of a long corridor, the nurse opened a door and stood back to let Maku enter. The first thing she saw when she walked in was Abra lying in a bed with a light cotton sheet draped over her small body. A thin oxygen tube was taped against her cheek, and Maku gasped and covered her mouth with her hands, shocked to see her little girl looking so vulnerable.

'Madam, she is doing well,' the nurse whispered. 'We've given her fluids, and her temperature is already lower than when she was admitted.'

Maku approached the bed gingerly. The nurse was right. Abra was fast asleep and although her breathing was harsh, it sounded less raspy than when they had arrived. She stroked her baby's tiny hand and ran light fingers over her damp silky curls.

After a few moments, Maku raised her head to survey her surroundings, immediately feeling out of place in her dusty flip-flops and tatty house dress. The room was spacious, with tasteful furnishings that included a low-slung leather sofa and two matching armchairs. The television screen mounted on the wall was switched off, and on the sideboard beside the sofa, she could see a tray filled with cups and saucers and a plate of wrapped biscuits. Next to the snacks was a stainless-steel flask and a bowl filled with a variety of teabags. This place looks more like a hotel room than a hospital, Maku observed, wondering exactly how much Theresa would have to pay for this luxury. If this was how the other half lived, then it was high time she, Maku, joined them.

The nurse dimmed the overhead light, and suddenly Maku felt wrung out from the kaleidoscope of emotions she had experienced since Nortey had brought the children home. A single bed had been made up alongside Abra's, and Maku slipped off her flip-flops and stretched out along its length, facing her daughter. She watched the steady rise and fall of the small chest under the sheet, and the panic that had clutched her heart slowly began to ease. After a few minutes, taking care not to disturb the sleeping child, Maku slid her phone out of her bag to dial Nortey's number.

* * *

As the doctor predicted, Abra responded quickly to the treatment, and by mid-morning her temperature had fallen enough for him to confidently discharge her. With Theresa by Maku's side, and Joseph behind the wheel to navigate the light Sunday traffic, they drove through the quiet city streets back to Kaneshie.

Desperately tired and struggling to keep her eyes open after her sleepless night, Maku held Abra tightly against her. Despite the comfort of the hospital bed, she had stayed awake throughout the night, watching the nurse with eagle eyes whenever she came in to check Abra's temperature, and quizzing Dr Eshun relentlessly during his visits to monitor the baby's progress.

Nortey had clearly been waiting for them and his face was pinched with anxiety as he held open the door for an exhausted Maku, closely followed by Theresa. The high-pitched yelps of Scooby-Doo and his pals floated down the corridor from the living room, answering Maku's unspoken question about the whereabouts of her sons and Isabelle.

Nortey gently lifted the sleeping child from his wife's arms, and kissed Abra's soft cheeks with exquisite gentleness. Then he raised his head to meet Maku's weary gaze, and she could have wept at the depth of love she saw in his eyes.

'I'm so sorry,' he said quietly.

Maku nodded. Nortey might be irresponsible at times,

but she knew how much he adored his children.

Nortey turned to Theresa and, to Maku's astonishment, his eyes glistened with unshed tears that turned his deep voice husky. 'I can't thank you enough for what you've done for Abra and – and for *us*.'

For a moment, Maku wondered if she was dreaming. Nortey, who *never* had a good word to say about Theresa, was gazing at her as if he had come face to face with his personal saviour. Which she probably was, come to think of it.

Theresa smiled cheerfully and patted Nortey's arm. 'I'd better go and give Joseph a chance to enjoy the rest of his day off. *You*,' – she looked pointedly at Maku – 'need to get some sleep. Abra needs her mum to be healthy.'

Maku nodded and reached up to gently extricate her daughter from Nortey's arms. Theresa turned towards the door and then hesitated. Turning back, she looked directly at Nortey and said softly, 'Look after her.'

Nortey closed the door behind Theresa, and Maku yawned widely. She dropped a light kiss on Abra's head and shuffled slowly towards the bedroom, grateful it wasn't a working day.

'Don't worry about the kids, okay?' Nortey called after her. 'I'll get them dressed and take them out so you and Abra can have some peace.'

Maku nodded, too bone-weary to reply. Gently placing the sleeping child in her cot, she marvelled at the rapid turn of events of the past few hours. The luxury hospital/ hotel already felt like a dream, and she stripped off her clothes and slipped an old T-shirt over her head before crawling under the bed covers.

As she drifted off to sleep, her mind went back to the look she had seen on Nortey's face, and the love that she knew was hers. Whatever their situation, she had never doubted how much he cared for her and their children, and she snuggled into her pillow feeling overcome by intense gratitude for what she had. Maybe being married – *properly* married, that is – wasn't all that it was cracked up to be. There had been no sign of Kwesi at the baptism, or afterwards at Theresa's house, and Lyla had looked the picture of guilt when she'd finally turned up at the hospital. Lyla was so clearly unhappy in her marriage that if her cousin hadn't been such a religious fanatic, Maku would have sworn she had something going on the side.

She rolled over and plumped up the pillow under her head to get a better view of Abra in her cot. Maybe it was time to accept her marital arrangement, and just be thankful she had wonderful friends and a good man who loved her. As Maku's eyelids drooped, something niggled at the edge of her memory, something she knew she had to take care of. But she couldn't quite push through the heavy barrier of fatigue, and within seconds she was fast asleep.

Nortey

Nortey seized the remote control in exasperation, lowering the volume of the television until he could make himself heard. Ignoring Samuel's outraged protest, he turned his attention back to Elijah, and tried again.

'Son, be a good boy and wear these trousers, okay? Look, I know you love your Transformers pyjamas, but if I take you out wearing them, your mother will kill me.'

Elijah thrust out his lower lip stubbornly, and Nortey tried to tamp down his growing frustration. *Christ! How on earth did Maku manage this?* After protracted negotiations with the children over who should take their bath first, who was – or wasn't – wearing what, and which one of them could choose the TV programme, Nortey's brain was about to explode. And it was still only eleven o'clock! Conscious that he hadn't yet fed the children, Nortey gave up the pyjamas battle and went to sort out breakfast.

He pushed open the kitchen door and came to an abrupt halt at the sight of an elderly woman unloading a stack of food containers onto the kitchen counter from a striped nylon bag. He hadn't heard the gate opening, which meant Qasim must have snuck her in. Judging from the woman's furtive expression and her apparent familiarity with his kitchen, Nortey would have laid bets it wasn't for the first time.

As soon as he walked in, she stood to attention, smoothing down her traditional skirt and top and deftly tightening the matching wrapper around her waist. Although her eyes widened as Nortey slowly approached her, she said nothing. Turning his attention to the items on the counter, he inspected the tubs of food and then glanced down at the half-empty bag before returning his gaze to the woman. She stood silently, her guarded expression issuing an unspoken challenge.

The stand-off continued for a full minute. Then, still too stunned to utter a word, Nortey bent to carefully lift the remaining containers out of the bag. While he did so, the woman opened the freezer and neatly stacked the tubs on the counter inside the almost empty compartment. He handed over what was left, and she arranged them carefully before closing the door with a firm thud.

'How much?' Nortey finally broke the silence, reaching into the back pocket of his denims to pull out his wallet.

Auntie Lizzie's eyes brightened. She quickly named her price and then watched intently as he counted out the notes and handed them over. Thrusting the money inside her bodice, she gave a nod of thanks, scooping up the empty bag and folding it roughly.

'*Nyame nhyira wo!*' she exclaimed. With a wink followed by a cheeky smile, she scurried out before he could say a word.

Nortey chuckled softly and, as the absurdity of what had just transpired struck him afresh, he burst into loud guffaws, almost choking with laughter. *God bless me, indeed!* He shook his head in rueful disbelief. Maku never *ever* failed to surprise him! Wondering how long his wife had been outsourcing the cooking, he was still chuckling as he opened the cupboard to retrieve Isabelle's cornflakes and a cereal bowl. He hesitated, and then brought out two more bowls. Enough was enough. If Isabelle could enjoy expensive cereal, his boys deserved no less. It was time for things to change.

When breakfast was over, Nortey shooed the children outside to wait in the car and tiptoed into the silent bedroom. Abra was fast asleep, and he gently laid his hand against her face. Her skin felt cool and her breathing was even. After a moment, satisfied that her temperature seemed relatively normal, he turned to where Maku snored softly under the light covers. His eyes softened as his gaze moved over her face, and he noticed for the first time the fine wrinkles around her eyes.

He bent to pick up Maku's precious accounting textbook from the floor and placed it on the bedside table with a sigh. How had he become so wrapped up in his activities that he hadn't realised what was going on in his own home? Seeing the lines of exhaustion on Maku's face left him with an overwhelming sense of sadness and shame. How could he have failed to notice how much it took for her to look after four kids, and not even suspect his wife was so overloaded with work and her course that she had to pay someone to help her out? He knew Maku was studying so she could earn more money to supplement his salary – an amount so meagre he would have been embarrassed to admit it to anyone – and yet he had been so caught up in his selfish plans, he hadn't even noticed his daughter was burning up with a fever.

Coming home to find his children in tears at being left

inside on their own had felt like a kick in the stomach. But it had been nothing compared to the utter helplessness he had felt while listening to Maku's tearfully whispered reports from Abra's bedside throughout the night. Unable to leave the children so he could comfort his wife and see his daughter, Nortey had berated himself mercilessly for his blind self-centredness.

He ran his fingers lightly over Maku's wiry braids, smiling at how smartly she had pulled the wool over his eyes about the food, which she always earnestly assured him was home cooked. Which it was, he conceded wryly, just not in *his* home. He remembered the apprehension on the woman's face when he'd caught her in the kitchen – she had clearly expected him to blow up at her and lose his temper. After all, why else would a wife hide what she was doing from her husband? But there was no way on earth he could be annoyed at his magnificent wife. He was already worn out after a few hours of managing the children alone; a task, he reminded himself soberly, which Maku performed every single day – on top of studying to give them all a better life. Theresa was right; he needed to do a better job of taking care of his wife. It really was time for things to change.

* * *

'*Moses!* Didn't I warn you not to disturb me?'

George opened the door and blinked rapidly with the bleary-eyed look of someone who had just been rudely awakened. As his eyes focused on Nortey standing on the doorstep, one hand holding Isabelle's and the other a bulging suitcase, George quickly pulled together the silk

321

dressing gown he had plainly thrown on in a hurry, while Isabelle, her pink school bag strapped securely on her back, beamed at her father.

'*Nortey!* What – what are you doing here?' George stammered, evidently too stunned to greet his daughter. His stubbly cheeks sagged in dismay as his gaze darted frantically between his child and his brother-in-law.

But Nortey's attention was momentarily diverted as his eyes fixed upon a silver Golf – a car which did not belong to his sister – parked under the carport next to George's Mercedes. He swivelled back to look pointedly at George, and the fearful expression that met him instantly confirmed the car's ownership. Without answering, Nortey pushed past his brother-in-law and led his niece into the hallway, propping the suitcase against the wall.

'Isabelle, take your bag up to your room. Your daddy and I need to talk.'

The two men watched in silence as the little girl skipped up the wide staircase, her curly braids bouncing up and down in rhythm.

As soon as she was out of earshot, George hissed fiercely, 'Nortey, what the *hell* are you playing at? Why didn't you call me?'

'Are you *insane? I* should have called *you*. The same person who totally ignores me whenever I ring?' Nortey glared at him furiously, and only the thought of his mission held him back from punching George on his large, smug nose.

'Is it about money? Look, if you need more money for Isabelle...,' George blustered, wrapping his dressing gown tightly around him and tying the cord over his protruding stomach.

'No, it's not about money. At least not money for your daughter. It's time Isabelle came home. Abra has been seriously ill and Maku has her hands full, so you need to take care of your own child. My wife does too much already, and with all the bills we have to cover, we're stretched to the max.'

'I've just told you I can give you money for Isabelle,' George said defensively. 'Whatever you need, just tell me.'

Nortey looked at him, unimpressed. Where was this burst of generosity during all those months when he and Maku had desperately needed it?

Despite the air conditioning blasting through the hallway, George was visibly sweating, and his eyes darted nervously towards the upstairs landing. Nortey shook his head in disgust. It didn't take a genius to conclude there was someone else in the house, and it was time to come to the point.

'I'm glad you've mentioned money because I need a loan from you,' Nortey said bluntly.

George looked at him warily. 'A *loan*? If you're returning my daughter, what do you need a loan for?'

'For my wife.'

George looked baffled, and Nortey continued, 'I've decided to have a church wedding, and I need you to lend me the money. I want to give Maku the best surprise she could imagine.'

'You must be crazy!' George scoffed. 'Mama has told everyone she will boycott any such wedding.'

'Then we'll do it without her,' Nortey said equably. 'But if I know my mother, she'll show up and act like she never said anything of the sort. So, all I need from you is twenty thousand cedis.'

George spluttered. 'Are you *joking*? Do you think I'm made of money! Besides, why the hell would I risk my mother-in-law's anger by lending you money?'

Nortey shrugged. 'It's up to you. If you're prepared to risk your wife's anger instead when she hears about your mistress, then that's your choice. But I think we both know Adoley will kick you out in a heartbeat if she finds out what you've been up to. She's already complaining she can never get hold of you, and knowing my sister's temper, if she hears about your "friend" I can guarantee you'll be spending a lot more than twenty thousand to pay your divorce bill and cough up alimony.'

George narrowed his eyes. 'You're bluffing! You wouldn't dare cause problems between Adoley and me. Your mother would kill you!'

Nortey blinked innocently. 'Oh, *I* wouldn't need to tell my sister a thing. I could just go upstairs right now and introduce Isabelle to your friend, and I'm pretty sure she'll tell her mother how she found a strange woman in Mummy's bed. Your playmate is up there, isn't she? So why don't we go and make the introductions, huh?'

George's face was instantly suffused with panic, and he rushed to plant himself at the bottom of the stairs, stretching out his arms to block access to the staircase. Barely suppressing his fury, Nortey swatted him out of the way.

The minute Nortey's foot hit the bottom step, George hissed, 'Okay, *okay!* I'll give you the money!'

'Great. Get your chequebook now, because I'm not leaving without it. Oh, and make it out for cash. Since you like shopping at Swanson's, I'm sure you're good for it.'

In less than five minutes, George had written out the cheque. He scribbled his signature at the bottom with a shaking hand and ripped it out of the book to hand over to Nortey, adding bitterly, 'And don't you dare tell your mother you got the money from me!'

Nortey tucked the slip of paper into the breast pocket of his shirt without comment and called up the stairs. 'Isabelle! Come down and let's go for a car ride while Daddy has a shower and gets your room ready. I promised to buy the boys some sweets – and we can get you some cornflakes while we're at it.'

Nortey watched the little girl bound down the stairs and out of the front door before turning to George. 'We'll be back in an hour. Make sure that woman and everything belonging to her is out of my sister's house by the time I'm back. And if I *ever* catch sight of you with her again – money or no money, I'll tell Adoley myself!'

With that, Nortey strode outside. Taking Isabelle's hand, he whistled all the way to his car.

Lyla

Lyla narrowly avoided stepping on the dirty nappy, and she bent to pick it up with a grunt of disgust. She held it gingerly between two fingers and retrieved an empty plastic bag from the items carelessly strewn across the dining table, dropping the nappy inside and tying the contents securely. Looking around the messy living room, she sucked her teeth in irritation and took the bag to the kitchen to dump on top of the overflowing bin by the back door. You could take the girl out of the village but getting the village out of this girl was clearly never going to happen. If living with Mama for years hadn't erased Maku's chronic untidiness, then nothing would.

'*Ma-ku!* Hurry up, will you?' Lyla yelled from the kitchen doorway in the general direction of her cousin's bedroom. 'Theresa's waiting in the car and we should have left ages ago!'

A muffled shout was soon followed by the sound of Maku's bedroom door opening and then slamming shut. 'Cuz, I'm *coming!* I'm sorry, I thought I'd have more time to get ready, but Nortey and the kids only left a few minutes before you guys got here.'

Lyla returned to the living room to collect her bag and follow her cousin out of the house, waiting impatiently while a clearly flustered Maku fumbled with her key and locked the front door behind her. Lyla felt a pang of guilt for being so judgemental. The poor girl had been through so much recently and, if her house was a mess, it was also because Maku was a busy working mother with no domestic help.

Lyla linked her arm affectionately through her cousin's as they strolled towards the car. 'I'm sorry for shouting – I know you have a lot on your plate.'

Maku grinned cheerfully, looking relieved that Lyla sounded like her normal self. 'It's okay. Things have been a bit tough but – can you believe Nortey actually took the kids out this evening without me having to beg him? I nearly fainted when he said I deserved a night out with the girls.'

They giggled and climbed into the car to join Theresa. Lyla drove off, turning up the music so they could all sing along to the songs blaring from the radio. It was a warm, dry evening – perfect for a night on the town – and heading into the brightly lit city centre, the three women laughed and talked over each other excitedly.

'So, where are we going then?' Maku demanded from the back seat. Decked out in a silky black dress she rarely got the chance to wear, she was enjoying the air-conditioned luxury of Lyla's Audi. 'It had better be somewhere posh now I'm able to squeeze myself back into this dress!'

Theresa turned around to scrutinise Maku. 'You know, you actually *have* lost weight.'

'Yeah, well, I should be skin and bone after the two weeks of hell I've been through. D'you know that, apart from going to work, this is the first time I've left Abra since she got sick?'

Lyla glanced over her shoulder to flash a sympathetic smile. 'Nortey's right, you do deserve a night out. And don't worry; we're going somewhere *very* posh. I've booked us a table at The Embassy hotel. They do a buffet, so you can eat as much as you like. That said,' she eyed Maku through the rear-view mirror, 'if you're happy you've lost weight, you might want to go easy on the food.'

Maku snorted. '*Please*! I can diet tomorrow. Tonight, it's all about having fun – which means eating and drinking as much as I like.'

An hour and a half, and two heaped plates of food later, Maku was groaning in her seat and struggling to breathe after her assault on the buffet.

Lyla rolled her eyes in good-humoured exasperation. 'Are you familiar with the word moderation?'

Maku was too stuffed to retaliate, and half-heartedly pulled a face that made Theresa splutter with laughter. Lyla smiled. It was good to see Theresa looking like her old self again. Her fears that her best friend's marriage was heading for the rocks had receded, and Tee looked happier than ever.

'You're not missing Ben tonight, then?' Lyla teased.

'Nope.' Theresa didn't hesitate. 'I spent all afternoon with him and Tyler's on duty now.'

A mental picture of the soon-to-be baby that was dominating her own life popped into Lyla's mind, and she swirled her fork around her half-eaten plate of food, her appetite vanishing as she remembered the stand-off with Ma Abena.

'Do you two realise how lucky you are to have children? I want one so badly that I'm considering doing something I never thought I could.'

She must have sounded more wistful than she realised

because both Maku and Theresa looked up sharply.

Maku spoke first. 'Okay, Lyla, what's going on?'

No matter how hard you tried, you couldn't hide the existence of a real live person forever, Lyla thought wryly. It was time to tell the truth – after all, if she couldn't trust her sisters, who else was there? She dropped her fork onto the plate and dabbed at her lips with the white linen napkin embossed with The Embassy's logo, sneaking a quick glance around the room. The restaurant was busy, but the tables were set well apart and there was no chance of being overheard. Nevertheless, Lyla lowered her voice and leaned forward, and the other two immediately followed suit.

'There's no easy way to say this, so I'll just spit it out.' She took a deep breath and tried to inject a light-hearted note into her voice, despite the pain lodged deep in her heart. 'Kwesi has been having an affair, and the woman is pregnant.'

Theresa blinked in shock and then gasped and covered her mouth with her hand. '*Lyla!* Oh my God, no!'

Maku's eyes hardened and she reached out to cover Lyla's hand with her own. 'Who is she, Cuz? Who's the woman? Tell me, and I'll beat her myself!'

Lyla squeezed her cousin's hand gently. 'It's okay. I've known for a while, although I must admit I'm still struggling to get my head around it all. She's only a young girl and—'

'If she's old enough to get pregnant, then she's old enough to know what she was doing with your husband is wrong,' Maku broke in grimly. 'Wait a minute; have you actually *met* her?'

Lyla nodded. 'Yes, she came to the house and told me herself.'

Theresa's jaw dropped. 'I don't believe it! The *bloody nerve* of the girl! Lyla, what are you going to do? You can't stay with Kwesi after this, surely?'

'He's begged me not to leave him. He says it was a mistake and that he loves me.'

'What does he think was the mistake? What he did – or the getting caught part?' Theresa said savagely, and Lyla sighed. This was exactly why she had procrastinated about sharing the news with her closest friends. She was still torn about what to do and, justified though they were, Theresa and Maku being furious at Kwesi didn't help the difficult decision she had yet to make.

'Girls, believe me, there's nothing you can say that I haven't already thought about both Kwesi and Nadia – that's her name, by the way. She looks like a twelve-year-old kid with big boobs who's raided her mother's make-up bag and slapped everything she could find on her face. She's barely educated. I just don't get what Kwesi saw in her.'

Maku raised a sardonic eyebrow. 'Cuz, I hate to say it, but I really don't think Kwesi slept with her because he wanted to discuss her insights into world politics.'

Lyla shuddered. 'Ugh – I really don't want to think about it.'

'Well, if the twelve-year-old is having a baby, you're going to have to,' Maku said in a hard voice. 'Not that there's much to think about. Just get rid of the bastard – and I mean Kwesi, not the baby.'

'I wish it was that simple.' Lyla raised a hand to stop her

as Maku tried to interrupt. 'Look, I know what Kwesi did was reprehensible, and I'm not condoning any of it, but—'

'But what? You're still going to carry on living with him and being the good Christian wife?' Theresa stared at her in disbelief, disgust written all over face. 'His affairs were one thing, but a *baby*? Especially after everything you've gone through to have your own – that's just *despicable*!'

Lyla winced. 'I get it, Tee, trust me. You both know how much I want a child and,' she took a deep breath and the words tumbled out one after the other, 'and that's why I'm thinking about Kwesi's mother's suggestion.'

Maku forgot the discomfort of the dress squeezing her abdomen and sat bolt upright to inspect Lyla through narrowed eyes.

'And what exactly did that old witch have to say?'

Lyla carefully avoided making eye contact with either of them. 'Ma Abena thinks, when the baby is born, that Kwesi and I should take it and bring it up as ours.'

Theresa inhaled sharply but seemed too stunned to speak, while Maku's face remained expressionless. Lyla chewed on her lower lip, pleating her napkin between fingers that were suddenly shaking, while her eyes darted from one woman to the other.

'Will one of you *please* say something? I nearly slapped the old woman when she first came out with it, but the more time I've spent thinking about the whole situation, the less ridiculous it sounds.'

She turned to Theresa in a naked plea for understanding. 'Come on, Tee! We know of so many cases where kids from different mothers all live together as one blended family. This wouldn't be so different, would it?'

Theresa stared back stonily, and then reached for her glass and took a sip. 'Lyla, what do you want me to tell you? What message do you think you're sending Kwesi if you agree to look after a kid he's had with his mistress?'

'I don't know – maybe, that I've forgiven him?' Lyla said hesitantly. 'I knew he wasn't a saint when I married him, but then again, who says *I* am?'

'Oh, *please*! There's nothing you've done that even comes close to what Kwesi has got away with.'

While the two women were sparring, Maku had been lost in thought. Suddenly, she cut across Theresa's angry protests.

'Maybe it's not such a bad idea.'

Theresa turned on her indignantly. 'What are you talking about? It's an *awful* idea.'

Maku tutted in irritation. 'The trouble with you is that your head is full of all these English ideas about love and romance – not that it seems to stop people over there from also having affairs, mind you. There's no point looking at me like that, Tee, this is *Africa*. As I keep telling you, we look at these things differently here.'

She turned to Lyla and her tone was as practical as if she were discussing the weather. 'Let's face it, Cuz, you want a baby. Now, we all agree Kwesi is a dog who deserves a good kicking, but if there's a chance he can give you what you want, then you should take it. But you'll need to be *very* careful.'

She strained forward, her voice almost a whisper, and the other two leaned in. 'I saw this Nigerian movie once where the man brought home a baby girl and forced his wife to look after it. When the girl grew up, she and her birth mother plotted to poison the wife so the husband could marry his former mistress. So, Lyla, I'm just saying. Look after the kid, yes, but keep a close eye on it. You don't want to spend years raising this baby, and then have it turn around and try to murder you!'

With a look that clearly said, *'Don't say I didn't warn you'*, Maku leaned back and gently massaged her bulging tummy.

Nonplussed, Lyla and Theresa looked at each other for a moment, and then burst out laughing. Almost hysterical with laughter despite the gravity of her situation, Lyla ignored Maku's pout and gestured to the waiter to bring the bill.

* * *

Driving home after dropping off Maku and Theresa, Lyla's thoughts returned to the conversation at the restaurant. Turning to her friends for advice hadn't helped to bring her any closer to a decision; by the time they'd parted company, Theresa had been vehemently against the idea of taking in Kwesi's child, and Maku had stuck equally firmly to her guns.

Lyla glanced at the clock on the dashboard. Ten o'clock. She really ought to go home, but she knew she wasn't going back to Marula Heights, at least not yet. She smiled as she turned the car towards the highway leading to Reuben's mansion which felt far more like home to her than the silent, sterile house where she was forced to confront a husband she could barely bring herself to speak to.

Her confession to Theresa and Maku about Nadia's baby was one thing, but Reuben was a secret that Lyla wasn't ready to share. The relationship was much too complicated to explain, and even talking about him would force her to confront the contradictions between her religious beliefs and her actions. How on earth could she explain to Theresa that she loved this man but couldn't let herself be with him fully? How would she make Maku understand that, after that first magical time, she and Reuben had never again made love, but instead spent countless hours talking, laughing and sharing their hopes and dreams? Occasionally, the temptation for them to touch and to kiss became too strong to overcome. But in Lyla's mind, however irrational it sounded, by not having sex with him, her relationship with Reuben was not an affair.

Lyla sighed quietly. How indeed could she expect her friends to understand that Reuben had created a haven of safety, warmth and love for her, when she couldn't quite comprehend it herself? All she knew was that this magnificent man had coaxed her back to life. That when she had been at her lowest and unable to eat, sleep or see a way forward, Reuben had literally nursed her back to health. When she spoke, he listened so intently that Lyla knew he heard both what she said and what she left unsaid. His rudimentary attempts at cooking when they were alone had left them both helpless with laughter but had also encouraged her to see making food as a joy, and not simply penance for an errant husband. Eating better and feeling loved, the energy and spirit of the old Lyla had blossomed, slowly pushing through the heavy layer of self-loathing and despair.

Nothing felt better than the evenings spent with

Reuben on the huge, squashy sofa, cradled up against him as they listened to music and talked about their day. The naked admiration in his eyes whenever he looked at her acted like rain showers over her parched self-esteem, and her renewed confidence was reflected in a rejuvenated wardrobe now filled with sassy clothes in bold colours. No longer the wilting and abandoned flower she had once been, Reuben's care and laughter, as well as his sheer presence, had *refreshed* her.

Lyla waited for the guard to open the gates, and then drove inside to park her car next to Reuben's. With a wide smile, she hurried up the steps to the front door, desperate to see the man she had been thinking about all day.

* * *

The kiss deepened, and Lyla moaned, wrenching herself away from him before the passion racing through her body burned through her weakened defences. Her pulse was racing furiously but she steeled herself against Reuben's anguished groan of protest. Evading his outstretched arms, she pushed herself off the sofa to snuggle into the adjoining armchair, bringing her knees up to her chest and smoothing back her hair with a trembling hand as she tried to catch her breath.

The first, glorious, and only time she and Reuben had made love, Lyla had felt none of the guilt she expected would follow the flagrant breach of her marital vows. After each subsequent clandestine visit to Reuben's house, she'd waited expectantly for whatever barrier was holding back her conscience to crumble and leave her drowning in a swamp of shame and self-disgust for betraying her marriage. Instead, she left Reuben's house each night feeling more alive and more herself than she could ever remember. *And yet... and yet...*

Lyla sighed inwardly. No matter how much her heart yearned for this big, beautiful man gazing at her with such naked passion, she was a married woman and wasn't free to be his in the way they both wanted. Being with Reuben meant everything to her, but the idea of ending her marriage – imperfect as it was – was a struggle to contemplate.

'How long are you going to keep on torturing me?'

From where he lay sprawled along the length of the sofa, Reuben's breathing sounded even more ragged than her own.

She attempted a smile, but the look he gave her made it clear that he wasn't amused, and she bit her lip, still feeling the delicious pressure of his mouth against hers. Wrapping her arms tightly around her knees, she tried to cling on to rational thoughts before her physical and emotional frustration overwhelmed her. Reuben was right; she *was* torturing him – and tearing herself apart in the process. Her steadfast refusal to sleep with him again was, to Reuben's mind, both absurd and infuriating when, as he repeatedly pleaded, she could end her loveless marriage and commit to a new life with him. For Lyla, on the other hand, with every day they spent together, it became harder for her to make sense of the complicated situation she had allowed to develop.

'Lyla, I'm *begging* you! Leave Kwesi and come to me. You don't love him, and you know how I feel about you – why won't you trust me enough to let me take care of you?'

336

'Of course, I trust you! I trust you with my *life*, but that's not the point.'

'Then, what *is* the point? Because I'm struggling to understand why we are doing this to ourselves.'

He swung his legs off the sofa and leaned forward to gaze intently into her eyes. The music playing in the background ended, and the silky notes faded to a silence that amplified the tension between them.

Lyla broke the quiet with a whisper. 'I'm sorry. I don't want my being here to upset you. It's not easy for me, either, but you know my situation...'

Her voice tailed off miserably as she stared at him, wishing with every part of her being that she could take away the pain in his eyes. But this wasn't just about the two of them. There was also a child involved, even if that child wasn't hers – or, at least, not yet. She had walked away from having one child, and she simply couldn't do it again.

Lyla so wished that Reuben would understand why she couldn't reject this child, too. She had spent hours praying that he would see, just as she did, that God hadn't yet forgiven her and that this baby was a test, a chance to make amends for the awful sin she had committed. But beneath her conviction, a small, scared voice inside her whispered: *So then, why are you here?* What indeed was the point of being here with this man? If she wanted the baby enough to stay with Kwesi, then what about Reuben?

'What about me, Lyla?' The slight tremor in his voice gave lie to the apparent calmness of his question.

Her eyes fell. 'I don't know,' she whispered wretchedly. 'He's still my husband and I owe it to him to at least—'

'You owe him nothing!' Reuben ground out, his voice unusually harsh. 'He's cheated on you more times than you can count. He has lied to you almost every day since you married him – the man doesn't deserve you!'

Lyla looked up at him sadly. 'Maybe he does deserve me. I'm really no angel, and I so wish you could see that.'

How can I get you to understand? Her gaze shifted to the huge black and white portrait of the twins, and she felt her eyes mist over. Those beautiful, smiling babies, now gone through no fault of their own.

'Reuben, it's not just about him. There's a child involved who didn't ask to be born into these circumstances. Surely you must see that I can make amends by taking care of the baby and allowing something good to come out of all this?'

'My darling, even if you think it's the right thing to do, you have absolutely no idea if the girl will agree. If you were in her shoes, would you let someone else take your child?'

She winced, and his voice softened. He reached across the space dividing them and took one of her hands, caressing it gently between his.

'Sweet, sweet Lyla. I know you want to do the right thing by your conscience, but do you think it's fair to use this child to assuage your own sense of guilt?'

Shocked, Lyla pulled her hand away. 'Of all people, I thought you would understand about children and loss!'

Reuben inhaled sharply but he didn't take his eyes off her. 'This baby is not your responsibility – nor is it the cure for your ailing marriage.'

She shook her head stubbornly. 'You don't know that.'

Reuben looked ready to explode with frustration, and

she watched apprehensively as he got up to change the track, keeping his back to her while he fiddled with the controls on the high-tech sound system. Another song began to play, and he stood still, letting the soft strains of the music flood the room and cool the heated atmosphere.

After a couple of minutes, he turned back to Lyla. His eyes searched hers and she returned his gaze with a mixture of sadness and defiance.

Reuben shook his head slowly, and then his rich, deep tones cut across the music. 'I want to take care of you, Lyla. I love you.'

A jolt of electricity shot through her. Of course, she knew he had strong feelings for her, but this was the first time Reuben had used those words. Her heart melted at the vulnerability in his eyes and the sweetness of his voice. What in God's name had she ever done to deserve this wonderful human being standing in front of her declaring his love?

NOTHING!!! The harsh Voice, having gone quiet for ages, roared its unexpected return. A few months of bliss had lulled her into a security which Reuben's declaration suddenly ripped away, triggering an unexpected and savage frenzy of self-loathing. As if re-energised by its absence, the bitter, unforgiving Voice inside her head launched into a brutal and mocking tirade. *You dare to think you deserve this when you know what you've done? You are a lying cheat, just like Kwesi. No, you are even worse – at least he's not a murderer. Kwesi is the one you deserve, not Reuben!*

Unable to stop the vicious stream of abuse she was directing at herself, Lyla wailed in agony. An avalanche of hot tears coursed down her face and deep sobs wracked her body as she wept uncontrollably. It didn't matter how much Reuben loved her, it was never going to be enough to wipe away the shame or the pain that was so deeply seared into her soul. Why God? she sobbed. Why did you let me find this man only to have to let him go? Do you really hate me that much?

For a moment, Reuben stood frozen in bewilderment. Then with a muffled curse, he went to her and dropped to his knees to cradle her against him.

'No!' she protested. Furiously gulping back her sobs, she pushed his arms away with a fierce strength and scrambled up from the chair. She pressed a hand on his shoulder, urging him to stay put, and stared down at him with eyes swimming with tears.

'You *can't* love me. Even God doesn't, really. Why do you think He's punishing me like this?'

Reuben's face contorted with such pain that for a moment she feared he was about to cry.

'Lyla, please don't do this to yourself. Don't – don't do this to *us*!' he pleaded.

With the back of her hand, she swiped fiercely at the tears on her cheeks and bent to snatch her bag from the thick pile carpet. Reuben was still kneeling, and her heart almost burst inside her chest at the naked despair in his eyes.

She hesitated, praying for strength. Her chest was pounding with fear, but she knew what she had to do. She bit her lip so hard she could taste the blood in her mouth.

'I – I'm so sorry... for everything. I have to go.'

Driving back to Marula Heights tested Lyla's driving

skills to their limit. Between the dense blackness of the night and the tears that blurred her vision all the way home, she had no idea how she reached the gates to the estate. She stared unseeingly at the security guard who rushed to raise the barrier, and sped down the wide avenue to her house, heedless of the speed bumps scraping the chassis of her car.

She walked into the house and then stopped to dry her eyes and smooth her braids into some semblance of tidiness. Despite the lateness of the hour, she could hear noises coming from the kitchen, and her heart sank at the thought of seeing Kwesi. She felt drained after the scene with Reuben, and she wanted nothing more than to fall into bed and cry herself to sleep.

'Lyla?' Kwesi stood in the kitchen doorway, the light behind him outlining his slim silhouette. For a second, her mind flashed to the rugged muscularity of the man she had just left, and a fresh prickle of tears bit the back of her eyes.

'Um... are you hungry?' Kwesi sounded hesitant as he held up a sandwich he had clearly just finished assembling. 'I can make you one, if you like?'

Her stomach twisted violently at the thought of food, and she shook her head. 'No, it's fine. I – I had dinner with the girls.'

Kwesi nodded and she stood awkwardly, not sure whether to run past him and up to the safety of her bedroom or to engage in the stilted conversation that now passed for communication between them. Exhaustion won, and she gave up the struggle and made for the stairs. But, after a few paces, she changed her mind and swung round to look directly at him.

'I think it's time we decided what we're doing about Nadia and the baby, don't you?'

Ignoring the look of confusion that flooded Kwesi's handsome features, Lyla stood her ground. 'I know I didn't want to hear it before but, whether we like it or not, the fact is there's going to be a child. So, what are we going to do?'

Kwesi looked down at his sandwich as if it held the answer, and then back at his wife. After a moment, he shrugged helplessly.

'I don't know – whatever you want.'

Her eyes flashed with exasperated fury. 'What do you mean, "whatever I want"? Don't you care that you have a child on the way? Is it that easy for you to pass off a baby as if we were discussing a – a holiday or something?'

The hunted expression she knew so well settled on his face, and he shifted uneasily from one foot to the other.

'Look, all I meant is I'll do whatever makes you happy. If you want us to raise the child together, then I'll make it happen. The kid is mine as well as Nadia's, and we can fight for custody if she tries to be difficult.'

If you were in her shoes, would you let someone else take your child? Reuben's words sounded as clearly in her ears as if he was standing right next to her. However badly Nadia had behaved, was it fair to force her – or indeed anyone – to part with their child? Lyla shuddered inwardly at the thought of Kwesi using his charm to coax the girl, playing on her feelings for him with lies or, even worse, threatening her. All to achieve his own selfish ends of keeping his wife right where he wanted her. By going along with this, Lyla would be a party to any dirty tricks her husband used against a pregnant girl with precious few resources to fight back.

Apparently satisfied that he had resolved the problem, Kwesi bit into his sandwich, and it was that one mundane action that accomplished what nothing and no one else had been able to. The sight of Kwesi wolfing down the thick slices of bread, and the satisfaction with which he licked away the tomato sauce that had leaked onto his fingers, sent a tremor through her of utter revulsion.

Dear God, what was I thinking? How could she ever have considered a life with this man, or imagined raising a family with him? He didn't have a single, empathetic bone in his body! When she was blessed with children, she wanted them raised in a secure and loving home like she had experienced. What kind of foundation would a loveless, soulless marriage like hers and Kwesi's offer any child? Nadia might be poor, and live in a dilapidated house in Nima bursting at the seams with extended family, but it was a home filled with life and laughter – and people who would love the baby for itself, not as a panacea for past regrets or an inducement to keep an alienated spouse. Lyla shook her head in wonderment that she had ever considered this option. No, whatever God had in mind for her, it wasn't this. It *couldn't* be this.

'Kwesi, I'm leaving.' The words came out so calmly that it took him a few moments before they sank in.

Then he frowned and wiped his sticky hands down the sides of his trousers. 'What are you saying? I mean – *why?*'

'You know what I mean, and you know perfectly well why. Kwesi, be honest with me. Is this – this *arrangement* between us really the life you want for yourself? Because let me tell you, it's killing me! I've stood by for years and let you do exactly as you wanted because I told myself that one day we would have children – a family – and that things would be different.'

She gave a harsh, bitter laugh devoid of any humour. 'Although I really didn't expect you to go ahead and start our family without me.'

'Lyla, I'll sort it out – I promise!'

Lyla shook her head. There was nothing left for her here. 'Don't bother sorting anything out. I don't want to do this any more.'

'C'mon, Lyla – you *know* I love you!'

Kwesi's protestation meant nothing to her, because she had already seen real love this evening – just not in this house. She hesitated, trying to find the right words. Suddenly, a picture of Reuben's devastated face flashed through her mind and, as if a lighted match had been tossed onto the petrol-soaked rag of her battered emotions, Lyla exploded. *No!* She marched furiously towards Kwesi. He had no right to use that word after everything he had put her through, and she wouldn't allow him to get away with throwing it out to justify his – his utter *heartlessness*!

'You *love* me? You don't know the meaning of the word! If you did, you wouldn't have humiliated me all these years to the point where I can't even look our friends in the face.' The heated words gushed out from her pain like an erupting volcano. 'Do you think because I said nothing that I was too stupid to see what you were up to – that I didn't know each and every time you found a new woman? So, tell me, did you *love* me when you left me alone in this house night after night cooking food you never came home to eat? Did you *love* me when you stood by and let that awful mother of yours abuse and bully me because I couldn't keep a pregnancy? Tell me, Kwesi, did you *love* me when you were out screwing everything that moved – *did you?*'

She was almost up against his face and Kwesi's mouth fell open at her ferocity and the unmistakable contempt and disgust in Lyla's words.

He reached out a hand, but she slapped it aside and headed towards the staircase, unable to stand the sight of him for another second. Lunging forward, Kwesi grabbed her arm and forced her around to face him.

'Lyla, you *can't* leave me!'

She stared at him in silence and, as if emboldened by her lack of protest, Kwesi released his hold. Looking bewildered, he ran a hand over his neatly cropped hair, and she noted with satisfaction that he was trembling.

'I know things haven't been perfect between us, but – but you *can't!* You can't possibly be serious. What are you saying? That you would leave all this,' – he gestured around the spacious, beautifully decorated hallway – 'and – and *me?*'

His expression was an almost comical blend of incomprehension and incredulity, and Lyla watched the emotions flit across his face, appalled at how utterly shallow and conceited a man she had married. Did he honestly think she was such a walkover and could be so easily appeased? *Oh my God, you vain, pompous bastard! Do you think you and this house are such a catch that I'd stay with you just because of that?*

Goaded by the sheer audacity on display, Lyla opened

her mouth to release the scathing words rising in her throat. Then Kwesi took a step closer, and the overhead light shone directly on to his face. The words died on her lips as she recognised the emotion lurking in the depths of Kwesi's eyes. It wasn't arrogance she saw there; it was fear.

Kwesi

Kwesi slammed the car door angrily and gunned the engine into life. He screeched away from the kerb with only a cursory check for oncoming traffic, unable to contain his fury at the utter gall of the furniture supplier. How *dare* the man think he could screw him, Kwesi, over! He was bloody lucky that Kwesi had let him in on the deal in the first place, and instead of showing gratitude for the thirty per cent they'd originally agreed, the *bastard* now had the nerve to insist on fifty-fifty!

He pressed down hard on the accelerator, his anger further fuelled by impotence. Despite his bluster before storming off, both men knew the supplier had him over a barrel and he had no option but to agree to this blatant extortion. Because that was *exactly* what it was, he fumed. If he made any attempt to call the man's bluff by instructing Procurement to look elsewhere for cheaper priced wholesale furniture, he had no doubt the supplier would immediately inform his store's Head Office that their own General Manager had conspired with him to inflate his prices.

Damn it! Kwesi hit the steering wheel in frustration. He had been counting on that money and if he had to give half of it to that double-crossing weasel, he wouldn't have enough to pay the balance for the Swiss watch he'd already ordered. Nor could he afford to lose the hefty deposit he'd already paid if he cancelled the order.

All in all, this was absolutely the worst time for a cashflow shortage, Kwesi thought grimly. He hadn't spoken to Lyla since she'd moved out the week before and he had no idea if she would continue paying her share of the rent. It was only now dawning on Kwesi that he was liable for the payments being made in full, and on time, and he sorely regretted both negotiating a monthly payment schedule instead of an annual rent advance, and insisting the lease should be solely in his name. At the time he'd wanted to prove he was the man of the house, especially as Lyla paid far more towards the bills than he did.

But it wasn't just Lyla's contribution to the household expenses that he missed, Kwesi acknowledged moodily, as he drove down the busy dual carriageway from the supplier's factory in Dzorwulu into the city. Even when Lyla had been angry with him, at least she had been physically present. With her gone, he dreaded going home to an empty house. He hated the silence and walking through the door felt to him like entering a museum – a tribute to good taste maybe, but certainly not a home.

Kwesi was also hoping Lyla would return home before anyone noticed that she'd left. He was reluctant to tell his mother, or anyone, about their explosive quarrel, and indeed he was still astounded by the words his wife had screamed at him and how savagely she had ripped off the façade concealing their marital arrangements. He was particularly shocked by her admission that she had known about his indiscretions all along. *Why the hell had she never said anything?* Once again, his mind shied away uneasily from the painful possibility that she hadn't loved him enough to care.

Kwesi's frustration started to build up once again, and he drummed a restless tattoo on the steering wheel. He'd been prepared to give Lyla a bit of time to get over feeling upset, but this couldn't go on forever. He needed her to come back. They were Lyla and Kwesi, the beautiful couple, the envy of all their friends. He had his reputation to consider and he couldn't just stand by and let this stupid misunderstanding between them ruin everything. But what could he *do*? Lyla was almost certainly back in her mother's house, and the thought of facing his mother-in-law without knowing what Lyla would have told her, was another reason he hadn't dared to seek out his wife. In any case, he brooded, there was no point begging her to return without offering her something. Everyone had their price, and in Lyla's case there was no way she would refuse to come back to him if he brought home a baby. Kwesi sighed deeply. He had to get Nadia to play ball, and he had to do it now.

Lost in planning the best strategy for dealing with his former mistress, Kwesi's anger at the duplicitous furniture supplier was already a distant memory. A few minutes later, he turned into the road leading to Nima, tutting with irritation as his car bounced over a pothole that had appeared from nowhere. *Why the hell did I get involved with someone who lives in such a shit area?*

His nose twitched at the stench from the sun-dried gutters creeping through the car vent, and he hastily turned up the dial on the air conditioner. It had only been a few months since he had last driven down this road and it looked even rougher than he remembered. The latest heavy downpours had washed away part of the road surface, and Kwesi drove cautiously, cursing the foreign firms that charged a fortune for shoddy workmanship, and his corrupt government that took on extortionate loans which benefited foreign workers instead of their own hard-working citizens. All any politician was interested in was collecting bribes, he thought in disgust, the irony of his recent transaction with the furniture supplier completely lost on him.

Kwesi pulled up outside Nadia's house and switched off the engine. He slipped on his designer sunglasses and checked his wallet was securely inside his jacket. Swinging open the car door, he stepped out and looked up and down the road. Other than a group of boys kicking their football around a patch of dried grass, the area was deserted. Hopefully his car would be safe here, but he didn't plan on hanging around for long. He'd had enough of people messing him around today, and Nadia was going to have to listen to reason.

The door was wide open and Kwesi pushed aside the multicoloured bead curtain hanging across the doorway to walk into the hair salon. The room was gloomy and lit by dimly burning light bulbs studded around the ceiling. It felt almost as warm inside as it was on the street, and the acrid smell of chemicals was overpowering. Nadia was bent over a plastic sink at the far end of the tiny salon washing a woman's hair, while a couple of feet away another woman, engrossed in a video on her phone, sat under a hairdryer attached to a stand leaning drunkenly against the pock-marked wall. A small radio blaring local music shared a dusty shelf with an assortment of hair and beauty products.

Kwesi slipped off his glasses and, as his eyes met Nadia's,

he caught the flash of happiness on her face before she quickly scowled and looked down again, rubbing her client's scalp with renewed vigour.

Clearing his throat loudly, he raised his voice to be heard above the music. 'Hello, Nadia.'

At first she ignored him, and then after a minute she raised her head and said sullenly, 'What do you want?'

'I need to talk to you.' He smiled warmly, and seeing her frown falter, he wanted to laugh. This would be easier than he'd thought – it was so obvious she still cared for him.

'Wait there.' She nodded towards an empty chair by the door. He hesitated, and then sat down as instructed and watched her rinse the woman's hair and wrap a large dark towel around her head like a turban.

Excusing herself, Nadia stepped out from behind the sink and Kwesi's genial smile froze at the sight of the conspicuous bulge clearly outlined beneath her stretchy top. She walked slowly towards him, and her heavy movements were in such stark contrast to her former sexy litheness that he struggled to hide his horror. *Jesus, the girl was fat!*

He stood up as she approached and, as if she could read his thoughts, her lips tightened. The revolving fan in the corner was no match for the warmth of the salon and up close, with her long extensions tied back in a loose ponytail, he could see the beads of perspiration on her face.

'What do you want?' she repeated.

Kwesi steered her towards the doorway, trying to hide his distaste as his fingers touched her shoulder and the dampness of her sweaty T-shirt.

'Can we speak privately outside?' He forced a smile which he hoped would soften her up.

She hesitated, and then led the way, pushing aside the bead curtain and deliberately letting it fall back in his face as she walked through. Swallowing his irritation, he followed her outside.

The afternoon heat was punishing, and Kwesi pushed his glasses back onto his face to protect his eyes from the harsh glare of the sun. Nadia shaded her eyes with her hand and looked up at him. The heavy perspiration had wiped away whatever make-up she had been wearing and, in the stark sunlight, she suddenly looked very young. He felt an unaccustomed pang of conscience at what he was here to do – until he remembered Lyla. He had to get her back, whatever it took.

'Look Nadia, I know you're busy, so I don't want to take up your time.' He hesitated and curved his lips into the smile she had never been able to resist. 'You look beautiful, do you know that? Pregnancy suits you – you're blooming.'

Clearly unnerved by the direction of the conversation, Nadia looked confused.

'Kwesi, I don't understand why you have come here. After what you said to me when I came to your office, you should be ashamed to come and face me.'

'Believe me, I'm sorry,' he said earnestly, steeling himself to take her hand. He looked her straight in the eye and said softly, 'Nadia, I didn't mean to hurt you. Lyla was putting so much pressure on me I couldn't think straight. I know I should have been in touch these past few weeks – believe me, I've been thinking about you all the time – but Lyla has been threatening all kinds of hell if I continue to see you.'

She looked uncertain and he pressed on. 'I'm sorry I put you through all of that – please, please forgive me?

Look, whatever has happened was in the past and is water under the bridge. Let's look to the future, shall we? After all,' he increased the intensity of his smile and rubbed the palm of her hand softly with his thumb, 'we're about to be parents, you and I.'

Nadia's eyes lit up, and she looked down at the hand holding hers, and then back up at him. 'Kwesi, do you really mean that?'

'Of course, I do,' he said smoothly. 'We'll always be connected through the baby. No matter what happens.'

Nadia snatched her hand away, suspicion dropping like a mask over her face. '*No matter what happens?* What are you talking about?'

She stepped away from him and her hand moved to cover her stomach in an instinctive gesture of protection.

'Kwesi, tell me the truth! Why have you come here?'

The mirrored sunglasses provided a poor barrier as, without warning, she leaned forward and spat in his face.

'You *bastard*! Do you take me for a fool? You think you can take my child, so you and your wife can live in your big house with *my* baby?'

Kwesi pulled out his handkerchief and wiped his glasses gingerly, his face twisted in disgust. 'I can't believe you did that!'

'I'll do a lot worse if you don't get out of here!' she shouted angrily.

The boys playing football across the road stopped their game and turned to watch, cackling as an irate, pregnant Nadia hurled insults at Kwesi. The sweltering heat, combined with his embarrassment at being so publicly chastised, was bringing Kwesi out in a sweat and, beneath his jacket, his shirt stuck uncomfortably to his back. He ran a finger around the inside of his collar as his eyes darted around nervously.

'Nadia, for God's sake, be reasonable!'

He dropped his voice, hoping she would do the same. 'You barely make enough money to take care of yourself and your family. If you let Lyla and me—'

'I've already told you! I want the house you promised me, and an allowance every month to help me look after your child.'

Clearly, the carrot strategy wasn't working, Kwesi decided. It was time for the stick. He narrowed his eyes and looked her up and down, no longer bothering to hide his repulsion.

'Yes, that's right, *my* child! And if I take you to court, who do you think the judge is going to decide should bring up the baby, huh? A professional married couple with their own home and plenty of money to provide a decent education, or a young girl with no husband who works in a hair salon in Nima?'

Nadia gasped in outrage and, before he could dodge, she raised her hand and slapped him hard across his face. The boys watching the drama from across the road whistled and whooped loudly, shouting across catcalls of encouragement to Nadia who looked ready to scratch Kwesi's eyes out.

Kwesi had had enough. He turned and strode back to his car, his jaw stinging from the surprisingly powerful blow. He couldn't get out of here fast enough. Baby or no baby, this was the last time he was coming back to this godforsaken *dump*.

Nadia shouted after his retreating back, 'If you think this is over, you are dreaming! I know where you work, and I know where you live. And when this baby comes, you will *pay*! If you don't know what I am capable of, you will soon find out!'

FEBRUARY

**MARRIAGE ENDS A PERFECT
ROMANCE AND STARTS REAL LIFE**

Theresa

Back from her two week holiday in London, Theresa felt energised and ready to get back to work. Humming softly to herself, she slipped a paper knife under the flap of the envelope and neatly slid it across. Pulling out the sheets of paper, she skimmed the bank statement and smiled. Thanks to Margaret's tireless efforts and young Clara's creative digital campaigns, TB Communications was now on a steady footing with very buoyant finances.

Clara's easy familiarity with social media had proved a godsend. Since she'd joined, her creative ideas for podcasts and blogs, as well as her ability to write engaging content for their clients' digital communications, had brought a fresh dimension to their business pitches, adding new services and increased billings.

Theresa dropped the statement onto her desk and sat in her leather armchair, swivelling slowly while she surveyed her office. Her recent trip had banished any lingering doubts about their momentous decision to leave London. While it had been fun to revisit her old haunts and introduce Ben to her friends, she was relieved to be back home – which was most definitely how she now saw Ghana. Tramping through the streets of London wrapped up in a thick winter coat and praying her son didn't catch a chill from the bitter wind and never-ending rain of a British winter, she had longed for the warmth of the tropical sun. The irritated glances from restaurant staff and other diners when she attempted to soothe a fractious Ben during mealtimes had not gone unnoticed, and she'd badly missed the welcoming Ghanaian service staff who invariably cooed over her son.

One of the best parts of her trip had been dinner with Melanie, once her best friend at Cromwell McIntosh. Leaving Ben at home with her mother, Theresa had met Melanie at an Italian restaurant off Sloane Street.

'You are so lucky, Theresa.' Melanie had cast an envious glance at her over the glass of vodka and orange she had refilled twice at the bar before they'd been ushered to their table. 'You've got a gorgeous baby, you look amazing, and you're running your own business. It's *incredible* what you've achieved in a year!'

Theresa smiled and sipped the sparkling, chilled Prosecco she'd ordered. Put like that, it did sound rather impressive. Not wanting to appear boastful, she murmured something non-committal and quickly forked another mouthful of the delicious bruschetta into her mouth.

'No, really, I mean it,' Melanie persisted. 'I always knew you'd do well, but...' She ignored her seafood starter and took another sip of her drink. 'You know we lost the WonderChild account and Lennon's Pizza after you left? They weren't in the least bit impressed with any of the campaigns we pitched, and even that bitch Jess admitted she should have fought harder to stop you leaving.'

Theresa laughed aloud. Just knowing that Jess McIntosh had finally come round to recognising her value made the whole trip worthwhile.

'You'd never have guessed it from her reaction when I quit. Honestly, Mel, after she read my resignation letter, she just looked at me over the top of her glasses and barked, "You'll regret it", and then went straight back to reading her emails.'

Finally picking up her fork, Mel took a large bite of a garlicky prawn. Chewing vigorously, she swallowed quickly before replying. 'Yeah, well, she's the one regretting it now. It's such a shame you're not in London, because I bet all your old clients would grab you in a heartbeat. The Comms Director at WonderChild sent Jess an email after they dropped us saying it was thanks to your campaign ideas that they'd received so much media coverage. She was right – no one writes copy like you!'

'Mel, that's lovely to hear but, if I'm honest, the thought of working for Cromwell McIntosh – or any company for that matter – makes my stomach churn. I'm *so* loving the freedom to work on brands that I really care about, and with clients I like, instead of coming up with ideas people shoot down as if you're an idiot, and then take the credit for when they work out brilliantly.'

Melanie gave a sympathetic nod. 'That's classic CM for you. Those two are geniuses when it comes to making you feel like shit, and then shamelessly rake in all the dough. You know they've told us there are no pay rises this year? You should have heard Ian: *"PR isn't all glamour and liquid lunches, guys. We're in a highly competitive and volatile climate, and we all have to tighten our belts."'*

She pulled a face and Theresa cracked up at the wicked impersonation of Ian Cromwell's almost impenetrable Scottish accent.

'He's such a smug *git*! From what I've heard, the volatile climate' – Melanie dropped her fork to draw air quotes – 'didn't stop him and Jess paying themselves huge, bloody bonuses!'

She took another sip of her drink and shook her head dismissively.

'Enough about that lot. Tell me more about Ghana. How's the gorgeous Tyler – is he loving it there as well?'

'Well, he's had a few ups and downs, but hopefully things are now going in the right direction,' Theresa said carefully. She had avoided telling people about Tyler's new circumstances, not wanting to jinx anything just as things were picking up. It was his story, and he would tell it himself when he was ready.

The most memorable part of her trip, however, had occurred while staying with her mother – the first time she'd lived under her mother's roof since leaving home to move in with Tyler. The exquisitely decorated bedroom, now furnished with a cot for Ben, with its charming en-suite bathroom that Ludmila, her mother's long-suffering cleaner, had been ordered to scrub until every tile sparkled, had been as comfortable as ever. Less comfortable was the all too familiar sense of feeling smothered, a sensation which too much time spent around her domineering mother tended to generate. Back in her childhood room, Theresa had struggled not to slip into her old role of dutiful daughter to forceful parent. In preparation for her grandson, Clementyne had packed away all her precious china figurines as well as the large glass centre table that dominated her spacious living room. When Theresa had protested that Ben was nowhere near walking,

Clementyne's reply had been an acerbic 'Darling, babies are magnets for accidents, whatever their size'.

The first few days in London had passed without incident. An enchanted Clementyne had bonded instantly with her grandson, and it had warmed Theresa's heart to see her poised, elegant mother down on all fours on her cream shagpile rug, roaring like a lion to make Ben chuckle.

It was on one such occasion that Theresa had laughingly suggested that her mother consider a visit to Ghana.

'You'll love it, Mama. You haven't been there for years, and there've been so many changes! And just think, you'd get to spend loads of time with Ben – and Tyler,' she added hopefully.

Clementyne's response had been to pick up Ben and blow loud kisses against his chubby, velvety cheeks.

'Hmm. I suppose that's what they mean by every silver lining has a cloud, doesn't it, my little darling?'

And that was when it had happened.

'Mama, don't you *dare* talk about my husband like that!'

Clementyne's mouth fell open, and she almost dropped the baby in shock at her daughter's furious rebuke. Theresa was equally stunned by her response to her mother's flippant comment, but having spoken up, she wasn't going to back down.

'I mean it, Mama. Tyler's the man I *chose* to marry. Not only do I love him to death, but he's the father of my son and your grandson, and if you can't understand that and give him the respect he deserves, then I don't want you around Ben.'

Theresa fixed her mother with an uncompromising stare, and Clementyne, plainly flustered by the forthright ultimatum, flushed and dropped her gaze on to the baby on her lap. Without her usual confident smile, her cheeks sagged, making the tiny wrinkles around her eyes more pronounced, and Theresa took a deep breath to steel herself against the pity threatening to undo her resolve. Her mother had been allowed to get away with far too much over the years, and the damage she had inflicted on Theresa's childhood would never fully heal. Glancing at her son's innocent face, she was determined that, unlike her, Ben would not be used as a pawn between two people he loved.

'I'm sorry, Mama, but I won't have Ben feeling torn between his father and you – I had enough of that growing up and I'm not going to allow you to do that to my kids. If you can't have a healthy relationship with my husband, then you're not welcome in our home. I'm deadly serious, Mama. I don't want you to come to Ghana if you're not prepared to treat Tyler decently.'

The room went deathly silent, and Theresa waited with bated breath for the explosion. *No one* spoke to Clementyne Curtis like that, especially her own daughter. It took almost a full minute before it dawned on Theresa that the unfamiliar look on her mother's face was one of... respect.

'I see you've finally grown up and learned to stand up for yourself.'

Her mother's wry tone was as close as she would ever come to an apology. With a sigh, Clementyne planted a quick kiss on Ben's cheek and inclined her head in a gracious nod. 'Very well. I accept your terms and I will do my best to refrain from saying or doing anything that will upset you or – or Tyler.'

Theresa blinked. It was the first time in years that her mother had referred to her husband by name, usually describing him as 'that man you married' or 'the one that stole you away from me'.

Apparently deciding to show magnanimity in defeat, Clementyne continued, 'Maybe it *is* time I paid a visit to Ghana – goodness knows Pat's been nagging me for years to come and stay with her. I'd love to see what you've done with your house and your business. I always knew you'd make a success of it.' She paused for a moment before adding with satisfaction, 'Now, *that* comes from my side of the family!'

With that, she'd returned to playing with Ben, leaving Theresa to roll her eyes in amused exasperation. Only Clementyne would have the audacity to take credit for something she'd so adamantly opposed.

'Please, madam, are you ready for us to leave?' Joseph hovered hesitantly in the doorway.

Theresa blinked. Immersed in her memories, she had lost all track of time, and she glanced at her watch and exclaimed.

'Oh, my goodness! Thanks for reminding me, Joseph. I'm supposed to meet Margaret at Watts Industries at ten o'clock.'

She scrambled to her feet and picked up the open file on her desk. 'I'll see you at the car – I just need to let Auntie Sisi know I'm leaving.'

Sitting in the back seat a few minutes later with the usual soundtrack playing of Joseph's favourite phone-in radio station, Theresa smiled ruefully at the realisation she wasn't the only one who had missed Ghana. When she'd popped into the den to kiss him goodbye, Ben had been gurgling with laughter while playing peek-a-boo with a doting Auntie Sisi and had barely spared his mother a glance. Only hoping her housekeeper would tear herself away from the child long enough to make dinner, Theresa flicked through the papers in her lap and tried to get up to speed with the agenda for the upcoming meeting.

Joseph pulled up at a set of traffic lights and her attention was distracted by the sound of tapping against her window. Rolling it down, she scrabbled in her bag and dropped some coins into the outstretched hand of a disabled beggar, paying no attention to the irritated tut from her driver. While she loved being back home, she wasn't blind to her privileges or the struggles of those simply trying to survive. She rolled up the window and looked out thoughtfully at the young boys and girls milling between the stationary cars to hawk cheap, mass-produced items. It was youngsters like these Reuben was so keen to help – entrepreneurial, gutsy and energetic, but with neither the support nor the connections to turn their innate skills into financial success.

While the focus of Reuben's foundation was backing scalable and profitable tech-based projects, he had requested today's meeting to plan the launch of a scheme to train street kids to start small businesses. Theresa read through Margaret's neatly typed notes and sighed with satisfaction. It was meaningful projects like these that made her job worthwhile, not slogging her guts out to provide Ian Cromwell and Jess McIntosh with fatter bonuses. If her business grew as she hoped, Theresa dreamed of setting up a not-for-profit programme at

TB Communications, which would offer top-quality PR services to young entrepreneurs at a fraction of the cost.

After a further twenty minutes in traffic, Joseph pulled up in front of the building that housed Watts Industries, and Theresa gathered up her notes and thrust them into her briefcase. She ran lightly up the steps and into the cool lobby where a quick check of her watch showed the time to be quarter past ten. She grinned and punched the button to call the lift. She had most definitely acclimatised to life in Ghana, even to the point of being fashionably late.

* * *

The steady drumbeat of rain against the roof woke Theresa up from a deep sleep and a jumbled dream, the only part of which she could remember involved an irate Auntie Sisi and a room full of cooking pots. With so much of their housekeeper's time now spent looking after Ben, maybe the dream was a sign it was time to get someone else in to help with the cooking, she wondered blearily.

A loud rumble of thunder drove away any vestiges of sleep, and she sat up and propped up her pillow against the headboard. It was still early, and Tyler was snoring gently beside her. She stole a peek at Ben in his cot alongside their bed and smiled at the sight of him curled up in a perfect imitation of his father.

Feeling too restless to stay in bed, Theresa slipped out quietly from between the sheets and shrugged on a light cotton robe. Clutching her slippers in one hand, she tiptoed out of the room and padded downstairs and into the kitchen. Yawning widely and suddenly desperate for a cup of tea, she switched on the kettle and filled a mug with

369

her favourite blackcurrant infusion. Drink in hand, she wandered into the living room and pulled open a louvre window, scanning the overcast sky dubiously. The rain wasn't coming down quite as hard as she'd feared, and she offered up a silent prayer that it would have stopped altogether by the time she had to leave the house.

Theresa was dreading having to drive, but she'd promised to take Maku to her dressmaker for the final fitting of her long-awaited wedding dress, and not even a tropical monsoon would dissuade her friend from making the trip. Besides, with the big day now only two weeks away, Maku's excitement about her forthcoming wedding was infectious and Theresa was secretly longing to see the dress. Despite Maku's increasingly exasperating bridezilla antics, it was hard to begrudge her determination to have her perfect white wedding – she'd certainly waited long enough and deserved whatever she asked for.

Theresa carried her brimming mug over to the sofa and settled herself onto the soft cushions to sip her tea and enjoy the serenity of an early Saturday morning. Her thoughts turned to her husband and son sleeping upstairs, and a deep feeling of peace and gratitude stole over her. The past year had brought its challenges but thankfully they had come through them as a family, and their lives were finally falling into place.

* * *

By mid-morning the rain had petered out and Theresa set off with Maku firmly ensconced in the front passenger seat. At the last minute, Lyla, equally excited to see the wedding dress, had demanded they pick her up on the way.

'Try not to hit the gatepost,' Maku said caustically as she watched Theresa manoeuvre the car through the narrow opening into Auntie Pat's driveway. 'I don't know why you didn't get your driver to take us.'

'Shut up, there's nothing wrong with my driving,' Theresa muttered, bringing the car to a jerky halt. 'I told you last week that Joseph has a family funeral today, so either I drive, or you pay for a taxi!'

Lyla's appearance and cheery greeting put an end to their bickering. As if sensing the tension in the air, Lyla said nothing as Theresa painstakingly reversed the car, narrowly missing Auntie Pat's prized hibiscus bush, and drove slowly back out through the gates. Once they were safely on the main road, Theresa settled back in her seat and threw an irritated glance at Maku who was gripping the handle above her door.

'Will you calm down and stop acting like you're about to die at any moment!'

'Can you blame me? I've been waiting for years to get married – imagine if your driving killed me now, just as I'm about to get my wish? I saw this movie where—'

Leaning forward, Lyla broke in quickly. 'Stop being so dramatic, Maku. No one's getting killed!'

'I wouldn't bet on that. If she keeps up this nonsense, I'll kill her myself,' Theresa muttered loudly, swerving as a taxi pulled out in front of her without warning.

Maku inhaled sharply, her knuckles almost white from the pressure of her grip, and wailed, '*Lyla*! You see what I mean?'

Lyla burst out laughing and Theresa and Maku exchanged startled glances. Since leaving Kwesi and moving into her mother's house, Lyla had grown increasingly sombre and withdrawn. For months, she had refused point blank to talk about the breakdown of her marriage and, when she wasn't at the office or in church, spent most of her time closeted in her bedroom. On the rare occasions when Theresa and Maku managed to drag her out of the house, Lyla would sit in near silence and exude a sadness so intense that it seemed to seep out of her skin.

Today, however, Lyla seemed happy, or at least a lot more like her old self than she had in weeks. While Theresa weighed up whether to comment, Maku blithely plunged in.

'It's good to hear you laughing, Cuz. If I'm honest, I really don't get why you've been so miserable. I mean, you should be happy you've left that piece of sh—'

'Don't rub it in, Maku,' Theresa interjected smoothly. 'I think she knows better than either of us what she's walked away from. But Lyla, it *is* lovely to hear you sound happy. Has something happened?'

Through the rear-view mirror she saw Lyla shrug lightly.

'Hey, it's a beautiful day and I'm out with my best friends in the world – what's not to be happy about?' Changing the subject, Lyla squeezed Maku's shoulder excitedly. 'And we're going to get your *wedding dress*! Isn't that amazing?'

Maku squealed with excitement and stamped her legs up and down in the confined space like an excited toddler. 'I know, *right?*'

Theresa grinned at her unbridled enthusiasm before turning her attention back to the teeming traffic on the road, determined not to give Maku the satisfaction of saying 'I told you so!' if she caused an accident.

While they waited for Maku to slip on the dress, Theresa and Lyla sat side by side on the dressmaker's sofa flicking through old copies of *Hello!* Glancing at the date on the magazine she was browsing, Theresa snorted with disgust and tossed it on the table where it landed face up. The cover was dominated by the picture of a glamorous couple sharing loving smiles as they cut into a frosted four-tier wedding cake.

'What *is* it with these celebrities and the way they hop in and out of marriage? Those pictures were only taken two years ago, and they're already divorced!' she exclaimed.

Immediately the words were out, she could have bitten off her tongue. She glanced hesitantly at Lyla, but her friend didn't appear troubled. Deciding to take no chances, Theresa quickly changed topic to a new healthcare pitch she was developing with Clara.

'The girl is turning into quite the superstar! She's as sharp as a tack and can spot opportunities to package ideas in an instant. I thought I was good with Twitter, but Clara's an absolute *genius* with social media. I put her on Reuben's account, and she's already pulled together a fantastic digital campaign which will be perfect for the young people he's targeting.'

Lyla flinched at the mention of Reuben's name and Theresa studied her with narrowed eyes. Since taking him on as a client, she had casually alluded to Reuben from time to time, but Lyla hadn't risen to the bait. For his part, Reuben had made no reference to Lyla and Theresa had no idea if he even knew they were friends. Ever since her initial confession about her feelings for Reuben, Lyla had steadfastly refused to be drawn into any discussion about their relationship – assuming, Theresa pondered, that there was even a relationship to talk about.

She was debating whether to simply ask her when Lyla cleared her throat and looked squarely at Theresa.

'Okay, so you know you said in the car I looked happy, and asked if something's happened? Well, I didn't want to say it in front of Maku because I don't want to cast a shadow over her wedding, but I've filed for divorce from Kwesi.'

Theresa gasped. 'Oh my God! Are you sure it's what you want?'

'Tee, *really?* Are you, of all people, suggesting I'm making a mistake?'

Theresa shook her head. 'No, of course not! Look, don't get me wrong, I've never thought Kwesi was good enough for you. It's just, well, is it too soon?'

Lyla laughed, sounding genuinely amused. 'Too *soon?* Theresa, I've invested far too many years already into trying to build a life with that man.' Her smile faded. 'The past few months have been really, *really* hard, for all sorts of reasons, but I've learned a lot about myself. I've also prayed for a long time over this decision, and I'm more than ready to move on.'

'*Well?* What do you think?' Maku marched into the room holding up the hem of her dress, and Theresa and Lyla gasped in unison.

Theresa was the first to speak, her voice husky as she fought the sudden constriction in her throat, and the tears that had welled up at the sight of Maku's radiant smile.

'You look... absolutely *beautiful!*'

* * *

Theresa clutched the steering wheel as she urged the car down the last short stretch of road, silently praying that the sharp stones hadn't shredded her tyres. Maku's street was a total nightmare!

'I love the girl, but this road is pure hell,' Theresa muttered under her breath. She turned on to the main road and once she felt confident there was no danger of a tyre exploding, she put her foot down and let the car accelerate down the highway.

Lyla chuckled in sympathy. 'Hopefully, now she's passed her exams and can be considered for promotion, they'll soon be able to afford a bigger house – or at least one on a better road!'

'It's so nice to see you smiling again. I know you've been through a really crappy time, but you've been incredibly brave and – and, well, it's time to get *you* back again.' Theresa chanced a quick glance at Lyla. 'D'you know what I mean?'

Lyla smiled and squeezed Theresa's knee gently. 'I'll be fine once the divorce is finalised, I promise. I found a great lawyer, and Kwesi's agreed to co-operate, so it should be done and dusted quite quickly. Now then, that's enough about me. Tell me how Tyler's getting on. It's wonderful that you and,' – there was an infinitesimal hesitation before she quickly continued – 'that you were able to help him.'

Theresa pulled a face. 'He knows Reuben's my client, but I still haven't let on to Tyler that it was my idea to approach the man about Sycamore House. To be honest, when I first pitched the idea, I was hoping Reuben might be interested in taking a couple of the units for the foundation's offices. I could *not* believe it when Tyler told me he'd sold him the entire property!'

Lyla shifted in her seat to look at Theresa. 'I'm curious about why you would keep it a secret from Tyler, though. What you did was a good thing.'

'I'm not sure, either,' Theresa confessed. 'I suppose he was so excited when he told me the news that I panicked in case he thought I'd muscled in on his business, or that I didn't respect or trust him enough to sort out his own problems. I didn't want him to feel – I don't know, emasculated or anything, because I'd found a way to help him out of his jam.'

She hesitated. 'We're in a good place again, and I don't want to rock the boat or make him feel bad about himself.'

Lyla raised a brow but said nothing. After a moment, she looked across at Theresa. 'You know, it's hard to believe you're the same person who was threatening to walk away from her marriage because she couldn't stand the idea her husband could be less than perfect.'

Theresa flushed, and gave a weak smile. 'You know me. It takes a while, but I usually get there in the end. When I think back to what a selfish cow I was before—'

'No, no, don't get me wrong, Tee. I think what you did, all the love and the compassion you've shown Tyler is – is *magnificent*!'

Theresa turned wide eyes on her friend, too startled to remember to keep her focus on the road. Lyla smiled and patted Theresa's arm in approval.

'I mean it. Not only did you finally put your mother in her place, you've overcome your demons enough to see that just because a man is going through tough times, it doesn't make him weak or disposable. Instead of blaming everything on Tyler, you've become a grown-up in your marriage – and I'm so, *so* proud of you!'

Feeling unexpected tears prickle behind her eyes, Theresa drew a sharp intake of breath and gave Lyla a shaky grin. 'Okay, well, I wasn't expecting *that*.'

'Tee, you're a changed woman, and just like you've created the business you dreamed of, it's up to you to define the marriage you want. I'm hardly the best person to give anyone relationship advice but trust me – Tyler's a good man and I honestly don't believe his ego's too fragile to value your support. So, maybe, give him a chance to prove it, hmm?'

Theresa nodded, and they drove in silence until they arrived at Lyla's.

'Do you think I should come in and say hello to Auntie Pat?' Theresa glanced at her watch, eager to get back to her boys and enjoy the rest of the weekend.

Lyla scoffed good-naturedly. 'Don't bother. She's out on a date, and I'm not expecting her back until tonight.'

Theresa's eyes widened. '*Really!* Who with? Not—'

Lyla nodded. 'Yep. That bald guy you and I bumped into when we came to visit her. His name's Robert, and he's a retired ophthalmologist. Anyway, they've gone off to Cape Coast for the day, and she probably won't get back until late.'

'Go, Auntie Pat!' Theresa crowed. She took in Lyla's resigned expression and added cautiously, 'How're you feeling about it?'

Lyla gave her a half-smile and shrugged. 'I'm just happy to be home, so whatever Mama does is fine with me.

Daddy's gone, and I have to accept she's a grown woman with the right to live her life however she wants.' She opened the door to step out of the car and then turned back. 'Just so long as he doesn't expect me to call him "Dad"!'

Theresa was still giggling when she pulled up to her house and turned into the driveway. She switched off the ignition and pulled out the key with a sigh of relief. Driving in Accra was way too stressful and, as far as she was concerned, Joseph couldn't come back soon enough. Tyler's dusty transit van, now his preferred mode of transport, was parked at the side of the house, and she felt the same thrill of excitement at the thought of seeing her husband as she'd felt the first moment they'd met. Despite all the challenges of the past year, her feelings for Tyler had never died, and she smiled. *'What doesn't kill you, makes you stronger!'* as *Mama would say.*

Theresa stepped out of the car and walked into her house, dropping her handbag onto the table inside the entrance. She hastened across the hallway, impatient to find her family, and was thankful to hear the sound of pots banging from behind the closed kitchen door, the signal that Auntie Sisi was back on cooking duty. Theresa pushed open the door to the den and smiled at the sight of Tyler sprawled across the sofa watching football with Ben in his arms, and loudly cheering on his team. Originally furnished with Auntie Sisi in mind, the den had turned into the de facto family room for everyone since Ben's arrival, the grey patterned sofa and chairs with their perky red throw cushions proving far more comfortable than the elegant cream-leather set in the living room.

'Hey, beautiful!'

With a huge grin, Tyler jumped to his feet and walked over to where Theresa stood in the doorway. Leaning down to kiss her, his lips lingered on hers until Ben squirmed in protest. His football game apparently forgotten, Tyler handed over the baby and enthusiastically launched into a rundown of progress at the project site.

'At this rate, the centre will be ready for us to use almost a month earlier than we'd planned. The crew are putting in extra hours like you wouldn't believe, and the engineers will be in soon to install the technology. The tech is going to be *unbelievable*! Total state-of-the-art stuff – Reuben reckons if we can give people a start in the best environment, they'll always aspire to be the best.'

Theresa cradled Ben and bounced him gently in her arms as she listened intently, hugely relieved to see Tyler back to being Mr Positivity.

'Reuben's found the first new business for the centre, and we met the guys earlier this afternoon. They only graduated three years ago, but they've got a really cool idea for an app that could totally revolutionise public transportation here and in other African cities. Once I've got Sycamore House up and running, Reuben and I have agreed to work with them to develop the prototype and get it launched.'

Theresa lowered her sleepy son carefully into his bouncer. Trying to sound non-committal, she murmured, 'Well, when you're ready, we can help them develop a PR plan or maybe source some sponsorship or crowdfunding – you know, do our bit for corporate social responsibility and all that.'

Tyler didn't reply, and she glanced up at him, trying not to betray her sudden anxiety. 'Would you be okay with me putting some ideas together?' she suggested tentatively.

He swooped upon her and pinned her arms to her sides as he wrapped her in a tight bear hug and nuzzled her neck with a fierce growl. She laughed and wriggled to loosen his grip.

'Um, okay, so I'll take that as a yes, then?'

'A *huge* yes – *and* a thank you! Do you have any idea how amazing you are, and how lucky I am that you're my wife?'

With a smile that was dazzling in its intensity, Tyler stroked Theresa's silky curls away from her brow and kissed her softly. She laid her head against his chest and relaxed into his arms. Lyla was right; there was nothing to feel anxious about because this relationship would be whatever she and Tyler wanted it to be. After the traumatic events of the past year, what she wanted – what she *needed* – in her marriage was a genuinely equal arrangement based not on hidden fears and superficial, unrealistic romantic expectations, but on an honest appreciation of each other's strengths, as well as their flaws.

After a moment, she looked up and said lightly, 'Margaret and I have been discussing moving the business out of here and into proper premises. We'll need to hire another exec soon to support Clara, and we've outgrown the space downstairs. Since property is your bag, would you mind helping us out with some ideas for our first office?'

Tyler raised an eyebrow and pretended to look shocked. 'You really want my opinion? I thought you didn't want me interfering in your business?' he added with a teasing smile.

Theresa's dimples deepened as she smiled up at her husband. Although the bitter words of the past would never be entirely forgotten, she knew the love they had rekindled, seemingly against all odds, would carry them through.

Eyes twinkling, she wound her arms around his neck and kissed him lightly. '*You* are my business. Besides, we're partners, aren't we?'

Tyler

Tyler mopped his brow once again, thankful he'd left his jacket back in the office. The afternoon sun blazed overhead, but it was a minor inconvenience compared to his excitement at seeing the project nearing completion. He waited impatiently for the project manager to finish his instructions to the site foreman, and as soon as the man walked off, Tyler resumed their conversation.

'I'll take a quick look around inside before I head back to the office, but I must say your team is doing a fantastic job, Gabriel. I can't tell you how relieved I was to get you all back on board.'

'Boss, like I told you before, once the money is there, we can get the materials. And once we get the materials—'

'We can get the job done. Yes, I know,' Tyler finished off the sentence with a grin.

Gabriel's catchphrase had become a standing joke between them since the stocky, no-nonsense manager had returned to direct the project. Finding a contractor with the right expertise was like playing the lottery and, having witnessed some horrors in the past, Tyler thanked his lucky stars that Gabriel had come to the job armed with a highly disciplined crew. Without being overbearing, the man ran a very tight ship, and instead of the typical problems of delays, missed deadlines and cost overruns that Tyler had experienced with building contractors in the past, Gabriel seamlessly directed the workflow on the site. Well versed in critical path scheduling, he quickly smoothed over any conflicts that arose between the different trades working in the building who were forced to compete for the same spaces at the same time.

Spotting a labourer signalling to him, Gabriel trundled off, leaving Tyler alone to complete his inspection. Dabbing his forehead with his now sodden handkerchief, Tyler pushed his hard hat down on his brow and ran up the low flight of steps, edging cautiously through the half-open smoky glass doors into Sycamore House. It was stunning to witness the pace at which the redesigned interiors were being completed and, as Tyler moved from room to room trying to get his head around the lightning changes in his life, he recalled the thrill of that momentous phone call from Watts Industries.

At his first meeting with Reuben a few days later, the two men had instantly bonded, and it had taken them less than an hour to agree on a deal. Sycamore House was now destined to be a business incubation and training centre and would house high-quality office units instead of luxury apartments. It had taken a further three meetings for a persistent Reuben to convince Tyler to partner with him on his new venture.

Tyler finished his examination of the three office suites on the ground floor before moving across the hallway to the smaller unit he had set aside for his own office once they started operations. Having salvaged Jeff's loan and his personal savings through the sale of Sycamore House, he had initially been reluctant to lose his independence –

the main attraction for leaving his job in London to set up in Ghana – and hesitant about joining forces with anyone. But Reuben had pulled out all the stops to overcome Tyler's objections, and been quick to reassure him he would have a free hand to run the incubation project.

'Look, I know we haven't known each other long, but I have a good instinct for people, and I have a feeling you and I can make something really good happen here. What do you say?'

Although his experience with JP Investments had left Tyler highly dubious about his own instincts, there was no doubting Reuben's passion for his foundation or the sincerity of his promises. This was no Jeff Parnell looking for a chance to make money from exploiting other people's ideas and having Reuben as a business partner would make a pleasant change from trying to go it alone in a new environment.

And so they agreed that while Watts Industries would provide the financial investment and Reuben would set the overall investment strategy, Tyler would lead the Watts Foundation's flagship project in Sycamore House – first managing the refurbishment, and then supporting the selected entrepreneurs with resources and expertise to create sustainable businesses. Once a business had achieved a scalable level of success, it would be moved on and a new entrepreneur brought in to take the space.

As Tyler later explained to Theresa, having your own business didn't mean you had to do it all by yourself. With Reuben as a partner, not only would he have someone with whom to share the risk, but also a unique opportunity to create something exciting and truly worthwhile.

Theresa. Tyler vaulted up the stairs to the first floor and smiled as his thoughts flipped to his wife. He dearly wished he could tell Theresa how much he loved her for coming to his rescue. But he had promised not to divulge Reuben's accidental slip-up, and if that meant keeping up the charade, then so be it. What mattered most was that she and Ben were back home after an absence that had felt more like two years than two weeks. And not only had his wife saved his bacon in Ghana, she also appeared to have worked her magic in London.

Shortly after her return to Ghana, as Theresa was ending a call with her mother, she'd handed him the phone, pointedly ignoring his frantic signals to pretend he was out. Bracing himself for Clementyne's usual jibes, his mother-in-law's cordial greeting and her enquiry after his health had left Tyler dumbfounded – an entirely justified reaction as Clementyne's only interest in his well-being generally centred on the vague hope he'd drop dead.

Back on the ground floor, Tyler walked around the empty unit trying to work out where to place Patience's desk. After a few minutes he gave up and made a mental note to bring her along on his next visit. As the about-to-be Office Manager of Sycamore House, his PA would have far better ideas than he for layouts, and the furniture needed for their new office.

With a nod of farewell to the decorators painting the hallway, he left the building to find Gabriel. After a quick discussion, Tyler returned to his van and tossed his safety hat onto the seat beside him. The transit van was now his vehicle of choice, and he had relinquished the car to Theresa, along with Joseph who was now officially an employee of TB Communications. He shifted the engine into gear and took a last long look at the hubbub of activity surrounding Sycamore House. Not a vulture in sight, he noted with satisfaction, before driving off with a cheery toot of his horn.

Bounding into his rented office suite, Tyler stopped short at the sight of Reuben chatting amiably with Patience.

'Well, this is a pleasant surprise. Have long have you been waiting?'

The two men shook hands and Tyler glanced down ruefully at his damp shirt. 'You'll have to excuse the state of me – I just left the site and it's sweltering outside.'

Reuben laughed and followed Tyler into his office, taking a seat in the leather chair facing the desk. 'Don't worry about it. You don't need a suit and tie to talk to me.'

Tyler extracted two bottles of water from his office fridge and handed one to Reuben before sitting down behind his desk. He twisted off the top, took a long swallow, and sighed with satisfaction. His eyes scanned the spacious office with its expensive leather furnishings and the deep mahogany bookcases that had never been used. Although he had possession of his swanky office for a few more weeks, he couldn't wait to move out. Turning his attention to his guest, Tyler raised his bottle in a silent toast.

'You've saved me a phone call by coming over, so let me give you an update on where things are.'

They chatted for over an hour until Reuben reluctantly rose to his feet. 'I'd better go if I want to avoid getting stuck in traffic. Give my best to Theresa when you get home, will you?'

Tyler grinned. 'Why don't you join us for dinner this evening and tell her yourself? Theresa would love to see you, and her friend Lyla's coming over – I'm sure the two of you would get on like a house on fire.'

Reuben froze, and appeared rooted to the spot. His mouth opened and shut without emitting a sound and then, with an inarticulate murmur, he dashed out of the room leaving a baffled Tyler still in his chair. Patience walked in with papers for his signature, distracting him from Reuben's odd behaviour, and as Tyler scanned the final document, an authority to his bank to repay the loan to the bank account of JP Investments, he wondered for the umpteenth time what had become of his original investor.

To all intents and purposes, Jeff Parnell had disappeared into thin air since his midnight flit from Ghana. After concluding the sale of Sycamore House to the Foundation for a price that had been more than fair, Tyler's priority had been to repay Jeff's seed capital and sever all ties with the man. But with no reply to his emails or to the letters he'd sent to the company address, he had finally decided to transfer the money back to the account from which it had been received.

'Thanks, Patience.' He replaced the cap firmly on his pen and stood up, reaching for the jacket hanging on the coat stand. 'You've done more than enough for today. It's time we went home.'

With a smiling 'Yes, sir,' Patience picked up the signed papers and left the room.

Tyler was almost at the door when his phone rang, and he stopped to pull the mobile from his pocket. He glanced at the screen and rolled his eyes good-naturedly.

Since joining forces with Reuben, Tyler had been fending off Nortey's constant invitations to meet for drinks at Jake's so Nortey could sound him out on a brilliant business proposition. Bringing the handset up to his ear, Tyler listened patiently to Nortey's earnest request, and then shook his head with a chuckle.

'No, my brother, not tonight. What do you mean, why not? Because I'm going straight home to my beautiful wife and our gorgeous son.'

Nortey's voice squawked in loud protest through the handset, but Tyler simply grinned and punched the button decisively to end the call.

Switching off the lights, he shut the office door firmly behind him.

Maku

'Don't you *dare* cry! I mean it, Cuz, I don't want your mascara leaking all over my wedding dress!'

With that, Maku turned back to admiring her reflection in the full-length mirror in Auntie Pat's guest room, raising her arms to better marvel at the slender waist created by the sturdy corset the dressmaker had built into the white lace confection. The sweetheart neckline modestly displayed her curvaceous breasts and Auntie Pat's borrowed pearl necklace, while the full skirt skimmed over Maku's broad hips, creating the perfect hourglass silhouette.

Lyla sniffed, and Maku glanced at her warily. Theresa, who was clearly trying to stifle her giggles at Lyla's outraged expression, quickly handed her friend a tissue, and Lyla dabbed at her eyes, careful not to smudge Joanna's carefully applied make-up.

Having finally convinced her father that she would never make an accountant, Maku's former classmate was now enrolled on a beauty course which she'd taken to like a duck to water. To show off her newly acquired skills, Joanna had volunteered to tackle the make-up for the bridal party, and Maku had ordered her dismayed girlfriends to accept the offer.

'Stop grumbling! Joanna's been very good to me, and she's doing us a massive favour giving us her father's car and driver for the day. Theresa, you never wear much make-up, so you definitely need some help. And as for you, Lyla – the less said, the better. For God's sake, let the girl do it, if that's what she wants – it's not like she'd do a worse job than either of you.'

Eunice, who had been drafted in from Theresa's hair salon for the day, had been waiting patiently for Maku to finish preening and now gave a discreet cough. 'Please, madam, let me finish your hair so we are not late.'

With a final twirl, Maku plumped herself on a chair and submitted to the hairdresser's deft fingers. Eunice neatly twisted the long braids into a circular crown before carefully pinning the white lace veil into place.

'*Oh Maku!*' Disregarding the earlier instruction, Lyla's eyes welled up as she looked at her cousin's reflection in the mirror above the dressing table. 'You look so *beautiful!*'

Maku blinked rapidly to clear her own threatening tears. Lyla was right; the face looking back at her was almost unrecognisable. Her skin appeared satin smooth and the clever shading highlighted cheekbones that generally went unnoticed. Thanks to Joanna's surprisingly skilful application of eyeshadow and lashings of mascara, Maku's dark eyes looked enormous. The plum-tinted gloss applied to her full lips completed the picture. This was how she had always dreamed she could look, Maku thought. Just like the bride at the wedding she'd attended with Auntie Pat all those years ago.

Theresa cleared her throat and her voice emerged huskily. 'You look amazing. I can't wait to see Nortey's face when you walk down the aisle.'

Maku bit her lip, and a hint of anxiety crept into her

eyes. 'He'd better show up after all this. I mean, can you *imagine* if he stood me up? I was watching this Nigerian movie on TV last week and—'

Recovering fast, Lyla jumped in before Maku could get into her stride.

'Don't be silly, I'm sure he's already at the church,' – she glanced at her watch – 'and we need to leave. I know it's your prerogative to be late, but let's get a move on and put poor Nortey out of his misery!'

Maku took a deep breath and then stood up and slipped her feet into a pair of cream court shoes. She ran her eyes over Lyla and Theresa and gave a nod of approval.

'You both look very nice,' she pronounced, quickly adding, 'not as gorgeous as me, mind you, but I'm glad I chose that pinky colour. It suits you both and goes very well with my flowers.'

Ignoring their exasperated sighs, Maku lifted her dress and swept grandly out of the room, leaving her two matrons of honour to follow in her wake.

Auntie Pat had offered her house for the bridal party's preparations, and she stood waiting at the foot of the stairs dressed in a traditional Ghanaian outfit made from exquisite gold lace. Maku trod carefully down the polished steps in her unfamiliar heels and posed while the photographer took a series of shots.

'You look so beautiful, my dear,' Auntie Pat said tearfully. 'It's a pity your parents can't be here, but we'll send them some pictures.'

Maku sighed. 'If Ma sees me dressed like this, she'll only start complaining that I should be sending her money instead of wasting it on fancy clothes.'

Lyla held open the front door and Maku stepped out into the bright afternoon sunshine. A slight breeze lifted her gossamer light veil but, when she looked up, there was no hint of cloud in the clear blue sky and she sighed with satisfaction. *Today was going to be perfect!*

Joanna's driver was waiting in a sleek grey Lexus and, as soon as he spotted the bride, he sprang out to open the car doors. Once Maku was settled in the back, Lyla slipped in beside her and Theresa took the front seat.

The car moved out on to the main road and Maku sat up straight so as not to dislodge the short veil. She glanced out of the window and noted with a gratified smile the number of passers-by who stopped to watch the luxury vehicle with its ostentatious cream ribbons sail past. Spotting two girls stop mid-chatter to openly gawk at the bridal car and flashing headlights, Maku graciously inclined her head and gave them a regal wave.

Lyla spluttered with laughter. 'Maku, you are *impossible*! You're getting married, not being crowned queen.'

Theresa turned around in her seat to exchange an amused glance with Lyla. Maku airily ignored their teasing. 'You can laugh all you like, but it's my day, and I'm making the most of it.'

Theresa's phone pinged, and she quickly scrolled through the text message. 'Tyler's wondering where we are. He says the church is packed and everyone's waiting.'

She tapped out a quick response and continued, 'I still can't get over Adoley volunteering to look after Abra. When did she suddenly become so helpful?'

Maku chuckled. 'She probably thought it was the least she could do after I chose her daughter to be my bridesmaid. To be fair, she's been a lot nicer to me since she got back from Paris – quite frankly, I think she was relieved when Nortey took Isabelle back home and she could finally get George to answer her calls.'

The car pulled up to a set of traffic lights and Maku returned to her waving duties, smiling benevolently at the hawkers clustering around to peer through the windows. She knew she looked every inch the beautiful bride and, no matter how much Lyla or anyone laughed, she wanted to treasure these moments in her memory forever. Even now on her way to the church, it still felt unbelievable that her laid-back Nortey had made such an effort to fulfil her dream. It felt like only yesterday when he'd announced he had booked a church and its adjoining hall for their wedding, causing her to shriek so loudly with excitement that the boys had abandoned their beloved cartoons – and baby sister – to race down to Maku and Nortey's room.

The moment Maku broke the news to her incredulous friends, offers of help had flooded in from all sides as if the universe had simply been waiting to grant her wish. At Maku's tearful request to be her matrons of honour, Theresa and Lyla had promptly insisted on paying for their own dresses, Theresa also offering to cover the cost of the flowers, while Lyla promised a photographer and the services of her church choir. Auntie Pat had sifted through her latest stock to find outfits for Abra and the boys, as well as a knee-length white lace dress with a pale pink sash for Isabelle. Nortey, determined to spare Maku the burden of organising their big day, took charge of the catering, even presenting her with a comprehensive guest list for her approval. Joanna's enthusiastic offer of her father's deluxe car, along with her free cosmetics services, had been the icing on a most delicious cake.

All that was left was the dress. Reverently removing the length of beautiful white lace from its secret hiding place at the bottom of her drawer, Maku had anxiously handed the now fully paid-up fabric over to the dressmaker Lyla had recommended. It had taken multiple drawings and two mock-ups before Maku had pronounced herself satisfied with the design and allowed the relieved seamstress to get on with the job.

Maku was enjoying the drive immensely, and she was almost sorry when they pulled into the car park of the church. The front doors of the low, square building were wide open, and she could see Adoley standing with Abra at the entrance and chatting to the priest. Isabelle was standing next to her mother, and she squealed with excitement and pulled on Adoley's arm the instant she spotted the bridal car.

Suddenly Maku's hands were clammy with nerves as the enormity of the moment struck her. Her heartbeat quickened to a rapid tattoo at the same time as a host of butterflies fluttered beneath her tightly corseted waist. As if sensing her cousin's inner turmoil, Lyla laid a warm, reassuring hand on Maku's arm.

'It'll be fine. Nortey's here, and it's your day, so enjoy it.' She smiled and reached for the door handle. 'Come on, Cuz, let's get you married!'

Maku's nerves vanished as rapidly as they had appeared, and she was almost squirming with anticipation as she waited for the driver to open her door. She took Lyla's outstretched hand and stepped out of the car, and within moments Auntie Pat, who had been following in her own car, was by her side. She handed Maku her bouquet, a beribboned cascade of vibrantly coloured blooms mixed with green ferns and sprigs of white baby's breath, and draped the translucent veil carefully over her face, stepping back with a satisfied smile.

'All right, ladies, she's ready. Lyla, pick up the hem of her dress, and Theresa, give her a hand up the steps. I'm going to fetch Isabelle's basket from the car.'

Fizzing with excitement, Maku forced herself to walk slowly up the short flight of steps. She almost laughed aloud at the astonished look on Adoley's face as her gaze travelled up and down Maku's immaculately made-up face and exquisite wedding finery. Returning the priest's greeting, Maku waited impatiently until he went into the church and, moments later, the sound of organ music swelled and rolled out to the front door. At Auntie Pat's signal, Isabelle marched forward slowly, her little face solemn as she clutched her straw basket of flower petals.

It had never crossed Maku's mind to ask her father to give her away, knowing full well he had no patience for any traditions that didn't originate in Biorkor. Tyler had cheerfully offered to take his place, but Maku had turned him down, insisting there were only two people she wanted by her side when she walked down the aisle. With a tremulous smile, she turned to Lyla and Theresa who were standing on either side and cleared her throat.

'Okay, girls, let's do this!'

Together, the three women walked slowly, arm-in-arm, down the aisle. After her first few shaky steps, Maku relaxed and scanned the full pews on either side. Bubbling with joy at the familiar faces grinning back at her, only the bouquet in her arms and the restraining hold of her matrons of honour prevented her from waving madly at everyone.

As she neared the altar, her eyes fell on Nortey standing tall in a new grey suit with Samuel and Elijah at his side, both looking solemn in equally smart suits. As proud as she was of her handsome sons, it was the naked love and admiration in the eyes of the man waiting for her that took Maku's breath away.

Theresa and Lyla released her and stepped aside, and it felt like the world had shrunk to her and Nortey. Maku's eyes locked on to his, and for a moment everything else fell away: the music, the people, and even the priest waiting to begin the service. If Nortey was nervous, he gave no sign of it. Instead he carefully peeled back Maku's veil and bent to kiss her gently on both cheeks before taking her hand.

Lyla retrieved Maku's bouquet and tweaked the back of her veil, and the couple moved forward to stand in front of the priest while the choir began the first hymn.

'*Our God reigns! Our God reigns!*' the congregation sang loudly. As the song came to an end, the priest reached for the thick book he had placed on the altar. Opening it to a page marked with a red ribbon, he bowed his head and the tortoiseshell glasses he'd slipped on slid slowly down his broad nose.

Nortey tightened his hold on Maku's hand, and she took a deep breath as the priest cleared his throat loudly.

'Dearly beloved, we are gathered together here in the

sight of God, and in the face of this congregation, to join this man and this woman in holy matrimony...'

Maku glanced up at Nortey, who returned her gaze with a smile and a reassuring squeeze of her hand and then returned her attention to the priest whose glasses were now almost at the tip of his nose.

'And therefore, is not by any to be enterprised, nor taken in hand, unadvisedly, lightly, or wantonly, to satisfy men's carnal lusts and appetites, but reverently, discreetly, advisedly, soberly, and in the fear of God.'

While most of the traditional language sailed over Maku's head, she did briefly wonder if Nortey's insatiable desire for sex counted as carnal lust.

The priest continued, 'First, it was ordained for the procreation of children, to be brought up in the fear and nurture of the Lord.'

We certainly have enough children. Maku flicked a wry glance at her two sons and at Abra, now sleepily ensconced in Adoley's arms.

'Secondly,' the priest intoned, 'it was ordained for a remedy against sin, and to avoid fornication. Thirdly, it was ordained for the mutual society, help and comfort, that the one ought to have of the other, both in prosperity and adversity.'

Help and comfort... in prosperity and adversity. They had yet to be tested on coping with prosperity, Maku mused, but Nortey had proved both helpful and comforting through all kinds of adversity. He had comforted her after her unexpected pregnancy with Samuel when another man might have abandoned her, he had helped lighten her burden by insisting that Isabelle return to her father, and by caring for the children almost single-handedly in the weeks leading up to her exams. And he had definitely comforted her by organising this wedding. Nortey had already done all this and watching the priest rescue his glasses before they slipped off his face, Maku couldn't help feeling the tiniest bit underwhelmed. For the first time, she wondered if Theresa and Lyla hadn't been right all along. If this was all real marriage was about, then she already had it. She sighed inwardly. *Oh well, at least there's the party to look forward to.*

When the priest invited anyone who knew just cause why she and Nortey should not be married to speak or forever hold their peace, Maku bit her lip nervously, her mind flying to the dramatically interrupted wedding scene in one of her favourite movies. She breathed a sigh of relief when the congregation remained silent, and the priest turned to Nortey.

'Wilt thou have this woman to thy wedded wife, to live together after God's ordinance in the holy estate of matrimony? Wilt thou love her, comfort her, honour and keep her, in sickness and in health and, forsaking all others, keep thee only unto her, so long as ye both shall live?'

Maku gazed shyly at Nortey who smiled at her before turning to the priest with a firm 'I will.'

Now it was her turn, and suddenly Maku's knees began to tremble. She stared at the priest and tried to focus on his words while inside she could feel her heart swelling as if it were about to invade her entire body.

'And wilt thou obey him, and serve him, love, honour and keep him, in sickness and in health, and, forsaking all others, keep thee only unto him, so long as ye both shall live?'

Maku glanced at Nortey and then stared dumbly at the priest and shook her head, terrified of bursting into tears if she opened her mouth.

For a tense moment during which the sound of a pin dropping would have been heard in the silent church, Maku couldn't answer. Then, once again, she looked up at Nortey. He gently stroked his thumb across the palm of her hand, and, at the sight of his reassuring smile, she felt her panic recede.

She could hear the collective release of breath from the congregation as she croaked, 'I will.'

The rest of the ceremony passed in a blur and she dutifully repeated her vows, stumbling only slightly over the long sentences. Nortey, on the other hand, sounded completely assured and she knew she would never forget the look in his eyes as he solemnly promised to love and cherish her 'till death us do part.'

A moment later, he slipped a gold band onto her finger, softly repeating the words, 'With this ring I thee wed, with my body I thee worship, and with all my worldly goods I thee endow.'

By this point, any cynicism about the magic of the ceremony had vanished, and Maku had to swallow hard to remove the lump in her throat. *Maybe there is something to this wedding thing after all!*

'I pronounce that they be man and wife together, in the name of the Father, and of the Son, and of the Holy Ghost. Amen!' The minute the words left the priest's mouth, the congregation stood and clapped. Nortey stooped to gently kiss her lips and Maku blushed with embarrassed pride at the tumult of foot stamping and whistling that ensued. Chuckling at the commotion, the priest raised his hand for calm before continuing with a prayer.

Maku sang along happily as the choir burst into their final song, all the while stealing glances at the shiny gold band on her finger. *Finally!*

As the organ began to thunder out the triumphant recessional, Maku and Nortey turned hand in hand to walk down the aisle. Waiting for Isabelle to lead the way, Maku took in the packed church with a radiant smile. The goodwill swirling around the room felt so intense, so *physical* she could almost touch it. Her smile stayed in place even when her eyes fell upon Nortey's mother standing next to Adoley. The older woman's lips were as tightly compressed as if she'd just sucked a lemon but, as their eyes met, she inclined her head in a grudging nod of respect. George, who was standing in the pew directly behind his mother-in-law, looked decidedly uneasy when Maku's eyes met his and promptly dropped his gaze, his shifty expression immediately reminding her of the serial killer in the last episode of her favourite crime series.

Isabelle was several paces ahead, and Maku smiled indulgently at the little girl carefully scattering flower petals from her white wicker basket. Isabelle wasn't a bad kid, she thought fondly; she just needed to remember she was an African – and eat something else besides bloody cornflakes!

Nortey's hand tugging hers brought Maku out of her reverie and together they set off behind their flower girl. Part way down the aisle, she spotted Mr Danso and waved vigorously at her boss who returned the gesture with a broad smile. She was rather less excited to see Rita standing next to him decked out in a low-cut red bandage dress that left little to the imagination. Still, it had been worth wasting an invitation on her annoying colleague just to watch the wind being taken out of the woman's uppity sails. Rita's discomfited expression when Maku presented her with one of the gold embossed wedding invitation cards, provided by Nortey's friend who managed a print shop, had been priceless. But what had been even more satisfying was Rita's disgruntled face when Maku triumphantly reminded her before sailing out of work on her last day, 'Don't forget when I come back after my honeymoon that it's *Mrs Quarshie* to you!'

Still tickled by the memory, she chuckled to herself, anticipating with relish Rita's reaction when she discovered Mr Danso had recommended Maku, his star employee, for a promotion.

* * *

Maku raised her glass as Nortey's best friend finished his speech and brought everyone to their feet to toast the newly-weds. She took an appreciative sip of the sparkling wine, wondering yet again where her husband – *husband...* she savoured the word for a moment – had found the money for all this. The hall looked beautiful, and the girls had gone to great lengths with the flowers and decorations. Theresa had supplied a celebrity DJ for the music, but that still left the cost of the drinks and the delicious catering they had just enjoyed, none of which would have come cheap.

Maku glanced at Nortey clapping Roland on the back and chuckling over his rather raunchy best man's speech and returned to her train of thought. Reluctantly discarding the idea that her new husband had robbed a bank – even Nortey wouldn't be that daft – she grudgingly concluded that his story about one of his ideas finally making money must be true. Maybe it was time she treated the half-baked schemes that emerged from his drinking sessions at Jake's a bit more seriously.

From the stage, Maku scanned the hall in awe at the sheer number of people who had turned up to help them celebrate the day. The children's table was just below, and she could see Adoley fussing over her boys and cutting Elijah's chicken into manageable pieces while soothing a fractious Abra. Her sister-in-law had offered to keep the children while Maku and Nortey went on their short honeymoon, courtesy of Tyler, who had refused to take no for an answer: 'If I can't be the father of the bride, at least let me pay for the two of you to have a couple of nights away at a decent hotel.'

Adoley's offer was one that Maku would never in her wildest dreams have imagined, but, if absence had made her sister-in-law's heart grow fonder, Maku was more than happy to be the beneficiary. After all, there had to be some reward for the months of hard work involved in looking after her daughter.

'Hey, snap out of it!' Lyla nudged her playfully in the ribs.

'*Ow!*' Maku inhaled sharply, and then winced. While the built-in corset did an excellent job of sucking in excess flesh, after a generous plate of food and two glasses of wine, the pressure from the body-hugging dress was making Maku distinctly light-headed. But with the bridal table in full view of everyone, she had little choice but to grin and bear it.

'What's wrong with you?' Theresa leaned across Lyla to interrogate her. 'I hope you're not getting drunk.'

'I couldn't even if I wanted to,' Maku grumbled. 'This dress is so tight, there's no room even for a drink.'

'Too bad, my friend. You're the one who insisted the dress should be like a second skin. Cheer up, we're going to be dancing soon – and I've told the DJ we want some hot numbers!'

Maku groaned and straightened up in her seat, trying to breathe normally despite the corset bones digging between each rib like mini daggers.

Theresa's lips twitched as she eyed Maku unsympathetically. 'Look on the bright side. You look fabulous, so just—'

'Suck it up!' Lyla chortled. 'Don't look like that, Cuz. We're not laughing at you – we're laughing *with* you!'

Theresa promptly cracked up and Maku glared at them. Whatever she planned to say was forestalled by Nortey rising to his feet and tapping his fork against a glass.

The high-pitched ping cut across the hubbub of conversation and, within moments, the room had fallen silent. Now he had the floor, Nortey cleared his throat and rather shakily placed his glass back on the table, and Maku reached out to briefly squeeze his hand. He looked at her and, apparently reassured by her smile of encouragement, nodded and pulled out a sheet of paper from inside his jacket and picked up the microphone.

Exactly five and a half minutes later, Maku was dabbing at her eyes with her napkin, not caring who could see her. In all the years they'd been together, Nortey had *never* poured his heart out to her as he had just done in front of a roomful of people, and it took all her crumbling self-control not to burst into big, noisy sobs. Once again, the guests were on their feet as Nortey turned towards her and held up his glass.

'Family, friends, treasured guests, may I ask you to please raise your glasses to the love of my life and my best friend – to my beautiful bride, Maku!'

'*Hear, hear!*' Lyla and Theresa crowed in unison, echoing the voices around the hall.

Maku swallowed a huge gulp of wine to stop from crying and spluttered when some of it went down the wrong way. In the commotion of people retaking their seats, Lyla slapped her hard on the back and smiled unrepentantly at Maku's angry glare.

'*What?* Would you prefer to choke to death on your wedding day? On second thoughts, that might make a good plot for one of those movies you love so much!'

After cutting the frosted three-tier cake – courtesy of Auntie Lizzie who had come out of the shadows and was now paid directly by Nortey – the newly-weds took to the dance floor. In Nortey's arms, swaying to the music, Maku put aside the discomfort of the boned corset and clung to the tall smiling man she had just *really* married.

Pulling her closer, Nortey whispered, 'So, *Mrs Quarshie*, are you happy?'

Maku giggled, and then heaved a happy sigh that came from the very depths of her heart. '*Very* happy,

Mr Quarshie. Thank you for doing all this – I still can't believe it! I know you didn't think us having a proper wedding was a priority, and I'd given up hoping I would ever get a day like this.'

When he didn't reply, she glanced up and for once Nortey's expression was serious.

'You deserve it, Maku. I meant everything I said up there on the stage. You really are the best woman a man could ask for and I'm so lucky to have you. Having a wedding wasn't really a priority for me because I've always felt married to you, but,' he shrugged, 'this is what you've always wanted, and I wanted to prove to you that *you* are my biggest priority.'

Maku tucked her head under his chin and reflected on Nortey's words as the other guests joined them on the dance floor. No matter how silly it might sound to other people, it *was* satisfying to now be a Mrs instead of a Miss. But the more she thought about the blessings she already had in her life, the more she realised that she and Nortey were already experiencing their happy ever after. A marriage is more than a wedding, she mused, and seeing Nortey defy his mother in order to give Maku what she really wanted, she now felt confident that her man would always put her first.

Nortey twirled her around, and Maku laughed as he pulled her back into his arms. She looked up at her 'new' husband and shook her head with a rueful smile. Technically they had been married for only a few hours, but unlike many brides, she already knew the man she had married inside and out. Perhaps he wasn't as handsome as Kwesi, or as financially successful as Tyler now looked set to be, but Nortey loved her unconditionally. From the very beginning, he had seen past her humble origins and her lack of polish to appreciate her for exactly who she was and when it came down to it, *that* was what really mattered.

Maku looked up and spotted Mr Danso across the dance floor. Opposite him was Rita, her full breasts in danger of spilling out of her dress as she bobbed up and down, throwing herself into the upbeat, pulsating rhythms of the music.

With a mischievous smile, Maku steered Nortey towards the couple, making sure she positioned herself at *exactly* the right angle to flash her wedding ring.

Nortey

'Ah, Mr Quarshie!'

'Professor,' Nortey murmured, trying to edge past his boss.

With an affable smile, Professor Ghartey moved smoothly to block him. Fussily adjusting his patterned bow tie, he saw off a speck of lint from his jacket sleeve with an imperious brush of his hand before returning his attention to Nortey.

'Congratulations, once again. I have to say it was an absolutely splendid wedding!'

Nortey blinked at the unaccustomed sight of his boss looking pleased with him and nodded politely, struggling not to laugh. *Thank God for Maku!* Once again, his wife had been right on the money. When he had protested about sending a wedding invitation to Professor Ghartey, she had dismissed his objections out of hand.

'Of course, you must invite your boss.' Grinning wickedly, she'd added, 'You've said yourself the university has funding problems. Trust me, after you've entertained him and introduced him to your wife and children, you'll be the last on the list if he has to cut his staff.'

Plainly in an expansive mood, the professor hadn't finished. 'Mrs Ghartey and I enjoyed the day very much. A wonderful atmosphere, if I may say so. Kindly convey my thanks to your wife.'

If the old man was wearing a bowler hat, he would have tipped it, Nortey thought with a wry shake of his head as he watched his boss saunter down the corridor. How a mere twelve months spent in a foreign country could give someone such pretensions, he would never know!

He strode into the empty lecture hall and was pulling his notes from his battered briefcase when a tentative knock sounded. He glanced up to see one of his students hovering by the doorway and repressed a sigh. While he enjoyed the financial benefits of his promotion, the increased demands that came with it still irked him. Nortey didn't hate his job quite enough to go in search of a new profession because, if he was honest, his ideal occupation was anything that would pay enough money to take care of his family while allowing him plenty of free time to socialise with his friends. Nevertheless, he disliked pandering to the high-maintenance students who attended his university, many of whom came from well-to-do families and were often far more ambitious than he had ever been.

Nortey gestured to the girl to enter. The deliberate way she shut the door behind her and the guarded expression with which she approached him immediately sent his antennae shooting straight up. He straightened with a frown. *Ivy,* that was her name. If the ambitious students irritated him, the lazy, self-entitled ones drove him insane. Ivy was frequently late to his classes and had yet to deliver an assignment on time. Judging by her heavy make-up and long painted fingernails, it was clear she spent little time typing economics essays.

'Good morning, sir.' The patterned silky dress she

wore swished softly as she walked right up to his desk and smiled at him, her red lips parting to show perfect white teeth.

'Good morning, Ivy. You're early today.'

She ignored the observation and tightened her hold on the strap of her roomy leather bag. 'Sir, I need to ask you a favour.'

Nortey's eyebrows rose. She certainly wasn't wasting time beating about the bush. 'And what is that?'

'Sir, I'm... well, the thing is... um, I was wondering if we could come to an arrangement.'

'About what?'

Ivy's radiant smile faltered, and the heavily mascaraed eyes narrowed. Nortey's studied neutral expression apparently offered her no clues to his thinking and, after a tiny hesitation, she ploughed on.

'My boyfriend wants me to travel with him to the States for a few weeks, which means I will miss some classes.'

She paused and Nortey waited in silence. With an impatient flick of her long glossy hair, she added, 'I'm prepared to pay if you can – you know, take care of it so that my grades are good enough for me to graduate at the end of the year.'

'*Take care of it?*' Nortey repeated carefully. 'Let me make sure I understand what you're asking. Are you suggesting I take money from you to alter the grades for your work or, to be precise, for work you don't actually submit, so you can graduate under false pretences?'

If Ivy felt any embarrassment, it was hard to tell. She stared at him impassively, letting her silence confirm he had hit the nail on the head. Although it wasn't the first time he had fielded an offer of money in exchange for grades, it had never been made quite so blatantly and for a moment Nortey felt a flash of sympathy for Professor Ghartey. It must be a nightmare trying to run an ethical department when you had people like Ivy on the lookout for lecturers like Tony Tagoe who grasped any opportunity to wring money out of their students. Unfortunately for Ivy, he was no Tony, and she had picked the wrong person to bribe.

Nortey folded his arms and glared at her, channelling his boss as he adopted his sternest expression. 'I see. Well then, Ivy, let me also make myself perfectly clear. If you want to graduate this year, you will show up for every one of my classes without exception *and* submit all the required coursework within the deadlines I set my students. For your sake, I will forget your proposed "arrangement" but make no mistake – if you don't deliver, you will *not* be graduating.'

Ivy's nostrils flared like a startled stallion and her eyes flashed with outrage. She gripped her handbag tightly and her voice trembled with barely suppressed fury.

'*Sir!* All I'm asking is that—'

'One more word, Ivy, just *one* more word and I will report you to the head of department for attempting to bribe a faculty member which, in case you are not aware, would mean your immediate expulsion from the University. Now, kindly open that door and take your seat.'

Nortey shook his head as he watched her stalk off and fling the door open before stomping right to the back of the lecture room. He would never claim to be an angel, but he had enough integrity not to give a pass to an undeserving student. While he was always open to a good deal, his unwillingness to be involved in anything shady was probably why he would never be rich, he acknowledged wryly as he removed the rest of his paperwork from his bag. It was just as well his wife had enough ambition for both of them because, knowing Maku as he did, he had no doubt that nothing would stop her from reaching the top of her chosen profession.

* * *

With his lectures over for the day and the hands of the clock safely past the five-thirty mark, Nortey took a leisurely stroll through the university grounds to his car. Brushing the discarded sweet wrappers on the back seat onto the floor to join the rest of his children's litter, he dumped his briefcase and lowered himself into the car, tossing his phone onto the seat beside him. As he grasped the steering wheel, his eyes fell upon the shiny gold ring on his left hand and he flexed his fingers, still not entirely used to the feel of the metal. This was probably the only thing that was different about his relationship, he pondered. Although he had never doubted his commitment to Maku, it did feel good to have this visible symbol she had insisted upon. When he had jokingly pointed out that it might make him more attractive to a certain type of woman, she had clearly and succinctly outlined the fate that awaited him if he ever dared, as she called it, 'to do a Kwesi on me.'

Nortey chuckled at the memory and pulled out of the parking space, braking sharply as his phone rang. He glanced down at the screen and shook his head in exasperation. After an extended period of frostiness intended to underline her displeasure at her objection to his wedding being ignored, his mother had finally resumed normal communications. But having relished the brief period of peace from her incessant demands, Nortey was determined not to be sucked back into the role of unpaid handyman and general dogsbody. He cut off the insistent ringtone and, shifting the car back into gear, drove out of the car park and on to the main road, tapping his ring finger against the steering wheel. He would deal with his mother later; having defied her with his newly found independence, they both knew where his loyalties lay if it ever came to a choice between her and his wife.

Maku. Nortey grinned at the mental image of his feisty, smart and deliciously curvy wife. He really was a lucky man to have found someone who loved him, warts and all. He was under no illusion that he was a great catch, but Maku never made him feel judged or a disappointment. He might irritate her intensely at times, but she always allowed him to be exactly who he was. As much as he liked Lyla for her kindness, and respected Theresa for her loyalty and support, there was something very daunting about the idea of being married to either woman. The pressure of trying to meet their expectations, financial or otherwise, would totally stress him out. No, his only job was to keep his wife happy, because when Maku was in good spirits she was more than content to leave him to his own devices.

Nortey drew up behind the cars waiting at the crossroads and pursed his lips in thought. It was still early, and if he stopped at Jake's Joint he might be able to catch Frank Appiah before his evening shift at

The Embassy hotel. While serving drinks to a couple of German diplomatic staff a couple of weeks earlier, Frank had overheard them discussing a shipping handling contract, and he was seriously considering putting in a bid. Nortey had always got on well with Frank and was hoping to persuade him to cut him into the deal.

The lights changed and the traffic surged forward. Nortey glanced at his watch and tapped the steering wheel in an agony of indecision. Maku and the kids wouldn't be home yet, and Frank had sounded very excited about the contract.

Nortey took a deep breath and indicated left, pressing hard on the accelerator as he sped towards Jake's Joint. I won't stay long, he promised himself. Just a quick drink.

Lyla

It was finally over. Desperate to keep his situation under wraps, Kwesi had reluctantly agreed to the speedy and uncontested divorce. Having signed the court papers, Lyla was eager to escape the lawyer's office before her excitement burst out of her throat into an unrestrained shriek of sheer, heady joy.

Freedom! Was this how convicts felt when they emerged from prison into the world? So joyful at walking free from jail that absolutely nothing could dampen their spirits? Out on the street, even the oppressive humidity felt like a warm embrace. She inhaled deeply, and never had the pungent aroma of petrol fumes, fried street food and the mass of human traffic smelled so sweet. Hugging herself with glee, she forced a path through the heavy flow of people, scarcely registering the raucous cries from the hawkers adding to the congestion of the dusty pavements.

For weeks she had fantasised about finally being free of her husband, but in none of those scenarios had she imagined the riot of emotions exploding through her like lava from a volcano. And she had certainly not anticipated the sheer bliss of finally reclaiming Lyla Blankson. Just the act of scrawling her signature on the legal documents that erased her horrible decision to marry Kwesi had expelled the festering remnants of pain, guilt and anger. It was, she thought, like shedding a coat whose weight you'd grown so used to that you'd forgotten quite how heavy it was. In the blink of an eye, in the scribble of a pen, everything felt utterly different.

Reaching the traffic lights, Lyla crossed the street to wave down a taxi. She had left her car at home, knowing it would be next to impossible to find parking in the city's busy central district. A gleaming Toyota sedan with distinctive red and yellow taxi markings pulled up and she slid into the back seat, relishing the unexpected coolness that greeted her. She couldn't remember the last time she'd taken a regular taxi that deigned to use its air conditioning. She leaned forward to ask the driver to take her home, but then glanced at her watch and changed her mind. It was just after five o'clock and the traffic was moving so slowly, she'd be lucky to get back to her mother's house within the hour. It made more sense to go straight to church for choir practice and then take a cab home – or maybe get a lift from one of the choristers. With a shiver that had nothing to do with the air conditioning, she quickly instructed the cabbie and then leaned back against the pristine upholstery. *One of the choristers, indeed! Who are you kidding, Lyla?* The Voice piped up pointedly.

Today was the first day she would speak properly to Reuben since the afternoon he had appeared at her mother's house a few days after the awful scene in his house. Once again, he had pleaded with her to come to him, but after fleeing her house and her husband, Lyla had felt too raw and fragile to countenance another relationship. Tearfully but firmly, she'd pointed out that she was still married and needed time to work out what she wanted to do.

'If I decide to come to you – or to anyone – I need to do so with clean hands, Reuben,' she'd said wretchedly, her heart breaking at the sadness in his eyes as she rejected his offer. But as much as she knew she loved this man, and as grateful as she was to Reuben for helping her climb out of the pit of despair into which her marriage had driven her, Lyla knew she needed to be alone.

It was past time to face the memories she had buried and to own up to the choices she had made. It was up to her to rediscover who she really was and, however bruised or broken, to nurture what was left of the once strong and independent Lyla back to life. Reuben had begged to take care of her, but that wasn't Reuben's job to do, it was hers. She had allowed the men in her past to pull her down and she wasn't going to rely on another one to be responsible for her happiness. She was a woman, not a child, and she would have to take care of herself.

The taxi inched forward at a sluggish pace, and Lyla curled up in the back and gazed blindly out of the tinted windows. The refreshing coolness acted like a balm, gently soothing her feverish exhilaration into a satisfyingly warm glow in the pit of her stomach. It was hard to believe that in a few short weeks, when the final decree came through, she would officially no longer be married! But mingled with her relief at closing this painful and destructive chapter of her life was also a quiet sadness, and for a few moments Lyla allowed herself to feel the loss of what might have been.

Notwithstanding Kwesi's failings, divorce for Lyla represented a rebuke for her own shortcomings. Marrying Kwesi to ease the pain of Ravi's abandonment was something she should never have done. She had always known she didn't love Kwesi in the way marriage demanded and trying to use him to father a child, as redemption for the one she had lost, had been grossly unfair. While Kwesi had never been a saint when it came to women, perhaps if she had loved him enough he wouldn't have needed the self-validation that came from going after other women. Perhaps if he had felt wanted and cherished for himself, perhaps if she had railed louder against his affairs and fought harder for them as a couple, perhaps then... maybe... *maybe* Kwesi would have felt sufficiently committed to building a strong marriage with her.

Lyla sighed. The only problem with that argument was that in order to fight for something, you had to really want it. And this, more than anything, had been at the heart of her apathy towards Kwesi's conduct. Yes, his affairs had been humiliating, but she hadn't loved him enough to really *care* about what he was doing with women. Lying alone in her bed at night, she had burned in anger at her husband's blatant lies, but that wasn't the same as agonising over mental images of him making love to someone else or feeling tortured by the idea of him caressing another woman's skin or whispering words of love in her ear.

The taxi driver slammed on his brakes and the ear-splitting car horn startled her out of her thoughts. Cursing furiously, the driver rolled down his window to shout at the sheepish looking man he had narrowly avoided running into, before restarting his engine and driving on. Lyla released her hold on the seat belt she had gripped reflexively and shook herself out of the gloomy fog that was threatening to descend. It's all over, she reminded herself. Whatever the rights and wrongs on both sides, you and Kwesi were not good together. God has given you a chance to put it in the past and start a new chapter, so look on the bright side.

An impish smile crept across her face. The first bright spot was knowing she would never again have to deal with Ma Abena, although her last encounter with her soon-to-be ex-mother-in-law could still make her chuckle. Having finally dragged the information that Lyla had left him out of a reluctant Kwesi, Ma Abena had arrived unannounced at the Blankson house a few days later. Alerted by the gardener that she had a visitor, Lyla had walked outside the gate to find the older woman waiting on the pavement beside a taxi, her arms folded imperiously.

'My son tells me you have left the marital home,' Ma Abena said without preamble. The woman was clearly livid. Her lips were tight, and every inch of her small frame vibrated with anger.

Lyla stared at her curiously, feeling not the slightest bit intimidated. 'Did he tell you why?'

'He said you were *angry* with him.'

It was obvious from Ma Abena's incredulous tone that no amount of rage could possibly justify leaving her son, and Lyla almost laughed. She had to wonder what Kwesi's mother must have put up with in her own marriage.

'Well, he's right. I'm furious with him – and with myself for ever marrying him. Enough people warned me that Kwesi would never settle down, including his own brother.'

Ma Abena's lips tightened further at the reference to Papa Kwame, and her eyes flashed with spite.

'Maybe my son would not have felt the need to look

elsewhere if you had given him children – like Violet has done for his brother.'

Secretly astonished at how the woman's words now completely failed to wound her, Lyla tilted her head to one side and stared at Kwesi's mother as intently as a scientist might study a new strain of bacteria. The woman shifted uncomfortably under the probing gaze, but nonetheless raised her chin defiantly.

After a moment, Lyla shook her head and asked softly, 'Tell me, Ma, why do you hate me so much?'

For a second, a flicker of what might have been shame crossed Ma Abena's face before her features hardened. Clearly rattled and, as if to make up for any momentary lapse, she raised her voice angrily.

'Does wanting my son to have the joy of a child mean I hate you? Do you know how your *failure* – yes, you can shake your head at me if you like – but your failure to have children has embarrassed my family? And now, when you have a chance to be a mother to his child, look at how you are behaving.'

Out of the corner of her eye, Lyla could see the taxi driver who had been slouched in his seat jerk upright to stare at the tiny woman ranting and gesticulating wildly.

'Kwesi is a handsome man,' Ma Abena shouted. 'He could have married any girl he wanted, and yet he chose *you*! I warned him that you were too book-long. All that university education and foreign training and – and big jobs you think are so *important*.' She struggled for breath as she spat the words out. 'What use is all of that when you can't have a simple baby!'

Lyla's eyes widened as she fastened on to the clear

resentment bubbling like hot tar beneath the woman's words. *Hold on a minute, is Ma Abena* jealous *of me?* Snippets of conversation with Kwesi about his mother floated through her mind. How she had left school without qualifications to work as a trader in the local market until she met his father, a junior civil servant in one of the government ministries. How her attempts to improve her education had stalled when she fell pregnant with the first of their four children. And then there was Violet's tearful recounting of Ma Abena's scathing criticism of their spending money on private school fees for their children. Her mother-in-law's constant digs that Lyla was overeducated made a warped kind of sense if the old woman's vitriol sprang from frustration at her own curtailed ambitions.

'I feel sorry for you.'

The words slipped out before Lyla could stop them, and the older woman's features contorted so savagely that for a moment Lyla feared Ma Abena would slap her. Instead, her mouth worked furiously but no sound emerged, and then, with what looked like a herculean effort, she drew herself up.

'I came here to talk sense into you, but as usual you are too stubborn and wilful to listen to your elders and betters. My son has given you everything, and for *what*? For you to stand there and insult me? I don't understand girls like you and if you ask me, I blame the mothers!'

Whatever vestige of sympathy Lyla may have felt for her mother-in-law vanished in a heartbeat.

'You are my elder, Ma Abena, but you are *not* my better! Your precious son gave me nothing. Do you hear me?

No-thing! Unless, of course you count his lies and his cheating with any woman who would look at him twice – now that, he certainly gave me plenty of! Oh, I know I'm not perfect, but Kwesi is a spoilt, immature, self-obsessed liar who has been so pampered his whole life that he thinks he's entitled to behave exactly as he likes without any thought for anyone else!'

She paused for breath, her heart racing furiously as the pent-up feelings she had suppressed for years poured out. 'But you know what? You and I can most definitely agree on one thing, Ma Abena. I *also* blame the mother!'

Slamming the gates firmly behind her gave Lyla the most satisfying moment she had experienced in a very long time. Even now the memory of Ma Abena's stunned expression brought a smile to her face, a smile that widened at the thought of the old woman and a fiery Nadia battling it out with Kwesi caught in the middle. It couldn't happen to a nicer family.

'Please, madam, should I take this road for the church?'

Lyla leaned forward to direct the taxi driver and, after reassuring herself that he was on the right track, she pulled out her phone to text her mother not to expect her for dinner. *Why aren't you going home for dinner?* The Voice probed, but Lyla ignored it. The only voice she was prepared to listen to now was her own, not the imposter that spoke up only to belittle her.

To his credit, Reuben had respected her wishes and, other than polite greetings, he had kept his distance at choir practice and during church services. In turn, she had made every effort to avoid being alone with him or giving him any false encouragement. But today, Lyla thought, today was different. Today, she knew exactly what she wanted, and she was ready to ask God for it.

The taxi pulled into the church car park and Lyla pulled a few notes out of her purse and handed them to the driver with a grateful smile. She hurried into the building, relieved to see that she wasn't the first to arrive. There was no sign of Reuben, and she slipped into the pew to stand next to James who greeted her with his now customary peck on each cheek.

'You're looking very well, Sister Lyla,' James murmured, his gaze travelling up and down her lilac shift dress.

'Thank you, Brother James,' she retorted with a demure smile. The dress was short, but she no longer felt self-conscious about displaying her legs. *If you've got it, flaunt it, as Auntie Clementyne would say.*

Lyla's self-assurance took a rapid nose dive twenty minutes later when a tall, broad figure entered the church and strode towards the assembled group of choristers. Reuben's presence felt so powerful that he might as well have been standing right next to her instead of two rows behind, and Lyla's heart pumped so fast she gripped the bench in front to steady herself. His arrival signalled the start of practice, and over the next hour Lyla tried her best to forget the man and focus on her God. Rehearsing the solo she would be singing at the Sunday service allowed her to clear her mind and let the pure, soaring notes connect her to the spiritual source that had sustained her through so much.

But all too soon choir practice was over, and it was time to face a different kind of music. Following James out of their pew, Lyla waited while Reuben exchanged words with the chorister next to him and then shook hands and made to leave.

Don't waste your time; he's probably found someone else by now! As quickly as it piped up, Lyla banished The Voice. Reuben started towards the aisle and she took a deep breath and moved forward to block his path, her heart beating in rapid time as she looked up into his achingly familiar and beloved face.

At the sight of her tentative smile, Reuben's expression moved swiftly from astonishment to bewilderment and then, to her intense relief, to hope. The other choir members nudged past them, and he gently pulled her aside.

'How are you, Lyla?' The low, vibrant voice sent shivers through her.

'Much better than I was when we last spoke,' Lyla said candidly. 'May I ask a favour? I came straight from town and I don't have my car. Would you—?'

'It would be my pleasure.' He cut in before she could say another word and gestured to her to lead the way. Lyla walked down the aisle with Reuben close behind her and she ruthlessly suppressed the mental image that immediately crossed her mind. *How about letting one marriage go before you plan the next, Lyla!*

Once outside, she hung back and let him stride ahead to his car and he opened the door and helped her in without a word. He walked round to his side and climbed in and, still without speaking, turned the key in the ignition and rolled down the windows to let the stuffy air out of the vehicle. Only then did he look at Lyla, and she nodded in answer to his unspoken question.

'Can we go to your house? I'd really like us to talk.'

Reuben continued to look at her in silence and feeling slightly panicked, she added quickly, 'I mean, only if that's okay with you? If you'd rather—'

'It's fine with me. I'm waiting for you to wear your seat belt.' He gave a small smile and nodded towards the strap by her side and she smiled back shakily and quickly clipped it into place. Rolling up the windows, he turned on the air conditioning and drove slowly out of the car park.

During the drive, neither of them spoke, instead allowing the music to fill the space that was not quite ready for words. The soft jazz melodies were so soothing that Lyla's jangled nerves had settled into a calm, Zen-like state by the time Reuben parked in his driveway. Lyla reached for the door handle and slipped off the high seat onto the fine gravel, her footsteps crunching behind his as they walked up to the palatial porch and into the house.

Once inside, she stood still and looked around her, taking in the serenity of Reuben's home with its familiar decor. Unconsciously, she released a sigh of pleasure and Reuben, who had been watching her thoughtfully, smiled.

'Welcome back. The house and I have missed you.'

Lyla spun around and burst into a smile of unconcealed joy. 'I've missed it – and you – so very much!'

It was Reuben's turn to sigh; a deep exhalation that seemed to emerge from the very heart of him. In two quick steps, he was by her side and sweeping her into his arms.

She nestled against him as a feeling of indescribable peace came over her. Liberated from the shackles of her unhappy marriage, she was finally free to love this man. *I'm home; Reuben is my home!* This was where she belonged,

Lyla realised, and she clung on tightly, revelling in the sheer muscularity of his body as he caressed her and murmured feverishly into her hair. No words were needed as he cupped her face and kissed her lips with such aching tenderness she could feel the tears prickling behind her eyes. None were needed when he took her hand and led her up the wide staircase, nor when they entered his room and slowly undressed each other. And no words would have made an iota of sense as she took him into her with an urgency and intensity of pleasure that only he knew how to bring.

* * *

Much later, as they lay between the tangle of sheets on his massive bed, Lyla thought back to the first time she and Reuben had made love. For a moment, she wondered if Kwesi had felt that magic with Nadia. That inexorable pull that made it impossible for reason to enter your brain. When all you wanted was to comfort and be comforted. When, even though you knew it was wrong, every fibre in your body strained towards another and no amount of willpower or prayer could stop you. But, instinctively, she knew Kwesi had not been driven by any of that.

Weaving her fingers between Reuben's, Lyla chewed her lip thoughtfully. If that had been the case, she could certainly have understood and probably even forgiven it. But Kwesi's transgression wasn't because of the type of love she felt for this beautiful man beside her. His affair with Nadia had been only one of many, and any feelings he'd held for the girl were probably long extinguished. There really was no comparison and for a bizarre moment she felt sorry Kwesi would never know the joy of truly loving and being loved.

'What are you thinking about, my darling?' Reuben turned on his side to face her.

Prudently deciding that no man, however enlightened, would want to hear the woman in his bed was thinking about his predecessor, Lyla contented herself with a smile as she leaned across to kiss him. Stroking his soft beard lovingly, she said with a mischievous grin, 'Just reminding myself how lucky I am that I found you.'

Reuben sighed. 'You could have found me a lot sooner. These past weeks without you have been pure hell. You'll never know how hard it's been to keep my distance from you at church when all I wanted to do was scoop you up, bundle you into my car, and take you away.'

'I don't think the pastor would have been too impressed by that,' Lyla giggled.

Reuben chuckled for a moment and then said soberly, 'Somehow, I don't think Pastor Jeremiah would have been too surprised. I've spoken to him about my feelings for you and he has given me a lot of counsel.'

Lyla arched her eyebrows in astonishment. '*Really?* What on earth did he say? I can't imagine what he thinks of me!'

'You aren't the first woman who has been in a marriage that didn't work out, Lyla, and the pastor doesn't think any the less of you for that. It takes two people to make a marriage work, and Pastor Jeremiah knows you and knows your heart.'

Lyla remained silent for a moment. 'So, what counsel did he give you?'

Reuben gave a short laugh. 'To be patient. He knows about Eva and what happened to our children, and I suspect he had a shrewd idea of what your marriage was like. He told me that if being together was God's plan for us, I needed to step back and let God do the work of bringing you to me, which pretty much put an end to my kidnapping strategy. I'm not sure he'd approve of what we're doing right now, but I'm only human...'

He tailed off with a wry chuckle and pulled her close, and she smiled and burrowed into him. It couldn't have been easy for Reuben to confess to their pastor that he loved a married woman. And she was intensely grateful that he had been given advice that came without judgement. *God truly does perform miracles!*

After a moment, Lyla pulled away and propped herself up on one elbow, sweeping her long braids away from her face. 'I'm so glad he gave you that advice – and that you listened to him.'

Reuben examined her solemn expression and then nodded. 'Even though I was desperate to help you and it was tough to just sit and wait, I forced myself to give you the space you wanted. Although I have to say it sometimes felt like God was making the challenge even harder. Can you believe Tyler invited me to dinner one evening and wanted to introduce us? I'm sure the guy thought I'd lost my mind when I just raced out of his office!'

Lyla giggled. 'Oh, my goodness, you poor thing! When was this?'

He shrugged. 'I don't know – a couple of weeks ago, maybe. I didn't want you to feel I'd ambushed you in their house, and to be totally honest I wasn't sure I was strong enough to be in such close proximity to you and then have to watch you walk away again.'

She kissed him softly and they both fell silent, reflecting on the time they had spent apart.

Then Reuben stroked her cheek and said gently, 'So, my darling Lyla, what finally changed your mind and brought you back to me, hmm?'

She gazed at him while she considered her answer. How could she explain the anguish, tears and self-recrimination of those first few weeks after leaving Kwesi? When she had been racked with guilt despite knowing she had finally done the right thing. Would Reuben – or anyone – understand the long hours of prayer and self-reflection which had slowly pulled her out of the darkness that had engulfed her for so many years? Spending those weeks alone, peeling back the layers of what she had become and making the painful journey to find out who she truly was had been hard. It had also been unavoidable, because without fully accepting herself, it would have been impossible to share that self with someone else.

'I didn't want to come to you until I truly believed I deserved to be happy,' she confessed. 'Love like yours is a gift from God, but I was such a mess in every way possible that I couldn't appreciate the gift. I needed time to sort myself out and, you know, *really* think about everything I'd done and come to terms with it all. Until I did that, I knew I would never feel... I don't know, good enough to deserve happiness – or you, because you *are* my happiness.'

Reuben looked pensive. 'Lyla, none of us is perfect. Isn't that what our religion teaches us – that we are sinners? Isn't that why we seek forgiveness?'

She nodded and said softly, 'God forgave me a long time ago. I was the one who couldn't forgive myself.'

With that, she moved back into his arms and into the peace of being in the right place at last. It had been hard to face up to the past, but here in Reuben's arms and knowing she could now reconcile herself with all her choices – both good and bad – she was so thankful she had.

With Kwesi, she'd chosen marriage for all the wrong reasons, ending up with a painful and destructive bargain and an arrangement which had brought out the worst in both of them. With Reuben, however, Lyla knew with all her heart it would be different. Their life together would be founded on deep, genuine love and a mutual respect, and she snuggled against the man she adored, knowing that finally she could be happy.

Kwesi

Leaving the hospital, Kwesi didn't know whether to feel elated or depressed. On one hand, he was now the father of a beautiful baby daughter. But on the other hand, he hadn't been able to get away from Nadia fast enough. Watching her cradle their newborn, his triumphant mistress had looked so smug that Kwesi had felt like crying along with the infant.

Re-establishing communications a few weeks before she'd given birth, Nadia had proceeded to issue instructions that included a long list of items for the child, and threatening all manner of dire consequences if he skimped on the purchases or turned up with, as she put it, 'those cheap things you sell in your shop!'

There was nothing cheap about the items in his store, Kwesi thought irritably as he drove back to his house. Lyla had always appreciated the pieces he brought home, courtesy of his employee discount. Not that Nadia would know quality if she met it, considering her background. Her insistence that the baby should be named Diamond – *after a TV soap character, for Christ's sake!* – said it all. He had absolutely no idea how he was going to explain that to his mother. Why didn't the stupid girl understand that tradition gave *him* the right to choose the name? Kwesi sighed miserably; there was very little that was traditional about his current situation.

He slowed down to cruise through the main gates into Marula Heights and gave the gatekeeper a cursory nod before speeding off and then cursing as he drove too quickly over a speed bump. *Damn!* All he needed now was a damaged vehicle to add to his troubles.

Solomon ran to open the gate, and Kwesi swept up the incline and parked at an angle in front of the house. He no longer needed to leave space for Lyla's car, and occupying the otherwise empty part of the driveway felt like the kind of gesture which would help obliterate the memory of his soon-to-be ex-wife. In the same way, he'd made a point of sleeping in the middle of their huge bed for weeks, although that particular luxury had been denied him since Nadia moved in.

Installing his mistress in his home had not been Kwesi's idea. Having resumed contact, Nadia had also steadfastly renewed her clamouring for the house he'd promised her.

'Kwesi, there are too many people in my family house for me to be comfortable living there with a new baby – there isn't even enough space for the cot I've told you to buy! You live alone in that big house now, so if you're not going to rent me my own place then you'll just have to make room for us there. Don't forget, I'm the mother of your child and it's your responsibility to take care of me and the baby.'

Kwesi couldn't forget, and in an unguarded moment he'd complained to his mother about Nadia's unreasonable demands. To his horror, instead of the maternal sympathy he'd been expecting, his mother had immediately taken Nadia's side.

'For God's sake, son, do you think I want my grandchild

to grow up in Nima, of all places?' had been her scornful response. 'The girl is right; it's not good for you to live alone – and it will also show that ungrateful wife of yours that she is of no importance! Bring the child here and at least we can make sure it is brought up properly. You made your bed with this girl, so make the best of it – you never know, after you've had more children together you may feel differently about her.'

Feeling nothing but gloomy at the prospect of Nadia's return in only two short days, and this time with a baby, Kwesi let himself into the silent house that would soon cease to be his sanctuary. Wandering into the kitchen, he pulled open the fridge to retrieve a bottle of beer, levered off the metal cap and cleaned the rim with his shirt sleeve. Gulping down the icy brew, he wiped his mouth and then rummaged in the cupboard for a glass to pour out the rest.

Glass in hand, he leaned against the counter and let his mind wander back to the squirming baby with the thick shock of hair. When the nurse had handed her over, the infant had sleepily opened big brown eyes to squint up at him and Kwesi had been shocked by the surge of fierce protectiveness that shot through him. Examining her tiny features and marvelling at how vulnerable she looked in his arms, his stomach had clenched at the thought of anyone ever hurting her. Given his track record with women, he thought, it was somewhat ironic that he now had to worry about how men would treat his daughter in the future.

Not liking the direction his thoughts were taking and anxious for distraction, Kwesi carried his glass to the living room and turned on the television, struggling to focus on the football game he had rushed home to watch. He glanced around the living room that Lyla had decorated so tastefully and wondered how long he could continue living here. The houses in Marula Heights were in high demand and rents didn't come cheap. Without Lyla's contribution, he would soon be forced to find somewhere less costly to live.

He twisted his lips into a humourless smile and took a long sip of his beer. His newly acquired family was fast becoming a drain on his finances. Nadia had closed her salon shortly after moving in, much to his annoyance, even though the paltry income from her business was nowhere close to what he needed to maintain his lifestyle. To make matters worse, she was fast developing expensive tastes and showed little interest in economising, despite his protests that his divorce lawyer was costing him a fortune. Only last week, she'd dismissed his suggestion they stick with terry cloth nappies for the baby out of hand – 'Do you want your only child to look like a beggar on the streets!' – and had defiantly grabbed the largest bag of imported Pampers off the shelf at Swanson's.

Agreeing to Lyla's offer to end the marriage quietly in exchange for a quick, hassle-free divorce had sounded fine until he'd felt the full brunt of the legal fees. But he was desperate to stop the news from spreading around town – at least, until he could explain it on his own terms. After that scene in his office, it had taken him weeks to persuade Jessie that Nadia meant nothing to him, and he dreaded his friends and colleagues gossiping over his stupidity in going from sophisticated, classy Lyla to... well, *Nadia,* with her crass comments, local accent and tight, revealing clothes.

There was no question in his mind this was how people would judge his changed circumstances as even he still found the whole situation a puzzle. And yet curiously, buried beneath the fear and embarrassment caused by Lyla's abrupt departure from his life, was a feeling akin to relief. Deep down, it was as if something he had long feared would happen had finally come to pass. Not because of his womanising, but because he had never felt good enough for Lyla.

Kwesi pushed the uncomfortable truth away with a long swig of beer. There was no point dwelling on the past, he told himself firmly. What mattered now was finding the money to deal with his present financial pressures. He brightened as he remembered his arrangement with the furniture supplier and the new order going through procurement. Even allowing for the greedy bastard's insistence on fifty per cent of the inflated amount, the extra money would be very welcome indeed.

Feeling rather more cheerful, Kwesi strolled to the kitchen for another bottle before returning to the football game, and soon he was caught up in the match between his favourite team and their biggest rivals. The teams were drawn at one goal each with a minute remaining when his phone pinged with a rapid series of text messages. Kwesi growled in irritation and reluctantly tore his eyes from the screen to reach for the mobile. He glanced down distractedly and groaned at the sight of three messages from Nadia. *Damn the girl!* He returned his gaze to the TV, but the damage had been done and his excitement leaked away like fizz from an open can of soda. Seconds later, a last-minute goal consigned his team to defeat.

Kwesi clicked off the television in disgust and scrolled through the messages. *Christ, does she think I'm made of money?* He scanned the extended shopping list and swallowed his distaste at the last item – *Nipple cream! Ugh!* There was no way he was wasting money at the overpriced pharmacy in the mini mall down the road, leaving him with no choice but to make another trip into town. He was in no mood to go out again, but Nadia would give him no peace until he'd delivered everything she demanded. Slipping on his shoes, he was struck by a more pleasant prospect; while he was in the city, he could phone Jessie and arrange to see her after he left the hospital.

He shrugged on his jacket, picked up his keys from the table in the hall and thumbed through the rapidly shrinking pile of notes in his wallet, mentally calculating the cost of Nadia's shopping. *Damn!* Romancing Jessie would have to wait until his share of the money from the furniture deal came through. Besides, it made sense to cool things with her for a while as keeping the affair going would be a struggle once Nadia was home from the hospital. She had made it crystal clear when she moved in that she knew every one of his moves from first-hand experience and, unlike Lyla, she had no intention of turning a blind eye and letting him get away with murder. He glanced at his watch and shoved the wallet into his jacket pocket. If he didn't get a move on, the shops would be shut by the time he got to town.

Traffic into the city was relatively light, and within the hour Kwesi had stowed his purchases in his car boot and was struggling to control his ire at Nadia's persistent texts demanding to know when he would get to the hospital. He settled himself into the driving seat and switched on the ignition, sucking his teeth in frustration as the fuel light began to flash. *Christ! Was there no end to this?*

He pulled out of the supermarket car park and slid open his window to let out the stifling air. The air conditioner guzzled petrol and he was in no mood for the added expense of filling his tank. His wallet was haemorrhaging money and he still had to buy the copy of *OK!* magazine Nadia had insisted upon.

The intense heat, the acrid smell of engine fumes, and the plaintive cries of hawkers plying the congested city streets, all wafted unfiltered through the open window into Kwesi's car. Eventually escaping the busy city centre, he turned into the gravelled car park of The Embassy hotel and parked under the shade of an aged baobab tree. He hurried inside, pausing to savour the cool serenity of the quiet hotel lobby, before entering the glass-fronted gift shop next to the restaurant.

A quick scan of the shelves revealed a stack of magazines in sealed cellophane covers and he snatched the copy at the top of the pile and tossed it onto the counter, along with a small pack of spearmint gum. Opening his wallet, he reluctantly pulled out a note from the once healthy wad and handed it to the cashier. He gave a cursory glance at the change she dropped into his hand and picked up the magazine and gum. His attention was on the skimpily dressed model on the magazine cover as he turned to leave the shop, and he cannoned into a petite, dark-skinned woman standing close behind him.

'Oh, I'm so sorry!' Kwesi exclaimed, instinctively reaching out to steady her. 'Please excuse me – I should have been looking where I was going.'

'Hey, don't worry about it. No harm done.'

Even in her high heels, the woman barely reached his shoulder and when he released her, she smiled up at him with twinkling eyes. Her voice held a strong American twang and he hesitated, intrigued by the combination of her luminous chocolate-coloured skin and the vivid flame of her silk dress. Equally intriguing was the bold confidence she exuded.

Ignoring the voice in his head shrieking at him to keep walking, Kwesi returned her smile at full wattage and watched with satisfaction as the woman's hand crept up to smooth the short pixie haircut framing her heart-shaped face. This was just too easy.

He tilted his head to one side and modulated his voice to its huskiest pitch. 'I know we haven't been properly introduced, but I hope you'll allow me to apologise for my clumsiness by buying you a drink?'

* * *

Kwesi shut the car door and started the engine, his excitement at getting Karen's number momentarily overriding his discomfort from the blistering heat inside the vehicle. She had proved even more charming than he'd suspected and after a couple of drinks she'd left him in no doubt the attraction was mutual. While the cash he'd just spent at the bar was well worth it, the money from his deal with the supplier couldn't come soon enough. Karen was pure class and wouldn't be fobbed off by the second-rate restaurants that appeased Nadia. Relieved not to have wasted time and money calling Jessie for a date, he put the car into gear and was about to move off when his phone rang.

Bloody Nadia! Tempted to ignore the insistent ringtone, Kwesi knew she would only persist if he didn't answer. He pulled the phone from his pocket, the intrusion already dampening the high from his encounter with Karen. He glanced at the screen and frowned in puzzlement before hastily switching off the engine and answering the call.

'Chris! This is a surprise. I've been meaning to call you to set up another game of tennis,' Kwesi chuckled. 'If you're lucky, maybe this time I'll let you win.'

But instead of the friendly banter he was accustomed to exchanging with his boss, the icy tone in which the Operations Director demanded Kwesi report to head office, immediately, set alarm bells ringing and brought a sick feeling to the pit of Kwesi's stomach.

'Just so you understand, Mr Amoah, I'm here with the Head of Procurement and the Group Finance Director – and we expect to see you within the hour. Is that clear?'

Kwesi blanched, his gut twisting as if he'd been punched. His heart was racing, and he forced himself to take a deep breath. *This cannot be happening.* Not to him. Not *now*! Despite the warmth of the car, his body felt icy. He could hear the panic in his voice as he stammered out a reply.

'Yes, *yes*, of course, sir. I'm on my way. But—'

'*Mr Amoah*! Please don't waste my time. We're waiting for you – do you understand?'

Too shocked to offer more than an inarticulate murmur, Kwesi dropped the phone onto his lap and gripped the steering wheel convulsively. *How the hell had they found out?* And – more importantly – what in God's name was he going to do?

EPILOGUE

**IT'S BETTER TO BE GOOD THAN
FAIL TO BE PERFECT**

Lyla gave the flowers in the crystal vase a final tweak and stepped back to admire the effect. The starched ivory tablecloth was the perfect setting for the gold-trimmed white dinner plates she'd picked up from Swanson's the week before. Adding the silver cutlery and sparkling crystal glasses she had unearthed from the boxes of Reuben's belongings from America, she had created a table set for a king. Or queens, she corrected herself happily. She couldn't wait for the girls to get here and to catch up on everyone's news – with all three of them having been so busy lately, their girls' nights were more important than ever.

After making a tiny adjustment to the bouquet of creamy orchids and green ferns, Lyla set the vase in the middle of the table and returned to the kitchen to put the finishing touches to dinner. She inspected the roasting chicken and adjusted the oven temperature, smiling at the memory of the first time she had used the hi-tech cooker and incinerated the food. She poked a fork into the pot of steaming jollof and sampled a few grains of the spicy rice before firmly pushing down the lid, and then stirred the rich tomato sauce simmering on the front burner.

The sound of the gate clanging open heralded the arrival of the girls and Lyla hurried excitedly to Reuben's front door. She corrected herself again; Reuben's and *her* front door. Even now, eight months after their quiet, low-key ceremony, she found it hard to believe she was married to the man she loved and living in this beautiful house.

Theresa was the first in, bursting through to fold Lyla into an enthusiastic hug accompanied by loud squeals of delight.

'Enough! It's my turn,' Maku protested, dragging Theresa aside. Lyla seized her cousin in a tight bear hug and the two women held each other for a long moment. Stepping back, Maku's gaze raked Lyla from head to toe.

'Cuz, look at you! I can't believe that skinny old you could actually get this big – do you think it might be twins?'

Lyla laughed and stroked her rounded belly. 'Okay, so now you sound like Reuben – you know he has twins in his family. No, I promise it's just one baby. Come on, let's go and sit down; I've been *so* excited all day. It feels like ages since we got together, and I want to hear all about everything.'

Theresa linked her arm through Lyla's, giving it an affectionate squeeze as they followed Maku into the living room. Maku made an instant beeline for the enormous sofa and plumped herself down, slipping off her sandals to rest her feet on the suede footrest, while Theresa snuggled into the far corner of the sofa and tucked her legs up under her.

With a sigh, Lyla sank into an armchair and propped a cushion behind her.

'Let me get my breath back and then I'll get us some drinks. I've been on my feet for ages and carrying this little one is getting exhausting.'

'Take your time, Cuz, we're not going anywhere.' Maku picked up a bowl of nuts and crispy plantain chips which Lyla had set out earlier and tossed a few into her mouth. She looked appraisingly at her cousin's bump which

444

bulged even more conspicuously now she was seated. 'Are you sure you can keep working for another two months? You know what they say about first babies, don't you? I saw this programme on TV where—'

With a groan, Theresa cut Maku off without ceremony. 'Knowing Lyla, I'll bet she's already got her hospital bag packed and ready to go.'

'*We-ell*,' Lyla laughed. 'Okay, you've got me there. Reuben thinks I'm mad but I'm positive this child is coming early. Which is another reason I've decided to start my maternity leave sooner than I'd planned. Driving to work is getting uncomfortable and my team's going to have to do without me while I'm on leave, so they may as well start getting used to it.'

'Why do you even need to go back to work?' Maku interjected, ignoring Theresa's exasperated tut. 'Reuben's *loaded*. I don't think I'd want the hassle of working if Nortey was a multimillionaire – not that I'm ever likely to find out.'

'Maku, you're a career girl through and through, and there's no way you'd enjoy sitting at home being a rich man's wife,' was Lyla's dry response. 'And, yes, even you would get sick of watching movies all day.'

'You're probably right – have I told you guys I've been promoted again and I'm now Accounts Manager?'

'Um, only about ten times at the last count,' Theresa said with a deadpan expression, and she and Lyla immediately burst into laughter.

Maku pursed her lips. 'Laugh all you want but getting that diploma has really paid off. I've decided I'm going to study for the chartered qualification once Abra starts school. *That* will put me in line to become the Finance Director one day.'

She brightened. 'The best thing about the new promotion – apart from the money, of course – is that I can delegate work to that silly cow, Rita. I still get a kick from remembering her face when Mr Danso made the announcement. You should have seen her – I thought she was going to faint!'

'God help her,' Lyla muttered, hauling herself to her feet. 'Stop crowing and come and get yourselves a drink while I check on the food. I've told Reuben he's not allowed back until eleven at the earliest, so we have the house to ourselves for the evening.'

An hour later, the three women were seated around the dining table in animated conversation tucking into the meal Lyla had prepared. The perfume from the display of orchids, now relegated to the sideboard, blended into the spicy aromas from the roast chicken and fragrantly flavoured rice.

Maku speared a piece of fried plantain into her mouth and chewed slowly on the sweet delicacy. '*Mmm*, Cuz, I swear no one except Auntie Pat makes better fried plantain than you.'

'When you eat it as often as Lyla does, you'd better know how to make it.' Theresa remarked. She gestured with her fork towards the large serving bowl. 'D'you remember how we used to fight over this stuff when we were kids?'

'When we were kids – or a few months ago?' Lyla snorted with derision. 'Please don't think anyone's forgotten your disgraceful behaviour at lunch after we left the registry office.'

Theresa gurgled with laughter and spooned a few more pieces of plantain on to her plate. 'I know, right? Tyler was horrified, although you'd think he'd be used to it by now. Gosh, Lyla, that was *such* a lovely day, and definitely the smallest wedding I've attended in Ghana.'

'That's what made it so special. I wanted to keep it as intimate as possible, especially after the circus with Kwesi when I didn't have a clue who half the guests were. Besides it was the second time around for me and Reuben, and we didn't want to make a fuss.'

Lyla passed the jollof rice to Maku and then turned back to Theresa. 'Speaking of Tyler, it sounds like he's doing some great work with the Foundation. You'd think he walks on water the way Reuben goes on about him.'

'Tyler's really enjoying it, and absolutely loves mentoring the young entrepreneurs. He's just persuaded one of the banks to approve a loan for the first business they moved into Sycamore House. I know he can be a bit over the top sometimes, but it's good to see him so excited and – and fulfilled.'

'So, now you're both sorted, is it time to start working on baby number two?' Lyla teased, nibbling on the remains of her chicken drumstick.

'I'd take my time if I were you,' Maku warned. 'Kids are hard work and your business is still young.'

Theresa took a sip of water and pleated her napkin between her fingers. 'We-ell, that's true, but… is there *ever* a perfect time to have kids? I mean—'

Maku's fork dropped onto her plate with a forceful clatter and she stared at her friend open-mouthed, her eyes zeroing in on the water in Theresa's glass.

'Oh my God! You're *pregnant*?'

At Theresa's sheepish smile, Maku shrieked and jumped to her feet, bombarding Theresa with questions. Lyla struggled out of her chair to embrace her friend.

'I'm so happy for you, Tee! When are you due? Why didn't you say anything? Why—?'

'*Whoa!* Hold on a minute!'

Laughing, Theresa held up a hand in protest until the other two fell silent. 'I was going to tell you tonight, anyway. I've been feeling so tired and run down lately that I went to see Dr Owusu yesterday, and he confirmed it. I told Tyler last night and – surprise, surprise – he's over the moon.'

Maku beamed. 'Just imagine – all our kids will play together, just like we did.'

After even Maku had declared herself unable to eat another bite, they moved back into the living room. From where she lay sprawled on the sofa, Maku took a large gulp from her wine glass and stared up at the huge black and white portrait on the wall.

'Lyla, tell the truth, doesn't it feel weird having a picture of your man's dead children looking at you all the time?'

Theresa choked on the water she'd been swallowing and glared at Maku, but the other woman's eyes were still fixed on the image of the smiling twins.

Lyla turned to follow Maku's gaze and said softly, 'No, it doesn't. It's actually rather nice to have it up there – it feels a little like Max and Leah are with us, and I know it comforts Reuben to see it. He's such a sweet and loving man that whatever makes him happy is fine with me. Besides, I don't believe in forgetting the past – at least, not the good bits.'

448

Theresa cleared her throat. 'Talking of your past, Margaret heard from one of her contacts why Kwesi was sacked from the store. Her friend didn't know all the details, but it was something to do with fraud and taking kickbacks. Turns out your ex-husband's brother is on their board, which is why the company kept it all hush-hush and didn't prosecute. He might have escaped jail, but apparently Kwesi's still struggling to find a job.'

'Ah, Kwesi... the gift that keeps on giving,' Lyla murmured resignedly. 'Why does that not surprise me?'

'Because you know what a dishonest person he is. As my dear Mama always says, once people reveal their true character, you should always expect they'll do it again.'

'Well, it serves him right, if you ask me,' Maku said viciously. 'The lying bastard deserves everything he's got. Nortey says he's living with his baby mama on the old housing estate behind the industrial area. It's even worse than where we used to live.'

Lyla gave a wan smile and stroked her stomach with slow, gentle movements. 'I don't wish him any harm, girls. It wasn't all his fault and, as I keep reminding you, I wasn't perfect either. The truth is I should never have married him. I'm just grateful I don't have to deal with that evil witch Ma Abena ever again.'

Maku chuckled. 'That woman makes Nortey's mum look like an angel. Mind you, since we got *properly* married,' – she ignored Theresa's anguished groan – 'my mother-in-law is almost friendly when she sees me.'

She glanced at her watch and frowned. 'Nortey had better have remembered to pick the kids up from her house – he's supposed to have them home and in bed by nine. Mind you, he's also promised to limit Jake's Joint to three times a week, max, so we'll see how that works out.'

Lyla topped up Maku's glass. 'Relax, Cuz, it's your night off. You know Nortey's a good guy and he'll take care of the kids, don't you, *Mrs Quarshie*?'

'Yeah, I suppose you're right. He's not perfect but he steps up when I need him to, and I'd much rather deal with his faults than some of the other guys out there.'

Maku took a big sip of wine and giggled tipsily. 'Just look at us – all grown up, and wives and mothers now. We've seen each other through some crazy times, haven't we?'

She swallowed another mouthful and smiled at them with misty eyes. 'I *love* you guys. You're the best sister-friends any girl could have... *I know!* Let's make a toast – like they did in that movie with Whitney Houston.'

She staggered to her feet and raised her glass with an unsteady hand. 'Right, let's do this properly. Lyla, where's your glass? Come on, Tee, *up!*'

With an indulgent smile, Theresa left the armchair she had snuggled into and joined the other two. On Maku's order, they raised their glasses.

'To sisters!' Maku exclaimed.

As one, they echoed, '*To sisters!*'

Acknowledgements

I cannot write a book about sister-friends without acknowledging the women who support, encourage and uplift me on this journey of life.

So, in no particular order because you're ALL fab, here goes: Helen, Angela, Caite, Simi, Elizabeth, Kassiani, Mallie, Nana Afraks, Ophelia, Emma, Terhas, Landé, Wendie, Opokua, Patti, Esther, Betty, Tosin, Melissa, Maxine, Marian, Maama, Grace, Jill, Rosemary and Kay. For anyone I've left out, the next drink is on me.

A special thank you to Elvina for your patience, optimism and unfailing faith in my independence adventure. And Marcelle, you've been pivotal to my writing career and I can't thank you enough.

Thank you to the superbly talented Dorothy Koomson for taking the time to read this manuscript and for your wonderful feedback. You are an inspiration – and I can't tell you how excited I was to get that email!

Thank you to Ayesha Harruna Attah for so graciously agreeing to read the draft and for your lovely review which almost made me cry. To the super triple-threat Chibundu Onuzo, thank you for your time, talent and support.

To Catriona Robb, I'm in awe of your editorial skills and so grateful for your insights and patience. To Aimee Dewar, my heartfelt thanks for the typesetting and hand holding on this new adventure. To Kate Forrester, another phenomenal cover, and my immense gratitude for taking this on and producing such a beautiful design.

To Jazzmine and Valerie at Jacaranda Books, eternal thanks for believing in me and setting me on my path as a novelist.

To my own little women, Seena and Khaya. The love is real.

There are sister-friends, but there are also mothers. To Akosua Mensah, who has been mine for the longest time... what can I say? Thank you for everything.

TGBTG!

A Message from Frances

If you enjoyed reading *Imperfect Arrangements*, I would like to ask you a small favour.

We all want to read a book that someone else has loved, so please take a moment to share your thoughts with a short review on Amazon, Goodreads, BookBub or any other platforms you use. Even if it's only a line or two, I'd really appreciate it.

If you'd like to find out more about me and my work, please visit my website at www.francesmensahwilliams.com and join my FREE book club to receive regular newsletters, exclusive free downloads, sneak previews of books and events... and a whole lot more.

Connect with me on Facebook: www.facebook.com/francesmensahwilliams

Follow me on Twitter @FrancesMensahW and on Instagram at francesmensahw

I'd love to hear from you!

Fancy a FREE story?

To say thank you for buying *Imperfect Arrangements*, I'd like to offer you a free short story called *Sweet Mercy*.

What's it about? Well, remember Mercy – the woman Theresa and Lyla were discussing in *Imperfect Arrangements*? No, don't flick back! Let me tell you her story FOR FREE!

All you need to do is visit my website, join my Book Club and download the story: www.francesmensahwilliams.com. As simple as that.

Coming in 2020!

Hot Sauce and Croquet
by Frances Mensah Williams

Falling in love was the easy part...

When self-appointed fix-it queen Cara Nightingale met Henry Fitzherbert, it was love at first sight. But his rural aristocratic background is a far cry from her blended North London family with its mix of English cream, African chilli and Caribbean spice – and enough drama for their own reality show.

While Cara struggles to fit in to Henry's casually affluent lifestyle of country houses, horse trials and croquet, her gorgeous and infuriating first love Ryan unexpectedly reappears, fully intent on winning her back. But Ryan brings with him deeply painful memories Cara has tried to forget. Can she really forgive Ryan and let go of the past or is Henry still the man for her? When the only thing she and Henry have in common is love, can Cara trust her judgement and risk her heart again?

Sorting out the predicaments of friends and family is one thing, but, as Cara discovers, it's quite another to fix yourself. Confronting tough choices and the secret that still haunts her, choosing her future forces Cara to face her past – and discover what *really* matters.

Pre-order your copy of *Hot Sauce and Croquet* via my website www.francesmensahwilliams.com

About the Author

Born in Ghana, Frances spent her early childhood between the USA, Austria and Ghana before settling in the UK. After building her career in London, she moved to Ghana for several years before returning to set up a consultancy to manage Human Resources and skills development projects across Africa.

Frances's first book, *Everyday Heroes: Learning from the Careers of Successful Black Professionals*, was followed by the careers guide, *I Want to Work in Africa: How to Move Your Career to the World's Most Exciting Continent.*

An avid scribbler, in 2015 Frances's acclaimed first novel *From Pasta to Pigfoot* was published by Jacaranda Books and selected by WH Smith Travel as one of the top 25 of its 100 Summer Reads. Described by the novelist Lesley Lokko as 'a warm and poignant coming-of-culture' novel, it features under-achieving PA and pasta fanatic Faye Bonsu and chronicles her attempts to find her cultural niche as she explores contemporary Ghana. The sequel, *From Pasta to Pigfoot: Second Helpings,* continues Faye's adventures of self-discovery and self-acceptance.

Frances is a passionate advocate for building skills and capacity in Africa and writes extensively on issues relating to Africa and the African diaspora. She is the founder and publisher of ReConnect Africa.com, an online portal for professionals of African origin, and was a speaker at TEDx Euston on the challenges of belonging and finding your place in an unfamiliar culture with her talk *Where is Home?*

Frances was awarded a CBE by Her Majesty the Queen in the 2020 New Year Honours list for supporting young people in the African community in the UK and helping them to share their skills within Africa.

Frances lives in London with her family.

Other Books
by Frances Mensah Williams

From Pasta to Pigfoot

On a mission to find love, a disastrous night out leaves pasta-fanatic Faye's romantic dreams in tatters and underscores her alienation from her African heritage. Leaving London to find out what she's missing, Faye is whisked into the hectic social whirlpool of Ghana and into a world of food, fun and sun to face choices she had never thought possible.

*From Pasta to Pigfoot:
Second Helpings*

Pasta fanatic Faye Bonsu seems to have it all; a drop-dead gorgeous boyfriend, a bourgeoning new career and a rent-free mansion to call home. But with friends shifting into yummy mummy mode, a man with no desire to put a ring on it, tricky clients, and an attractive and very single boss, things are not exactly straightforward. Faye returns to sunny Ghana, but life doesn't always offer second chances.

Non-Fiction

I Want to Work in Africa: How to Move Your Career to the World's Most Exciting Continent

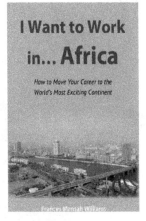

A practical, invaluable guide to the African job market, the industries and professions in demand, how to put in place a winning strategy, write a compelling CV, make the right connections, and find a job in Africa that builds on your career and talents. Illustrated with personal stories and full of practical advice from recruiters and professionals who work in Africa.

Everyday Heroes: Learning from the Careers of Successful Black Professionals

A collection of interviews with sixteen professionals with different careers including law, accountancy, music, publishing, medicine, banking and architecture. These 'everyday heroes' talk about what it takes to succeed in their careers, their own influences and the life lessons they have learned along the way.

CPSIA information can be obtained
at www.ICGtesting.com
Printed in the USA
LVHW040200221120
672341LV00002B/16

9 780956 917546